LEOPARD IV

BEARING WITNESS

In the same series

LEOPARD I
Dissonant Voices: The New Russian Fiction

LEOPARD II
Turning the Page

LEOPARD III
Frontiers

LEOPARD IV

˻BEARING WITNESS˼

THE HARVILL PRESS
LONDON

First published in Great Britain in 1999 by
The Harvill Press
2 Aztec Row, Berners Road
London N1 0PW

www.harvill.com

1 3 5 7 9 8 6 4 2

A CIP catalogue record for this title is
available from the British Library

ISBN 1 86046 067 4

Designed and typeset in Galliard
at Libanus Press, Marlborough, Wiltshire

Printed and bound in Great Britain by Butler & Tanner Ltd
at Selwood Printing, Burgess Hill

CONTENTS

Acknowledgements   ix

Editors' Preface   xi

ESSAYS

Jenefer Coates
Bearing Witness: Leopold Labedz (1920–93)   3

Stephen Becker
On Being a Patient   69

Julio Cortázar
from *Portrait of Keats*   83

Julien Gracq
Caen   111

Ismail Kadare
A Proscribed People and Its Spokesman   116

Anna Maria Ortese
The Involuntary City   127

Jonathan Raban
Seagoing   146

José Saramago
Nobel Lecture 1998: *How the Character became
  the Teacher and the Author His Apprentice*   153
and *From Poem to Novel, from Novel to Poem*   165

Adriaan van Dis
Stolen Languages   170

Claudio Magris
Caffè San Marco   178

Carol Brown Janeway
For Erwin Glikes   199

PHOTOGRAPHY
Robert Mort
Burmese Journey (1990–96)   211

POETRY
Gesualdo Bufalino
"To My River Ippari"   215

Ernst Jandl
"Still Life"   216
"to remember"   216
"asleep"   217

Bruno K. Öijer
Three Poems   218

Paul Durcan
"The Bloomsday Murders, 16 June 1997"   220

Aleksandr Pushkin
The Bronze Horseman   222

STORIES
James Salter,
My Lord You   237

Ludmilla Ulitskaya
Genele – the "Handbag" Lady   250

Ken Saro-Wiwa
On the Death of Ken Saro-Wiwa   261

Starling Lawrence
The Crown of Light   270

Javier Marías
Lord Rendall's Song   288

Luigi Malerba
Silvercap   295

Julian Mazor
The Lost Cause   300

Neva Mullins
Dinner at Natalia's   317

Yi Mun-yol
The Knife-grinder   330

Murray Bail
The Seduction of My Sister   340

EXTRACTS FROM NOVELS
Lionel Abrahams
from *The Celibacy of Felix Greenspan*   357

Slobodan Selenić
from *Fathers and Forefathers*   365

Notes on the Authors   383
Notes on the Translators   387

ACKNOWLEDGEMENTS

The Publisher would like to thank all those who gave permission for the inclusion of the following material in this anthology:

LIONEL ABRAHAMS: extract from *The Celibacy of Felix Greenspan*, Bateleur Press, Johannesburg, 1977. © Lionel Abrahams, 1977; MURRAY BAIL: "The Seduction of My Sister". First published in *Picador New Writing 3*, Sydney, 1995. © Murray Bail, 1995; STEPHEN BECKER: "On Being a Patient". First published in *Atlantic Monthly*, July 1967. © Stephen Becker, 1967, 1999; CAROL BROWN JANEWAY: "For Erwin Glikes". © Carol Brown Janeway, © Erwin A. Glikes, 1993, 1995; GESUALDO BUFALINO: "To My River Íppari". From *Amaro miele*, Einaudi, Turin, 1982. © Giulio Einaudi, Turin, 1982. Translation © Patrick Creagh, 1999; JENEFER COATES: "Bearing Witness: Leopold Labedz (1920–93)". © Jenefer Coates, 1999; JULIO CORTÁZAR: "Portrait of Keats". From *Imagen de John Keats*, Alfaguara, Madrid, 1996. © Julio Cortázar and Heirs of Julio Cortázar, 1996. Translation © The Harvill Press, 1999; ADRIAAN VAN DIS: "Stolen Languages". © Adriaan van Dis, 1995. Translation © Charlie Murphy, 1999; PAUL DURCAN: "The Bloomsday Murders". First published in the *Sunday Independent*, Dublin, 1997. This revised version from *Greetings to Our Friends in Brazil*, Harvill, 1999. © Paul Durcan, 1997, 1999; JULIEN GRACQ: "Caen". From *Carnets du grand chemin*, Librairie José Corti, Paris, 1992. © Librairie José Corti, 1992. Translation © The Harvill Press, 1999; ERNST JANDL: "Still Life", "to remember", and "asleep". © Luchterhand Literaturverlag, Munich, 1985. © Ernst Jandl, 1999. Translation © Michael Hamburger, 1999. © Daedalus Press, Dublin, 1999; ISMAIL KADARE: "A Proscribed People and its Spokesman". Introduction by Ismail Kadare to the French edition of Rexhep Qosja's *La Mort vient de ces yeux-là*, Editions Gallimard, Paris, 1994. Introduction and French translation © Edition Gallimard, 1994. Lightly abridged English version of the French © The Harvill Press, 1999; STARLING LAWRENCE: "The Crown of Light". First

EDITORS' PREFACE

In this edition of *Leopard* Ismail Kadare speaks of the need for every writer "to bear witness, to assert that it is sometimes less a question of not knowing than of not wanting to know". Internationally-acclaimed authors, poets and translators from around the world are assembled here to a similar purpose. Each has entered the witness box to relive their experience, to give their testimony.

The reader will discover how the best witnesses can descry what lies ahead by interrogating the past, whether it be José Saramago looking at the future of the novel, Ismail Kadare revealing the inexorable context of the war in Kosovo, or Ken Saro-Wiwa's disturbing fictional prediction of his own death. Jenefer Coates's memoir of Leopold Labedz reminds us that we have a duty to speak out on behalf of the Winston Smiths of this post-*1984* world, while Robert Mort's photographs are eloquent witnesses to the struggle of the community that surrounds Aung San Sun Kyi for democracy in Burma.

There are personal testimonies too. Preparing to set sail, Jonathan Raban considers sea travel as a metaphor for life's journey; Julien Gracq conjures up the ghosts of ancient Caen, the university town that stood in the path of war; Julio Cortázar brings a luminous latin appreciation to the most romantic of English poets, Keats; and the late Stephen Becker shares with us what it is to come to terms with paralysis.

Also to be found in this *Leopard* are Carol Brown Janeway's moving recollection of the publisher Erwin Glikes; Claudio Magris on his native Trieste; Anna Maria Ortese's account of a Neapolitan slum housing estate; Adriaan van Dis on the transformative power of translations; fine stories by Murray Bail, James Salter, Ludmilla Ulitskaya, Starling Lawrence, Luigi Malerba, Javier Marías, Julian Mazor, Neva Mullins and Yi Mun-yol; poems in translation by Gesualdo Bufalino, Ernst Jandl, Bruno K. Öijer, and by Paul Durcan, and a new translation by Peter Norman of Aleksandr Pushkin's *The Bronze Horseman*; and extracts from fiction by Slobodan Selenić and Lionel Abrahams.

This completes the fourth *Leopard*, the first since The Harvill Press became again an independent house, and one in which we are especially proud to publish José Saramago's Nobel Prize address.

Leopard will henceforward be published annually and will continue to draw from new writing in translation, as in English, from all over the world.

THE HARVILL EDITORS

ESSAYS

JENEFER COATES

Bearing Witness:
Leopold Labedz
1920−93

As murderers, victims or bystanders, men in the final analysis
always act individually, subjectively; and they and their deeds
should be judged likewise.

JOSEPH BRODSKY

The fate of a book lies with its readers.

TERENTIANUS MAURUS

My interview with Mr Labedz was arranged for 3 o'clock at the *Survey*
office. This turned out to be in a shabby Edwardian block at the
eastern end of Oxford Street, midway between academic Bloomsbury
and marketeering Soho. High, heavy doors opened from the bright
pavement into the gloom of an entrance hall. Metallic lift-gates glinted
through the shadows, and the liftman, as we rose up, thoughtfully
intoned over and again from beneath his white moustache the
name of the journal, stressing it *Sir Vay*, as though questing a lost
knight. Released onto the topmost floor, I followed a maze of empty
corridors round a dingy light-well. At the far end of a cul-de-sac were
two doors: one marked *Survey*, the other *Editor*. No one answered.
A single chair had been placed outside them – an ominous sign –
and I sat on it facing the corridor just passed along. All down one
side, icy August radiators stood at intervals beneath windows that
filtered poor light onto the unkempt marble floor; there was no
human sound, either inside the building or from outside in the
streets below.

This would be my first real job: fresh with my degree in Russian,
I had been recommended as assistant to one of the most controversial
figures in East European studies whose unique reputation balzed

before him: Leopold Labedz was editor of the leading journal in
the field, a writer of fierce polemics and a fiery opponent in argument.
I sat and waited . . . and waited . . . but for how long was one
supposed to wait?

At last the lift could be heard creaking up, its metal concertinas
opening, then closing, and fast light footsteps approaching. Round
the corner at the far end hurried, almost scurried, a compact,
rotund figure, intent, his hand tapping, counting each stretch of
wall between the windows: a regular, private habit. He hadn't
seen me yet. He was dressed formally despite the summer heat. I
deliberately stirred to attract attention and he looked up surprised.
A broad twinkly smile spread over his round face, diffusing the
momentary ghost of consternation at having been observed whilst
lost in his own thoughts. Elaborate courtesies ensued: the cheerful
exchange of introductions was soon accomplished, the doors were
unlocked with great ceremony and the offices of *Survey* were
thrown open.

What a contrast with the gloomy entrance! The little rooms were
tucked in cosily under the roof. They were cottagey and rainbow-
bright with books. Every surface was piled with paper of some
kind – a bibliophile's dream, a librarian's nightmare. From floor to
ceiling, the walls were lined with shelves which sagged in the
effort to accommodate the hundreds of volumes that stood and
lay and leaned along them, some banked in double rows, others
crammed in sideways across the tops. Printed matter was piled on
top of filing cabinets and across desks and grew up in staglagmites
along the tatty carpets. Close to the walls, paper rose in tottering
columns that were starting to resemble the trees they once had
been. Yet books, I would find out, most certainly did not just
furnish a room here – vanity played little part in Leo's mentality
and he was indifferent to surroundings – this was a place of industry.
The rooms were unexpectedly sunny: the windows peered westwards
across a London roofscape of grey slate and pink brick. Leo's
attention seldom wandered out of doors, however, and he certainly
never heeded the grime that crept in through those ill-fitting panes,
coating all the surfaces unreachable by the succession of unsuccessful
cleaners.

Yet despite the startling appearance of chaos, everything was in
fact arranged, if that is the right word, in a kind of organic order,
though few ever discerned the principles that governed it. Over
time it became apparent that those papery accumulations, gathered

and hoarded from all corners of the earth, mapped Leo's thought processes. That mass of diverse print – far more precious to him than conventional objects of value – were an outward sign of the eclectic reaches of his innermost mind, tokens of his true estate. Since he kept no journal, each yellowing sheet of print came to hold the power of a crumbling madeleine: the key to his own history and to images and arguments otherwise locked away from even his remarkable powers of recall. And therefore when, finally many years later, this unique archive had to be dispersed, scattered among libraries, lofts and dustbins, a large part of his memory was sadly lost with it.

We sat and chatted amiably for a couple of hours. Conversations with Leo, I was to find out, tended to ignite and spread like bush fire until a vast area had been set going in a matter of minutes. Once started, a dialogue could smoulder on for weeks, and, even if interrupted by days at a time, it could resume just where it had left off. Topics would range widely and wildly, punctuated with funny stories, gossip, abstruse quotes, sage observations and anecdotes: it was inspired and inspiring, challenging and entertaining.

But that first day I had come to talk about work and we had touched on nothing practical. Time was passing and I had to go. "But of course you've got the job," he exclaimed, incredulous that I needed to ask. "However. Next week I'm going to France. For a holiday. For three weeks. Come in and read the files while I'm away. Then when I get back," he beamed, "you'll know where everything is. Here's the key." Thus I began at *Survey*.

At that time, in 1969, *Survey* was approaching its most successful period as a quarterly on Soviet and East European affairs. But it was no ordinary academic journal. Its three decades of publication, from 1956 until 1989, coincided with the struggle for human rights and democratic freedom that had begun after the end of Stalinism and year by year gathered strength across the countries of Eastern Europe. From early on, *Survey* was one of the small handful of western publications prepared to print consistent evidence and analysis of Soviet deception and violations, and its pages therefore now provide a unique record of the era, chronicling the steady, sober opposition to communism by both experts and scholars in the West and dissident intellectuals throughout the Soviet bloc. It bore witness to the activity of individuals who called, with immense personal courage, for freedom within a totalitarian state; nor did it flinch from recording every detail of the measures used to crush them. Through his own publication and the publicity of others, Leo kept persecution and resistance before the eyes of the world, fostering an international sense of solidarity. From every angle, *Survey* probed a vast empire and the ideological system that had created it. Even for those discomfited by its unremitting assault on communist thinking, the journal was indispensable, and will stand as a lasting tribute to the singlemindedness of Leo Labedz. But he was much more than an editor: "scholar-activist" is more apt for one who tirelessly deployed the force of his intellect to bring about change. It was commonly acknowledged that he had "read everything and knew everything" about the world of communism."I learned early," he wrote, "the lessons of comparative totalitarianism," and he used that knowledge to devastating effect. But although his whole working life was devoted to the cause of greater freedom, he was little known to those outside his own field.

Leo was a complex person, one of those cosmopolitan figures who act as leaven in all societies. He was a naturalized Briton yet happily different, a writer of English who was fluent in six languages, a familiar of London and a hero among Poles, and one who lived in England yet who regularly skipped around the globe, his eagle vision fixed unblinkingly in a dual perspective from East to West and back again. He was a catalyst who brought news from elsewhere – indeed from everywhere else – creating a bridge across cultures through his writing and publishing, and through translating and broadcasting the ideas and testimonies of those who would otherwise have remained unheard behind the double wall of foreign language and political suppression. He kept cause with men and women he never met and who remained in countries he could not visit. The debt of gratitude he is owed remains unrecognised today and is unlikely ever to be truly measured.

Some years before his death in 1993, Leo reluctantly bowed to affectionate pressure from friends (most notably Mark Bonham Carter) and agreed to write his memoirs. He was fighting serious illness by then: a heart attack had been followed by diabetes which had necessitated operations for amputation of each leg in turn below the knee. Confined to a wheelchair, he was living alone in conditions of appalling difficulty. Yet despite all this, he was outwardly cheerful, his spirits lifting at the ring of phone or door-bell in his little sheltered flat in Ealing.

I worked twice on *Survey*: first in the early 1970s, during its years of vigorous success, and then in the late 1980s when both Leo and his journal were in decline. When *Survey* finally folded, I was to assist him with his memoirs. A plan was drawn up: structured conversations would be recorded on tape, transcribed, and then shaped between us into a "life". Yet even with every reserve of goodwill and patience, this proved impossible to realize. He managed with a certain diffidence to record a few hours of reminiscences about his early years, but the details eluded him. His memory, long commanded to such devastating effect, had grown fallible. For decades it had been his chief weapon, relied upon to produce a quote or a quip, deadly as a grenade, to be lobbed at the opposition. His memoirs, written in the fullness of health, would surely have been among the most fascinating of our times. But the attempt to compose them was undertaken when prolonged medication, the depredations of age and too many upheavals had taken their toll.

Other reasons doubtlessly inhibited their completion: revisiting past tragedies inevitably involved pain. Leo was a modest man, and the object of any story was to illustrate an abstract or moral point about "the world", not to vaunt himself. Reflective, even obsessive, he was not self-obsessed and only referred to himself obliquely. Memoirs are conclusive, they make summations; they are a leave-taking written in retirement. Leo had no concept of retiring, nor had he the will to reflect upon his own life. He was tragically caught out and forced to leave the game before he was ready to do so. Besides, the year 1990 was not the time for introspection: almost overnight, his own private story had become past history together with the communist era, and the New Order required fresh mental adjustments almost daily. The focus of interest had shifted away from the past and onto the future.

What follows is but the palest substitute for the brilliant memoirs we shall never have. It is not so much a portrait in oils as a mosaic pieced together from Leo's recollections, his published writings and from anecdotes by and about him which were rescued from the memories of friends and family. It is impossible to reproduce the vivacity of his own story-telling: his style was rich and distinctive. He was a sharp mimic. He displayed, with impish wit, impressive mastery over a vast sphere of learning that was enlivened by first-hand experience of the central events of this century. Seven decades of intense activity have been reduced here to a mere hour or two's reading.

May his shade therefore forgive the innumerable omissions

and errors in an account which regrettably found form too late to be embellished by his red-inked scrawls of incisive editorial improvement.

EARLY DAYS

Leopold Labedz was born on 22 January 1920 in Simbirsk, a small town in Russia on the river Volga near Kazan. It was also the birthplace of Lenin and Kerensky. Leo's parents were Polish, both doctors studying for higher medical diplomas at the University of Kazan when they met. Thus Leo was born "in exile", far from the Warsaw where he would grow up.

Leo – the name by which he was known the world over, except among Polish speakers, who used their own range of affectionate diminutives – was born in times of great turbulence. In 1920 the tremendous upheavals in the aftermath of the Bolshevik revolution were still continuing. There were post-war border disputes in almost every surrounding country, while Lenin's Red Army was preparing to crush Poland's attempts at independence. The populations were exhausted; there was famine and disease.

When Leo was only a few months old, his mother, who had been working in a Red Cross hospital in Kazan, caught typhus in an epidemic and suddenly died. Cut off from Poland by the hostilities, Leo's father found himself unable to return to his family in Warsaw, and had to wait several months for the first opportunity of repatriation. When he at last obtained the necessary papers, however, he faced fresh problems. Crossing Russia by train would have been arduous enough at any time, but with a young baby and in conditions of war it was hazardous too: there were severe shortages as well as physical risks. With a resourcefulness that would prove vital in times ahead, Dr Labedz found a way to feed the infant. He bought a goat, a bale of hay and a stove, and so it was that Leo, with his fresh supply of milk, lived to tell the tale of his first great journey in life. Survival and travel, he later observed, would set a pattern to be repeated throughout the following decades.

Leo was brought back to Warsaw to grow up among his father's large family. His grandmother was particularly doting and quick to protect the motherless child – though Leo claimed she did not spoil him. The family was close-knit and cultured: assimilated, middle-class Jews who spoke only Polish and knew, or acknowledged, little Yiddish. While not denying their origins, they observed no religious rituals, and Leo was taught no Hebrew and little about Jewish culture, absorbing humanistic values at home together with the canons of high European culture in the course of a normal Polish education of the time. Leo's grandfather was a businessman (whom Leo recalled being preoccupied with charities), but the next generation down, taking advantage of the lifting of Jewish quotas in the universities, had entered the professions. They were not tempted to switch to Catholicism, despite the promise of professional surety it offered against rising anti-Semitism. Poland at this time had the highest concentration of Jews anywhere in the world and the fact that almost half its lawyers and doctors were, by the 1930s, of Jewish origin, was reflected in Leo's own family, seven of whom had medical qualifications. It was assumed that Leo would follow suit. This, however, was not to be.

An only child, Leo grew up surrounded by a warm family and affectionate attentions, but oddly for one who later grew so voluble, he was slow to start talking. By the time his third birthday was approaching, the adults, fearing retardation or deafness, were growing alarmed. But then suddenly little Leo spoke, uttering his first full sentence. This great event was prompted by the family's pet fox-terrier called Lalouche. When the dog leapt up and snatched food from the child's plate, the outrage stung him into shouting: "My cutlet's gone!" The silence was broken and Leo would be an unstoppable talker from that moment on. A lifetime of using words as weapons, particularly against injustice, had just begun.

Leo was a voracious reader from an early age (and often in trouble for reading through the night – a practice he was never to abandon). Precocious and forthright, he tested the patience of teachers by quoting from his own independent reading. Wide interests were encouraged from the start: he was taken on a Grand Tour of Europe at the age of eleven with his father and aunt. He nurtured an ambition to visit every country represented in his stamp album (which he almost achieved, failing to reach only a handful of the more exotic places).

At the Kreczmar Gymnasium, one of the best secondary schools in Warsaw at that time, Leo proved an exceptionally able pupil, a good all-rounder. One friendly rival in his class was Leopold Tyrmand, later well-known as an émigré, his satirical essay "The Hairstyles of Mieczyslaw Rakowski" becoming a Polish classic. Four years below him was another boy destined to become a close friend and colleague in emigration, Richard Pipes, later Professor of Russian History at Harvard.

The school had some imaginative teachers. When the Nazis occupied Poland during the war, the geography teacher, a genial and popular figure, was appointed director of the Warsaw Zoo, and famously managed to save a number of Jews by hiding them in the monkey cages. The history teacher had been an early underground communist but, having sensed the growing dangers of Stalinism, had left the party. From him Leo learned much about the early political developments in Russia.

By the time Leo reached his teens, anti-Semitism was on the increase. With the death of Pilsudski in 1935, Polish national sentiments were sliding towards fascism and many Poles looked to Germany to save them from communism, which they generally blamed on the Jews. Many Jews had espoused communism in the hope it would offer them protection from Hitler. Leo later wrote: "This was not an unusual evolution. Many members of the Jewish intelligentsia looked to communism for a solution of the 'Jewish question' in a country where anti-Semitism was endemic, where discrimination barred the way to a career, and poverty and obscurantism were rampant."

School life reflected these tensions: a once-liberal and tolerant institution turned authoritarian and exclusionary; Jews were denied free access. A stringent new deputy director was appointed. He did not disguise his dislike of Leo and repeatedly censored or confiscated the school newspaper which the boy edited. This same man taught Polish literature and soon took exception to Leo's cheeky brilliance in class. One day he asked the boy to read his homework essay aloud. Leo raised his book and started to "read", but the essay did not exist, as he had done no homework. Concealing that blank page from the teacher's malevolent gaze was, Leo later recalled, one of the tensest experiences of his life.

As the political atmosphere deteriorated, Leo grew increasingly mutinous and the director finally threatened him with grades so low he could have been expelled. Nevertheless, Leo matriculated in 1937 with the highest marks of his year, enabling him to pass straight to university without sitting an entrance examination. He enrolled in the department of law – not because he wished to become a lawyer but as an alternative to medicine, which his family was keen for him to study, since a doctor could work anywhere in the world.

At university, Leo's independent views brought him into conflict on all sides, not least among students. He used the Show Trials then being staged in Moscow as a litmus test for gauging the opinions of leftist sympathizers (these trials he would describe, much later, as Stalin's "morality plays *pour décourager les autres*"). While some considered the Trial victims' so-called confessions authentic and believed there must be good reasons for them, Leo remained unconvinced, and thus, not for the first time and most certainly not the last, found himself in a minority of one. He was impervious to the climate of opinion, no matter what issue was at stake.

Increasing violence by gangs of right-wing students – which the authorities made no attempt to curb – aimed to keep Jews out of the university. But they refused to be intimidated and one day Leo arrived home dripping with blood after an attack with knuckledusters and razors. This was the last straw: with great reluctance, his family finally agreed to let him go to Paris, where he was first supposed to learn French and then to follow in his father's footsteps by pursuing medicine (his father had qualified in Paris). Leo would be accompanied by his closest friend, Jurek Rozenat.

PARIS

The two eighteen-year-olds set off for France in 1938 in a spirit of adventure, despite leaving Poland trapped between the double threat of Hitler from the west and Stalin from the east. As the train crossed Germany, Leo observed SS men strutting menacingly in black uniform. At certain stations along the way, large boards displayed instructions to the refugees who had started fleeing from the Sudetenland. In Paris, they found the Gare du Nord plastered with posters announcing the *mobilisation générale*. Europe was preparing for war.

Nevertheless, there was still much to be enjoyed in Paris: Leo had always felt a strong lure towards Western Europe and it was exhilarating to be "out of the provinces". To his schoolboy English, Latin and German, Leo now added French, in the first instance attending the *Alliance française*, where he caused much hilarity among teachers, who could normally pinpoint nationality through a student's pronunciation, by speaking with an accent so strange no one could guess his origins. Later, at the Sorbonne, among lectures he attended were some by future black leaders in Africa and North Africa.

Paris was a place of refuge for many nationalities. He met Spaniards who had fled the Civil War, and, while acquiring a smattering of Spanish, he more significantly acquired insight into political events through personal accounts: ideology for Leo would always be weighed against empirical evidence.

Leo and Jurek did the usual rounds of museums, galleries and cinemas. The songs of Edith Piaf and Charles Trenet would forever thereafter recall months that had been carefree and light-hearted. Occasionally they glimpsed a famous face: Ilya Ehrenburg was pointed out in a café on one occasion. Another time Leo was walking along the street with his head in a book when he collided with somebody and looked up to find himself apologizing to Marlene Dietrich.

Though many other East European émigrés had settled in Paris (might they have unknowingly glimpsed Bruno Schulz prowling the streets on his visit that year?), the two students had no contact with them and assumed, like most people away from home, that their own language was incomprehensible to everyone else – with occasionally comic results. In the *metro* one day the two boys, speaking Polish and not bothering to lower their voices, began assessing one by one the attractive points of two pretty girls seated nearby. As the girls rose to leave they came over and roundly told them off – in Polish.

Leo meanwhile devoured every kind of publication he could lay hands on, trying to keep up with each stage of the worsening political situation: the *Anschluss*, the crisis in Czechoslovakia, *Kristallnacht*. From the French press he formed clear views of French rightist sympathies, while noting the split between French Stalinists and Trotskyites caused by the Moscow trials. (Later he would discover these splits had occurred everywhere else.) He read Ante Ciliga and Boris Souvarine (founder of the French Communist Party, expelled from the Politburo in 1924) on the political struggles surrounding Stalin, details of which were not fully revealed in print for decades. Soviet publications, available in French translation – Leo's acquisition of Russian still lay ahead – formed part of his insatiable diet of reading and would provide him with an exceptionally rich field of reference later. Little was ever lost, every detail being squirrelled away for later use, though at this stage Leo was not consciously preparing the "great case" with which he would find himself constantly preoccupied after the war.

Although to some extent Paris offered relief from the increasingly ugly political climate that Leo and Jurek had left behind, it was no moral holiday: they discussed and decided everything together, weighing up all the possibilities for the next step. Should they return to Warsaw or escape elsewhere? How to survive? Could they work? Should they join the Polish Army in France? (This would, in fact, have led to Swiss internment.) They discussed returning to Poland via Romania, to avoid Germany: the Nazi regime, they were both agreed, offered no haven. But in the end they decided, as Leo later put it, "to share the same destiny as everyone else" and set off back to their families in Warsaw.

On the worrying return journey through Germany – it was now August 1939 – they witnessed signs of increased militarization. The SS and uniformed soldiers behaved with greater brutality than ever at the stations they passed through. Reaching Poland with grim forebodings, Leo did not go directly home, but met his family by the lakes in eastern Poland, hoping to spend a short vacation with them before returning to Warsaw. News of the Stalin-Hitler Pact broadcast on 23 August, however, made it clear that the Germans were about to attack Poland. In the rush to get back to the capital, panicking holidaymakers, fearful of being stranded, filled the trains to bursting point. In desperation, Leo's family hired a taxi to drive them the several hundred miles back to Warsaw, but on arrival they discovered Leo's father had already left. As a radiologist, he had immediately been drafted into the army and put in charge of a military hospital.

WAR BEGINS

The next days were frantic. Leo's family was torn: some felt safety lay with "civilized" Germany; others thought greater chances lay with the Russians and their "progressive anti-fascism". On 1 September, German bombs began falling on Warsaw and by 7 September the radio was reporting the advance of German columns. All young men able to take up arms were called upon to march east. Leo left Warsaw in great haste with an uncle, a distinguished veterinary surgeon, who was taking his own wife and son with him. They carried minimal baggage: a few clothes but no books. Fleeing Poles teemed and straggled all along the roads towards Brest-Litovsk (where Leo hoped to trace his father). The German Army meanwhile crossed the Vistula from the west on 10 September and by 23 September had taken Warsaw. By this time Leo was attached to his uncle's unit in eastern

Poland. The Polish Army, despite being virtually destroyed, continued to offer pockets of resistance until 3 October. When the order came to regroup, Leo's unit was evacuated from Biala Podlaska and Leo found himself travelling on top of the baggage in an unsprung peasant cart: the incessant jolting and battering for mile upon mile, as they hurtled further east, compounded his anguish. But by now there was no escape: too far north to reach Romania or Hungary, they were already cut off by the invading Red Army, which had started to attack eastern Poland on 17 September.

Leo was sometimes billeted with officers in private houses, sometimes with the soldiers in barracks. One night, they were invited into a farm house with the officers and were just enjoying the hospitality of food and beer when suddenly there was a sound of shooting outside. Out of the darkness came four or five armed Soviet soldiers, ordering the Poles to lie down. Prodding their backs with the points of their bayonets, the soldiers shouted "*oruzhia, oruzhia*" which Leo, in confusion, misheard as "roses" in Polish – it was Russian for "weapons".

All the Polish officers were arrested and disarmed, and taken several miles away (Leo with them, once more in a cart) to spend the rest of the night in a schoolhouse under Red Army guard. The next morning any remaining ordinary Polish soldiers who had not already managed to escape were released and Leo found himself free once again. But the Polish officers were kept under arrest and marched off in the direction of Brest Litovsk. Leo's uncle was never seen again: transported to a Soviet camp he either died there, or met a violent end at the massacre in Katyn Forest in April 1940. He was one of an estimated 26,000 Polish officers and intellectuals whose extermination in the course of the following months would only come to light later.

Leo now found himself on his own with his cousin, having to rely on wits and luck to get by. It was a myth, he would conclude, that survival was a matter of will or determination: it largely depended on chance, on being in the right place at the right time – though the right opportunity might be taken for the wrong reasons, and vice versa. Certainly, in Leo's narrative of survival, only a few strokes of luck, mostly in the form of coincidence, spared him the worst. It is ironic that Pasternak was later castigated for contriving too many improbable coincidences in his fictional *Doctor Zhivago*, whereas in a real case such as Leo's, genuine coincidence played a crucial part in a story which took place against a similar backdrop of chaos, with millions of people scattered by force across many thousands of square miles.

Leo somehow managed to reach Brest Litovsk. He found it milling with fleeing humanity, everyone struggling with bundles and packages, frantic to avoid being parted from each other, holding on against the tides of fate. In fleeing the threat of Nazi horrors they were facing others yet unknown. At every point there were fresh problems: Red Army soldiers confiscated passports and papers, which was to cause many obstacles from then on. Leo had to beg from house to house in search of shelter. When at last he and his cousin were taken in, they sent the address back to the family assumed to be still in Warsaw. Private entrepreneurs were charging increasingly exorbitant amounts for the delivery of letters. But money was rapidly ceasing to have real value. The scarcity of food was causing prices to soar: soon a gold watch would buy only half a loaf of bread.

In the daytime Leo went around seeking news of his father: finally at the military fortress he came upon a Polish janitor who had heard of a Major Labedz, but could only report that the soldiers who had been there had been taken eastward. Meanwhile people started improvising notice boards by posting up scraps of paper seeking news of lost relatives. As Leo was pinning up his own note about his father, a man nearby happened to glance at it. He was sure there had been a Major Labedz in a military hospital in the town of Kovel, where he had just been. All the other Polish officers had been arrested by the Red Army and sent into Russia but the surgeon and the X-ray specialist had apparently been kept back as prisoners to treat the wounded. The man was hoping to return to Kovel and offered to take a message from Leo.

As soon as he had word from Leo, Dr Labedz immediately set about escaping from the hospital. He bought a greatcoat at the market to cover his uniform (the sight of which would have led to instant rearrest, or worse, by the Russians) and managed to find a truck driver willing to risk giving him a lift. The truck was delivering vegetables to Brest Litovsk, so the doctor travelled the whole way hidden beneath a pile of cucumbers. Two or three days later at dawn he was furtively knocking on Leo's door.

Their next escape was assisted by further acts of kindness from local people: someone gave Dr Labedz the civilian clothes he needed. (In recalling this many years later, Leo realized with regret that, in the rush of events, they had never been able to thank properly the various anonymous men and women whose generosity had helped save their lives along the way.)

Still riven by uncertainties, Leo and his father even discussed making their way back to the family that remained in Nazi-occupied Warsaw. But Leo, with terrifying impressions of SS officers still fresh in his memory, was adamantly opposed. Poland, its army now destroyed, had been effectively crushed: Hitler had swallowed the west and now Stalin, having marched into the east, was intent on annihilating those Poles who had fled. One and a quarter million Polish people were about to be deported to the farthest-flung corners of Russia. Polish nationalism had simply been an inconvenient obstacle to both forces.

Leo and his father eventually made their way down to Lvov where they knew people who could take them in and where Jurek, Leo's closest friend, with whom he had managed to keep contact, had also landed up. The young men first stayed in a student hostel until the Soviet NKVD got wind of them, then they found refuge in a monastery. Leo's father found shelter elsewhere. The young men were given the job of lighting the monastery boilers, which meant getting up at two in the morning. Leo enjoyed ripping up old *Pravdas* but, despite much puffing and fanning, even these failed to catch fire. They were paid ten rubles a day. With a loaf of bread at that time costing fifty rubles on the black market, they often went hungry. This was typical: those who were deported all over the Soviet Union to collective farms and forced labour camps were paid less than survival rates for their work and thus effectively became slaves and starvation and cruelty were to account for the deaths of millions in this period.

After some time, Leo's father came to report that he had heard of a possible job at a newly built sanatorium (*zdravnitsa*) about 80 kilometres away. Jurek, however, was still determined to escape and set off for Romania on his own.

UNDER ARREST

When Leo and his father finally reached the sanatorium, they were taken to report their arrival. Ushered in to the director's presence, they were stunned to be confronted by the very man who had been in charge of the hospital back in Kovel, from which Dr Labedz had made his escape. It would have been easy for the director, Colonel Silenko, to hand them straight over to the NKVD at this point, but fortunately he was under pressures of his own: the sanatorium had to be ready and working as soon as possible and he urgently needed staff to run it. Therefore Leo and his father were held under arrest and put to work. Dr. Labedz was appointed medical head while Leo was given the job of librarian. In due course they would receive news from Jurek: he never got as far as Romania but had been arrested and deported to the Gulag.

The sanatorium was a wartime anomaly. Designed as a health retreat for Stalin's ruling party elite, it was as lavishly appointed as a hotel. For the time being, Leo found himself imprisoned in one of the most luxurious places in the Soviet empire, an oasis of comfort within a vast desert of unimaginable harshness and deprivation. It was a symbol of the secret sphere of privilege almost unknown to outsiders. To Leo it offered an incomparable window onto a separate world, but living there was dangerous and marked the true end to his adolescence.

Party officials came to stay at the sanatorium for one or two weeks at a time. With plenty of human material to be observed at close quarters, Leo set about making comparisons with what he already knew about the Soviet system through reading and hearsay. Most of the "guests" came from the *verkhushka*, the upper echelon occupying the highest level of power immediately below the Great Leader himself, though few of them worked in the Politburo.

Leo observed three types of "guest": older members of the pre-revolutionary intelligentsia who, by fair means or foul, had managed to survive not only the Lenin years but also Stalin's purges, which only the war had recently brought to a halt. Then there were opportunists who had "benefited" from the purges, gaining promotion onward and upward through vacancies left by those who had disappeared into the Gulag or grave. These could often barely read or write and characteristically developed a "patrimony of illiteracy", by claiming their fathers had been shepherds (rather as Bazarov in Turgenev's *Fathers and Sons* claimed his grandfather had "tilled the earth"). They were coarse and crude, unaccustomed to living in decent surroundings or to the niceties of civilized behaviour, and would treat the place roughly – stubbing out cigarettes on the furniture. Then finally there were members of the new Soviet intelligentsia, *homo sovieticus*, members of the *nomenklatura* who were high in aspiration, low in culture and ideologically blinkered. These were literate but poorly read – having digested only the restricted canon of approved Russian texts, with little by foreign authors – yet they paraded their meagre attainments arrogantly. If, Leo felt, man is what he reads, then he, as librarian, was in a good position to assess what these men were.

Such first-hand observation of Stalin's henchmen was to provide Leo with further evidence of the workings of the communist world: the significance of an unacknowledged, secret class enjoying a way of life denied to the slave-citizens of that era would strengthen his arguments about the discrepancy between theory and reality. His understanding of Stalin's Terror was based on contact not only with those who had lived through it, but also with those who had helped to carry it out.

People at the sanatorium revealed more than they suspected in conversation with this bookish young Pole. Leo's Russian quickly became fluent and he even acquired some local Ukrainian, too. There was considerable irony in working through the standard texts of Marx and Lenin in the confinement of a Stalinist prison of privilege and in later life Leo enjoyed trouncing opponents by quoting them chapter and verse – a familiarity usually misattributed to the devotions of a former Party member.

Sometimes, driven by morbid curiosity, he found himself playing snooker with local members of the NKVD until late into the night. He recalled once suggesting it was perhaps time to pack up, whereupon they said, "Oh no, we're not going to bed tonight – we're working." By then Leo knew the dark implications of such words only too well. Despite the veneer of bonhomie, he never forgot his precarious position – a single slip could have had fatal consequences and as a foreigner, furthermore, he was under constant scrutiny and suspicion.

Amongst those who stayed at the sanatorium were certain notables from the artistic sphere, including the film director Pudovkin, then as famous as Eisenstein. But probably one of the most formative, and informative, characters Leo was ever to encounter was a Jewish scriptwriter, Alexei Kapler, who during that period was working directly with Stalin himself. Then aged about thirty and utterly cynical, Kapler took Leo into his confidence, and with a mixture of daring and foolishness, revealed all he knew about the tyrant whose absoluteness of power had no parallel. Kapler took immense risks in doing this: he knew almost nothing about Leo except that he had been a student in Paris. But a cameraderie developed between the two, and they would go for long walks in the surrounding woods to avoid being overheard, for both knew the price of a joke about Stalin. What especially interested Leo were the sorts of thing that people scarcely dared think, let alone discuss aloud, at that time: he wanted to know about Stalin's psychology, what it was like to live and deal with such a man at close quarters. Kapler described Stalin's behaviour, his moods and dispositions, the style in which he lived, his manners, the way he talked and conducted himself with others, and so on. Since eye witness reports always counted for much with Leo, Kapler's were especially valuable: Stalin was clearly in the grip of deep paranoia, with boundless power to indulge his murderous whims and unpredictable furies. Leo heard about the appalling effects on Stalin's family as well as his close entourage: the violence and drunkenness, the disappearances, and the suicide of his wife. (Details of life *chez* Stalin would in due course be verified in various published accounts.) Yet all was then concealed by the powerful and persuasive propaganda that projected Josef Stalin world-wide in the smiling image of the Great Father Protector of Nations.

Kapler's work as a professional film-maker was crucial to this process of political image-making. He had worked with Stalin personally as scriptwriter for the film versions of the February and October Revolutions. These were in fact screen adaptations of *A Short Course in the History of the Communist Party* – "the Bible of Stalin's era" which every Soviet child was made to learn by heart – in other words, elaborately stage-managed versions of historical truth. As Leo wrote many years later, "Kapler was perfectly aware that the *Short Course* was a concoction of lies, historical fabrications, and surrealistic distortions. But needless to say Kapler did what Stalin 'suggested' to him and in our own conversations he was quite cynical about it. His was not a case of 'double-think'; he was conscious of the falsification of history involved in his work." This manipulation was a strategic part of Soviet propaganda: Kapler explained how genuine film footage and stills were edited and doctored to accord with the Stalinist version of events. It was just one link in the chain of deceptions that Leo was to spend his life tracking from their fabrication at the highest levels down to their ultimate consumption by the unquestioning, near and far.

As a shrewd member of the *privilegentsia*, Kapler was one of the few who managed to survive proximity to the Great Protector long enough to die a natural death. When his stay at the sanatorium came to an end, there was no question of further contact with Leo. Yet by the strangest chance, their paths were to cross many years later.

Only two members of the staff at the sanatorium came from the "lower classes", one of these being a Jewish barber from Leningrad. It was from this man that Leo first heard about a ghetto being constructed in Warsaw, its walls, in the words of *Pravda*, "cemented in blood". "It was clear to me then," Leo commented, "that the Nazis were qualitatively different from anything we had known before. With the ghetto, we were taken way past the perspectives of the nineteenth century." The family that Leo left behind in Warsaw did not survive: they were deported to Germany and were among the three million Poles who perished in Nazi death camps.

On 22 June 1941 the period of nerve-wracking but easeful imprisonment came to an end when the Germans attacked Russia. The attack prompted a mass evacuation, in which Leo and his father managed to escape by obtaining forged papers and crushing themselves into one of the last overloaded trains going east towards Asia.

THE POLISH ARMY

When General Anders was permitted to start organizing a Polish army on Soviet territory, both Leo and his father enlisted in Kuybyshev. It was at this point discovered that many thousands of men were missing from the officer lists. The cream of Polish officers and intellectuals, it later transpired, had either been "liquidated" in regional camps or killed in cold blood – mostly shot with a single bullet in the back of the head, sometimes bludgeoned or bayonetted to death – at Katyn Forest. Their fate was suspected at the time, but it took many years to establish the truth and apportion blame officially. The whole tragedy has since been fully reconstructed from all kinds of grim evidence, including, most recently (1997), Soviet archive film of the mass graves. The callousness of the massacre was exacerbated by the Soviets' repeated denials of guilt and their cynical attempt to blame it on the Nazis (who had been nowhere near Katyn in April 1940 when the killings took place). "It was decided by the victorious governments," wrote Churchill, "that the issue should be avoided, and the crime of Katyn was never probed in detail." Nearly half a century was to pass before a full international investigation found the Soviet NKVD culpable.

Leo was one of those who for years would independently amass quantities of evidence both on the crime itself and on what he and many others felt was inexcusable softness by western powers towards the perpetrators. The final laying of blame in 1989 came too late to assuage a long-standing sense of betrayal. Destroying the intelligentsia had struck a double blow at both the Polish nation and its army, and forced General Anders' army to abandon any attempt to re-enter

Poland and to depart for the Middle East with the Allies.

Leo now found himself in Tashkent in Uzbekistan. Here he heard about the fate of the other million or more Poles who had fled to the "safety" of the Soviet Union: over half of them had been sent to "corrective" labour camps, and the remainder to prisoner-of-war camps or enforced settlements in remote and inhospitable regions of the south-eastern provinces, to live in cruel conditions in which brutality, starvation and sheer exhaustion claimed the lives of a high proportion. Making the reality of the Gulag known to the West was to be a slow and thankless process. Leo would be one of a small band who relentlessly fought to establish unwelcome facts. Another was Robert Conquest, whose *Great Terror* (1968) would mark a turning point in post-war Western understanding, though it would take a Solzhenitsyn to make Gulag an international term.

General Anders' army had more hopes than means: ill-equipped, underfunded and underfed, it managed to organize itself from Polish population scattered far and wide in deserts, villages and remote rural areas. Once Dr Labedz was drafted into the army as medical officer, Leo again lost contact. During this period soldiers had to fend for themselves. There was no pay, they could not work and they joined queues where there was rumour of food. They foraged. Many starved. Leo recalled once spying windfallen pears on the ground in a small orchard. Creeping in to pick one up, he was confronted by a peasant armed with a gun. This small event, he wryly observed years later, gave him first hand experience of the *kulaks'* tenacious sense of ownership, which even Stalin had not managed to stamp out among the Uzbeks. (In fact, however, in 1932, at the height of the famine, a Soviet law had been passed making it illegal for citizens to pick up a single piece of fallen fruit, grains of wheat or unharvested produce left in the fields – doing so constituted theft from the state and was punishable by forced labour or worse) This period of acute privation may have caused, or at any rate aggravated, Leo's curious eating habits in later life – an utter aversion to vegetables, for example, compelled him to remove even the green specks of parsley garnishing a dish – and it may well have contributed to his fatal diabetes.

Though he grew skeletal from starvation, he would never dwell on his suffering: many, after all, did not survive. He was, on the contrary, often ready to make light of things, and once remarked that on the matter of instinct, Freud had it all wrong: the primary instinct for survival concerned not sex, but food – its acquisition became the total obsession of everyone he encountered at that time.

One recollection from this period illustrates Leo's capacity to rise above circumstance. In Tashkent, between wanderings in search of food, the soldiers would huddle inside the library for warmth. Leo, ragged and weak with malnutrition, also demanded books to read. In his affectionate portrait, published in *The American Scholar* 63 (1994), his friend Edward Shils reconstructed the scene from Leo's anecdote:

Seeing the library, a single dim light in a dusty lifeless scene, he went in. However disorderly it might have been within, it was a nearly divine order compared with the outside. Leopold began to order all sorts of books to be brought to him. After a time, the clerks refused to bring any more books for him. Where books were concerned, Leopold was even more ravenous than he was for meat. He was not one to accept refusals. Weak though he was, Leopold could raise his voice. He demanded to see the head of the library. After some squabbling, he was ushered into that person's presence. The director was an oldish man, probably in his sixties, bent, thin, unsympathetic, his coldness of mien emphasised by his pince-nez. He was obviously a man who did not want any commotion around him. All else might be disregarded but not commotion. And here was Leopold, a creator of commotion. The librarian appeared to be a traditional Tsarist, and then Communist, *tchinovnik*. The librarian weakened to the extent of asking Leopold why he wished to read so many books. Leopold told him what little there was to tell about his academic career. When Leopold mentioned his studies at the Sorbonne, the old librarian broke down. He too had studied in Paris, before the First World War. He began to reminisce: it had been the happiest time of his life; he recalled streets and cafés and bookshops. He began to sob. Russia, when he returned, went to war; then came the succession of the revolution, the civil war, famines, epidemics, trials – it was all too much for him. He could not stand the turmoil, so he withdrew to what he thought would be the peace and quiet of the librarianship of Tashkent. But here was no escape from the cruel, dusty, broken treadmill of Soviet society. Recollections of Paris had brought before his mind reminders of a now impossible happiness . . . Pulling himself together, he told Leopold: "You will be free to read any books, periodicals, or papers in the library except *Pravda* or *Izvestia* from

1918 to 1920. Please do not ask for my permission to read those papers. [It would be more than my life is worth] to give you permission to see them. So, please do not ask me to allow you to do so.

This apparently inconsequential period of study – yet another stage in his unsentimental education – provided Leo with a chance to immerse himself in pre-war Soviet writing from which he would draw, in typical feats of memory in later life, detailed evidence of pro-Stalinist apologists.

Illness followed hard on the heels of persistent malnutrition, and Leo fell prey to serious disease for many of the following months. In 1942 he collapsed with typhus. An army field hospital had been set up in a converted mosque, where the sick were carried in and left lying on the floor, mostly until they died. Lying there, Leo tried to reconcile himself to dying alone, never learning what had become of his father, or what fate his family had met.

Then one day a very sick young man was placed beside Leo. The seemingly impossible had occurred: out of all the thousands of people scattered across those vast eastern territories, "chance, or providence, or God" had brought his closest friend, Jurek. After deportation, Jurek had somehow made contact with Leo at the sanatorium, from which Leo had managed to send parcels to the Gulag. But then they had lost touch. Both had been transported east in the evacuation and both had duly joined General Anders' army from different points. And now, starving, both had succumbed to typhus. But Jurek had been brought in too late and was already very weak – too weak, in fact, to be helped. After three days, he finally expired in Leo's arms. This, Leo confessed, was one of the lowest points in his life. Alone and ill, with everything and everyone lost, he had little reason to live. There seemed to be no point in going on.

At this point, however, the Russians agreed to allow the British to move the troops under their command over the Caspian Sea: in the summer of 1942, therefore, General Anders' army prepared to leave Russia for Iran.

The journey required an overnight march to the port. Still in poor health, Leo was unfit for such strenuous activity. Nevertheless, when the order came to march, he struggled along under the great weight of his kit bag, a bag that contained all his worldly possessions which included the valuable tinned food and provisions issued by the army for the journey. The longer they marched, the slower Leo plodded, dropping farther and farther behind with every step. Finally, utterly exhausted, he sat down at the side of the road in despair. Failing to reach the ship would mean falling into Soviet hands and almost certain death. An Uzbek youth, however, approached and offered to carry his bag. Leo feared that once he had let it go, he would never see the bag again. Yet without it, he would have a better chance of reaching the ship in time. Reluctantly, he handed it over and watched the young man stride off into the distance. Leo's worst fears were confirmed: he now owned absolutely nothing in the world.

Trudging through the night with a heavy heart, he reached the port at dawn and dragged himself to the docks. There was the ship, preparing to set sail. And there too was the young man, waiting with the bag. It had not even been opened, nothing had been touched. Even the food was intact, despite the young Uzbek doubtlessly being as hungry as everyone else at that time. For Leo, this gesture of altruism shone like a beacon after the dark chaos of the previous months. It taught him another lasting lesson in trust, and in the value of decency among ordinary people, even *in extremis*.

By the time the ship docked in the Iranian port, Leo was in a state of complete collapse. He lay among the massed bodies on the beach, dehydrated, exhausted, and close to death – many were already dead. Surveying this terrible scene, one Polish officer, Misza Wolach, noticed small signs of life. Coming closer he recognized the living corpse as the son of his friend, Dr Labedz. He said: "Leo, what are you doing here?" Ever quick-witted, Leo gasped: "Well, dying actually."

By another stroke of great good fortune, the officer knew that Dr Labedz was in Tehran in charge of a field hospital. Leo was duly transported and remained there until the end of the year, recovering from pellagra and the effects of severe malnutrition.

In due course, Leo received basic military training, though stories suggest that as a soldier his conduct was professorial rather than professional. He claimed to have been a surprisingly good shot (now unverifiable). But he was still prey to illness. One evening he turned up at the officers' mess. "Anyone for bridge?" he asked. But the pack was barely dealt before he slumped onto the table: this time it was malaria.

In 1943–5, as part of the 2nd Polish Corps of the 8th Army, Leo was sent through the Middle East, via Iraq, Palestine and Egypt. He took part in the Italian campaign, eventually seeing action at Monte

Cassino. Here again he displayed unconventional military behaviour: aghast at the destruction and looting of villas and palazzi, where treasures, especially books, had been left to rot among the rubble, Leo determined to salvage what he could. Emptying ammunition from the tank to which he was attached, he dismayed and angered his fellow soldiers by stowing as many books as he could manage in its place. These fine, ancient volumes he later handed over to a library in Rome. In the city, he was put on guard duty at one of the great museums and often found himself sole custodian of priceless treasures. Possibly as a result of this work, he became friendly with the Italian painter Giorgio de Chirico. Some affinity of spirit may be glimpsed in de Chirico's memoirs where, recalling a moment in childhood when left to face some youthful bullies, he wrote: "I was the monomachist, the one who remained to fight alone." It evokes a personal determination he must have recognized in Leo.

THE WAR ENDS

When the war came to an end, members of the liberating army were offered the chance to enter the university of their choice. Studying at the oldest university in Europe attracted Leo and he enrolled in the faculty of law at Bologna University, though with no desire to become a lawyer – where his career was concerned he was only ever certain that he most emphatically did not wish to become a doctor. His legal studies would, however, always bolster his belief in legitimacy, especially political legitimacy.

Bologna, a haven of civilized life, offered balm to the horrors and loss of the previous years. Leo now acquired yet another language and, with it, affection for a country to which he subsequently returned whenever possible. (He had a hand in bringing Giuseppe Tomasi di Lampedusa's *Il Gattopardo – The Leopard* – back to England after one summer trip in the late 1950s, urging Manya Harari and Marjorie Villiers to publish it, as they did, at The Harvill Press.) His Italian studies did not go to waste: right to the end of his life he would still be reaching back to texts read as a student and once famously clinched an argument with Leon Radzinowicz, the great authority on criminal law, by triumphantly quoting from Beccaria's *Dei delitti e delle pene* in the original. And in his last years, when confined to a wheelchair, he requested a volume of Guicciardini from the London Library to confirm a quote, and found unexpected pleasure in leafing through their fine leather bound copy kindling fond memories of far-off student days.

If Leo made little of what he endured, it was less out of modesty than recognition of his relative good fortune. Of the millions displaced in Eastern Europe, most had perished and, of those who survived and escaped to tell their stories, many were regarded with scorn or disbelief in the West, sometimes with tragic consequences (as in the case of Victor Kravchenko, who killed himself in Paris in 1966 after his accounts of the Russian camps were treated with public contempt and ridicule). Such experiences set people apart from those they came to live among, and formed a basis for a tacit mutual understanding among themselves. Like most exiles down the ages, Leo would never abandon his sense of loyalty to those lost or left behind. He unavoidably perceived past events through the prism of his own life, and possessed a grasp of the realities of twentieth-century events in Eastern Europe that few were prepared to acknowledge in these early post-war years. It required a mental balancing act to command both a western and eastern perspective, as simultaneous insider and outsider. Leo belonged, as Robert Kostrzewa wrote in a foreword to the leading émigré Polish intellectual journal, *Between East and West – Writings from "Kultura"* 1990, "to that generation of Polish intellectuals who stayed in the West after World War II when it became clear that the catastrophe of the Nazi destruction was going to be followed by another national calamity – the Soviet occupation. They were driven to exile by bitter necessity and the desire to oppose defeat in the hope of ultimate victory."

ENGLAND

While Leo remained in Bologna, Dr Labedz went on to London where he succeeded in finding a job at the Polish Hospital. Leo joined him in spring 1946 and for the next three years was to remain attached to the Polish Resettlement Corps, part of the Polish Army, improving his English and studying economics at the University of London. In 1950 he embarked on a degree in sociology at the London School of Economics.

Here Leo was distinguished by his breadth of knowledge and a seemingly indefatigable capacity for argument. He seldom alluded to personal loss or experience – indeed, all his life he only ever revealed snippets of personal history through rare anecdotes to close friends.

He could never, for example, speak about the fate of his family who died in Nazi death camps, though he once remarked, in the days before the plethora of Holocaust literature, that "This Way to the Gas, Ladies and Gentlemen", the shockingly cynical short story by Tadeusz Borowski, seemed to say it all. At the deepest levels, however, loss surely drove his convictions.

In the formal atmosphere of post-war Britain, Leo was a highly energized enigma: people often wondered "What made him tick?", for here was an articulate, multilingual émigré who, paradoxically, was explosively emotional in the cause of rationality. He was a militant liberal. Leo always gave an impression of unbounded energy and his lively, cheerful spirit seemed uncrushable, though it could be clouded by anger. Even when debating matters of gravity he appeared deceptively playful, and although he could leave an opponent bloodied, he was fated to be underestimated for much of his life, often taken for a mere irritant – "a thorn in the flesh of politicians and policy makers" – or affectionately dismissed as a snapping terrier or bouncing ball, chiefly on account of his fast, and often furious, argumentation both in speech and print.

Dialogue – argument – was for Leo not only fundamental to democratic debate, it was a way of life. His intense analysis resembled a secularized form of traditional interrogation and commentary practised for centuries in the communities from which his fully-assimilated Jewish family had sprung. Only the texts had changed. He drew on the most diverse of sources: the shallows of pamphlets were trawled as thoroughly as the deeper waters of canonical tracts. His passion for detail, however, made heavy demands on anyone less familiar with a given subject than himself, while the fervour with which he attacked "misguided theories and their adherents" was characteristic of a religious fanatic. But Leo had little feeling for religion: as a young man, he had admired the passionate atheist Bertrand Russell (though he came to deplore his pacifist views) and similarly maintained steadfast "faith" in the power of reason. He acknowledged, however, that in Eastern Europe the persecution of the Church and other organized religious groups in the name of state atheism had driven many to seek refuge in alternative ethical systems and spiritual beliefs, while the authority of the Catholic Church in Poland, boosted by the appointment of a Polish Pope, came to play a key role in political opposition in the 1970s.

As a student Leo was assiduous but too self-willed for a permanent life within ivory towers. He resisted timetables and schedules. He needed to be in the flow of things, taking the broad view. All that he read and thought was informed by what he had already seen and continued to see and hear for himself: his insistence on weighing the theoretical against the empirical nwould bring him into conflict with orthodoxies of all kinds, from the academic to the political. And the quest for further evidence never ceased. The gathering of information, eye-witness accounts, personal stories, anecdotes and jokes went on to the end, side by side with scholarly pursuits. How he would have relished the rich cornucopia of vindicating evidence that poured from the communist archives made accessible in the 1990s.

First as a student and later as an editor, Leo sought, or was himself constantly sought by, an unending stream of people from all walks of life whose stories he heard and committed to memory. Unfazed by reputation or status, Leo's constant measure was personal integrity, especially of those who held positions of power or influence. Ignorance or irresponsibility were unpardonable in his eyes, and nothing heightened his sense of outrage more than those in the West willing to turn a deaf ear or find excuses for the excesses of totalitarianism. The faddish flight from objective truth that ultimately evolved, via relativism, into contemporary notions of "social construction" especially drew his fire, for they denied, just as Soviet Communism denied, the reality and experience he knew to be true. His intellect was fuelled by knowing how it *really* was (*Wie es eigentlich gewesen ist*), his notion of an incontrovertible *reality* drawing him into permanent battles with those whose views were shaped by ideas alone.

By the mid-1950s, Leo was capable of reading and arguing in six languages, while schoolboy Latin ensured the grammatical correctness of tags. His voracious reading habits were to become legendary. One friend commented: "He reads all night and talks all day," while another who shared a house with him as a student recalled a kind of scaffolding constructed all round the bathroom which allowed Leo to continue reading for as much time as humanly possible. "Leo read everything and anything," wrote his friend Edward Shils. "Print at any angle drew him as by a magnet. When he came into a room to see a person seated at a paper- or book-littered desk, he read all that was open there – even upside down!"

Being at last offered an opportunity for years of uninterrupted study, Leo was fermenting with ideas: intellectual ebullience would always cause an overflow of both deadlines as well as the pint pots of print. One of his first reviews, of Burnham's *Managerial Revolution*, elicited sixty handwritten pages of foolscap. Tracing the interconnectedness of things could be risky, however, and no matter how outstandingly he spoke at university seminars and tutorials, Leo proved an unruly candidate in examinations. In one finals degree paper, instead of answering three questions, he produced just one exceedingly lengthy disquisition. His examiners thus faced a dilemma: a student of undoubted brilliance had failed to comply with the regulations. Though some wished to fail him, his case was supported by Jean Floud, then a lecturer at LSE, and a compromise was finally reached by awarding him a lower second. Unbowed, he registered for a doctoral thesis on Soviet social structure and policy, but was never to complete it.

Leo's path was guided less by self-advancement than by tenacious adherence to principles and a sense of loyalty to the "cause". This cause was, in its broadest terms, a struggle against political extremism, but more specifically – particularly in the early years after the war – spoke on behalf of the victims of extremism, those who no longer had a voice, having been silenced forever in camps, in gas chambers or other unimaginable places, and those who were still deprived of a voice through continuing political repression. Leo felt under an unshakeable compulsion to place his learning and great intellectual dynamism at the service of exposing those injustices. Pure scholarship was not enough, he needed to be active. With such a sense of mission, it was natural that he should gravitate towards a phenomenon of that era which has still received scant historical assessment: the Congress for Cultural Freedom. In 1956 he joined the staff of the publication that was about to become the journal *Survey*. Having found his métier as editor, he would from then on channel his energies into a broader kind of scholarly activity.

THE CONGRESS FOR CULTURAL FREEDOM

The Congress for Cultural Freedom was an intellectual crusade of the twentieth century. It still tends to be dismissed as a regrettable and embarrassing aspect of the Cold War – but this masks a confusion. For while the stand against Nazism had been fairly straightforward, opposition to Communism was always complicated by old loyalties and unresolved conflicts. "The sin of nearly all left-wingers from 1933 onwards," Orwell once wrote, "is that they have wanted to be anti-fascist without being anti-totalitarian." However, at the time, anyone pointing to the remaining delusions and omissions of conscience was fated, like Cassandra, not only to speak the truth but also to be disbelieved.

The Congress for Cultural Freedom was intended as an organized retaliation by the democratic non-communist left to powerful, organized communist propaganda, the battle lines being drawn between democracy and individualism against tyranny and collectivism. Its ambition was to create a global alignment of intellectuals united against an ideology in the name of which more than fifty million had already been murdered in Eastern Europe alone, and which was bent on spreading its influence further across the post-war world.

Ostensibly the impetus to form the Congress was provided in 1946 by the sight of refugees being forcibly repatriated to Eastern Europe, where, as war-time "traitors", they would mostly be sentenced to forced labour camps or death. Formally, however, the Congress sprang from a conference held in Berlin in 1950 at which Arthur Koestler, one of the organizers together with Melvin Lasky and Irving Brown, had rallied the assembled intellectuals with the slogan: "Friends, freedom has seized the offensive!". This was in response to two "world peace" Congresses orchestrated the previous year in New York and Paris to celebrate the triumphs and joys of Stalinism, and which included among their large numbers delegations of "reliable" intellectuals from the Soviet Union.

From its beginnings the Congress was to attract liberal-left intellectuals, but it was also a station of disenchantment for a generation which, having joined or travelled with the Party between the wars, had undergone a process of painful disillusionment when their god had failed. "When all is said," wrote Koestler, "we ex-Communists are the only people . . . who know what it's all about." Nevertheless, there were plenty of others such as Leo for whom the Party had never offered a temptation and who still knew "what it was all about" – having learned personally how *les extrèmes se touchent* through harsh experience at Nazi or Soviet hands. The Congress for Cultural Freedom was not the monolith that accounts have suggested hitherto, but it embraced a range of views, from aggressive pessimists, who called for uncompromising opposition to the captive minds of the Party, to gentle optimists, who advocated a slow erosion through dialogue and contact. By distancing itself from the hysterical witch-hunts of McCarthyism, the Congress hoped to provide a platform for "the rational and truthful understanding of the contemporary world" and for those who sought to "protect intellectual integrity".

By the early 1950s, the Congress was fully established under the directorship of Michael Josselson, with the composer Nicolas Nabokov as Secretary-General. It was soon publishing a network of literary and cultural journals across the globe, while organizing international conferences and seminars with a wide-reaching translation programme. The grander dialectic of which the Congress was a part traced its origins via both French and Russian revolutions back to the Enlightenment, with fundamental questions of freedom, progress, science and history being placed within the larger framework of what constituted a just and free society and how it should be achieved. As Edward Shils, a long-standing member of the Congress, wrote:

> The belief that the "noble experiment" undertaken by the Soviet Union was by and large the model which all societies should follow for the benefit of the human race has been one of the most tenacious and widely accepted beliefs of the educated classes through most of the 20th century . . . The Congress for Cultural Freedom took as its main task the assertion of the value of intellectual and artistic freedom at a time when in the Soviet Union and Eastern Europe and China, these did not exist . . . It was also an address to the intellectuals of Western countries to remove the blinkers from their eyes and to see the Communist societies as they really were.

Founded on the belief that true democracy could only exist with the free exchange of higher ideas that would eventually "trickle down", the Congress was formed as "an act of solidarity with the intellectual victims of the repressive imposition of Communism and 'people's democracy'". But this avowed elitism would find itself swimming against a double current: on the one hand, the growing egalitarianism of mass and pop cultures worldwide, and on the other the increasing agitation of youthful radicalism, which was about to attack the very foundations of liberalism on which the Congress was based.

By the 1960s, more than twenty Congress publications were in production: *Encounter* was the leading monthly intellectual review of the arts, edited in London initially by Stephen Spender and Irving Kristol. *Survey*, originally started by Walter Laqueur, soon joined by Jane Degras and later by Leo Labedz, focused on Eastern European affairs, while *Minerva*, the brainchild of Edward Shils, dealt with

science and social policy, and the suppression of intellectual freedom
was monitored in *Censorship* edited by Murray Mindlin. *China
Quarterly* and *New African* were both edited in London, whereas
Preuves and *Der Monat* were established in Paris and Berlin, with
others in English and foreign languages across the continents.

For more than a decade, polemic poured forth in print and speech:
the magazines and journals flourished, conferences great and small
were staged in capital cities, while lectures, seminars and symposia
were held at universities round the world. Leo Labedz was particularly involved in two of these: "Contemporary History in the Soviet
Mirror" and "Literature and Revolution in Soviet Russia" with Max
Hayward at St Antony's College, Oxford.

The more the Congress expanded, however, the louder the rumours
grew about who or what lay behind it. Even so, when it was publicly
revealed in 1967 that the CIA had secretly funded the whole enterprise
by channelling funds through private foundations, the Congress
was rocked to its core. The revelations triggered deep acrimony and
a lasting schism in its membership. For this was the unkindest cut
of all: an organization aimed at unmasking the Great Lie turned out
itself to have been founded on deception. Protestations of ignorance
at the top were inadmissible. People felt used, despite having joined
of their own volition. The eventual collapse of the Congress caused
unpleasant political reverberations around the world, since all its
activities had become associated with an American foreign policy
which by then had brought about unpopular military involvement
in Vietnam. Not only did that policy split liberal-left opinion, it also
confused western opposition to communist oppression. The resulting
disarray baffled dissidents struggling for basic democratic rights
inside communist countries, but no doubt gave cause for rejoicing
to their oppressors.

The Congress requires fuller consideration in the longer perspective. What it tried to reveal about communist societies appeared
to be so unwelcome in the West that shooting the messenger was
apparently preferable to heeding the message, and the hostility and
suspicion besieging even the most successful of its initiatives point
to continuing contradictions in attitudes prevalent in the second half
of this century. People may have "deprecated Stalinist malevolence,"
wrote Leo, "but [they deprecated] even more the aggrieved outcries
on behalf of its victims by the 'cold-warriors' and the 'anti-communist
crusaders.'"

The Congress is commonly portrayed as a covert transatlantic operation, peddling western propaganda to "save Europe from itself". Even Peter Coleman's sympathetic profile was entitled *The Liberal Conspiracy*, to which a former member replied: "Liberal? Yes. Conspiracy? No." Yet it never sought total unanimity: with such a diversity of vociferous men (and women), each prizing independence of mind above all else, such an aim, in any case, would have been unfeasible. It was a loose, humanistic enterprise in which a disparate network of intellectuals was united by broad but firmly held objectives. Its supporters were not mouthpieces, they felt they were acting freely. Nevertheless, its chief memorial has remained the taint of its funding – with Stephen Spender's famous resignation as editor of *Encounter* signalling the deep outrage that was felt far beyond the Congress itself.

The Congress's fall from grace gratified many – in particular the younger generation and the New Left who resented American policies – but it made harder the job of speaking out about communist outrages, and thereafter any independent liberal initiative was easily stigmatized by hints at CIA backing. Those who refused to abandon the aims of the Congress, irrespective of who bankrolled it, suffered an unrelieved sense of betrayal, which in Leo's case would infuse his writing with further acerbity, particularly towards erstwhile intellectual allies. The threat of communism, from the perspective of his own experience and understanding, could never be underestimated. It led him to draw a comparison, in an essay entitled "Holocaust: Myths & Horrors" (1980), between "Commu-Nazi" genocides and the atrocities perpetrated by the Khmer Rouge: "One day perhaps we will have a comparative study of genocide, and the story would be incomplete without a picture of the international reactions in the outside world to these atrocities. It is striking what great, evidently deep-seated, reluctance there was in each historical case of genocide to accept the hard facts and recognize them for what they were. Universal condemnation was delayed on each occasion by a tendency to ignore, obfuscate, or rationalize the facts. Were those who denied them anything but moral accomplices?"

Despite a change of name and genuine, clean funding from the Ford Foundation, the International Association for Cultural Freedom that rose in the late 1960s from the ashes of the old Congress was unsteady from the start. The fissures in its base mirrored those that had come to divide the intellectual world at large, due to the Vietnam War and New Leftism. The deep diffrences that finally broke up the Association also broke up long-standing friendships. Leo's hopes for creating a strong and vital centre had been dashed by what he disparaged as "the long march through the universities".

Although the greater "family" of the old Congress fell apart, a special kinship remained among certain former members, especially Leo, Edward Shils and Melvin Lasky, now the editor of *Encounter*. Though their publications were independent, the three men braced themselves against the dangers they detected in the resurgent extremism of Sixties radicalism, and, yoked to a common cause, they formed a troika of ebullient war-horses, spurred on as much by cerebral rivalry as by a spirit of fraternity. Drifting almost daily to the *Encounter* offices, Leo must have spent months of his life sparring (mostly) amicably with "Mel" and anyone else he found there. "Ed", on the other hand, was solicitous, even protective, towards Leo, whom he captured in a moving memoir shortly before his own death.

EDITING SURVEY

Survey had started life in the early 1950s as a flimsy Congress for Cultural Freedom newsletter entitled *Information Bulletin on the Soviet Union*. Edited by Walter Laqueur with the assistance of Jane Degras, it consisted of news items on the cultural life burgeoning in the thaw that followed Stalin's death in 1953. By the time Leo joined as associate editor in 1956, it had become a slim pamphlet called *Soviet Culture*, soon to assume the plumper form of a conventional-looking academic journal which it would retain unchanged from then on. Elegance of design was not considered important and all attempts to prettify its plain and unpretentious format were firmly resisted; any excitement was to be found inside the covers. When Walter Laqueur left to become director of the Wiener Library in 1966, Leo became sole editor of what was now called *Survey*, and remained in that post for the next 23 years. It was produced with one full-time assistant and a proofreader.

Leo was a brilliant editor. He had a sharp instinct for commissioning and for perceiving the silk purses in the sow's ears that flopped unbidden onto his desk; he was a master in the art of assemblage. Through tentacular connections, he would always try to enrich each issue with at least a couple of plums – and often held up production to include them. Most of the time, he was merrily provocative, courteous and cheerfully uninterested in "the practicalities". Inspired, lively, amusing and knowledgeable, he was possessed of deep insights and a phenomenal memory. But he was also volatile, unpunctual, disorganized, argumentative, resistant to compromise, and could be maddeningly, or endearingly, punctilious. His erratic habits wrecked timetables and schedules. He was neither a good manager nor an easy colleague. His buoyant demeanour counterbalanced a propensity for violent disagreement – which he would generously term "misunderstanding" – and he was pleased as a puppy if a reconciliation could take place. Friends found their patience and affection tested to the utmost and usually forgave him his trespasses. Foes did not.

In Leo's hands *Survey* was not so much a journal as a one-man campaign. It will remain his enduring monument. He never doubted the uniqueness of its role and was never swayed by any consideration other than the pursuit of the truth: "I have nothing to lose," he once wrote, "but my integrity." Through *Survey*'s pages he aimed to bear witness to the present partly through analysis of the past – for the past and its horrors were never to be forgotten. Yet this was no exercise in nostalgia; it was an attempt to set straight a record that had been, and continued for most of the century to be, subject to all manner of falsification. The contents of *Survey*'s 130 issues reflected all aspects of life and thought, culture and politics, and the developing voice of opposition within the Soviet bloc. All the key names, ideas, texts and events of the period found their place in astutely arranged editions that crossed like stepping stones over a vast river of gradual historical change. *Survey* will be of immense value to posterity as a chronicle of the epoch.

Leo quickly fastened on to emerging issues, observing how they fitted into existing patterns or broke with precedent. Civil protest, *samizdat*, historiography, nationalism, censorship, cultural freedom, psychiatric abuse . . . each milestone in the battle for human rights and political independence in post-war Eastern Europe was marked in *Survey*'s pages. Often a whole issue was devoted to a single topic: the Hungarian Uprising in 1956, the Prague Spring in 1968, Poland in the 1970s and again in the 1980s, Yugoslavia, Romania, Afghanistan, the Baltic states, and so on. Wave after slow wave of change rolled on until suddenly the pace quickened after *glasnost* and *perestroika* – and the Wall was down. Dissident intellectuals in one era became presidents and leaders in the next. Yet despite its close analysis, not even *Survey* could foresee the swift final domino effect of the Gorbachev era; not even the best informed Kremlinologists were prepared for the way things finally went, though of course many problems, such as nationalism, were always simmering beneath the

Stalinist "solutions". As Leo wrote in 1972: "When Clio is raped she takes her revenge. In all the countries where major revolutions have taken place . . . continuity reasserted itself with a vengeance after a time. Perhaps to reassert their identity, the societies in question cling even more closely to their traditions whatever they are, when their evolution has been interrupted by a revolutionary 'jump'. . . It also reinforces the nationalism of these societies, making a mockery of revolutionary professions of friendships towards other peoples." Even with the communist chapter (presumably) closed, *Survey* still has things to say and certainly has a role to play for historians wishing to fill in what Gorbachev called the "blank spots" of Soviet history (eerily echoing Orwell's "memory hole", a term that makes frequent appearances in Leo's own writing).

When financial support for *Survey* withered away with the demise of the International Association for Cultural Freedom in the 1970s, Leo was forced to begin an unending quest for the ideal sponsor to relieve him of worry about balance sheets. Yet, despite the long years of financial and editorial independence that were to follow, *Survey* would never fully cast off the suspicion that surrounded its early associations. And even the best arrangements – such as those with the university presses of both Oxford and Stanford – foundered. Though often disheartened, Leo was not one to give up and he resigned himself to paying a price for singlemindedness – to him, *Survey* had always been a matter of conscience, not commerce. Leo had in any case little business sense: finance was less of a moral issue and more a matter of contempt for the material realities which he left to others – he himself was absolved by working for the higher good. This disdain for the quotidian was unwise and often brought *Survey* to the brink. But it was no different in the personal sphere: Leo's negligence was infamous. Demands from utility companies threatening disconnection would be habitually ignored or stuffed unopened into his battered briefcase. Once, a friend staying overnight at Leo's house found no hot water – the gas had been cut off. The phone likewise would go dead. On the other hand, also discovered among his old papers were several uncashed cheques, fees he had never collected for freelance work.

Even at its most successful *Survey* never aimed at a mass reader-ship – its circulation barely exceeded a few thousand. But an excep-tionally high proportion of its readers were specialists, journalists and policy-makers in positions of power and influence worldwide. Leo's command of his subject, his widely respected knowledge of the history, theory and practice of communism made him uniquely qualified as editor. Knowing personally, at *Survey*'s height, a great proportion of the leading international scholars in the field, he could commission articles and essays from the whole range of expertise. Many voices from the dissident movement in Eastern Europe also appeared in translation: a single issue might contain pieces from as many as six languages.

Every issue, usually of around 200 pages, was typically shaped into three or four sections, each containing comment and original research, important source material and data, and the history and analysis of current developments on a given subject in the news, often focused on a single country in the Soviet bloc. In a BBC interview on his highly successful issues on Polish *Solidarity* in the 1980s, for example, Leo explained that he had "selected, from the enormous amount of material available, what would give the cultural and historical background necessary to understand the intricacies of the Polish situation, and what would introduce into the picture the human element, conveying to the reader not only dry political analysis but also a flavour of reality." The topics ranged across politics and ideology to history and historiography, social policy, contemporary developments and strategic issues, diplomatic relations, censorship, intellectual repression and the politicization of cultural life – above all, the conflict between the state and the individual, between political institutions and writers and artists who were forced to surrender their individual voices to political demands.

One section that may possibly be of greatest value to historians was simply entitled: "Documents". This charted the steady struggle for human rights through numerous sober, often personal, testimonies – transcripts of trials, declarations, documentary evidence relating to the suppression of intellectual freedom, imprisonment, illegal torture and psychiatric abuse, legal statements, open letters demanding rights, and protests against criminal prosecutions for civil acts – all of these having been smuggled out at great risk from courts, prisons, camps and other institutions, past the strict controls of and officials, prying border guards and vindictive customs men.

Like an intellectual seismograph, Leo gauged each sign of coming change from the most insignificant ripple in the affairs of Eastern Europe. Much of his information derived from reading continuously in six languages, devouring perhaps fifteen newspapers daily along with all the available journals and periodicals, press and information reports and broadcasting transcripts he could lay hands on; for the rest he relied on correspondence and conversation. He always tried to keep *Survey* one step ahead of actual developments and generally predicted events with such accuracy it was said (and may now perhaps be verified) that the Kremlin arranged for its regular translation into Russian so that the *Politburo* too could discover what was really going on. (An émigré cartoon once depicted Soviet *apparatchiki* in a meeting consulting a copy of *Survey* to find out what decision they had just reached.) Despite its reputation as the most influential publication in the field, however, *Survey* kept a low profile and was sold almost entirely on subscription. But every so often an issue would produce a flurry of publicity that boosted sales and even called for a reprint (as, for example, with the number containing Andrei Amalrik's prescient essay "Will the USSR Survive until 1984?" and the special issues on Poland). Leo also edited many successful books, such as *Revisionism* and *The Sino-Soviet Conflict*, many of which were translated into other languages.

With roughly each decade, the journal indicated a widening of its scope by a slight change of title. Originally called *Soviet Survey, a Quarterly Review of Cultural Trends*, it broadened into *Survey, a Journal of Soviet and East European Studies* in the 1960s, becoming finally *Survey, Journal of East and West Studies* in the 1970s. Its span coincided with the period of liberalization that began with Khrushchev's Twentieth Party Congress speech in 1956 and ended with Gorbachev's era of *glasnost* in the late 1980s. Liberalization was not a smooth process but a confused policy of stop-go. The apparently liberal Soviet gesture, for example, of publishing Solzhenitsyn's *One Day in the Life of Ivan Denisovich* in 1962 was followed by a hardening of official attitudes towards intellectuals, with formal prosecutions for publishing texts considered anti-Soviet. Although the use of law could be seen as a step away from tyranny, harsh oppression continued. Attempts to "legitimize" intellectual persecution by recourse to the law had transformed the act of writing into political activism, and likewise transformed the activities of translating and publishing outside the Soviet Union into acts of solidarity with persecuted authors. International publicity became a powerful tool for supporting internal opposition.

It was here that Leo came into his own. He acted as a key point of transfer, his address books testifying to the range of contacts he could call upon across the media. He employed every possible means to draw attention to what was happening in Eastern Europe, issuing press releases or occasionally calling a press conference. He was tireless in support of a cause, aligning allies (and enemies) with the strategic sense of a chess-player.

If he himself could not publish a work that found its way to the West, he found translators and publishers elsewhere who could – he sought an American publisher for Solzhenitsyn's *One Day in the Life of Ivan Denisovich* and wrote the foreword together with Max Hayward, one of its translators. But however adept he became at feeding information into print, there were setbacks too: he found it hard to forgive the last-minute axing of a *Panorama* programme about the treatment of Andrei Sakharov, the physicist turned human rights campaigner, just because the available visuals were not right. If this had been Robert Oppenheimer (Sakharov's American "counterpart" in developing the atom bomb), Leo complained, the issue would have been aired in full.

News from underground in Eastern Europe was dependent on a small number of courageous individuals: the obstacles were formidable. Strict security prevented the flow of printed matter between countries, telephone lines were bugged, scrambled or simply cut, the mail was of course intercepted, and travel highly restricted with visitors subject to close surveillance. Contacts with certain countries, such as Poland, however, were easier and the Polish émigré community was larger and better organized than most. Leo naturally played a key role within that world, but his energies tended to be directed at the source of all power in the Soviet bloc: the Moscow Kremlin. Besides, since so few Russians of his own generation had managed to emigrate, Leo often assumed the role of Russian opposition spokesman himself.

A constant stream of people, packages and phone calls led to the offices in Oxford Street. If a newly arrived émigré or exile was not brought to *Survey*, Leo would soon be taken to them. He was one of the first to be called about an arrest, sent an important statement or shown a smuggled text. His briefcase was often the first port of call for some secret smudgy typescript. (How often did those vast photocopiers of yesteryear sulk like Sparky's piano at the worst possible moment, or spew out sooty pages that grew pale at human touch? And how often did Leo heap every conspiracy theory in the book onto the hapless engineers from Xerox?)

News flowed in both directions: as fast as he gathered it, Leo passed it on. Always a reliable source for producers to approach out of the blue for instant comment, he frequently found himself in a radio or TV studio, even when abroad. His was a familiar voice on the

BBC World Service and Radio Free Europe. How often would some political stir prompt a last-minute call for a sound bite, a brief paragraph, or clarification within the hour. He once completed an urgent feature article in a taxi speeding him from his office to *The Sunday Times*. Shifts in Eastern Europe that seemed obscure to some had long been anticipated by Leo. In interviews, a single question would let loose from him a fast-falling torrent of words in response, animated by a keenness to explain everything dow to the last detail and at top speed – his voice slightly raised, Polish inflections growing stronger under stress, and his syntax growing more pedantic, leaving no dangling threads to chance misunderstanding. The excitement of urgency suited his high energy. Or was it perhaps that, always with too much to do and too little time to do it in, his way of life created situations that could only be met with adrenalin?

Though highly convivial, Leo guarded his privacy. He would return home late in the evening after some work-connected activity and would then read long into the night, usually falling asleep at dawn. His manner of living was eccentric: every room in his house was as stuffed with print as his office. At some early point, he had begun a habit of collecting – or perhaps refusing to part with – newpaper cuttings, pamphlets, magazines, handouts and every imaginable kind of printed matter. These he sorted into a range of specific topics, which included the Katyn massacre, the Holocaust, genocide, forced labour camps in Eastern Europe, and other grim subjects that in the post-war decades were seldom aired in public, being either denied completely or considered too sensitive to explore in depth. These multifarious papers were at first collected in large envelopes, but then Leo discovered the dustbin bag. In due course these shiny black rotundities swelled up year by year with their yellowing contents, and came to be banked in orderly rows all along the walls of his entire house, as well as the walls of his office. Sometimes retrieving a quote or passage from these bags was successful, but mostly it was not: the method was not efficient, but that was possibly beside the point. It was as though he was devoutly amassing huge quantities of evidence in a great, continuing case against the injustices of the twentieth century.

These materials formed a link with his past and with his experience of that past. They were part of his testimony as a witness to the twentieth century. "And when the contemporary witnesses are dead," he wrote, "who knows what effect . . . obnoxious and cranky falsifications may have in undermining the historical truth about genocidal abominations? With the passage of time the traumatic impact of such crimes and their memories fades, and myths will increasingly encroach on authentic history." Those papers were memorials. They preserved the memories, the soundless thoughts and voices of the millions condemned by death to silence, whose tireless advocate Leo had become in the land of the living. He spoke because they could not. His own griefs he rehearsed in private, but they continued to furnish him with an inner code of moral absolutes. He had known both evil and goodness, and this certain knowledge enabled him to pass judgement with an almost biblical authority. Every "case" that came before him was assessed, pure gold or the gold of fools, weighed and valued and duly assigned its place – for or against. Leo's life and values had been directly shaped by the events of the twentieth century. History was not confined by the endpapers of a book – it flowed into the present moment where Leo was actively playing his part, affirming reality and truth as he understood them.

ACTIVISM

Leo's skill as an activist was nowhere better illustrated than in his efforts on behalf of the writers Andrei Sinyavsky and Yuli Daniel, who had been arrested in 1965 after publishing work abroad under pseudonyms. Together with Mark Bonham Carter and David Carver, then secretary of International PEN, Leo travelled to Stockholm to organize a huge protest demonstration designed to coincide with the ceremony for awarding the Nobel Prize for Literature to the officially-blessed Soviet writer, Mikhail Sholokhov. The stark counterpoint – between the bleak fate of two writers of integrity held under arrest on the one hand, and the glorification of the Party's voice on the other – was not lost on the international press, which gave the case widespread coverage and raised an immense outcry from intellectuals the world over. "The fate of Sinyavsky and Daniel," Leo wrote, "has a bearing not only on the struggle between Russian literary 'liberals' and 'die-hards' but on the whole internal evolution of the Soviet Union." The unwelcome glare of attention forced the Soviet authorities to hold their trial the following year virtually in secret, yet that did not prevent transcripts being smuggled out.

The 1966 Sinyavsky-Daniel case proved a turning point in the persecution of intellectuals. Although publishing abroad had never been technically illegal, the Soviet legal code had been amended so that writers could now be charged with producing "propaganda that undermined the state". This new, flexible legal instrument was designed to strengthen control already exercised through state censorship and the powerful Writers' Union which had been enforcing the narrow doctrine of socialist realism since the 1930s. This doctrine required all forms of artistic and intellectual expression to be positivistic and optimistic in content and outlook, and emphasized social utility at the expense of individual experience and imagination. It turned Soviet culture in on itself and away from foreign influence, and attempted to force the development of a popular (proletarian-socialist) national art form. But its grip was strangulating – humour, satire, irony were all more or less proscribed – and the results were largely stillborn.

Once the breaking of these cultural strictures became a matter for state prosecution, both the writer and the written text could be deemed criminal. Thus the exchanges that took place between judge and accused in the courtroom became dramatic enactments of the ideological conflict between political power and artistic expression. As Leo observed, it was not the authors so much as "literature itself that was on trial". "In Russia," commented Lydia Chukovskaya, "there is only one crime for which the authorities never pardon anybody. This one law, the strictest of all, lays down that every person must be severely punished for the slightest attempt to think for himself. To think aloud, that is."

When Sinyavsky and Daniel were handed down harsh sentences in a strict regime labour camp, the Russian intelligentsia were outraged. The Soviet Union was bombarded with telegrams, petitions and letters of protest from around the world; Leo was again involved behind the scenes in mobilizing support, and also in the unsuccessful attempts to obtain clemency. In the book of the transcripts and testimonies that he edited jointly with Max Hayward under the title *On Trial*, Leo concluded his epilogue with a quote from Sinyavsky (Tertz)'s own writing: "The Court is in session, it is in session throughout the world . . . all of us, however many we may be, are being daily, nightly, tried and questioned. This is called history." *On Trial* was the first of several such books that Leo was to produce – the fruit of insight and scholarship combined with a fine sense of timing.

The next decades would see a series of prosecutions and new

forms of persecution arising from different aspects of the struggle for democratic rights, and Leo continued to play a prominent role in supporting their cause.

SURVEYING WEST AND EAST

The intellectual climate of the 1960s and 1970s produced many anomalies. The fall of the Congress for Cultural Freedom and the rise of the New Left were part of the same polarizing phenomenon that brought youthful rebellion around the world. In America, anti-war protest led to wider confrontations within the universities and elsewhere; Paris 1968 saw the dawn of student unrest across Western Europe, while in China, young Red Guards were encouraged to overturn the authority of their elders in the Cultural Revolution. Yet these years also saw the quiet flourishing of the European Court of Human Rights, Amnesty International, *Index on Censorship*, and other organisations concerned with individual freedoms. Meanwhile the democratic movements that arose in many countries of Eastern Europe, in Poland, Hungary and Czechoslovakia for example, were brutally and cruelly crushed. The Soviets adopted new tactics: they attempted to silence criticism by sending Brodsky and Solzhenitsyn, for example, into foreign exile and Sakharov into internal exile, while the superficially liberal gesture of allowing Jews to emigrate to the West in fact masked the very anti-Semitism which the Jews were trying to escape.

Leo grew ever more irritated by modish western intellectuals who condemned the Soviet invasion of Czechoslovakia, yet displayed "political schizophrenia" by refusing to abandon Marxist loyalties. "You can't be a little bit pregnant," he would quip. He now became a political Janus – as stridently unforgiving of the masters of unfreedom in the East as those who appeared to condone them in the West.

He was especially scathing of western intellectuals who "point out, perhaps with a touch of jealousy", as he wrote in 1972 in an essay entitled *On Literature and Revolution*, "that in Communist countries, unlike in the West, writers 'are at least taken seriously' . . . There is an ironical contrast between the mortality rates of pro-revolutionary artists and writers under revolutionary and non-revolutionary regimes . . . The contrast between the intelligentsia East and West is striking indeed. What divides them more than anything else is life-experience: first-hand knowledge in the one case, theoretical knowledge in the other."

Leo's experience of life similarly divided him from many in the West, and his subject broadened beyond Soviet communism to embrace the wider issues of revolution and utopianism. Student activism, for example, appalled him by its "playful flirtations with revolutionary ideas". The mass "actions" of rainbow-arrayed, chanting and (mostly) young people bent on destroying the canons of civilization represented the "barbarism of the New Left". It was here, he felt, that, far from there being *pas d'ennemis*, the true enemies lay. Radical youth was identified as the offspring of the fellow travellers of his own generation, with whose weaknesses he was already familiar. "If one is too long on a bleak diet of the dead past and mediocre present, one turns to a bright future for psychic sustenance. Yet the paradox of Utopianism is that historically it has invariably led to results grimly at variance with the ideals of the true believers . . . In such movements, realizable goals are irrelevant, and Utopia (i.e. fantasy) is the only satisfactory symbol. This is the emotional background behind the current ideological hotch-potch in which the 'one-dimensional pessimisim' of Marcuse is combined with the 'revolutionary optimism' of Mao. It is a mixture in which, ironically, élitist philosophy and dictatorial practice are supposed to serve as a guide to 'participatory democracy' in a permissive society . . . Those who are now longing for Utopia turn away from those who had a long experience of living with it. They feel uncomfortable when with the historical evidence which may adduce a sceptical corrective to their messianic fervour and deflate their ideological perspective." The radicals' undermining of authority and debunking of history in the West mimicked the heartless humiliations that were inflicted in the name of the Cultural Revolution in China, with the struggle for civil and human rights being derided as "bourgeois reactionary". Yet it would take only a few short years for memories of those sentiments to fade. The condescension with which the vociferous New Left dismissed the actions of hundreds of individuals, such as Litvinov, Bukovsky, Sakharov – and numerous others all across the Soviet bloc equally courageous but less celebrated – has been swiftly disremembered if not revised. During those turbulent decades real risks were taken in challenging the Soviet system through public demonstrations, clandestine publication, secret universities, and so on, not to mention all the other unofficial activities and writings such as the *Chronicle of Current Events*, circulated in *samizdat*. Yet in the West such activities were often suspected (by those who should have known better) of being CIA provocations – as though these East European cousins were incapable of thinking for themselves, and were supposed moreover to ignore not only their own "experience of how Utopia works in practice . . . [but also their awareness] of the yawning chasm between the ideological abstractions and the personal lessons of their daily life".

Leo habitually cut out reviews and kept them folded inside the covers of newly published books for later reference: revisiting some twenty or thirty years later those hostile opinions with their pervasive resistance to self-evident truths provides today a reminder of what provoked Leo's outbursts then. As if he was not nuisance enough to the Left, however, Leo also embarrassed the Right too by persistently calling for recognition of the West's betrayal in "having handed over Eastern Europe to Stalin". This noisy émigré protested too much. *Private Eye* once described him as "five embittered Poles rolled into one". The jibe advertised more than it intended: the English-speaking establishment still fell on any excuse for unthinking xenophobia, of which discreet anti-Semitism was another typical facet. Little wonder therefore that Leo often appeared to generate the energy of five people.

LITERATURE AND TRANSLATION

Translation is a complex process which involves the work of many people. Leo frequently worked in collaboration with a small group of scholars, translators and editors who shared an understanding of the twists and turns of contemporary East European society and recognized the significance of the writings that began to emerge in the post-Stalin thaw. Max Hayward was central to this group and was a close friend and colleague of Leo's until his death in 1979. As the leading translator of his generation, Max Hayward had brought Pasternak, Solzhenitsyn, Nadezhda Mandelstam and many others to English readers, and was once described as "the custodian of Russian literature in the West until it could be restored to Russia". Leo was proud of being instrumental in the passage of *Doctor Zhivago* into English, and involved in its translation, which was undertaken jointly by Max Hayward and Manya Harari in an authorized version completed with regrettable haste in a race to bring it out before an unauthorized version could appear in Italy. The result had been, the translators felt, the best they could achieve in the circumstances, and hoped it might one day be worked again, free from such constraints. The case illustrated the personal pressures and political minefield that continued to surround publication of sensitive material. Looking over your shoulder for KGB informers was "normal", a daily reality, in Eastern Europe. It was little understood, however, that a similar need for vigilance extended into the West, resulting in a cloak-and-dagger atmosphere around activities furthering dissidence, especially where the publication of banned texts was concerned. Incriminating evidence was constantly being sought by the KGB to help mount legal prosecutions against dissidents in the Soviet Union. Powerful mutual suspicions thus arose between the two main groups involved in the West: on the one side were those working to the advantage of beleaguered authors whose intentions were scrupulously sought and respected and whose personal interests were set before other considerations in publishing their writings abroad; and, on the other, there were suave "émigrés" with undissolved Soviet links, who often achieved unauthorised publication by enlisting the help of naïve but well-connected westerners, who, with a misplaced sense of their own "heroism", could end up, wittingly or otherwise, further endangering Eastern European authors. Sometimes these battles over authorization led to legal action in Western courts, but questions of authority went far beyond the airy conceits of literary theorists or even the weightier deliberations of jurists – their implications could put real lives at serious risk. Western publishers thus found themselves drawn into the politics of the "Cold War" while their promotion of banned texts was sometimes misguidedly criticized as opportunistic and politically sensationalist. Once again, a gulf lay between those who understood the real situation and those who did not.

Few were aware of the subterranean literary wars and publishing scandals being played out in this period. Patricia Blake was a close ally of Leo's, for years contributing to the cause through her adroit publicity in leading American magazines; she also co-edited important anthologies of anti-Soviet writing in translation. Manya Harari was another close friend and source of great inspiration who, together with Marjorie Villiers, had founded The Harvill Press, which co-published *Doctor Zhivago* with Collins. The fine qualities which Leo recalled in Manya Harari's obituary in 1969 bore a close resemblance, in fact, to some of his own:

She was always ready to help with any action which would make the public understand the issues involved in the struggle of Soviet writers and intellectuals for self-expression and put into this cause her heart and intellect . . . She had two instruments at her disposal: the telephone to her very many friends in public life, and her pen. She used both very effectively . . . Ultimately human illness . . . and social illness, dictatorship, raise the same question of the need for spiritual courage. Manya Harari had this courage.

The sense of drama that infused many ventures in those days seldom reached the heights of the great collaborative effort that went into preparing *Solzhenitsyn: A Documentary Record*. The day the Nobel Prize committee announced the award of its 1970 prize for literature to Aleksandr Solzhenitsyn, Leo – recalling the way the Soviet authorities had humiliated Pasternak by forcing him to refuse that prize in 1958 – conceived the idea of presenting a collection of materials, speeches, letters, interviews and other documentary evidence that would offer a background to Solzhenitsyn's life and work, so that the general reader "could gauge the full significance of his fate as an individual and as a writer". It would also alert the world to the serious threats being made against Solzhenitsyn, even on his life, in Russia at that time. The book aimed to inhibit a repetition of the Pasternak scandal.

Leo's inspiration occurred six weeks before the Nobel Prize ceremony in Stockholm was due to take place, and the book had to be ready in time or would lose its impact. By dint of tremendous cooperation, copies were flown to Sweden at the eleventh hour. During the preceding weeks of production, however, the usually quiet offices in Oxford Street were abuzz with an enthusiastic rush of mostly young Russianists trailing paper of one kind or another. Though some documents had already appeared in *Survey,* the original texts of many others had first to be obtained in full, then translated, edited and finally annotated. Some helpers from outside London slept overnight on the floor in the space left between the piles of proofs and manuscripts (an issue of *Survey* was meant to be in production at the same time). In those pre-computerized days, the word "record" in the book's subtitle, *A Documentary Record,* came to hold a secondary meaning for everyone involved.

When the deadline for writing the introduction loomed, Leo also decided, as he occasionally did under such pressure, to camp overnight on a wooden armchair that unfolded to make an angular, punishing bed. Sometimes these overnight sessions bore fruit, but usually not. By morning he would be found red-eyed, surrounded by open books and loose sheets with false beginnings and odd paragraphs. But the ideas would be ordered in his head. Often he would write the whole thing out longhand and, after it had been typed, would decorate the margins of the typescript with scrawly additions that flowed down the sides and onto additional sheets that were sellotaped onto each other, so that long white scrolls of paper would unfurl from the final sheaf of manuscript. Galley proofs and even page proofs were subject to similar accretions: Leo had to include everything, be it an argument or the latest political development. How sweet his telephonic tones would become when begging indulgence from the long-suffering gentlemen at the Eastern Press, who naturally never passed on the reactions of the compositors, those much-lamented anonymous craftsmen who bore the brunt of additional typographic changes.

Occasionally, though, Leo would dictate an article straight on to the typewriter, the typist being required to intervene by reordering his gnarled syntax or untangling the charming "foreignisms" that entered a prose distinguished for the most part by its clarity. Though grateful for the improvements, Leo would typically challenge them one by one, demanding proof from a dictionary, for he hated being even slightly wrong. Verification of quotes often entailed a trip to his beloved London Library, but if someone else went, he quickly grew impatient at the delay. He would therefore gleefully absent himself from the office, taking the opportunity to drop in at *Encounter* on his way.

Leo's daily timetable was highly idiosyncratic. He seldom put in an appearance at the office before mid-morning. When he did come in "early", he would sit at his desk to eat his lunch of a bagel, ham and Diet Coke – an emblematic meal of Jewish, Polish and American elements that well represented Leo himself. He would prefer it, however, if he could go straight to a lunch appointment, and not arrive at the office until late in the afternoon. On those days, any work needing his attention had to be rushed through in the last couple of hours of the day, or the evening. Not everyone was prepared to stay late. Found among the papers in Leo's desk was a little note written (by my predecessor), preserved for thirty years. It had probably been written at six o'clock in the evening. Leo had most likely burst in one or two hours earlier, dived immediately into his room, picked up the phone and become engrossed in one conversation after another, each of greater urgency than the last. No doubt when the writer of the note had put her face round his door, mouthing the time or pointing to her wristwatch, he had waved his free hand while smiling disingenuously and rolling his eyes ceilingward in mock suffrance. The little note read:

> Goodnight Leo
> I am going
> See you tomorrow.

But maybe the sound of the door closing had prompted him to bark suddenly into the mouthpiece, "Just a minute!" and, throwing the receiver onto his desk, he had darted out of his office to call goodnight somewhat sheepishly to the figure retreating down the corridor. Leo was genial and fascinating, he was kind to young people, but he could also be exasperating to work with, and his assistants always left for new jobs with a mixture of regret and relief.

The phone would ring incessantly throughout Leo's day. It was not unusual for Leo to accept a call while a visitor was already installed before him, growing increasingly irritated by the minute, until Leo offered appeasement by wordlessly handing across his desk some enticing recent publication. This sometimes resulted in his commissioning reviews from unlikely quarters. But . . . O, those phone calls! It would be hard to imagine Leo without that instrument to hand. It was literally his life-line – professionally so when *Survey* was in its heyday and personally so later, when he was isolated and ill. Each of his friends could recall hours and hours of arm-achingly protracted conversations. At the end of his life, throughout the long periods in hospital, he would reverse charges, which for some technical reason caused an unstoppable little cuckoo to sing down the line the whole time. To this day, that sound recalls his voice, lonely yet spirited against encroaching illness. The great rambling dialogues ended only when he could no longer draw breath.

EDITING SURVEY

Leo kept tight control over *Survey*'s editorial content, but relied on the help of others to organize its production as smoothly as his erratic habits would allow. Once, in the early 1970s, he had to leave for a PEN conference in Asia before the final proofs for the summer issue had arrived, and, although it was unnecessary, he insisted on seeing them before allowing the issue to go to press. Elaborate arrangements were made to find another delegate willing to take him a set at the conference. All went according to plan: but the days passed and no word came back. The printers were waiting. A telegram was sent. Still no word. Finally a second telegram went off, this time threatening to go ahead without his agreement. It worked. His reply read: PROOFS OK REMOVE COMMA SECOND PARAGRAPH PAGE EIGHTY LOVE LEO. This change not only made no difference whatsoever, it must have been the most expensive comma in *Survey*'s history.

Although little details might cause protracted niggling, Leo remained surprisingly insouciant when it came to the bigger things. One morning in November 1969, he was taking a morning flight from London to New York, having sent to the printers the night before his editorial pages, "Quarterly Notes", which were always written at the last minute. On this occasion they referred to the anticipated outcome of a crucial imminent meeting at which the Italian Communist Party was expected to expel three of its members. By lunchtime, when Leo should have been safely on his way across the Atlantic, however, the news placards in Oxford Street were screaming: PLANE EXPLODES MID-AIR. It was Leo's plane. Shortly after take-off, the paper said, first one engine had fallen off, then a second one had exploded. The airline would only reveal that the plane had made a successful emergency landing without casualties and that passengers had immediately been put on a new plane to New York.

Leo's letter arrived the next day. He had written it when he was on his way for the second time to New York. As the first plane was taking off, he wrote, he had just noticed in the newspaper that his prediction about the Italian Communist Party expulsions had indeed been right, and he had therefore started to write a letter to the printers, instructing them to change the wording of his editorial accordingly. But that letter had been interrupted by the mid-air dramas.

> There was of course great tension with the emergency drill, a few hysterical females, etc. But [returning to the airport] gave me a chance to phone Mr Martin at the Eastern Press to dictate him an additional sentence . . . At least I put this "providential" landing to good use . . . but I would have preferred for once not to be quite so up-to-date [in my "Quarterly Notes"] if the price had to be so excessive.

The remainder of this letter throws considerable light on his own cast of mind during the emergency:

> After the [second] explosion a large black lady sitting near me got very upset and asked me whether the plane had lost power and how could it land on two engines only. I was tempted to say that black power would not help either but desisted as people did not seem to be in the mood to appreciate jokes at that moment. The other neighbour, a chap with moustaches and pinky face, was even less self-composed though he looked to me somewhat like a Powellite. Well, all's well that ends well. After the happy landing, the pinkish white Powell man and the very Black Power lady embraced and the conversation on the plane acquired a distinct tone of a *Gemeinschaft* solidarity rite, with everybody being terribly cool and collected and cheerful and jocular and minimizing the danger just faced. I did not have time to become any of these things because I rushed to the phone . . . (in this case the near accident was a near-hit as well as a near-miss).
>
>   Love Leo, the near Icarus.

While many articles were written to commission, *Survey* was constantly bombarded with unsolicited material, easily recognizable by their large buff envelopes, usually bearing the return address of a university. The reading of this material became a familiar ritual. Leo would assume the air of the surgeon he never became and, wielding a small dagger-shaped letter opener with precise and dainty gestures (he had small, fluttery hands), he would slit across the envelope, carefully gathering up any tiny torn pieces that had fallen off and placing them meticulously in the bin (a futile gesture of refinement amid the surrounding clutter). Then, after a glance at the covering letter's heading and signature, Leo would peel it back. The main operation now commenced. Skimming through the introductory paragraphs, he would cut incisively to the intellectual viscera and rapidly turn the pages, testing and probing structure and soundness of arguments as if gauging pulse and vitality. He would pause at the conclusions and then scan the bibliography with small noises of approval or disgust. Then he would seal it with a verdict: "Primitive" (drawn out and dismissive), or "Trotskysant" (scornfully, falling tone), or "Quite good" (surprised, with rising tone), or, the highest accolade, "Not at all bad" (voice and eyebrows rising together slowly in pleased surprise). Finally, he would replace the article in its envelope, allocating it to a specific position in one of the ever-growing piles of manilla paper: near the top meant future publication, near the bottom meant rejection – reasons for which he always shrank from articulating, although such evasion often caused greater offence than frankness might have done. Despite superficial details of author's name, address, etc. being entered in a leather-bound volume marked "Manuscripts Received", Leo's own memory would have filed a far more telling record which could later be recalled with little prompting: a phrase, argument or reference would have tagged it forever. Even many months after receiving it, he could retrieve an article from its pile in order, perhaps, to combine it with other materials, collected from various sources, that dealt with the same subject, which might suddenly have acquired topicality through actual events in the real world. And so it would duly appear in another well-orchestrated issue of *Survey*.

Leo's influence as editor went well beyond the pages of his journal. He was a font of ideas for all kinds of projects – seminars, conferences, symposia, as well as books and articles. Among his papers were endless drafts of lists of participants and speakers to be invited to this or that gathering, with notes and ideas for shaping themes. His library contained a large number of scholarly volumes inscribed by their authors with affectionate thanks for his inspiration and encouragement. Authors took intellectual courage in both hands before sending him a manuscript or consulting him, though, since as a critic he pulled no punches. Discussions were apt to turn into tutorial sessions. How often did he make the charge of "obfuscation" or "muddled thinking" because someone had not "done their homework", or because they clung to old loyalties that left "inconsistencies", another favourite term of disapproval.

Leo quickly formed friendships wherever he went. His desk drawers overflowed with dog-eared address books, visiting cards and hundreds of scraps of paper on which were scribbled names – many well-known – with appointments at myriad offices, restaurants, universities or homes in countless cities. His diaries burst with appointments for meetings arranged almost round the clock. But not all his visitors were celebrated. Leo was an institution to whom many turned for help. Over the years a constant trickle of subdued and modest men and women, many leading the difficult and impoverished lives of exiles and refugees struggling to survive in a new country, made their way to his door. They were a less glamorous facet of the cause, to which much unseen effort was devoted. Many letters were written appealing on other people's behalf for a job, a contract, a grant, or a reference. Sometimes he would shake his head sadly when a visitor had left and discreetly hint at some past horror or misfortune endured. He never allowed himself to forget the painful price some people had paid for survival, and felt it part of his duty not to let others forget it either.

SOCIAL LIFE

Social life for Leo took place largely in public, as he went constantly from meeting to seminar to conference to reception to restaurant. He made no distinction between work and play, and many colleagues became life-long friends.

Jane Degras, for example, who worked on *Survey* in its early days, was a small and fearsome woman reputed to be the only person capable of keeping Leo to a printing schedule. As a Party member she had spent three years at the Marx-Engels Institute in Moscow, but, disillusioned by what she had seen of communism in practice, had returned to London in 1941, where she acquired distinction as a scholarly editor. Her disillusionment was a frequent topic of conversation. After leaving *Survey*, she worked with Walter Laqueur on the *Journal of Contemporary History* until her death in 1973.

Sometimes she accompanied Leo back to his office after attending some seminar, their duelling voices rising to a crescendo as they could be heard approaching down the corridor, with Jane's deep rasping tones drowning out Leo's increasing falsetto. The door would fly open and she would roar triumphantly: "Absolute rubbish, Leo!" As in many of Leo's friendships, their differences were based on great mutual affection and respect, although when they were partners at bridge, the table became a battlefield.

A sparkling dinner guest, Leo was a memorable raconteur and a constant source of fresh East European jokes. He especially appreciated the warmth of home life. With few relations of his own (a cousin survived in Israel), his closest friends were treated as family and, despite the inevitable storms, he was as fiercely loyal to them as he was to everything else he held to be good. Even ideological opponents acknowledged his integrity and honesty. His closest circle of friends in his last years included Lionel Bloch, Marion Bieber, David Floyd, Leszek Kolakowski, Melvin Lasky, Jan Pomian, Edward Shils and Andrzej and Irma Stypulkowski and their families. Leo seldom invited others to his home and few knew much about his private life. He had been deeply hurt by his divorce in the 1960s, but had retained custody of his beloved daughter Natalie. She was cared for by a nanny who provided, in the quiet London suburb of East Finchley, a little slice of vanished Poland. In spite of his constant busyness, Leo was an affectionate, protective father and he always remained close to Natalie, proud of her chosen profession. Growing up overwhelmed by books and print had left its mark, and she became a distinguished conservator of works of art on paper. When the time came to let go of his "Nataluska, the apple of his eye", he did so with admirable selflessness. Though still recovering from the first amputation and the unsettling move from his old house, he refused to put his own needs first. He found the strength to smile generously upon her plans to get married and spend the following year in America, where her husband, Ed Copeland, was to carry out research as a promising astro-physicist. The latter revived Leo's student interest in physics and he would gamely quiz Ed on the philosophical aspects of quantum theory. In his son-in-law, Leo was fortunate indeed – both Ed and Natalie showed exemplary kindness and gentleness of spirit throughout his last illness and Ed spoke sweetly at the funeral. Leo never lived to see his grandchildren.

LEO THE WRITER

The sluggish pace of a quarterly, with its lag of weeks between page proof and bound copy, was never fast enough to meet Leo's need to comment on actual events as they occured. Paradoxically, by holding up production in order to have the last and latest word, he would often make *Survey* later than ever. He therefore found other outlets better suited to his role as observer and analyst of *byt* (daily life) under communism, not just in the Soviet Union and China but all over the world. At one time he wrote a weekly column for the *Daily Telegraph* and another each month, under the title "From the Other Shore", for *Encounter*, besides a further stream of short pieces and occasional features, for the *Observer*, *The Times*, and other broadsheets, as well as regular items for the Polish press, which might well be translated later into English. His work was regularly translated – by himself or by others and then reworked by him – into French, Italian or German, and Russian or Polish for the émigré press. This role earned him the description by his friend Bernard Levin as an "East European Mr Pickwick".

He edited or contributed to upwards of thirty books in as many years. Magazine offprints and cuttings of his articles came to fill numerous boxes. Yet despite this impressive output, it was, he claimed, his contributions to the *Fontana Dictionary of Modern Thought* that possibly offered him most satisfaction (although since his copy was allegedly so late as to have held up production for several years, the satisfaction may have been somewhat one-sided).

Leo's prolific output took the form of densely-worded pieces barbed against the fools he would never suffer gladly or otherwise, many written in rapid response to the daily unfolding of events. Others were more considered, shaped into wide-ranging essays. The slower rolling thunder of composing a whole book did not appear to suit his temperament, though the dozen or more titles he edited all made useful and highly respected contributions to the field.

It was only when the best of his essays were gathered into a *Festschrift* issue of *Survey*, edited by Melvin Lasky and published in March 1988 under the title *The Use and Abuse of Sovietology* that Leo was fully revealed as a sharply sceptical pluralist, whose humanist liberalism, already hard enough to hear against the marching drums of totalitarianism, had almost been drowned out entirely by the hectoring of New Left radicalism. In these more reflective days, he would perhaps have received a more sympathetic hearing.

Everything Leo wrote and uttered resonated with polemic. He was naturally combative – the term "dialogism" could have been invented for him alone – and his texts powerfully evoke the polarities of the era. One chapter of his unwritten memoirs was to be called "Adventures of a *Zeitgeist*", and for anyone seeking a flavour of the times, his essays offer it *con brio*. But with so many specifics, so many enmities and arguments woven into the text, only readers with the sharpest memories or the most painstaking of researchers could now negotiate the thorny terrain he nimbly traversed, dealing blows to left and right. His copious footnotes fizz with compacted furies. He openly invested everything with anger, disappointment or bitterness, respect, admiration or applause and made no attempt to conceal judgements. "Neutral?" he once scoffed. "Neutered."

How should one summarize the outpourings of a man who took as his subject the overriding ideas of the century: the totality of communism, revolution and utopia, past and present? Two main threads run consistently through his work: memory and appropriation.

Sometimes they intertwine: "He who controls the past," as Orwell wrote, "controls the future."

> The most important defence against the Communist denial of "the right to reality" is memory, [Leo wrote apropos the Polish poet Czeslaw Milosz] both for the poet and for the people: they all need to retain their identity. Hence the primary task of a writer is to preserve memory as the first line of resistance against the enforced falsification of words, images, ideas. Whatever his subject, and whatever his mood, authenticity is his first duty. His individual awareness inevitably clashes with the fraudulent "truth" forced upon him by the state. The pressure is strong and the temptation to submit is great.

The pressure in this instance stemmed from the shackling of literature to political ends, primarily through the demands for social-ist realism which appropriated every aspect of cultural expression: it wiped memory clean by denying the pain of the past (the "memory hole"), it demanded a positivist "realist" representation of the present, and an optimistic view of "the radiant future". "When writers try to perceive things along expected lines, they have to deny their own authenticity," wrote Leo. "Censorship interferes only with freedom of expression; obligatory perception and self-censorship with creativity itself." Those who wrote as individuals (e.g. Mandelstam, Akhmatova, Pasternak, Brodsky), resisting interference in their creative vision, paid a high personal price for retaining their integrity, but they won lasting admiration and esteem for doing so.

"The writers caught between the Revolution and Utopia know that in practice they face a choice between intellectual prostitution and martyrdom," Leo wrote in the essay "Literature and Revolution" (1972).

> They know how difficult it is to avoid this choice. For a majority of them all sorts of compromises and rationalizations, from self-deception to Newspeak, are inevitable. The few heroic ones who choose martyrdom – like Solzhenitsyn – are the exceptions. It is extraordinary that this heroism of *chestnye pisateli* ("honest writers") is necessary to do what would after all be the most ordinary thing: to write as they really feel. This elementary prerequisite of the literary vocation requires almost superhuman courage, involving as it does a challenge to the state which imposes on the writer an ideological strait-jacket and an obligatory perception.

Leo's respect for Solzhenitsyn as a writer was profound:

> In the Soviet context his historical as well as literary
> significance cannot be exaggerated [he wrote in 1974]. He is
> the first great Russian writer to emerge after the Revolution
> whose humanity can be compared with that of Tolstoy, his
> awareness of suffering to that of Dostoyevsky, his lack of
> sentimentality to that of Chekhov . . . Like other major
> novelists Solzhenitsyn makes his own experience the centre
> of his literary work and the point of departure for its symbolic
> significance. The concentration camp and the cancer ward
> are for him places in which to reflect not just on the problems
> presented by "extreme situations", but on the wider questions
> of Soviet reality and of our epoch, of good and evil, in
> short *la condition humaine*. Like other great novelists he
> is uncompromising in his attitude to truth and he restores
> to Russian literature the moral universalism which had
> been lost during the Stalin era . . . One of the characters in
> *The First Circle* reflects that "for a country to have a great
> writer is like having another government". Solzhenitsyn is
> such a writer.

Though Leo admired the value of Solzhenitsyn's work – "civilization
lives on through its art" – he distinguished an artist's writing from
a historian's: "Historical truth and 'artistic truth' do not necessarily
coincide," he wrote.

> The first obligation of a historian is accuracy. Not dramatic
> effect, not wistful improvisation, not tidiness in constructing
> a story, and not passionate expression of hope, despair, or even
> of inner understanding – but the cool and sceptical discovery
> of evidence. Unless he distinguishes between fact and supposi-
> tion, not after deliberation but as a mental habit, his literary
> flair will betray him; and the line between history and fiction
> will be blurred.

Some of Leo's most impassioned and coruscating remarks are to
be found in essays on history and historians, particularly in his
broadsides on the determinism that pervades most accounts of Soviet
history: "Leo Tolstoy noticed that with the passage of time everything
in the past begins to seem inevitable. This 'deterministic effect' clashes
with the realization of choices – political, social, existentialist – with
which we are faced in our actions before they are taken. The paradox

is heightened when a deterministic theory of history is linked with a call to action."

Following his assertion that "historical alternatives do exist", Leo caused shockwaves by his savage assaults on the leading English-speaking historians of Eastern Europe. Isaac Deutscher was a fellow Pole of the older generation with whose background Leo was familiar: everything he had read, Leo had read too, but with more critical attention. Quarrying Deutscher from cradle virtually to grave, Leo marked his evolution from orthodox Jewish roots through Party membership to emigration, and even adduced as evidence along the way a pro-Stalinist poem the young Deutscher had once published, and which the young and starving Leo happened to have read nearly 40 years earlier in the Tashkent library and never forgotten. "Soviet historiography is the Eighth Wonder of the world," Leo wrote in "Isaac Deutscher: Historian, Prophet, Biographer" (1978), a two-part appraisal of Deutscher as a biographer of Stalin.

> Bending the historical evidence did not begin with Stalin, though the surrealistic falsification of historical facts certainly reached "yawning heights" under him. But the "memory hole" technique certainly did not end with him, and his treatment in Soviet history books under his successors is a vivid illustration of this . . . Confronted with a falsification of history on an unprecedented scale, the suppression of facts and the creation of myths on a conveyor-belt by state historians, it is not just an elementary duty of the historian to be pedantic about the facts, he has to re-establish the truth . . . Barbarism is barbarism, and history is not a detergent . . . Deutscher washes whiter than Clio allows. His anthropomorphic language only obscures the realization that "history" cannot "cleanse" anything. Stalin's victims are in their graves, millions of them unknown, and they cannot be raised from the dead. And a moral restitution involves not a historical apologia, but an unequivocal condemnation.

Another pillar of the historical establishment that he took to task for rejecting "moralism" was E. H. Carr. History, Leo complained, is transmogrified through "the identification of the historian's perspective with that of the ruler":

> Carr was only one of a number of intellectuals fascinated with power who at the time of its decline in Britain were looking

with nostalgic sympathy at the rising new [Soviet] empire. Only a few of them, in identifying with it so irrevocably, went so far as to commit actual treason, but many engaged in *la trahison des clercs* . . . Carr was among the ranks of those who are "satisfied with appearances". Indeed, he perpetuated the Soviet myth in the name of "realism". He was the spiritual product of an earlier era, and in effect he transposed the faith of an Edwardian "progressive" on to Marxist "progressivism". . . [and had] little real feeling for the transitoriness of things in human history, which is the mark of a true historical sensibility and which gives a really great historian his historical perspective.

In "Holocaust: Myths and Horrors" (1980) Leo berates once more those who ignore the evidence: "Santayana's acute characterization of 'those who do not learn from history' (being condemned to repeat it) and Hegel's melancholy reflection on 'the only thing we learn from history' (that we never learn from history) do not go far enough. It may be that each generation fails to learn from the experience of its predecessors, but some generations, one suspects, even fail to learn from their own experience."

Leo brought to his reading of literature and poetry a deep understanding of the constraints that power and authority imposed upon artistic expression. His introductions to the volumes he edited on Solzhenitsyn and Sinyavsky and Daniel illustrate his sensitivity to the subtleties of the predicament in which East European intellectuals found themselves, even in exile. His essay "Appreciating Milosz" opens with Czeslaw Milosz's own observation that "a newcomer from Eastern Europe notices that he is separated from his new environment by the store of his experience". There is indeed a gap, Leo agrees, "between the poet's vision, images and reflections, his references and allusions, and their reception by readers with a quite different 'store of experience'". This divergence between readers and writers is a fundamental problem in all literary criticism, but is perhaps greater for literature that crosses languages and cultures.

Though essentially a writer of English, Leo reflected a complex cluster of viewpoints – which he referred to as "the multiplicity of realities" – for he never abandoned the perspective of those whose understanding was based on experience that differed sharply from that of most speakers of the English language. His writing was a natural advertisement for pluralism, peppered with a diversity of references and untranslated expressions drawn from the cultures of Europe and put to new uses. He would, for example, stretch the term *die unbewältigte Vergangenheit*, meaning "the unmastered past", beyond its usual reference to the Germans' denial of guilt, to embrace a general refusal to accept historical responsibility; or he would leave *zakonomernost* in Russian, since no English equivalent (it means "conformity to laws or natural development") carried the force of political implications in the deterministic Soviet context.

George Orwell was one English author for whom Leo consistently showed immense respect, frequently quoting him in his own writing. There were affinities in their continual striving for intellectual integrity and clarity, and of course a shared preoccupation with fundamental political issues. (Leo regretted that they never met, as Orwell died in 1950.) In his essay "Will George Orwell Survive 1984?", while defending the unfading accuracy of Orwell's portrayal of the totalitarian state, Leo examined an exhaustive array of different readings of *1984* in the eponymous year – these "examples of the rubbish I have inflicted on the reader [being] just a small portion of the proliferation of 'Orwellian' folly occasioned by the advent of 1984".

This was an opportunity to rescue Orwell from the "bodysnatching" clutches of those on the left who, having once "snubbed him, now embrace him". Furthermore they had the audacity, quoted Leo with iron glee, to believe they were "reclaiming him from the Cold War fanatics". "It is difficult," he wrote, "to find a comparable case of ideological 'reinterpretation' where the message of the author has undergone such a degree of distortion and corruption so soon." When James Cameron, for example, proclaimed in the *Guardian* in 1984, "I always thought [Orwell's] prophecy was rather mild anyway. Big Brother was daunting but less boring than Small Sister, and I believe I would rather be bullied by a brute than patronized by a prig", Leo retorted by pointing to "the 'Winston Smiths' who survived Stalin's brain-washings and post-Stalin 'rehabilitations', who are talking to us with the chastened voice of historical experience. None of them is on record as preferring to be bullied by a brute than patronized by a prig. They know where Big Brother has his headquarters . . ." He then cited a passage from the introduction to a Czech *samizdat* edition of *1984* by Milan Simecka:

> When I read the story of Winston Smith, I received a shock, because . . . I realized that this was my own story I was reading . . . I have grown up in a world of forbidden books, a

world of omnipresent indoctrination, where the past was
being rewritten all the time . . . Can you wonder, given all this,
that Winston Smith came to seem to me like my own brother?

Leo later reminds the reader, in another quote from a then recent
Russian émigré, that "the Soviet authorities – our dear KGB – have
overtaken Orwell by four years. In 1980 Andrei Dmitrievich Sakharov
and his wife Elena Georgievna Bonner were plunged into a world
that surpassed Orwell's nightmarish fantasies . . ."
   Leo concludes his essay:

> It is a dispiriting spectacle to see so many of our Western
> contemporaries (who enjoy freedom) wailing that Orwell
> predicted their present terrible enslavement. Yet we can take
> heart at the stirring effort of so many libertarian dissidents
> (who are actually enslaved) as they turn to the message of a
> writer who offers them the spiritual weapons of clarity and
> integrity. George Orwell will survive 1984.

Perhaps too much in the world, or too busy, to be a philosopher
himself, Leo never attempted to produce a complete social or
political theoretical system, though consistent views run through his
work. But he enjoyed protracted arguments – never quarrels – with
Leszek Kolakowski, Poland's great contemporary philosopher, who
became a good friend in exile. In the intellectual portrait drawn
in his essay "Kolakowski: Marxism and Beyond" (1969), Leo plotted
Kolakowski's philosophical evolution, focusing on the spiritual
struggles involved in contemporary ethics and the problem of
"conscience and history".

> Like other good philosophers [wrote Leo] Kolakowski is
> caught between the necessity for ontological choice and the
> impossibility of epistemological proofs . . . Like Spinoza
> he not only made moral orientation the linchpin of his
> philosophy, but faced the political and social orthodoxy of
> his own time and place with courage and ethical determina-
> tion . . . Man is the centre of his philosophical concern but he
> makes metaphysics the basis of his ethics, although he does
> not accept religious assumptions for his metaphysical beliefs.
> He makes "anthropological realism" his philosophical plat-
> form, yet considers that "infinity is the only fatherland of
> man". He is a truly tragic philosopher who does not however
> surrender to despair.

To many, Leo appeared excessively vigilant over other people's mistakes, but as the historian Arnaldo Momigliano, whom Leo knew and esteemed, that it was "one of the consequences of any tyrannical regime observed, even its opponents are often short of constructive thought". Leo's constructive thought went into supporting the struggle for political change and that required constant offensives. If, during these still early days of establishing durable forms of democracy in Eastern Europe, the "martyrs" of the past are temporarily eclipsed, their crucial role will not in the long term be forgotten.

Indeed, by the end of the twentieth century, Leo and his allies – often dismissed as cold-warriors or reactionaries by those of more progressive outlook – have come to look rather modern, while the progressives themselves have acquired a somewhat doctrinaire aura. These "reactionaries" revealed the nature of Soviet imperialism by questioning its legitimacy and authority and calling for a reappraisal of history; they challenged prevailing myths and defended claims for recognition by all nationalities and minorities; they condemned the denial of individual rights and cultural freedom and called for the liberation of language from ideological and political hegemony. These might not have been the terms in which Leo would have expressed his views, but recast in terms of contemporary post-colonial discourse, the nature of Soviet imperialism and the role of the "dissident" movement may become clearer to sceptics. Indeed, far from being behind the times, Leo now seems ahead of them – or, to turn La Bruyère on his head: *"Nous qui sommes si anciens, serons modernes dans quelques siècles."*

IN PLACE OF A CAREER

Leo formed no "career plan" nor did he appear to harbour worldly ambitions. Friends (such as Zbigniew Brzezinski) ultimately held high office, or occupied distinguished chairs at great universities, but Leo never showed much keenness to follow. He was too much of a maverick for the constraints of institutional life (he would ironically refer to the "anarchy of the Poles"), yet while responsibility for *Survey* was always a burden, it gave him freedom as well. However, he was always to have some kind of academic status, even if never a full-time post: he was a Fellow at LSE, where for years he assisted at Leonard Schapiro's famous seminar on Soviet studies, and he was a regular presence at Chatham House. He later held fellowships and visiting professorships at Stanford, Columbia and Miami universities, giving countless lectures at other major universities around the world. His diaries burst with an extraordinary range of appointments – curiosity attracted him to odd places – as he was a lively speaker whether addressing a formal audience or a small special interest group. Leo constantly drew the real world into the academy. On one occasion in New York, he invited the elderly Alexander Kerensky, with whom he had been lunching, to accompany him to the seminar he was due to teach that afternoon. The students refused to believe that this was the Kerensky from the history books, for assumed he had been buried along with democracy over half a century earlier.

Although Leo enjoyed America and was tempted by the wider recognition and respect he earned there, he knew London was better located for contact with Eastern Europe. Keeping abreast of each minute development was his stock-in-trade, strengthening the unique authority of his analysis on which his formidable reputation, if not quite fame, came to rest.

Leo relished disputation, but even when it took him to the most exalted levels he remained modest: motivation sprang not from personal advancement but from an evangelical spirit to influence opinion, and the higher the sphere the better. His interrogation of those who had known Stalin, for example, was led by curiosity about the mentality of a tyrant and the implications this had on the grander scale: what drew him was not power itself but its abuse. Leo was twice invited officially to China in his capacity as expert on Sino-Soviet relations, but the half-hour interview with Deng in the 1970s he shrugged off, since the dialogue had been so predictable, no anecdote could be wrung from it. He was similarly dismissive of his longer confrontations with Chinese generals: "They just wanted to tell me how bad the Russians were – so what was new?" But he was quietly proud of two interventions he made during the era of *détente*. At one Helsinki briefing, he caused the Soviet delegates maximum embarrassment in front of the world's press by calmly asking why innocuous publications comparable with *Mechanics' Weekly* or *Ladies Home Journal* were still unavailable in the Soviet Union: censorship, he implied, was clearly continuing in defiance of the Accord. He made the same point more forcefully when asked to testify at the SALT 2 Hearings in Washington in 1979, arguing that "those who defend the policy of *détente* in the way in which it is understood in the Soviet Union argue that international negotiations between powers are simply a matter of realistic policies to which ethical issues are irrelevant". He deplored the way western powers shrank from making agreement conditional on an improvement in democratic rights, without which *détente* was little more than appeasement. "It is an ironical situation," he wrote, "in which Sakharov and Solzhenitsyn stand for the cultural values of the West . . . while Western statesmen are ready to sacrifice them for the sake of an unrealistic *Realpolitik*."

PATTERNS OF COINCIDENCE

With Leo's attention concentrated so intently on one area, a certain continuity was inevitable; however, a sequel to his brief war-time friendship with Stalin's scriptwriter, Alexei Kapler, came quite out of the blue. In the 1960s, Leo happened to notice in the then *Daily Worker*, which he read along with all the rest of the press, that Kapler was visiting London for a film festival. He rang his hotel. "Well, Mr Kapler," said Leo, "I don't suppose you remember the young man with whom you had some interesting conversations in 1939?" There followed what Leo said was "probably best described as a pregnant silence". Then Kapler started stammering: "*Da, da*, of course I remember you . . ." They spent the next evening together, walking round the streets of Bayswater in conversation. (It was still dangerous for Soviet citizens to make unauthorized contacts in the West and Leo would have been considered far more dangerous than simply "unauthorized".) When Leo started reeling off details of Kapler's life since they had met in 1941, the latter reacted with profound shock and disbelief: how could Leo possess so much information about the vicissitudes of his own life? Leo revealed that Kapler's dangerous liaison with Stalin's daughter Svetlana, when she was still a teenager, had earned him over eleven years in the camps (for Stalin would tolerate him as a clever and useful Jew but not one who fondled his daughter). There, during his long imprisonment, Kapler had behaved with notable kindness and decency, and had subsequently been rehabilitated in the post-Stalin era, receiving awards and prizes for services to film making.

Kapler was incredulous at this unexpected account. How had Leo heard it? Was he "Merlin the magician"? No, Leo replied, he had come across it in a book written by Antoni Ekart, a Pole whose relative had been in the same camp as Kapler and had witnessed his behaviour there. Kapler seized on this news: he had good reason for doing so. The younger generation of anti-Stalinists – this was in the mid-1960s – had become suspicious of his past status as one of Stalin's favourites, the long sentence in the Gulag notwithstanding, and he urgently needed proof of good character.

Next morning, Leo rang the Polish Library where he had read the book. "I need to steal your copy," he explained. And so a grateful Kapler returned to the Soviet Union with his unexpected testimony. Yet as he took his leave, it was Leo's turn to be surprised when the former cynic admonished: "Don't write slanders about the Soviet Union", from which further tergiversation Leo concluded that Kapler probably wished to die in peace.

Nevertheless, over the subsequent years Kapler sent Leo journals published in such out-of-the-way places as Baikal, where risky materials could evade the eyes of the Moscow censor. These items were nonconformist rather than dissident – examples of the "ideological schizophrenia" of that era, with loyalties divided between Party and intellectual freedom. In exchange, Leo sent him inoffensive cinematic materials, such as the script of *Les Enfants du Paradis*. (When Svetlana Alliluyeva [Stalin's daughter] escaped to the West she became friendly with Leo and kept up a long correspondence with him. But in her wish to cut herself off from her past, she was unwilling to talk about Kapler.)

An unexpected coda to the Kapler story illustrates the way patterns continued to emerge throughout Leo's life. In 1977, when again invited to China, he happened to notice that Shanghai cinemas were showing Kapler's films, about whose falsifications Leo knew more than most. Why on earth were the Chinese bothering to show such things? he asked. Didn't they realize they were based on Stalin's mendacious *Short Course*? But the accompanying member of the Chinese Revolutionary Committee explained that, since those films had now been banned by anti-Stalinists in the Soviet Union, the Chinese, considered "it was urgent to prevent the falsification of history by Soviet 'revisionists', who were refusing to show a true picture of the Soviet past . . . I felt" as Leo wrote later, "that the ghosts of Kafka and Pirandello were hovering in a surrealistic embrace over the scene."

The worst form of tyranny, as Jacob Burkhardt showed, is the denial of complexity. Leo's appreciation of each fresh convolution of truth and falsity increased his scorn for naive "simpletons" and in this he was perfectly on the wave-length of East Europeans themselves, whose habit of double- and treble-think formed the basis for a sophisticated and deeply cynical sense of humour that shocked pious ideologues in the West.

THE FINAL YEARS

Leo's illness marked the final decline of *Survey*. He was in hospital for long spells. During one of these, a flood at his house made his old way of life impossible. It was hard to tell which distressed him more, grave illness or the loss of his home and possessions. Eventually sheltered accommodation was found in Ealing where he could cope alone. Bereft of his home of thirty years, his cherished library and archives, he resigned himself without complaint to a drastically diminished life in his little flat. He showed the same outward courage and tenacity that he had always shown in adversity, but once quietly remarked that he had at last understood the meaning of Churchill's "black dog" of depression.

Natalie's spirit of conservation extended to Leo's enormous archive, and she threw herself into helping preserve it for posterity. What could be salvaged of his library went to Poland, while she herself kept the extensive private correspondence together with much of the unique printed material in the hope of one day finding it a more accessible resting place. Meanwhile, the office closed down and the bulk of the *Survey* papers was shipped to the Hoover Institution at Stanford University.

There were a few consolations: despite immobility, Leo accepted an invitation to visit free Poland. He received a hero's welcome, with television cameras greeting his arrival at the airport. Not only were his own books displayed in shop windows, he reported with delight, but they were honoured by standing alongside those of his great friend, the philosopher Leszek Kolakowski.

Leo lived simply and ascetically himself. His little flat soon started filling up with fresh accumulations of printed matter – the sofa and armchairs were rapidly turned into bookshelves so that visitors had to sit on the dining chairs tucked under the table, which was itself half buried beneath papers. Though things of beauty were of value in the abstract, Leo never needed them around him, yet small gifts could give him great pleasure. Once, I brought him a little book about Warsaw. Photos of the same scene were displayed in pairs: in one photo, ancient buildings were shown as heaps of rubble after war-time devastation, and facing it, the same buildings were shown fully restored following post-war reconstruction. The new buildings gave no sign of what had so recently befallen them. Leo excitedly pointed out where he had lived. How often he looked at those photos by himself, no one knows, but he liked to show them to visitors – the little book was granted a special place along the arm of a chair. Perhaps it gave him a sense of continuity with his own past, filling in his own blank spots, recalling lives obliterated by history.

When Leo became acutely ill, attempts were made to hand *Survey* to a new editor, but Leo balked. The journal had been an extension of the man, reflecting a cast of mind and a set of principles born out of particular experience and understanding. Rather than allow inevitable change by diluting its vision or altering its perspective, he preferred his "baby" – for which he had lived and struggled alone over the course of many long and difficult years – to expire with him. And so at the very moment when the communist regimes of Eastern Europe, objects of his unblinking scrutiny for over half a century, finally collapsed, *Survey*, too, fell silent. In many ways, of course, it seemed its job was done and its time was over. But how Leo would have savoured the symbolic significance of parcelling up old copies of *Survey* to be sent to libraries and universities all over Eastern Europe. Its task in fact was far from over: the real memories and history of the Soviet Union that *Survey* contained were finally being restored to their proper owners, on whose behalf Leo had been dutiful custodian for so long. *Survey* was in some sense going home, helping to fill the "memory hole". The moment had finally come for both Leo and his journal, having valiantly given voice to the disappeared, the forgotten and the unfree, to find their new place in the complete history of the twentieth century. His death in March 1993 was marked by many tributes and obituaries, and by memorial services in London and Washington.

Leo Labedz was both an idealist and a realist: the idealist kept faith with what he, in company with the few "over here" and the many "over there", believed to be right, while the realist fought the daily battles, interpreting the present through the complex filters of the past. The "unorthodox" views of historical events, which he and others like him refused to relinquish, are now slowly being rehabilitated – alternatives are being considered. Leo was often tolerated as a noisy iconoclast, and once wryly asked: "Is it ever good being prematurely right? Doesn't it always result in ever greater animus from those who were wrong and prefer never to be reminded of it?"

Yet despite the scorn and hostility, *Survey* has proved its worth and Leo has been proved correct. Men and women closer to the realities of the times, some of them tested by the worst of horrors, have recognized in Leo a man of vision and a champion of freedom: to those living in the long darkness of unfreedom he offered a candle of hope. To them, at least, he was speaking the truth.

One of the last articles he ever wrote concluded with the following passage:

> People who condemned Stalin's crimes before Khrushchev and Gorbachev granted permission to do so are still dismissed as "Cold Warriors", still beyond the pale to the *bien pensants*. I remember a letter to the then editor of *Encounter* in the fifties upbraiding me for being "uncivilized" in making a critical remark about Stalin's crimes in my monthly column "From the Other Shore". I wonder whether the letter-writer would still consider me uncivilized now.
>
> On 6th April [1990] both *Pravda* and *Izvestiya* openly indicated that the figure for Stalin's victims was close to 50 million (not including the war dead) . . .
>
> I am glad to have lived until this moment of truth. In this *hora de verdad* there really can no longer be any doubt about who was right and who was wrong.

STEPHEN BECKER

On Being a Patient

First I was a wizened man of ninety-five in Washington, D,C., wearing a brown gabardine suit and a Panama hat and sitting in a warm, humid greenhouse. To step outside, or smoke a cigar, was to die; but the inactivity galled, and fear was shameful, and I stepped outside and lit a cigar.

Then I was my own age, thirty-one, in a small town in upstate New York, and there was an epidemic, and our children were dying, and we could save them only by bringing wooden objects – furniture, crates, toys – to the schoolhouse. Snow fell. Soon there were no wooden objects to be found, and our children went on dying.

Then I was a helicopter pilot, and a space pilot (this was all in January 1959), and the manager of a theatrical troupe stranded in St Petersburg (not Leningrad; St Petersburg). I was the landlord of a boarding house on the West Coast, and my tenants were drunken, aged Bohemians, and I left because there were toads in the swimming pool. I lay on a couch in Salzburg – in the house where Mozart died – begging two beautiful women for another cup of cocoa, because the cocoa was drugged, and I needed it, and I offered them money. In Mexico we played a game with the bartender, and a blue bead curtain hung in the doorway; you won the game by smoking your cigarette, and drinking your tequila, in a mysterious and secret fashion. A man said, "Do you remember my name?" Back in New Bedford I signed off the whaler after a two-year voyage, but the house I lived in was gone. I was cold. I was in command of a Canadian corvette, but they had tied me to my bunk. On the islands between New York and France I sat down to a lavish dinner with many friends, and I was wearing a white gown, bloodstained, and my arms would not move, and I was freezing. A man said, "Do you remember my name?" I was the governor's cousin, and a car was coming for me. A lady told me to stop being silly, and I swore at her, viciously. I was in a bar in Chicago with Bao Dai, and a man was saying, "Do you remember my name?"

I finally remembered his name, and eventually got to know him fairly well. He was an intern, and he had been trying to rouse me from a week of coma. All those lovely, horrifying, claustrophobic hallucinations – many more than the few mentioned here – had come within two or three days, as consciousness nudged me. Over the next week they ceased to be deep hallucinations and became a fitful delirium, punctuated by my loud insistence that I be taken back to the hospital. Yes, yes, the nurses said; and I hollered some more, because here we were in Texas, or Italy, and I had to be back in the morning for a spinal tap. Sometimes my wife was there. Sometimes no one was there, and I held long conversations with I.V. bottles. But always I was cold; and often I was tied down, pinned, locked in. I wondered why.

One morning I found out. I woke up, and was calm and lucid and full of curiosity, and they told me I was paralysed to the neck. That surprised me. I was too depleted for feelings of shock or tragedy, but was capable of surprise and – the word seems frivolous, but is accurate – dismay. That something was wrong, I had known three weeks before: extreme weariness, explosive puffs of pain in the legs and feet, and a slack, red-eyed face. Just after the new year one of my normally efficient systems had ceased to function, and when the failure persisted I drove myself to the hospital and had myself admitted. I was, for the first time in my adult life, a patient.

That was on a Sunday evening, and I went home ten months later.

In those days the language requirements for visiting interns were elastic, and unless you were lucky your first interview was conducted in Anglo-Hungarian or pidgin Wendish. My own exhausted intern had been napping, and was not disposed to stretch his mind as far as English. We compromised on French, so the whole experience began for me in a surrealistic haze – the more so as my French was a lot better than his, and after a few moments I had to phrase the questions as well as the answers. When the history and symptoms were on the record I was put to bed; the intern said "Ciao", which took us another step away from the real. I awoke weak but refreshed, ate well enough, and was punctured here and there by the laboratory people. Shortly my doctor arrived, and then an internist, for an intensive interrogation. By the third day, when my legs would barely move, we knew that my spinal cord was burning away – some sort of myelitis had attacked me, and I learned that the plural of myelitis is myelitides. Wednesday night my wife fed me, and the next voice I heard, over a week later, was saying, "Do you remember my name?"

When I heard that voice I was in another hospital: a large institution run by the state and county jointly, with a good supply of the monstrous instruments that might become necessary, like iron lungs and wooden coffins. I had been rushed there late at night, a tube in every orifice and a gloomy anaesthesiologist beside me; had been amply furnished with oxygen and liquid refreshment; and had been fussed over for seven days by teams of young doctors and special nurses. The infection had started at the base of my spinal cord and moved upwards, paralysing me progressively; there was nothing anyone could do but keep me as strong as possible. If it died before reaching my upper cervical vertebrae I might live, and that was all they could hope for. My eyes were covered with moist cotton, to prevent their drying, and one resident, with a delicacy I am still grateful for, instructed the interns to remove the cotton as soon as I showed signs of life so that I wouldn't wake up and think I had gone blind. Meanwhile, my respiration was down to six per minute, and an iron lung stood ready.

I missed all that, of course, the drama, the tension. I might have died an easy death, unknowing, slipping from one blackness to another. Instead, my respiration went up and my pulse came down, the iron lung was wheeled away, and my wife was told that I would live. A day later I called for her, and I can remember the first sight of her, and her kiss, and myself asking, "Did I almost die?" and accepting her "Yes" as perfectly natural.

At that point I ceased to be an abstraction, and became again a patient. But you must know what I mean by the word: I was not a rich man in a private room with a light touch of gout. I was a pauper in the charity wards of a public hospital, and I was helpless. I slept away the days and nights, and drifted in and out of delirium; I could suck down baby food, but chewing exhausted me; I could talk, but only a phrase at a time. (My closest friend was permitted to see me, and stood silently, wearing a gauze mask, at the foot of the bed. I woke up, and we looked at each other for a while because there wasn't much to say, and finally I wheezed, "That's . . . the last . . . time . . . I ever . . . kiss . . . *your* wife.") Worst of all – and I remember this much more clearly than the rest – my arms were paralysed; my hair, after two such weeks, was filthy, and my head itched damnably, and I was unable to scratch it.

Slowly order returned, sequence, continuity. Nurses made mysterious adjustments, and I learned that a tracheotomy had been performed, early on; a metal tube in my windpipe, like a tap in a barrel of beer, had helped me to breathe without chest muscles, and had kept me from choking on my own humours. Without a cork in the tube, speech was impossible, and my first fight with bureaucracy was for free speech in the primary sense. I won. My insistence was taken for rebellion, and therefore high spirits. (I learned later that any patient who argues with the staff is presumed to be improving or senile.) An old friend brought me a sheaf of Utamaro prints; they were tacked to the wall, and I contemplated them thankfully for two weeks, but when I left the contagious ward they were burned. Delirium lessened. Messages reached me from the world at large, reminding me that a novel of mine had been published on the day I passed out. The reviews were mixed but generally good, and it might even earn its advance. (I wish for all harried writers the equanimity with which I received this news.) I ate better, and graduated to mashed potatoes. I was laved and anointed. I flirted with nurses. I was palped and prodded, and for all I know leeched and cupped. I remember little of the daily routine, because I was not active in it: I was an object and not a participant.

I learned, finally, what was wrong with me. It was something called Landry's Ascending Paralysis. That was the syndrome. The disease was just "some sort of myelitis" – a lesion of the spinal cord, an infection, probably viral, that started low and moved up. No one knew why or how I had contracted it. (No one knows yet. I like to think it was hard work and clean living.) The name of the disease meant nothing to me, but the prognosis was unnerving: "Anything is possible." I could go on for years as I was, a vegetable: I could recover entirely; I could be stabilized anywhere in between. At that news, my emotions were stirred for almost the first time. I was angry and depressed, and my first reactions were ordinary: self-pity; "why me?" (there are some fifty cases a year in the United States); and "what have I done to deserve this?" (an easy question, unfortunately, for any man to answer). But in one of my wakeful and lucid moments, late at night, as alone as I will ever be, I saw how useless my questions were, because I saw what had happened to me: I was smack up against the absurd. I had read about it for years; now I *was* it. That did not burst upon me with the force of a blinding revelation. It simply seemed true; perfectly true; so true that I took it for my answer, and stopped my foolish riddling. After that night a good part of the fight was over, and won, with the conscious decision to do what had to be done, take my lumps, and keep my mouth shut.

(That was seven years ago, and this is the first time I have written about it. I probably won't again.)

When the risk of contagion was gone we took a long step: I was moved to a ward full of people, and the special care ended. I was one of thirty then, cardiacs and auto accidents, cirrhosis and diabetes, strokes and fractures. It was a new world, and I was in it for what would doubtless be a long time. (Everyone was cheerful and optimistic in my presence; unintended irony, because after that solitary night I was beyond optimism or pessimism.) As soon as I could move my index finger – a sign that I might recover – I had to decide whether to join this world of strangers, or to remain aloof. The choice was not as simple as it may seem. Not since the war had I faced a long stay with a random crew of men. (A compulsory stay, and with my own countrymen. I had lived in Chinese dormitories and small French towns, but there was a romance to that kind of mingling, and the exits were never barred.) This new world was not brave: it was a world of rock 'n' roll (everyone seemed to have a small radio, and they all blared at once; for months I could name the top ten, and hated all ten of them), warriors' reminiscences, batting averages, drinkers' boasts, comic books, amatory exaggerations, Abbot and Costello, and racial, social, and religious pride and prejudice.

As the paralysis retreated, the unease advanced. Now, thank God, I could scratch my head. Soon I could touch my first three fingers with the thumb of the same hand; one triumphant morning I could join thumb and little finger. One day I actually sneezed, which is a work of serious proportions; my chest heaved and swelled, air whistled in, the convulsion came; and what emerged was an infinitesimal, barely audible sniff, the catarrhal whisper of a rheumy mouse. A few days later the therapist placed an object in my hand, and I identified it by feel as a roll of adhesive tape. Then, a giant stride: I distinguished a nickel from a dime. My bed was raised; I could sit up and look around without fainting. But I had no desire for company. The music drove me wild; the sounds of television were even more inane than the pictures. I made a comb case by threading a leather lace through holes. It was much admired. I drew a tree in crayon, and was pronounced talented. As soon as I could turn pages – a delicate and complex operation – I read. I could feed myself, and ate some food. I began to put names to the faces and voices around me, to nod, to say hello. I enjoyed visits from the doctors, and learned phrases like clonic spasm and paraesthesia; when the visiting specialists came on rounds, trailing interns like fat hens with innumerable chicks, I liked overhearing their consultations and arguments. But I was like a student misfit hanging around the faculty club. My wife came every day; I clung to her, and to my books and occupational therapy (always called, regardless of its nature, "basket-weaving"). In short, I was an uncertain intellectual snob. I was afraid of people.

Coffee and cigars brought me around. Hospital coffee is by definition terrible, weak and somehow salty, and one day a nurse brought me a jar of instant coffee with my breakfast. Someone at the other end of the ward had sent it along, and it transpired that he was the X-ray technician who had worked me over weeks before, at the first hospital. A week later a heart attack had brought him here; he was recovering well, possibly because here his wife was a dietitian (she too was very kind to me; we were a club within a club). I got myself cranked up and waved in thanks, an exuberant, abandoned three-inch wave. People looked at me and laughed. I grinned. Every morning Chris sent me coffee, and with every wave of thanks I was integrated a bit further. And then one evening a fellow named Nate dropped by to chat. He was in his late thirties, a diabetic who died within the year; his eyes were going bad and he squinted, and when I first saw him I thought he looked like a surly barfly, a hater. He was not. He was a soft-spoken and gentle man (a foundling, he told me) who spent his days doing small favours for the bedridden. As we talked, he lit a cigar. It was a White Owl and not an Upmann, but the smoke he blew my way was the most savoury I can remember. He offered to blow smoke at me after dinner every day, and I accepted with thanks. He was liked, and brought other men with him, and soon I was no longer a snob and no longer afraid.

The fear was strange; I like people and am gregarious enough normally. I think now that it was a projection of physical fears. When you are immobile, and have no sensation below the waist, any travelling object is a threat; any bump or sharp contact may do vast damage that you will not even feel. For a while I hated needles. Every morning a girl pricked me for blood; twice a week larger amounts were drawn from a vein in my arm. When internal infection set in, injections were the answer. For certain examinations the anaesthetic was given by needle. Needles everywhere. And visitors bumping against the bed, and nurses dropping things on my dead legs. But fear gave way finally to acceptance; I ceased to care about the needles, and I made friends. For the first weeks I may have been in a deeper and less obvious shock than simple physical shock, and perhaps that enabled me to assimilate the bad news without horror; and maybe I was afraid to come out of it, afraid of stimulation from needles or people, clinging to a defensive narcosis through the worst days.

In the streets outside any hospital are signs requesting quiet; but no room on earth is as consistently noisy as a hospital ward. Bustle is constant. My basic routine was unvarying: wake up, wash, breakfast, Chris's coffee, rest, therapy, lunch, rest, therapy, rest, supper, Nate's cigar, free time, sleep. But the variety of event superimposed upon that routine was limitless. Doctors sweeping on to the ward, interns being solemn, nurses gossiping. Visitors lost. A crew of plumbers trotting in like the Marx Brothers. Gray Ladies and social workers and veterans' advisers. The old patient's son and his lawyer, trying to make changes in the will. Admissions and discharges. The flower ladies: every week an orange-juice can full of lilies of the valley. Accidents: broken glass, silvery liquids, slippery floors. Bedpan jokes. The cloudy octogenarian, hairless and senile, who wanders the wards without pants. The specialist, brisk and imposing in street clothes. Sometimes the specialist was for me, a neurologist; he would poke and tap and stick me with pins and smile encouragingly. Once I lost my cork in the middle of the night and woke with a raging thirst but unable to holler for water. I fell in love with two or three nurses and was assured that it happened often. Once I woke up in London, which was only odd because I had never been in London and was supposed to be finished with hallucinations. A liver case had a nightmare and woke us all with endless, agonized, quavering shrieks. A nursing student gave me a dry shampoo. A Greek pilot with a bad heart gave me a book about Athens; it was in Greek but the photographs were pretty. The doctor in charge of physical medicine and rehabilitation decided I was ready for serious work. The nurses accused me of malingering. We were all very busy, and my emotions were working again. By then I had learned to be cheerful and polite except under extreme provocation, like being given someone else's medicine, but I had also learned to be angry. There were moments of bitterness, despair, hilarity; but my basic emotional state for the next nine months was simple: I was sore as hell.

Not that I lacked the calming and ennobling influence of spiritual advisers. There are many sorts in a hospital. I liked best the much-maligned Gray Ladies. They come by to ask how you are, and whether you want a book or some supplementary basket-weaving, and they chat briefly and go on, and there is no nonsense to them, no back-slapping, no inspirational inanities. Then the social workers are fairly good. Their job is to keep your family together, and eating, and they take you away from your own troubles. The man from the Veterans' Administration is always welcome because he is showing you either how to save some money or how to get some. When you are a freelance of any kind, dead broke, with three kids and no medical insurance, and no benevolent company to keep you on the payroll, and no "sick leave", and no stocks and bonds or sellable furniture, and no income whatever for what looks like a long time to come, these considerations become important. Worry is unhealthy, and retards convalescence. (I was very lucky here. Many sensible friends sent my wife small sums immediately, without even asking. Simon and Schuster, then my publishers, sent a handsome cheque – as a gift, mind you, and not an advance. So did the National Cartoonists Society, with whom I was then working on a book. And a small group of ruthless poker players I had been supporting for years established a kitty in my children's names.)

But man cannot live by bread alone, much as he may want to. I suppose every public hospital has its chaplains, and God knows I had mine. (We even had a choir. A group of ladies came around once a month with a portable clavier, or calliope, or harmonium, a gleaming percolator, and sang the great old songs like "The Lost Chord".) I had, to begin with, a crew of earnestly religious nurses, some evangelistic, and probably the battle between Lucifer and the Lord was joined when the first nurse said to me, "God works in mysterious ways his wonders to perform." My answer was doubtless a grunt, but at that moment the metaphysical me (a very little fellow; I am one of these *hommes moyens sensuels*) took up a classic stance: chin tucked into left shoulder, left jab on the way, right hand protecting head and ready to hook. My troubles had only begun.

My wife had filled out the admitting forms at the second hospital, and when she came to religion she conscientiously wrote NONE. I could not have done that myself; it is impossible for a Jew to avoid the word "Jewish" without a sense of betrayal, or at least a tedious explanation. But my wife and I are a very usual sort of casual and permissive unbeliever, and she was protecting me from sinister possi-bilities: that I would come out of the coma nose-to-nose with a stout, cheerful, disputatious reform rabbi from Princeton, who would beam upon me and inform me in cultured accents that God had chosen to spare me for the time; or that I would die in the repellent odour of suburban sanctity, without even a chance to fight back. (She had a more serious and immediate reason: a friend of ours had regained consciousness in the first hospital just as I was passing out, to find herself being given the last rites. A week later she was fine, but still quivering with horror.) My wife was right, but the results were bizarre: being, on paper at least, a lost soul, I was claimed by every-body, and suffered triple visitations.

Of them all I preferred the Roman Catholic priest. He was rotund and bespectacled, vaguely European, and evoked nicotine stains and fiascos of cheap wine. He would come to my bed, shake hands (always), and stand for a moment nodding, as if the NONE at the foot of my bed were no more than he had expected in this vale of pagan tribulations. "How are you today?" I was well; still working at it. "Good," he would say. "Keep it up. You may go all the way." With luck, I would say. Then he would smile, because we both knew he wanted to add "and with help from above", and was refraining only to show me that his sympathy was human as well as professional. "Do you need anything?" No; but thanks. Then a wave, perhaps a sketchy blessing, and he was gone. A good man.

The Episcopal priest was also a good man, but very different: lean and grey, an amateur of the arts, a medical theorist, doubtless a member of book clubs. When he heard that I was a writer he was suffused by a pinkish ecstasy. From then on his visits were cultural events. I dreaded them; but he was a busy man, and kept them short. Finally at home, and even respected, in daily arguments about Jack Dempsey and Joe Louis, Pie Traynor and Pinky Higgins, Jack Daniel's and Old Cirrhosis, I resented interruptions from Sinclair Lewis and Somerset Maugham, from Millet and Millais and Millay and Malotte – interruptions that sent my new friends wheelchairing off in mild terror. But these visits, too, were welcome, sometimes funny and always a test of my good nature, my moral fibre, my grace under pressure.

I saw the rabbi only once, and I was rude; perhaps it was the rudeness that we reserve for cousins and never indulge with strangers. At the time I was on a tilt-table. Bedridden patients, like rising politicians, must be brought to uprightness gradually. They are strapped to tilt-tables and raised towards the vertical until they pass out, which defines the limits. I had worked up to about 70 degrees, and daily spent a pleasant quarter of an hour at that angle, wrapped like a mummy and bound to the table, looking out over my ward like the figurehead of a garbage scow. It was hard work. It required neck muscles to keep the head from lolling, and concentration to keep the breathing steady. I was straining to make a success of this when the rabbi came along, and the first thing I knew I was in an old-fashioned disputation: a roaring discussion of omniscience, omnipotence, oceanic feeling, intercession, and so forth. It may have been simply the frustration of having to argue with my hands tethered, or it may have been that if there was a God I had good reason to be vexed with him, but I found myself informing the rabbi warmly that I was not interested in reform pieties, Sabbath hootenannies, or Rachel and Leah in wedgies; on the other hand, if he represented the old angry bearded Jehovah, I was at his service. He left soon after, and later I was ashamed. He was a young man, but he had probably spent twenty years ridding himself of the old anthropomorphic orthodoxy, and he had left his study to spend a day in Bedlam, and I had taken advantage of his good nature and rude health, and been a boor. He never came back, and I wish he had.

But I hope I may be forgiven; and then the anger was good for me. Getting well is a bitterly hard job. Recalcitrant nerves and muscles depress the spirit, and the work requires every shred of will; the possibility of a short, bedridden life hovers like a nightmare; moral despair and physical exhaustion battle for the soul. Under these conditions a good nurse is worth more than rubies, and a religious caterpillar more hurtful than boils. Unctuosity and inspirational twaddle can be vicious, and applied pity can be maddening. And the theological dice are always loaded: if you recover, then God is good; if not, then God works in mysterious ways his wonders to perform. It is Job, and theodicy, all over again, but no one will ever argue it on that level. What you get is metaphysical molasses. A blasted man should be spared such sticky nonsense.

More to the point, and infinitely more invigorating, was my transfer, at the end of the second month, to another ward. Here lived three groups: permanently bedridden charges of the state, terminal cases, and patients in physical medicine and rehabilitation. From this ward we went home or to the grave.

Rapid changes kept me busy. My lung capacity was now normal, and the tracheotomy tube was removed. I was to sleep on my stomach hereafter, mainly because of a bedsore, or sacral decubitus, which is the polite name for a hole in my lower back the size of a lime (the flesh, deprived of circulation and therefore nourishment, and under the constant pressure of my inert body, had simply disintegrated). Best of all, I was to be placed in a wheelchair for several minutes every day. (They forgot to strap me in the first time; I fainted and fell out. Scandal. Investigations.) Furthermore, my therapy was to be accelerated. No more nickels and dimes, and no more basket-weaving, but hard work with progressively heavier weights. The social problem had ceased to exist, by the way. I came onto the new ward as a veteran, and observed with delight only two radios and one television set. For a day or two I was exhilarated.

What happened next is what I will remember when the rest is forgotten. I was wrestled on to the tilt-table and wheeled down to the gym. I proceeded like a tourist through new and exotic corridors and elevators, past pipes and valves and vending machines. In the gym I was flipped over, still happy, and tilted up, and placed before a pair of wooden handles attached to pulleys. It seemed to me that the whole hospital was there watching. At the end of each cable was a weight of one half pound. My Herculean task was to grasp the handles and raise the weights.

I grasped, and pulled, and strained until I thought my bones would crack. Nothing happened. My therapist spoke soothing words, and helped by tugging at the cables herself, and with her strength the cables went up and down, up and down, up and down. Then we quit for the day, in gloomy silence, and on the way upstairs I burst into tears for the first, and as it turned out only, time. It was a violent and immitigable oppression of spirits; nothing in my life before or since compares with it. That was a unique moment of absolute and brutal disappointment; of utter and helpless despair; of a finality like that of death. I had made the mistake of hoping.

Six weeks later I was raising a thirty-pound weight twenty times with either hand.

The next seven or eight months were anticlimax. I was a professional patient. When a new nurse woke me too early I bawled her out. I wore an intern's jacket in place of the degrading patient's gown. (Hospital dress as status symbol, from the director on down, is worth a study.) I could go from bed to chair and back without help, using a small overhead trapeze. I had one great stroke of luck: the doctor in immediate charge of me was a polio victim, and lived in a wheel-chair, and was tough. He hounded me and harried me; he also played chess with me and made off with his share of the fancy edibles my friends kept sending me. He worked me hard, but the example was more important than the whip. At the very worst, I would live as he lived; and he was doing his job and living his life. There was no nonsense to him. He offered no pity and needed none.

I took to supervising my own care, which was not a bad idea. I recommend minor meddling and ready asperity. Patients are damaged, and occasionally killed, in hospitals (which is – obviously, I hope – not to condemn doctors and nurses). Twice I refused medicines, knowing they were not for me; twice I made mechanical adjustments neglected by the night nurse without which serious harm, and possibly death, would have resulted. More and more (outside the gym) I took charge of my own routine. I ate what I wanted, and rejected out of hand the beef lung prescribed. I napped when I wanted to. With permission, if not approval, I took a cigar after supper. (Havana, in those days. The first one, after three months without, tasted like straw, but they rapidly became my prime solace. Later a friend brought me Burmese cigarettes, each a simple brown leaf rolled small; I was accused of retreating into marijuana, and refused either to explain or to give them up, enjoying the small scandal.) I became the senior patient on the ward, and was consulted by frightened newcomers. I grew a bristly moustache, and my children, who had not seen me for months, failed to recognize me. I wheeled myself to the movies on Wednesday nights; they were all bad, but they were a distraction. I remember explaining to a nurse why a man with a bleeding ulcer should not have aspirin; such pomposities were, I am sorry to report, good for me. I even got back to work, with a tape recorder; I lay mouthing mysteries into a microphone while my fellow patients kept a respectful distance, and my wife bore home little reels of tape and typed up the day's ragged prose.

I also took to reading my own chart, which was strictly forbidden. The belief seems to be that if a patient is exposed to an accurate account of his troubles he will fall into an immediate decline, possibly even dying of chagrin. But the chart accompanies him everywhere, and it is impossible to keep a determined busybody from hiding in a corner now and then with the forbidden volume. I was pleased to learn that twice my savage outbursts (on the order of "called Dr W-a murderous quack") had been considered quotable, and that two doctors had concurred in deeming me "intelligent". I also learned that I had spoken French and Chinese while coming out of the coma. Why such absorbing gossip should be kept from the patient I do not know.

But my life was mainly exercise. The memories of these later months are few now, like those of a man of fifty who tells you of his wild times in high school and college, and then says that he has been with IBM ever since. For two and a half hours every morning, and for two and a half hours every afternoon, I stretched and strained, grunted and groaned, the star performer among ten to twenty paralytics, aphasics, and fractures; a veteran trouper, a senior outfielder, the Solomon of the charity wards, the Samson of the therapy room. My arms and shoulders became stronger than ever, and my legs began to respond, and finally I was permitted to spend weekends at home.

Which proved difficult. Removed from the womblike security of the hospital, I was frightened again. Anything might happen, a fall, a fracture, a fever; and there I was with no doctors, no nurses, no therapists, no orderlies. No Gray Ladies. Not even a rabbi. The first two or three weekends at home were exhilarating and nerve-racking at once, but the nervousness passed, and was replaced by a ferocious desire to get out of that hospital for good. I was fitted for braces, and taught to use crutches. I was even taught how to fall. Over the summer my world expanded again, and the ward began to seem very small; I wanted to be a little frog again in my old cosmopolitan pond. The state of my health became less important; aside from the clearly defined disability I had become quite strong, and I had been – the realization was sudden and forceful – too long confined. By August I was a rebel, a prisoner reminding himself that his first duty was to escape.

I learned later that the doctors had been waiting for my rebellion, and were pleased. Cleverly I managed excursions, wandering unsupervised through the wards, or outside the gym in the summer sun; but I was more supervised than I knew. They wanted to send me home; but there were unresolved problems of internal medicine, and there was the bedsore. They knew I was ready for the world, but were not sure that I could live with the uncertainties of recovery. There were mechanical aids and medications that I might need for months, or even years, and prognosis was, as it had always been, impossible. For eight months I had known that today, this moment, might define my condition for the rest of my life; but also that I might go on recovering indefinitely. To release me in that uncertainty was to risk neurosis – depression, withdrawal, bitterness, despair. But to keep me was to risk a surly resentment, a permanent low-level claustrophobia. The doctors were weighing those dangers before I was even aware of them.

They let me go in October, after a last annoyance: they insisted on a final internal examination during the last week, and the examination resulted, as always, in a couple of days of fever, and they hesitated to discharge a feverish patient. I stormed my way through that one, and persuaded them to sign the papers; and on a quiet Friday evening I said my good-byes, wheeled myself to the car, and went home without looking back. I never did recover fully, and had two major operations in the next couple of years, and my way of life was drastically altered. But at least I was no longer a patient; I was a cripple. (Even hardened hospital personnel dislike that word, and search for euphemisms; but it is a decent and accurate word.) The difference is, I suppose, that a patient has no real independence; his life is defined and regulated by other people. A cripple's life is defined and regulated to some extent by his disability, but after that he's on his own. I still can't walk without a cane, and I need hand controls to drive, but last year I swam a shallow river full of piranha and rays from Brazil to British Guyana, and for one idiotic moment in midstream I wished that all those doctors and nurses were watching, lined up on the far bank with their stethoscopes and thermometers and long faces.

There is no moral. You decide in the first month or two whether you want to live or die, and once the decision is made you are nothing special. If you decide to die no one can stop you. If you decide to live you must decide simultaneously not to ask favours and not to ask "why me?"; you must reject pity and singularity with equal and absolute indifference. I suppose I learned that much, and more about getting on with my fellow man. Otherwise it was not that I learned; it was simply that I knew better and more surely what I had known uncertainly before. That we are promised nothing. That one man's hangnail is another man's broken neck. That the great trick is not to keep hope alive, but to keep going without it in a random universe.

   That nature never rejoices, and never mourns.

JULIO CORTÁZAR

from Portrait of Keats

Between 1951 and 1952, having translated Lord Houghton's biography of Keats into Spanish, Julio Cortázar wrote his own Imagen de John Keats. *He wanted to write an "unmethodical" book about Keats that was "baggy and dishevelled, full of interjections and leaps and great flutterings and splashings". The result is a kind of autobiographical literary biography, an eclectic amalgam of literary criticism and biography, personal reminiscence and detailed analyses of the poems. These extracts are designed to give a taste of the full "baggy" 600 pages of the original, and of Cortázar's playful and infectious enthusiasm for Keats and his work.*

ROMANTICISM

The word "romanticism" tends to have unfortunate associations for readers on either side of the Pyrenees,

> Zorrilla, the Duque de Rivas,
> Espronceda,
> Hernani, the red shirts,
> Musset, Chopin, Georges Sand,
> not to mention the sorrows of young Werther,
> weeping willows, Amalia

which are of little real interest in these times of a more original romanticism ("original" in the sense of closer to the beginnings of things): surrealism, for example. I would remind them that English romanticism has particular characteristics which place it in relation to German or French romanticism rather as Mozart stands in relation to Beethoven. In the best of English romanticism there is none of the egotism so subjectively cultivated by Lamartine or Musset; there is no endemic *mal du siècle*. The general idea is that while the world may be awful, life – lived in the world or in opposition to it – is still beautiful and can, in personal terms, transform the world. Related to this is the idea that weeping should be replaced by shouting, the elegy of the ode, and nostalgia by conquest.

There is no trace of a "romantic school" in England. The writers involved were isolated, their only contact being the times they lived in and other common and reciprocal influences. Their "I" emerged with a freedom denied them by the eighteenth century, but never got locked into the self-pity so prevalent in the worst kind of Lamartinian whingeing; instead, they made of their pain a javelin (Byron), a pair of wax wings (Shelley), or a voice that wrapped around things and gave them their true, secret name – and that poet was Keats.

Here I will pass on some common-sense thinking, courtesy of B. Ifor Evans:

> This romanticism admits an idealisation of life, an assertion of a faith not fully substantiated by any basis in fact, that life has beauty, glamour, graciousness and an indefinite range of sensibility. It is the belief in courtesy as Chaucer understood the term, and in gentility, and the affirmation that man is more than a machine, or a collection of reflex actions. In his perception of the world, in his affections and in his passions, the romantic poet asserts that man is capable of magnificence. The satirist, even indeed the realist, can easily deny this vision, and much in the daily incident of life contradicts it. Only by holding to the rare moments when outward circumstance and inward feeling unite in some sensation of exaltation can this faith be maintained. The ugly shape of so much in modern life, and a genuine attachment to the realistic, have led many contemporary poets to deny this vision as a delusion and a weakness, and it must be admitted that at times romanticism has descended into the effete. Be that as it may, the presentation of the "holiness of the heart's affections" has been a theme of English poetry for over six hundred years and rises again in the poetry of W. B. Yeats. Even if the temper of our time and the convictions of the younger generation will not permit new poets to reproduce it, the tradition of English poetry would be weakened if this part of its attainment were lost. For nowhere has the substance of poetry affected the national spirit more

closely, and even those who have not heard the names of
Spenser or Shelley or Keats or Yeats have had their lives in
some intangible way transfigured by the fact that great minds
have captured this transient but recurring splendour of life
into poetry.
(*English Literature. British Life and Thought*, British Council,
pp. 25–6)

The whole of this passage stems directly from John Keats, the
source of that enthusiastic affirmation of "the holiness of the heart's
affections". A key phrase, the sign of a message. Let us look, then,
at the situation of the poet within the frame and order that his
particular time imposes. But first, since we will only catch up with
him when he is nearly twenty years old, the reader deserves a rapid
review of his childhood and adolescence. Author's note: Lord
Houghton, Sidney Colvin, Amy Lowell and Dorothy Hewlett all
provide excellent "lives" of the poet. I happily leave the full chronicle
to them and say only that Keats was born in the autumn – 31 October
1795 – the same year and season in which Wordsworth and Coleridge
met, with famous consequences; a year of guillotinings on the
opposite shore; in Frankfurt, a young man took up the post of tutor
in the house of the banker Gontard and found in the mother of
his pupil the soul of Diotima. Hölderlin was twenty-five and survived
Keats by another twenty-three years: they never knew anything
about each other . . . (Cocteau said that constellations do not know
what they are; you need to be outside them in order to create
them . . . William Blake was another star, a nova of eighteen – again
an ignorance of black, icy air stands between his light and that of
Keats. To think that in 1795 the *Songs of Innocence and Experience*
had already been written!) Keats was still at the crawling stage when
Robert Burns, drowning in alcohol and ballads, after confusing
immortality with a snowy night, was dying in the north. Shelley was
three, Byron seven. Some nursery!

Mother and father were very ordinary people. There is a dark side
to the Keats' family life which I leave to those more given to psychoanalysis. He surfaces from a confused childhood with close ties to
his two brothers, George and Tom (younger than him) and to the
baby of the family, Fanny, who, early on, places in John's mouth a
fateful name.

(It occurs to me too that he was ten years old when our own
Esteban Echeverría was born.)

Nothing of much note until 1812. While here we were having our week of May, Cabeza de Tigre and Vilcapujio, John was receiving an obscure education in Enfield. At that time, Napoleon discovered the game of snowballs outside Moscow and Dargelos-Kutuzov ground him down with his slow, silent strategy. And John (long hair, broad shoulders on a small, slight body) reaches adolescence with his first poem, an imitation of Spenser that begins:

> Now morning from her orient chamber came,
> And her first footsteps touch'd a verdant hill . . .

the second line of which, oddly enough, will be the germ of the poems published in 1817:

> I stood tip-toe upon a little hill . . .

That standing on tiptoes, that wanting to look into the deep,

> I gaze, I gaze!
> ("Ode to Fanny")

is prefigured by his Vasco Núñez de Balboa – he makes a mistake and calls him Cortés – gazing avidly out to sea,

> Silent, upon a peak in Darien
> ("On First Looking into Chapman's Homer")

More than that, Keats had resolved to climb the heights that his poetry had crowned first. He felt no vocation for his enforced medical studies; they drag on for a long time (two years is a long time when you only have seven more years to live) and one day – I am sure of this – he stuck his lancet in the trunk of a tree and went to his tutor to tell him that he preferred poetry to pharmacy. You can imagine the ensuing row.

He is twenty-one years old, it is 1816. He admires Leigh Hunt, knows Shelley, is a devourer of new books and new roads. He celebrates, he pours out his libations, he is happy. It is the time of the band of brothers, the constant presence of Tom, George, and Fanny, and of his friends, Cowden Clarke, Haydon, Hunt, Reynolds. For him, Hampstead (a London version of the Adrogué district in Buenos Aires) contains the whole of Greek mythology and in his sky there begins to loom the shadow of the god he will elect for suffering and redemption: Shakespeare. And that is where we first meet him. So, John, shall we walk along together?

SIENA EARTH

I had just spent a long time sitting by the Fonte Branda, then I walked up a street, although really the street walked me, I just let myself be carried along, contributing only the movement. Thus I reached the house where Saint Catherine of Siena had lived and I sat down in a doorway to rest, to imagine, to compare. The sun was at ten o'clock, a sun which, in Siena-of-the-shadows, is both yellower and bluer, breaking up the ground into brilliant strips like immaculate side-streets along which only a Caterina Benincasa would have had the right to walk.

Siena is quiet (as is the whole of Italy – the clichéd Baedeker view of Italy mistakes raucous tourism for a sense of the pure truth of place) and I was enjoying being immersed in that silent light, looking between my knees at the house of the saint, still hearing in my memory the clucking waters of the Fonte Branda. Then, from a window up above, a young girl's voice began to sketch (to use any other verb to describe it would be cowardly) a canzonetta that was, at once, tender and lively and from which the word *primavera* leapt like a rabbit. In the empty street, the voice was suddenly part of the sun and of the saint. Siena was singing its present as if to provide me with some contact with what had gone before, with what I had been pursuing almost desperately throughout Tuscany.

Keeping absolutely still, afraid to look up and risk interrupting that voice, I heard the clear song vanishing into the air. When it stopped, the street was different, for the disappearance of that voice returned the street suddenly to its stone opacity and form; it seemed to me that the past was closing about the street again like a hand about a fruit; zealous, restless, necessary. Then, oddly, I thought about Keats. What I had felt a moment before, the total structure of that feeling, the present that included so much more than the moment itself, was the perfect universe of the "Ode to Autumn", the "Ode on a Grecian Urn", "The Eve of St Agnes". And I realized then that Keats had done away with night, that his work represented the reclamation of all that was diurnal, that it was the loudest of proclamations of morning life. That street in Siena was pure Keats, in the way that the world can only be completely identified with a man when there is truth in both of them, when there is an eighth day of creation.

On another morning, in Rome, sitting in the sun on the steps of Santa Trinità dei Monti, which he must often have looked at in his last days, I found myself repeating two lines he had written when very young:

> There must be too a ruin dark and gloomy
> To say, "Joy not too much in all that's bloomy" . . .

and with those lines came the image of the romantic landscape, the emphasis on ruins and solitude. I thought of Keats' letters in which the landscape is so rarely nocturnal and in which – as in his poetry – there is even a noonday dazzle about the moonlight. Then I realized how wrong I was to make a distinction between his letters and his poems, and I saw that everything he wrote was a whole, that is, the sense remains the same as he moves from verse to prose, from song to narrative. Many poems were written mid-letter, continuing – along a necessary poetic route – the line of intuition and the advance in knowledge that Keats was developing in his correspondence. I imagined (below, a boy was crying his wares – trinkets and knick-knacks) an edition of Keats that would give the poems and the letters in their order of creation, returning the work to the flow of his life. Such an edition would, however, present practical and even aesthetic problems. "It should at least be possible," I thought, "to write a book about him that would have as a frame-work that continuous line of life and work." I imagined a similar edition of Baudelaire, another poet whose correspondence is almost fiercely interwoven with the substance of his poetry, in his case *Les Fleurs du mal*. The writer is the first to detach from the totality of his being a product destined to become a book that will continue on beyond him. Publishing always involves burning boats and bridges. That is why a contemporary knows far less about the writers whose latest books he or she is reading than a reader generations later; what we call posterity is simply a process of reintegration. It is true that the writer works for the future, because the future will be his present, the time in which he will achieve wholeness and truth. By my side, I have the letters and poems of a man who, in his own day, was recognized by very few, and in whom only a small number of friends could merge the various aspects of his personality. Sitting on the steps of Santa Trinità, I gauged the need to banish all scholarly tendencies in order to reach Keats as I wanted to reach him, as he saw himself and wanted to be seen. A bird is song and flight; and only for methodical reasons . . .

But my book will not be methodical; I know now that when I walked up the steps and looked from the Pincio down onto radiant noonday Rome, my desire had already created this night tonight in Buenos Aires in a twelfth-floor flat in Calle Lavalle, a haven for the pages I am writing now as I determined I would do then, as I sat overlooking Bernini the Elder's "Barcaccia" rowing across the Piazza di Spagna, once the site of mock sea-battles.

LOU'S STORY

I crossed to the Lido one cold February afternoon, after the wind along the Riva degli Schiavoni had cut my ears to ribbons, forcing me into a number of bars on the pretext of drinking *un bicchiere di rosso*, in order to imbibe the dense, fragrant heat of Venetian interiors and to fill up on warmth again. The vaporetto dropped me at a piazza that lay naked to the whipping winds, and I walked along a street flanked by defunct hotels towards the sea booming on the other side of the island.

When I got there, the Adriatic was yellow and angry, hurling itself on the beach with such force that it wore itself out, only to start up again with the obstinacy of the obsessed. My feet sank into the sand that let its cold seep through my shoes. I looked across at the horizon and imagined that my sight – gone from me for ever – could reach the archipelagos that I would not manage to visit on this particular trip. The vast *lungomare*, the promenade that comes into its own during summer on the Lido, seemed to go on for ever until, at last, exhausted, battling against that aggressively sad atmosphere, I reached the end, a square flailed by terrible whirlwinds. I realized that this was not the Lido, that places have their moment much as women and songs do. Everything was closed, the huge international hotels, the villas, the theatres. Overwhelmed by a sense of solitude, by the anxiety provoked by being all alone in that amphitheatre intended for absent multitudes, I fled the beach; I wandered along vague, tree-lined streets, I plunged down a serene, leafy lane where the wind suddenly dropped, where a private sky was growing blue among the trees, with children on bikes and families in their Sunday best walking hand-in-hand through their neighbourhood.

I did not want to go back to Venice just yet and when I caught sight of the lagoon down a side-street, I walked along it as far as the seafront which was lapped by an absurdly calm sea. (Only a short distance away, on the opposite shore, the sea was still pounding.) Everything here was serene, green, damp. Now that the wind had dropped, the lake gave off the warmth of a sun sliding over white crests which raced off, like joyful yachts, into the distance, among the mooring posts, across the tremulous lagoon, to where distant Venice rose up in golds and lemon-yellows, with its Riva, with the pink sugar cube of the Palazzo Ducale. I sat down on the ground, "in the friendship of my knees" to use St John Perse's words, and I started a sketch of Venice which, to my great surprise, actually looked very much like it.

She arrived, slightly hesitant, and remained standing a little way off. She was not beautiful, but she was smiling at me. I thought she was trying to see my sketch and, shutting my notebook, I asked her in French (why in French?) if she liked the colour of the water. She made a gesture of incomprehension. It was a very Anglo-Saxon gesture, and then we talked and Lou told me about her travels in Italy, her home in California, her need, day by day, to annex the world for herself.

When it grew dark, we caught the vaporetto. One could no longer speak of the blaze of evening, the flood of fiery feathers, of green metals, of dark mirages. We were standing in the prow of the boat and my hand found Lou's hand, small and cold.

"Can one be worthy of such a moment?" I asked.

Lou said nothing, watching the approaching cupolas, the figures on the dock gaining colour, movement, voice. I heard her say, almost in a whisper:

> "O, that our dreamings all, of sleep or wake
> Would all their colours from the sunset take:
> From something of material sublime,
> Rather than shadow our own soul's day-time
> In the dark void of night . . ."

"John Keats to Reynolds," I said superfluously.

Lou was watching the prow, its blade cutting almost tenderly through the twin flights of firm water. I felt her tremble with the intensity of her desire; she was struggling along with Keats to save the day, to absorb into her memory the colours of that sunset which, tomorrow, wherever she happened to be, would colour her dreams with truth.

AGAINST THE EMPTY DARKNESS
OF THE NIGHT

What Keats was saying to Lou is what Girri says to us today:

> No te entregues a las sombras,
> Que sean otros los que mueran y perezcan.
> ("La bailarina")

> Do not surrender to the shadows,
> Let it be others who die and perish.
> ("The Ballerina")

From the outset, Keats' message is diurnal, lucid – that is, he chooses brightness – and his aim, along with Wordsworth and Shelley, in a time darkened by the penetrating melancholy of Coleridge and Byron, seems to be to write a solar poetry, a vigilant affirmation of human life, a romanticism of direct vision. Of Keats' earliest poems (the volume published in March 1817, which includes work written from 1814 onwards), those that most clearly illustrate this sense of immediacy are the "Epistles" and the two long poems that open and close the volume: "I stood tip-toe upon a little hill" and "Sleep and Poetry". Since Lou quoted a few lines from "Epistle to J. H. Reynolds", which came after that first volume but is in the same vein, we will go off in search of Keats as he was when he was twenty, at the time when he wrote his first great poetry. In fact, the oldest letter we have of his (Margate, August 1816) includes, or rather is, the "Epistle" to his brother George. A sense of thirst, of yearning for poetic attack fills this poem which already embodies a programme of spiritual action, a first contact with reality. The poem opens with a confession of dullness, privation; the aridity that every poet knows. Then come the time, the place and the formula, the access to the secret domain: Keats is already drawing up the joyous inventory. Spenser, the poet of his adolescence, revealed to him the fact that sudden receptivity is the beacon that illumines vision, and Keats recalls

That when a Poet is in such a trance,
In air he sees white coursers paw, and prance . . .

(The perpetual birth of mythologies: what are desires but the ideas of the heart?)

Then you have to speak, to enumerate, and the word enters the world. "*Oh, palabra, patria de mi alma* . . ." ("Oh word, my soul's homeland") says Eduardo Jonquières in "Como el piño" ("Like the pine-tree"). Dizzyingly, urged on by a sense of utter saturation, Keats rushes, from the very first, into the crystallization of his universe; everything must be said at once, without pause; said to friends, organized into a poem, seen from the perspective of the word. His first youthful discovery is this, that the word sees. There is a substance essential to the world which only the word of the poet can place, separate, perfect, designate. It is the eighth day. "The dumb are liars: speak," Paul Eluard will tell us later on.

The "Epistle" is interesting too because Keats already dares (still such a youngster, such a beginner) to conjecture upon the truth of his destiny, to glimpse the form his future will take. Rather primly, he attributes these ideas to the poet in general, as an archetype, but neither George nor we are fooled, and he knows perfectly well that we are not. The *non omnis moriar* is embodied here in physical images, in the straightforward prediction of his permanence on the Earth. "Lays have I left of such a dear delight/That maids will sing them on their bridal-night." And the queen of the village festivities will read "a tale of hopes, and fears", and the baby will be lulled to sleep by the song his mother sings to him. All this forms part of the veil of Maya, but Keats does not deceive himself about the price he will have to pay today for lasting into tomorrow. He says it straight out to George (always bathed in golden mediocrity): "Ah, my dear friend and brother,/Could I, at once, my mad ambition smother,/For tasting joys like these, sure I should be/Happier, and dearer to society." (Bad poetry, incidentally, because it is mere explication.)

If man is that "ever future gap" which Paul Valéry described, the poet suspects that present and future are a system of communicating vessels and that the level in one will give the level in the other. What Keats notices now is the terrible truth about those vessels: the future vessel will only fill up when the present vessel tastes bitter to the lips that touch it, and yet it has been filled for them, here and now. It is not true that one writes for the future, nor that the unhappiness of the poet is the price he pays for his future glory. The poet is happy if he is a poet, he is happy as a poet; only his ordinary self, with his poor heart in love with the circumstances that will fill it to overflowing, suffers the poet's happiness, weeps for his joy, dies little by little of his life. Keats did not exchange his present for his future; all the sorrow that awaited him did not arise from his being a poet, but from the fact of being a man who was destined to be a poet. Sure of that, he says, laughing: "Could I, at once, my mad ambition smother . . ." And then he plunges back into the poem just as his Endymion will plunge into the ocean, head first, without a thought. Lying on his back on the cliffs at Margate, he looks and looks and looks; a seagull, a boat, the shadow cast by the stem of a flower, the poppies. He is slowly approaching the identifications that will fill the "Odes" of 1819. Now he only looks and describes. His goal is to fix things, but his word is not yet strong enough, for he is still distanced from that goal by mannerisms and rhetoric. He can only glimpse what, in two years' time, will become a reality, he is like this page from Maurice de Guérin's Diary: "If only we were capable of identifying with the spring to the point where we wanted to breathe into ourselves all of life, all of the love fermenting in nature, to be at once flower, leaf, bird, coolness, pliancy, pleasure, peace . . ."

Keats can wait. His poetry was a tree, biding its time.

MELANCHOLY

Then comes the "Ode on Melancholy", the poetic leap into the certainty that requires no explanations. That is simply what is there.

The "Ode" is like a summing-up of the debate plaguing Keats, expressing its ultimate significance and conclusion.

I

No, no, go not to Lethe, neither twist
   Wolf's bane, tight-rooted, for its poisonous wine;
Nor suffer thy pale forehead to be kiss'd
   By nightshade, ruby grape of Proserpine;
Make not your rosary of yew-berries,
   Nor let the beetle, nor the death-moth be
      Your mournful Psyche, nor the downy owl
A partner in your sorrow's mysteries;

For shade to shade will come too drowsily,
   And drown the wakeful anguish of the soul.

II

But when the melancholy fit shall fall
   Sudden from heaven like a weeping cloud,
That fosters the droop-headed flowers all,
   And hides the green hill in an April shroud;
Then glut thy sorrow on a morning rose,
   Or on the rainbow of the salt sand-wave,
   Or on the wealth of globèd peonies;
Or if thy mistress some rich anger shows,
   Emprison her soft hand, and let her rave,
   And feed deep, deep upon her peerless eyes.

III

She dwells with Beauty – Beauty that must die;
   And Joy, whose hand is ever at his lips
Bidding adieu; and aching Pleasure nigh,
   Turning to Poison while the bee-mouth sips:
Ay, in the very temple of Delight
   Veil'd Melancholy has her sovran shrine,
      Though seen of none save him whose strenuous
         tongue
Can burst Joy's grape against his palate fine;
   His soul shall taste the sadness of her might,
   And be among her cloudy trophies hung.

Go not to Lethe, neither twist wolf's-bane . . . This is a startlingly
violent introduction to the subject-matter being waved in front of
us by the poet. It is as if Keats did not want to waste any time, as if
the sudden battle being waged by his poem in the very heart of
melancholy required him not to lose a minute.

   Then, if you jump in too, you realize that you are looking at the
thing from the inside, that the poem is not seeking for effect, but
rather, that the initial blunt negative immediately does away with
all the ad hoc symbolism which, aesthetically speaking, might have
served to evoke melancholy. Keats lists these symbols merely in
order to reject them as too remote, unilateral, partial. They are the
nocturnal symbols of melancholy and he has already discovered the
fusion of opposites, its presence at midday, when wolf's-bane kisses

honeysuckle. The next two stanzas will seal this contact between
contraries, where, as Rilke put it in his first Duino Elegy:

> das Schöne ist nichts
> als des schrecklichen Anfang . . .
> Beauty is nothing
> but the beginning of terror

At the same time, Keats manages to entrap us with the inevitable
associations aroused by that catalogue of symbols in the first stanza,
by the universal echoes that each contains; while rejecting them as
imperfect, he nonetheless disdainfully shows them to us. Having
crossed this familiar territory, we come face to face with the great
shock of the second stanza.

Here we have proof of Keats' mastery: originally, the "Ode" had
four stanzas, but Keats suppressed the first, realizing that a dynamic
beginning, with no introduction, was much more effective. The
original opening lines were rather gruesome, a parade of the stark
symbols of all things mournful: "Though you should build a bark of
dead men's bones,/And rear a phantom gibbet for a mast . . . /you
would fail to find the Melancholy – whether she/Dreameth in any
isle of Lethe dull." And then came: "No, no, go not to Lethe, neither
twist/Wolf's-bane, tight-rooted . . ."

That shift from one stanza to the next was perfect and meant
moving on from those cruder symbols to a catalogue of plants and
animals associated with night and death. Keats, however, suppressed
the first stanza, and the opening invocation of the second stanza
immediately took on a penetratingly mysterious quality, an allusion to
Lethe when there has been no previous reference to it. Why shouldn't
we go to Lethe in search of oblivion? And, anyway, why that association between melancholy and the deep river?

As if taking advantage of that moment of doubt on the very
threshold of the poem, Keats rushes us into the evocations of
the first stanza – wolf's-bane, nightshade, Proserpine, yew, beetles,
the death-moth, mournful Psyche, the downy owl, in order to
insinuate something else beneath all the allegories. Let us leave
them to one side.

> For shade to shade will come too drowsily,
>   And drown the wakeful anguish of the soul.

that is, the heaping up of nocturnal symbols on the shadow of melancholy will drown that wakeful anguish in which the soul is actually
able to apprehend the deepest melancholy, the definitive melancholy
that is present in the brilliant light of day, in the midst of life.

"Wakeful anguish" – how could anyone put it better? Anguish,
because what one has discovered is so awful, but wakeful, alert,
clear-eyed, because that is what being a poet means. Go not to
Lethe, because Lethe is here – in your happiness, in your sweetest
hour. That is what melancholy is, the price we pay for being human.

Wakeful means being active, an actor. If melancholy rises up
within you, you must be the one to search it out, to drain it dry;
don't be beaten to it by mournful Psyche; if its most subtle poison
lies in its diurnal side, then seek it out in its opposites, on the
other side of despair: "Then glut thy sorrow on a morning rose."
Keats responds from a deeper level to "Gather ye rosebuds while ye
may" and "Cueillez dès l'aujourd'hui". The Anacreontic, Renaissance
melancholy rises above the ashes of the feast – the uninvited
guest who arrives at dawn and sits at the feet of the sated drinkers.
None of them noticed, as Keats did, that melancholy was the first
to arrive, that it does not wait for the petals to fall from the rose,
that it is there in the bud, in its perfume. And it is better to know
this and to mingle sadness and pleasure in one dawnless experience.

> Then glut thy sorrow on a morning rose
>   Or on the rainbow of the salt sand-wave,
>   Or on the wealth of globèd peonies.

And if Fanny grows angry,

> Emprison her soft hand, and let her rave,
>   And feed deep, deep upon her peerless eyes.

The final stanza takes a very extreme point of view. "On a Grecian
Urn" saw truth in eternal beauty, the beauty of the marble with
its perpetuated images. Here, in opposition to that, is transient
beauty, joy "whose hand is ever at his lips/Bidding adieu" over
which melancholy reigns supreme, mingling with the very essence
of that beauty and joy. Is Keats saying that there is a difference
between eternal beauty and temporal beauty? Is the former safe
from sadness?

No, it isn't. Re-read "On a Grecian Urn" in the same slightly sing-song voice in which Keats read the "Odes" to his friends:

> And, little town, thy streets for ever more
>   Will silent be; and not a soul to tell
>   Why thou art desolate, can e'er return.

All is melancholy, but the poet's melancholy is that of wakeful anguish, the lucid acceptance of one's fate as a lucid being:

> Ay, in the very temple of Delight
>   Veil'd Melancholy has her sovran shrine,
>   Though seen of none save him whose strenuous tongue
>   Can burst Joy's grape against his palate fine . . .

Every poet will be the voluntary victim of that more subtle *belle dame sans merci*, present even in absences, Melancholy. The soul of the poet will savour the sadness of her dominion, "And be among her cloudy trophies hung."

A BIRD SINGS

March begins today, a month of meadows and farewells. I woke up filled with premonitions, I dreamed of friends in Europe . . . It's eight o'clock, the sun is shining in on one of my ears; I drink bitter maté tea and I know that it is March, that the planet moved on last night like the hands on the clocks of vast railway stations: an abrupt leap, two minutes. February, then suddenly it's March.

A month had passed in the "Odes" too. April brought the first odes; May, the home of spring, will hear the nightingale sing in Keats' poetry. Wanting to put paid to mediocre poets with the death of that cliché, Cocteau said: the nightingale is a bad singer. But he also said that some things are neither good nor bad: they have other qualities. The bird's sweet song contains that something which so darkly penetrates the darkness of the writer. Luis Cernuda, who has such an affinity with these odes, finds it in solitude:

> Como el ruiseñor canta
> en la noche de estío,
> Porque su sino quiere
> Que cante, porque su amor le impulsa.

> Y en la gloria nocturna
> Divinamente solo
> Sube su canto puro a las estrellas.
> ("La realidad y el deseo")

> How the nightingale sings
> in the summer night,
> because his fate requires him to,
> because his love impels him.
> And in the nocturnal glory,
> his pure song, divinely alone,
> rises up to the stars.
> ("Reality and desire")

Jorge Guillén finds it in passion:

> Cantará el ruiseñor
> En la cima del ansia.
> ("Advenimiento")

> And on the peak of desire
> the nightingale will sing . . .
> ("Advent")

and Daniel Devoto in the love of the person listening:

> Siento cantar un ruiseñor, a veces,
> Sobre una rama, y es solo mi sangre
> Que está pensando en ti sin que lo sepa.
> ("Canciones contra mudanza")

> Sometimes I hear a nightingale, on a branch, singing,
> but it is only my blood,
> all unknowing, thinking of you.
> ("Songs against change")

and Juan Ramón Jiménez in pain:

> Y un ruiseñor, dulce y alto,
> Jime en el hondo silencio.

And a nightingale, sweet and high,
Moans in the deep silence.

Keats used to hear the nightingale in the Hampstead twilight, and
his ode, born out of a half-sleep, will embrace his surroundings, a
world which the bird sensitizes, brings totally awake. The most
various of all the odes, it opens out symphonically onto the sphere
that Keats is seeking to grasp; the ode is a summary of the poet's
own yearning, happy youth, a triumph of the "wakeful anguish"
before the approaching autumn.

The idea of the poem is born out of the sense that the nightingale –
who, according to Berceo, "canta por fina maestría" ("sings out
of sheer mastery") – wounds the poet in the midst of his sylvan
solitude with music and that such intense, sonorous joy pierces him,
not with envy, but with a superabundance of pleasure. The meeting
of opposites occurs again in the propitious half-sleep, and Keats
feels himself submerged in that total osmosis in which loss of identity
fuses sensations and feelings with the thing that provokes them; he
achieves the oneness in which subject and object merge. His heart
aches because no heart can feel extreme joy without experiencing
pain, that ineffable explanation of death, which, alas, will not be the
same as our own subdued death at some future date.

(I mean that point when death actually becomes necessary, except
that it never happens there and then; no nightingales will sing on
the day we die, nor will love hold us in its arms, nor will all our
debts be settled. Who better than Keats to know that, the Keats who
here falls in love with the death waiting for him elsewhere as it did
for the king's gardener.)

The poem begins:

My heart aches, and a drowsy numbness pains
  My sense, as though of hemlock I had drunk,
Or emptied some dull opiate to the drains
  One minute past, and Lethe-wards had sunk:
    'Tis not through envy of thy happy lot,
    But being too happy in thine happiness, –
      That thou, light-wingèd Dryad of the trees,
        In some melodious plot
    Of beechen green, and shadows numberless,
    Singest of summer in full-throated ease.

What a leap, what an explosion of pleasure! Immersed in images
that strikingly repeat those of the "Ode on Melancholy", Keats again
rejects them, this time not with a "No, go not to Lethe", but by
surrendering from where he sits in the depths of Lethe's waters to
the joy that is the nightingale. Melancholy is present here too, since
it dwells with beauty; the ode gives testimony to its presence in that
alternation between surrendering to happiness (lines 2, 4 and 5) and
the sorrowful recognition of its transitory embrace in the remaining
lines, as well as in the general "tone" of the poem. That alternation
is a brilliant technical device (don't let's be frightened of the words!)
that takes the reader to the very heart of the "melodious plot" where
joy and melancholy dance hand-in-hand. First, there is that passionate
reaction to the miracle of the song:

> O for a draught of vintage! that hath been
>   Cool'd a long age in the deep-delved earth,
> Tasting of Flora and the country green,
>   Dance, and Provençal song, and sunburnt mirth!

Because the lover of claret wants to dance the wine – Isadora
Duncan once said: "I could dance that armchair" – "the true, the
blushful Hippocrene"; he wants it "With beaded bubbles winking
at the brim/And purple-stainèd mouth". He wants it in order to
lose himself in the forest with his nightingale, oblivious to his
surroundings, "Here, where men sit and hear each other groan . . .
Where but to think is to be full of sorrow". With a mere allusion,
Keats restates his firm belief: the nightingale and the urn are voices
from eternity that seek to tear us from thought; the felt force of an
ineffable beginning, the path beyond thought along which the essence
fleetingly appears.

And again – ever since the first man asked the first question and
felt fear and joy – the poet is using his weapons to find that path:

> Away! away! for I will fly to thee,
>   Not charioted by Bacchus and his pards,
> But on the viewless wings of Poesy,
>   Though the dull brain perplexes and retards . . .

The invocation to wine was a starting point, the first, sensual invasion
of Panic nature. But Dionysus is not enough, one needs different
wings to reach the nightingale. Then come the fourth and fifth

stanzas, pure word, verbal joy in which John has nothing to say, except this, and in which lines like "The murmurous haunt of flies on summer eves" evoke images that defy translation. It is night, "But here there is no light,/Save what from heaven is with the breezes blown . . ."

A need to lose himself in the fragrant dark, to abandon the last trace of identity that binds him to his words; death suddenly has meaning, that of the ultimate surrender, of being no longer transitory but a full-fruited ripeness in the mouth that sweetly bites and tastes.

> Darkling I listen; and for many a time
> I have been half in love with easeful Death,
> Call'd him soft names in many a musèd rhyme,
> To take into the air my quiet breath;
> Now more than ever seems it rich to die,
> To cease upon the midnight with no pain . . .

"Now more than ever seems it rich to die . . ." One remembers the "Ode to Maia": ". . . my song should die away . . . rich is the simple worship of a day".

Solitude is painless, silence is the sphere at whose centre the nightingale's thread of a voice contains the whole world. Listening, transfixed, Keats could be a line by Hölderlin (so close to him, though he never knew him) which I remember in the French translation in which I first read it:

> Tu es seul au coeur de la beauté du monde

He, listening; and the bird too that was "not born for death" and that knows the solitude of being always the nightingale, of having no identity:

> The voice I hear this passing night was heard
> In ancient days by emperor and clown:
> Perhaps the self-same song that found a path
> Through the sad heart of Ruth, when, sick for home,
> She stood in tears amid the alien corn . . .

I make no attempt to translate the following three incantatory lines:

The same that oft-times hath
Charm'd magic casements, opening on the foam
Of perilous seas, in faery lands forlorn.

The nightingale flies off, its song fades and gradually disappears into the depths of the forest. The poet returns to himself like an enormous, present, thinking weight; he opens his eyes, re-reads what he has written, and begins to be aware of verbs and branches:

Was it a vision, or a waking dream?
Fled is that music: – Do I wake or sleep?

Now, thirty centimetres of lecture. It's worth reading what Garrod has to say about this ode, in which he points to Coleridge's probable influence on Keats; for my part, I see myself in Mendoza in 1944, walking along a canal path with a copy of the Everyman Coleridge in my hand, making the discovery that "The Nightingale", written in 1798, precedes Keats' vital revindication of the nightingale, putting paid to the idea that its song was a sad one.

And hark! the Nightingale begins its song,
"Most musical, most melancholy" bird!
A melancholy bird? Oh! idle thought!
In Nature there is nothing melancholy.

And good Coleridge proves it beautifully.

. . .'Tis the merry Nightingale
That crowds, and hurries, and precipitates
With fast thick warble his delicious notes
As he were fearful that an April night
Would be too short for him to utter forth
His love-chant, and disburthen his full soul
Of all its music!

Keats must have liked the intensity of that song which raises the lines above the rather flabby context, full of plunges into prosiness. His nightingale will grow out of the eighteenth-century idea of Philomela, approaching the living fountain that mysteriously makes that song so dear to man. His ode – the most invocatory, the most ode-ish in the scholarly sense of the word – replicates with magical sonority the erratic line of the nightingale shining bright as a star in the trees. I know of no other of Keats' poems which – if one had to choose one – brings us closest to his "wakeful anguish" of being, to his explosive surrendering of self, to his oblique way of apprehending the world. It is the lucid delirium of the lyric, the language that does not wait for thought, but takes flight through images and gains access through incantation. It transcends speech. I think of Keats lying face up, letting himself be carried along by the singing; I think of St John of the Cross:

> Que me quedé balbuciendo
> Toda ciencia trascendiendo.

> I was left there stammering,
> all knowledge transcending.

AUTUMN

Between the first five odes and the odes that Keats dedicated to autumn there is a gap of four months, a period that includes the poet's final work, to which this ode would be an unwitting farewell – though no less perfect for that in its serene acceptance, its heaped-up granary, an acceptance of fate at the very moment when his personal battle was at its bitterest.

Later, we will return to Keats' letters, between June – where we broke off – and this terrible month, September, in which everything conspires against him; his correspondence, both the love letters and the letters to his family, give testimony to his confusion, his lacerated feelings, his path through utter darkness. Between July and September he wrote "Lamia" and the attempt at drama that produced "Otho the Great"; and "Hyperion", abandoned after a year of intermittent work, was to be the subject of one last effort with "The Fall of Hyperion"; his poetry, in parallel with Keats' dark night, reveals how the final decision is mingled with the effort itself; in the storm of his turbulent life, his ode "To Autumn" is all serenity, pure praise.

I will skip over those months and talk now about that ode, partly to complete our view of a cycle, but also because it contains in its essence a message of final reconciliation which to me – seen in the light of so much unconfessed pain – provides its loveliest depths and is proof that everything that happened in those intervening months was of no real importance. Without the letters (their existence is an accident born of friendship and the habit of keeping old papers), there is nothing in the poem to betray the suffering he was going through at the time. Ah, the beauteous word – the man who goes out for a walk, takes a piece of paper out of his pocket and, at the hour of noonday languor, scribbles down this golden image, this celebration of ripeness, recalling Shakespeare's "ripeness is all". Or as our own Guillén put it, in his "Arból del otoño" ("Autumn Tree"):

> Ya madura
> la hoja para su tranquila caída justa . . .

> The leaf, ripe now
> for its calm and proper fall . . .

Autumn is ripeness and the completion of the wheel of the year. The encounter of this moment with its poet – who is also ripe, a voice that both reaches out and bids farewell – made of the ode a fruit and plucked it, final and golden, from a branch that was just beginning to wither.

I

Seasons of mists and mellow fruitfulness,
  Close bosom-friend of the maturing sun;
Conspiring with him how to load and bless
  With fruit the vines that round the thatch-eves run;
To bend with apples the moss'd cottage-trees,
  And fill all fruit with ripeness to the core;
  To swell the gourd, and plump the hazel shells
With a sweet kernel; to set budding more,
And still more, later flowers for the bees,
Until they think warm days will never cease,
  For Summer has o'er-brimm'd their clammy cells.

II

Who hath not seen thee oft amid thy store?
  Sometimes whoever seeks abroad may find
Thee sitting careless on a granary floor,
  Thy hair soft-lifted by the winnowing wind;
Or on a half-reap'd furrow sound asleep,
  Drowsed with the fumes of poppies, while thy hook

Spares the next swath and all its twinèd flowers:
And sometimes like a gleaner thou dost keep
  Steady thy laden head across a brook;
  Or by a cyder-press, with patient look,
    Thou watchest the last oozings hours by hours.

III
Where are the songs of Spring? Ay, where are they?
  Think not of them, thou hast thy music too, –
While barred clouds bloom the soft-dying day,
  And touch the stubble-plains with rosy hue;
Then in a wailful choir the small gnats mourn
  Among the river sallows, borne aloft
    Or sinking as the light wind lives or dies;
And full-grown lambs loud bleat from hilly bourn;
  Hedge-crickets sing; and now with treble soft
  The red-breast whistles from a garden-croft;
    And gathering swallows twitter in the skies.

Garrod writes: "Of the 'Ode to Autumn' I will say nothing – for what seems to me a very good reason: I have nothing to say about it, nothing that can make it more intelligible or stimulate reflections upon it . . ."

Indeed, there is nothing to be said about the poem. It is simply there, almost too perfect according to Robert Bridges. But how many echoes it evokes from its bell-like being, that form that creates sound out of bronze. How not to feel the almost physical presence of Keats in a poem that shows him leaning over his time, giving in to the warmth of autumn that his early youth had ignored in the leap into winter; praising the harvest after having been the Corybant of renewal and first fruits. Breaking the dry branch of tradition, he disassociates autumn from its usual sad connotations, from the tone that Baudelaire gives to his gloomy "Chant d'automne" ("Song of autumn"):

Bientôt nous plongerons dans les froides ténèbres;
Adieu, vive clarté de nos étés trop courts!

Soon we will plunge into the cold dark;
Farewell, bright light of our too brief summers.

and which, in Jules Laforgue – in "L'Hiver qui vient" ("The coming winter") – becomes a grimace:

> C'est la saison, c'est la saison, la rouille envahit
> les masses . . .

> It is the season, it is the season, when rust attacks
> the sledgehammers . . .

Keats puts up a contrary argument, that autumn too has its music, and again, oddly, he heralds the view of Mallarmé, that friend of winter and defender of winter's austere clarity:

> Le printemps maladif a chassé tristement
> L'hiver, saison de l'art serein, l'hiver lucide . . .
> ("Renouveau")

> The sickly spring has sadly chased away
> Winter, the season of serene art, lucid winter . . .
> ("Renewal")

In parallel to him, Hölderlin sees in autumn an approach, man's encounter with his chosen season:

> Es sieget sich mit einem goldnen Tage,
> Und die Vollkommenheit ist ohne Klage.
> ("Der Herbst")

> But with a golden day it does appear
> And perfection is without complaint.
> ("Autumn")

And perfection is without complaint. How difficult to conceive of a perfection – when it is Man one is talking about – that is not perched on the stalk of a complaint. It is wonderful to see how the "Odes" quietly keep pace with the march towards that final note of grave contentment. Indolence fertilizes the hymn to Psyche, the eternal affirmation of the urn, the reconciliation of contraries in melancholy fused with beauty, the leap into the absolute in the invocation to the nightingale. Now it is autumn, ripeness. Ripeness is all. Keats has felt all his poems arrive and has effortlessly, soberly pushed them into being. Storms and arguments lie outside; here everything is summed up, present, final; the bell again, which accepts the blow as the price one pays for the music.

DECEMBER

From the window of his room that looked directly onto the steps of Santa Trinità dei Monti, he would see the steps like someone on the parapet of a bridge watching the ribbon of river slip by. A man of rivers, waters, a friend of aquaria and algae, Keats might have seen his small enclosed panorama as, a century later, Jean Cocteau so eloquently put it: "Keats' house trapped on the steps of the Piazza di Espagna like a millwheel".

During his first days there, he would climb slowly up those steps, leaning on Severn's arm. At his feet, the "Barcaccia", that curious nautical fountain designed by Bernini the Elder, lay at anchor. Up above was the church, whose one attraction for Keats would have been the fact that it was some way off, higher up, and then being able to walk along the Pincio, that green bridge high above Rome, where, at every step, the view of the city expands and offers itself up, wrapped in the greys and gilts of morning, in the lilacs and old golds of twilight.

He would sit down on a step, unable to climb further, and he would look back at his window as if at some abomination, the eye of an abyss drawing him ever closer; soon he would have only one way to look, then he would have to exhaust his view of the steps, the people coming and going, the play of the cold, raw light, of the sun far from its zenith. He would look too long at each stone, each stretch of wall, listening to the domestic games going on in the other windows, in the houses opposite, the street criers, the calashes racing off down the Via del Babuino. Young girls would look at him pityingly, knowing from his devastated face and the dark fire in his eyes that the small, thoughtful man was merely the reflection of another far-off life, an image from a magic lantern, the shadow of a cloud that the first breeze would blow far from the steps.

The evenings, the sumptuous entry made by the Roman night, would arouse in him the bitterest tide of pain. At that hour, Severn would do his best to distract him and good Dr Clark would come with news to tell and little jokes. But the fountain would be fading down below while, his forehead resting on the window pane, John watched the slow shipwreck of the barge in the violet water rising up from the stones. The steps would drown one by one, he would see the feet of night climbing slowly up towards him, and then he would turn with a look of helplessness, rejecting both the catastrophe and the beauty of the world and accepting everything, his bed, the bleedings, Severn's St Bernard face, the awful fasting, the memories opening out like fans in the bare room of his insomnia.

What he managed to see in Rome during his first few days there, before he succumbed to his physical debility, could only sadden him with anticipated visions of death and ruin: the forum, the lunar circus games at the thermae, the intricate silence of the birds along the Appian Way, the petrified beauty and colour in the statues and paintings in the museums, so many silent signs pointing towards the sunset. He withdrew into himself, into the mouldy snail-shell of the Piazza. But at night, at the hour of the catalogues of absence, he would tremble to think of the nearness of a beauty he had for years yearned for and that would not now be his. Michelangelo, Raphael, the marbles in the Campidoglio, the columns and frescos. To have an imaginary memory of them, a mental construct of the days in Hampstead, and to lack now the strength and desire to make them his, to raise his eyes to the ceiling of the Sistine Chapel, to rest his fingers on the torsos of Praxiteles, on the thigh of the wounded Gaul . . .

Severn, who, at first, would return from the street full of exciting tales of dazzling aesthetic finds, would fall silent, convinced that they were harmful to the patient. What did they talk about in that high room, where the hours would pass so slowly, where they had barely enough money for essentials? From the street would erupt thunderous Roman exclamations, cheers and blasphemies. And sometimes the smell of fritters, or a breeze from the Tiber, the cold, yellow mists of January.

1821: JANUARY–FEBRUARY

Severn's letters to their friends in England chart week by week the decline of a man who now no longer even leaves his bed. Although his words – which Lord Houghton transcribes at the end of his biography – have all the truth of poverty and suffering and provide their own chronicle, nothing can bring us closer to John – since he himself keeps silent – than the page in a notebook where, during one lone night spent awake and watching, Severn drew the dying man's head: the head of a drowned man, his hair falling over his forehead in greasy clumps, his waxen skin with a rose of fire in each cheek, his mouth drawn tight in a rictus that is less a rictus of bitterness than of infinite disappointment, and the words of the artist at the bottom of the page: "Three o'clock in the morning. I drew this in order to keep awake. A deathly sweat drenched him all night."

Looking at that image, which has watched me writing all these months and travels with me from house to house, I am reminded today that Gide had it in his room too, that Rilke saw it and wrote those unforgettable lines about those lips:

> O Schwelle der Gesänge,
> O Jugendmund, für immer aufgegeben . . .

> O, threshold of songs,
> O, youthful mouth, for ever silenced now . . .

"Little or no change has taken place," writes Severn on 14 February, "except this beautiful one, that his mind is growing to great quietness and peace. I find this change has to do with the increasing weakness of his body, but to me it seems like a delightful sleep: I have been beating about in the tempest of his mind so long." It was during this time that John came up with his epitaph: HERE LIES ONE WHOSE NAME WAS WRIT IN WATER. As in a mysterious poem that no one would write, he was ordering the sepulchral images that were his only present peace. One day he said to Severn: "I can feel the flowers growing over me." And like someone deciding what to take with him in his luggage – thus the young Pharaoh went down into his burial chamber with all his favourite toys – he asks that the letters from the two Fannys stay with him in his coffin and then changes his mind and wants only one letter and a lock of his sister's hair, and one can gauge at that moment the horror of a passion that is afraid of enduring into the beyond, the horror of opening with that passion the doors of silence.

On 23 February, around four o'clock, John receives the sign. Severn, watching by his side, does not understand and John explains in words made hesitant only by his laboured breathing: "Severn – I – lift me up – I am dying – I shall die easy; don't be frightened – be firm, and thank

God it has come." What remained was his body, bereft of consciousness, sliding gently towards the moment when his chest would rise for the last time and then surrender effortlessly to stillness. Severn thought he had fallen asleep, as had happened so often before after such a crisis.

Afterwards came "Adonais", the solitary pain of the few who had known him in all his beauty, and then, slowly, a necessary oblivion, John Keats' night.

Once he had murmured: "I think I shall be among the English Poets after my death." Fifty years on, Matthew Arnold confirms the dawn: "He is. He is with Shakespeare."

Buenos Aires, 19 June 1951
Paris, May 1952

Translated from the Spanish by Margaret Jull Costa

The lines from Rilke (p. 95) were translated by Stephen Mitchell, the lines from Jules Laforgue (p. 106) by William Rees, the lines from Hölderlin (p. 106) by Michael Hamburger, and Anthea Bell advised me on my translation of the lines by Rilke on p. 109.

JULIEN GRACQ

Caen

Caen. The passage of these four years, 1942 to 1946, remains lodged in my memory: the first two with the ancient city still intact, though the recollection of it barely subsists among a handful of people; the last two amid the accumulated ridges of rubble. Even before, long before it was destroyed, the old university town had become somewhat disincarnate. Between Friday and Wednesday, as it was emptied of its teachers, who returned to Paris the moment their classes ended, and deserted by four-fifths of its students, who spent those five days in their living quarters, be it school or college, or back in their remote villages, the Faculty gaped absently as it awaited the fire from the heavens. Even on my first visit, in November 1942, on my way from Paris to my new posting, the train quite suddenly came under machine-gun attack from an aircraft – as it were an arm's-length clip on the ear. Amid the alerts so lightheartedly observed – each one marked by the fall of two or three bombs away in the distance – a gentle touch of autumn sent a kind of pleasant shiver through the town, and hung over its curving streets which were even then somewhat fitfully inhabited, and over the Prairie Caennaise with its broad, placid expanse of green abruptly edged by the naked cliff of masonry – the Hôtel Malherbe, such a novelty! – and over the age-old posting inn where I took my meals, with its inner courtyard all planted out and rimmed with a wooden gallery giving access to the rooms; it had a charming old-world name which I cannot clearly recall – something like Hôtel Saint Jean et de l'Image (or du Commerce). I was living on the city heights, in Place Saint Martin, a little house of but a single storey, covered in jasmine and reached through a scrap of garden. There my landlady, octogenarian Mme L., lived through all the air raids in 1944, and never sought any refuge beyond the treads of her wooden staircase; during the raids she would sit beneath them with her knitting. The house was spared by a miracle, and suffered nothing worse than a few scratches from shrapnel. To the left a promenade of fine trees dropped down towards rue du Château.

Somewhat further back stood the little railway station of Saint Martin; one of my students from that time wrote to tell me that, despite what I had imagined in *Lettrines 2*, it was not brought back into service at the Liberation. From almost in front of the house a paved road sloped away that brought me to the old Faculty and the cavernous depths of the Geography Department; with its gallery running at half wall-height, its grille-fronted cupboards, its dusty silence, its dark chocolate-coloured woodwork, it bore a resemblance to the admiralty chartroom. All of this, paving included, was long ago reduced to dust. Between Wednesday noon, which saw the boisterous descent of the Paris contingent from the train, with their wooden soles and empty knapsacks, and the Thursday evening when those teachers hoisted the self-same knapsacks back on board, this time bursting with provisions, the Faculty filled up and seethed like a lock when the gates open. The rest of the time, out in the torpid streets, or beneath the compacted ceiling of my vast room, I would walk and work very much on my own. I saw scarcely a soul other than my colleague in Geology. The showcases of mineral samples, the library, these were our almost daily meeting-points. Occasionally, along with some dozen students from the two faculties, we would go on excursions presided over by Professor D., a solid, god-fearing geologist; in his company we would periodically take to the road in the freshness of early morning, for a long day's hike. More often than not we would wend our way along the Normandy byways lined with hawthorn and with milk churns awaiting collection; we would bisect the lines marking some primary syncline, a prized regional speciality and inexhaustible source of papers read to the Société Linnéenne de Normandie. When weariness began to set in, the chorus of young acolytes from our remote Temple of the Sciences would embark (the entire Geology Faculty thought highly of the professor or at least recognized which way the wind was blowing where his convictions were concerned) on some Catholic Youth anthem, such as:

> It's the road of the paladins
> The warrior road;
> It has beheld the saints a-marching
> Towards the light.

And not unlike the Rogation Day procession, the little file would raise the pace and reduce the distance separating not Vézelay from Compostela but the surface ridges of Breton sandstone from the schist lines of *Calymène Tristani*. An amateur snapshot, doubtless a gift from a student, preserves for me the memory and the atmosphere of one of those lighthearted days, all steeped in the wind's cheerful bluster, the dust, the sunshine, days at once studious and carefree. Here is D. with his battered straw hat, his gaiters, his toothbrush moustache and his geologist's hammer; and here am I at his side, playing corporal to his sergeant-major; I'm dressed in my black overcoat and rucksack, and all around us we have the little troop of disciples, all harnessed up in rucksacks over their city coats; the sacks contain our picnic, and there are pouches for rock samples; they are sitting strung out like onions, at the foot of a railway embankment. In a corner H. sketches the ghost of a smile in his round dimpled cheeks, as though he were waiting to watch the birdie.

The students enrolled in Geology numbered scarcely four or five; there was even a year when there were only two (while the teaching staff, including the lab assistant, ran to four people); there were ten or a dozen in Geography, but normally just five or six, and even just a single one for the Friday Regional Geography course. There were a handful of city bachelors from well-to-do households, who were killing time with no very precise goal in view, or else they were eluding civilian conscription in Germany; a few village schoolmistresses alighting all mud-spattered from the Thursday bus; two or three teachers' sons who would come along sometimes to make up the numbers: these served as a pretext for classes staffed in numbers that represented an extraordinary luxury during this period of dearth – though the luxury was disguised behind the decrepitude and the ill-lit somnolence of those rue Pasteur classrooms, reminiscent of the musty apothecaries' converted into museums that are still open to the public in provincial hospices, with their shelves full of mortars and porcelain vases, each one labelled. All good things come to an end: the bombs that were going to put paid to this surreptitious cultural largesse were in the course of being primed. But in the interval there was pleasure to be had from this pursuit of education inside a vacuum; it enjoyed a reprieve that tended no further than its own quite Malthusian survival (and quality was assuredly maintained). Here it vegetated in well-respected decrepitude, all in the family, as it would be in this sleepy town, the haunt of scruffy lawyers and footling cases. The rivalries and intrigues kept long a-simmering within these closed confines – be it over the succession to a chair, the award of a Legion of Honour, an election to the governing body – partook in the eyes of an outsider (and as I was not involved I was sometimes entrusted with certain confidences) of the muffled sacristy atmosphere of the Curé de Tours. No doubt it would have its share of real drama; for a supply teacher with no ambition to climb the local career ladder, what emerged was a cosy monastic oasis of calm, silence, indulgent urbanity and – subject to temper – of leisure or facile study. Art for art's sake. Everything evolved in untroubled calm, the age-old traditional pursuits imposed their daily rhythm on this sleepy faculty; and yet, out of the four professors in the History and Geography departments, by 1943 two had already been shipped to Buchenwald without anyone seeming to have noticed. As I re-read certain scenes in Bernanos' *Dialogue des Carmélites*, where the nuns pick cherries and make jam while vague snatches of the Jacobins' *Carmagnole* come drifting more or less unnoticed over the garden wall, I found myself thinking back to the mini-faculty at Caen under the Occupation and on the eve of the Normandy landings. And not because of the tragedy, which it was spared by fate, but on account of the clausura.

When I returned to Caen in October 1944, after the Liberation, I succeeded first in reaching Paris from Angers on board a railcar commandeered by the local authority, a sort of administrative charter which landed us at our platform after a highly fanciful transit. The only way thence to reach Caen was to secure a place on one of the lorries leaving for the town: an authorised form of hitchhiking which for many months supplemented the paralysed railway system. We would take our station – some forty postulants for the journey – at one of the city gates, where the lorries were required to load passengers so far as lay within, or even beyond, their powers. After a morning's wait we would take the truck by storm, scrabbling with hands and feet to heave ourselves up on a shifting mountain of crates and sacks; then off we went, hair streaming, wind-whipped, a sort of layered sculptural group which might have been posing, were it not for the direction in which we were headed, for an allegory of June 1940. The reoccupation and the exodus relayed each other on these clapped-out lorries jagged with bouncing humanity atop the sacks and crates – and yet we had had four years' experience in which to hone our skill at packing to the gunwales. At first the October sunshine was cheerful and heartwarming. How pleasant it was to watch the villages and trees slip past as though from the open deck of a bus. But towards dusk we penetrated little by little into a mysterious countryside, a sort of *terra incognita* from which all the usual landmarks had suddenly vanished. Now and again by the roadside the dust-coated hedges stopped to give way without transition to two gap-toothed moraines in brick or dressed stone; here the sound of the motor would set the rats heaving in the semi-darkness. Not a trace of humans, nor of movement, just the enervating silence of a graveyard in the moonlight. In the rather spectral gloaming, with not a light showing anywhere, in the cold which hit suddenly and gnawed one to the bone, it felt as if the lorry, which gradually shed its human complement, was advancing towards the limit of the inhabited world; towards one of those frontiers from vampire films where the only light comes from will-o'-the-wisps dancing over the marshes, where little dead souls flit silently about on bat's wings.

I got down near the ruins of Caen station, clutching my suitcase in the advancing night. Sometimes there was not a scrap of wall left standing for hundreds of metres, no doubt because the tanks had seen to the bulldozing in order to complete the work of the bombs and shells. There was a moon; beneath this colourless and yet fully vital light the town seemed to be displaying the labyrinth of its collapsing trenches and rubble parapets with dramatic ostentation, much as a torture victim will show off his stigmata with just a touch of immodesty. Not a living soul amid the ruins, in the hollow of this moonlit night. The rue Saint Jean, a long street that might have served for guide as it cut through the town, had disappeared without leaving so much as a scar: it had been totally destroyed and, as it was somewhat twisting, it was decided in the interests of simplicity to bulldoze a straight line of clearance through it to facilitate the passage of the convoys. In search of points of reference I cut away towards the docks; I got lost, until the decapitated bell-tower of Saint Pierre finally identified itself and gave me a bearing. Beyond it re-emerged a few stretches of wall still upright, then some street corners standing proud, and before long some inhabited houses. Up on the heights of Saint Martin, which were virtually unscathed, I found my house with barely a scratch to it, a little ark grounded on the hillside after the waters had subsided.

From Journals of the High Road
Translated from the French by Guido Waldman

A Proscribed People and its Spokesman

Rexhep Qosja is the greatest writer in the community of Albanians who live outside their national borders, constituting as they do more than half of the Albanian nation. He is, furthermore, one of the most remarkable men this nation has produced in the course of its long history. He is a novelist, playwright, essayist, brilliant polemicist, academic and literary historian, and has long formed part of that small number of intellectuals who repair Albania's standing, which has, alas, suffered in the course of a century that has treated the nation so badly.

One of his books is entitled *The Proscribed People*. This is how he has described that part of the Albanian population that lives in Kosovo or in other areas of what used to be Yugoslavia. It is not a metaphor but a poignant truth, one of the most tragic of our time. We are used to the expression "banned writer" but the expression "banned nation's writer" has a strange ring in our ears. Unfortunately, it is true: a banned nation does exist in Europe! That is the cry of this writer, that is his summons. He has been issuing this call for the last quarter of a century, but those who pay heed to it are indeed few in number. There lives in Europe a people deprived of every right, without schools, without newspapers, without radio or television, a people whose lot is to be terrorized and persecuted by an alien police. And this people is one of the most ancient on the continent; they are the contemporaries and neighbours of the ancient Greeks, and had a hand in the creation of some of those treasures of classical culture which are the pride of world civilization.

As is often the way with major crimes, people may soon start to say: How could these horrors be perpetrated beneath our very eyes, how can there be this reversion to the Middle Ages only a step away from us without our having noticed, how can one of Europe's nations be thus proscribed without our knowledge? Rexhep Qosja's novel is there to bear witness, to assert that it is sometimes less a question of not knowing than of not wanting to know. It has been victim of a boycott for the twenty years since its publication: it is a novel that causes disquiet, disturbs repose, and as a rule such works are little appreciated by those who like to sleep peacefully without being troubled by shadows and external fears.

For years the very name of Kosovo remained unknown. In recent times some part of its tragedy has surfaced here and there – some part of the terror, the massacres, the torture, the agony it has endured. But what comes to light is little, all too little in comparison with the reality of the situation.

What has done more damage to the Albanians than Serb terror is Europe's protracted silence. And even worse, the doubly shameful silence of Albania itself, the motherland. For it is a silence which indicated that for the Albanian and Serb Communists, as for most communists, the true motherland was to be found in the inhuman dogma of Marx and Lenin, to which they were prepared to sacrifice everything, not excluding their own fellow countrymen. The silence about Kosovo has lasted forty years; apart from a short interval following the Brioni Plenum (1966) when Tito improved the situation, the country has known a terror beyond description. And meanwhile in Yugoslavia there were nothing but international assemblies, festivals, delegations, third-world congresses – a European paper described Yugoslavia as "the Festival State". Nowhere else did the communist display ever achieve the status it attained in Yugoslavia. Beguiled by Tito's "liberalism", the rest of the world forgot that his chief lieutenant, Ranković, the minister of the interior, was one of this century's worst criminals. Ranković was, among other things, the most ruthless executioner the Albanians ever had to endure. But in Yugoslavia it was all right to imprison, torture and kill Albanians. It was even an act of virtue. Moreover, when in 1966 Tito got rid of this butcher who bloodied his salons and festivities, he did not condemn him for his crimes against Albania.

It was during this post-1966 period, the period of relative calm, that *Death Comes to Me from Those Eyes* was published. But the novel is threaded through with a sinister presentiment; the author does not celebrate a liberalism which he distrusts. He foresees that terror and massacres are to return to Kosovo.

It took the spring of 1981 to fulfil Rexhep Qosja's prediction. Kosovo was once again steeped in blood. Something was said about it, in an undertone. The blood of a proscribed population did not have the same store set on it as that of other peoples. The Yugoslavs had made friends around the world and many politicians, many artists had taken holidays in the official villas of the Festival State; rose bushes had concealed the lies and a mere massacre was not going to prejudice any of that! The massacres were resumed in 1989. It was with them that Milosević began his career. Kosovo's autonomy was withdrawn, and while the Kosovans dressed their wounds, Yugoslav television showed pictures of the enclave's abolition being celebrated in Belgrade with champagne. Things were said this time too, but all too little when compared with what needed saying.

In 1992 the whole world was aghast at what was happening in Croatia and Bosnia. Nothing unusual here. The crime had its origins in Kosovo and only waits to return there to reach its apogee. Among themselves the Serbs do not deny it: they cannot wait for Kosovo's turn to come.

Rexhep Qosja's novel is steeped in Kafkaesque anguish. Everything falls apart, everywhere there is a presence, the intimation of terror. The novel is threaded through and through with a sardonic laughter which could as readily be taken for a lament. Elements of tragedy and farce blend in the most natural manner. The author foresees that Kosovo is to experience a new reign of terror; and he is in the grip of another sorrow – in Albania itself things are faring no better. The Albanian flag displays a two-headed eagle; similarly the Albanian tragedy is double-headed: a single nation under a double communist dictatorship, the Serb and the Albanian. That is a lot for a people already the victims of their history.

Today the press and the other media throughout the world only mention the Balkan peninsula in terms of condemnation: where, it is asked, does this primitive ferocity stem from all of a sudden, this cannibalism? Such words are repeated wholesale whenever the horrors of the conflict in ex-Yugoslavia are shown on television. The answer is simple: from nowhere! The barbarity, the cannibalism, the inferno was already there in place, carefully hidden but ready to explode. There are people, the sort who salve their consciences by playing blind and deaf, who are pleased to observe: "What's to be done? It's the Balkans, after all, they're used to it." Then they smile as they come out with their cynical aphorisms along the lines of "balkanisation", "parish-pump mentality", "yokels at odds". What is simply overlooked is that it was in these lands, among these peoples, that the civilization of present-day Europe found its origin. It was in this peninsula that three thousand years ago the most important, the sublimest discovery in human history was made; a guilty conscience. The day the Greeks repented of their ancient crime, the destruction of Troy, a new horizon opened for humankind. Without this repentance, there would have been no ancient Greek literature, out of which was to spring law and culture.

Today, three thousand years later, all of this seems to be lost. As in a fatal cycle, the primitive ferocity that the inhabitants of the peninsula repented in those distant days is triumphing anew. And just as their forebears turned to the gods to settle their quarrels, so now they turn to the rest of Europe. But Europe is in two minds, weighing up the advantages and drawbacks of the affair. Some Europeans perhaps consider it useless to bother all that much over those wretched Balkan peoples. But the best of them have arrived at the view that for a number of reasons Europe has to intervene, most of all because Europeans have a long-standing debt towards the peninsula which had taught them the examination of the conscience, which served to shed light and yet now languishes itself in darkness and ignominy.

Despite the insulting epithets cast at them, the Balkan people today have indisputable merits, whatever their faults, and they clearly deserve better of life. It must not be forgotten that they have suffered as few others have, and if the struggle against evil can prove ennobling, it can also have the opposite effect and increase barbarity. In a famous play devoted to a legendary war between cats and serpents, the Greek poet Seferis relates that when it came to an end, the cats had won but the poison had entered their blood. That is more or less what has happened in the Balkans after their long struggle against the Ottoman Empire. Besides, the life they lived under three of the harshest empires in history, the Roman, Byzantine and Ottoman, resulted in these Balkan peoples emerging transformed by the gears of these huge machines of state. State crime has been fatally added to the primitive, as it were naïve, coarseness, and the rise to power of the fourth empire, Russian then Soviet, was only to compound this evil.

The worst crimes tend to be the repetition of old crimes that recur in a cycle; their horror seems to vary in degree. In Yugoslavia genocide has a long history. Contrary to the sanitized Soviet historiography that presents the Slav incursion into the Balkans as a peaceful march accompanied by agricultural labours and the planting of apple orchards, the Slav settlement of these lands in the seventh and eighth centuries was in fact a bloody affair. The medieval Slav and Albanian epics bear witness to as much. This epic literature is perhaps the only one in the world that has been preserved for us in two languages of two nations in conflict for a thousand years. It is as if instead of one Iliad we had two, a Greek version and a Trojan version, each one seeing the truth through its own spectacles and offering entirely conflicting accounts. This contrast has its climax in regard to the origin of the epics, each side believing that the other has merely traduced its text in translating it. As native Balkan-dwellers the Albanians accuse the Slavs, ever since they invaded Illyrian-Albanian territory, of stealing not only their homes and their land but their epic literature as well, and the Slavs insist on denying this *more balcanico*.

One thing is certain, it would be hard to find anywhere in human history another example of a hatred as inveterate and tenacious as that which exists between Serbs and Albanians. Without making an autopsy of this ancestral loathing one will find it difficult to understand the other focuses of hate in ex-Yugoslavia. And without examining this scourge which is the hatred in this land one will find it difficult to trace out the path to peace. Hatred for the Albanian is now fundamental to the world-view of the Serb nationalists; it has been raised to the level of a dogma. No nationalist leader can make his way, no party, even in opposition, has any chance at the polls unless they wave this murky banner. Many a Serb intellectual has been infected by it. In recent times other voices have fortunately been raised, but such messages of harmony are still isolated. The majority of academics, writers, historians and, above all, the Orthodox Church incite the evil instead of holding it in check. Here we have a hatred that nobody even challenges. In 1937 Vaso Cubrilović, who had a hand in the Sarajevo assassination, presented to the Serb public his doctrine on the extermination of the Albanians in Yugoslavia. The anti-semitic projects of Himmler and Eichmann do not extend further. And yet, far from incurring criticism, this criminal rose to become one of the most highly respected academics in Tito's Yugoslavia, and even a member of the Academy of the USSR. A writer as distinguished as Ivo Andrić put his name to a book no less macabre on this very subject, but he attracted not the smallest criticism, at a time when the great Borges was being constantly taken to task over a simple conversation with Pinochet.

Communist Yugoslavia fanatically pursued this tradition. After its break with the Soviet Union in 1948, Tito was persuaded to liberalise his regime to make it more acceptable in Western eyes. But not in Kosovo, where crime and terror were installed and carefully displayed as in a sort of conservatory of evil. The Kosovo Albanians found themselves alone under the axe of the murderous Rankovic. The West made Tito almost a hero of liberalisation and closed its eyes to the Albanian tragedy. Later the West was to justify its indifferences to the fate of the Albanians living in Albania by the isolation in which this country was kept under Stalinism; but even to this day nobody has been able to explain the indifference the West showed for half of the Albanian population on whose fortunes it might have been able to exert some measure of influence.

The origin of the terrifying hatred between Serbs and Albanians is not yet known but must certainly be sought in the eighth and ninth centuries, the time of the Slav invasion that set out from the Ural steppes, reached the Albanian border, and exerted on the Albanians a pressure that increasingly eroded their territory. And yet I believe that this original hostility was not sufficient to generate the hatred that was later apparent, and that it can be explained only by an urge for revenge upon the Albanians. And this urge is one that the southern Slavs, or at least a proportion of them, nursed and kept on the boil for the five centuries during which the Turks occupied the Balkan peninsula; five centuries are quite enough to imbue a simple thirst for vengeance with catastrophic dimensions.

To understand what happened it is necessary to consult the Balkan chronicles. After the endless struggles between Slavs and Albanians, the Serbs contrived provisionally to occupy not only Kosovo but also a part of Albania, although this did not achieve their ambition to destroy the Albanian barrier that excluded them from the Adriatic. Then came disaster for both sides in the shape of the Ottoman occupation. The Balkan peoples realized the danger, left off quarrelling and in 1389 on the plain of Kosovo tried to make a united front against the Turks. But they were crushed and the one after the other, a little sooner or a little later (the last Albanian citadel capitulated in 1478!), they fell under the Turkish yoke along with their memories, their quarrels, their victories, their defeats, their pride, their wisdom and, of course, their folly.

One might have thought that after such a disaster the Balkan peoples would forget their age-old discords, and so they did for a while. But these are not people who forget easily, least of all offences. It was quickly realized that in the multi-national Ottoman Empire different nations were to receive different treatment. Some were particularly oppressed and despised while others were pandered to and received the best of treatment. This was a constant policy of the

Empire whose goal was, it seemed, to divert a part of the conquered peoples' energies into internecine strife. The result was brilliant: never, or almost never, was there an end to the hostilities, rancours and jealousies between the peoples over which the Sublime Porte exercised supreme authority. The advantages of such a situation are clear enough. Since the time of Christ, whose crucifixion at the hands of His compatriots was a sign of powerlessness and servility towards an undisputed Roman power, nations have often given bloody spectacles before the tribunals on which the powerful flaunt themselves.

The Turkish Empire was a permanent cockpit for disputes. One pasha's army would leave to crush a rebellion in another's fiefdom. Cypriot officers would go to war against Walachians, Albanian pashas against Slavs, Bosnian beys against Greeks, and so on. All these initiatives left people disorientated, diverted their anger in unexpected directions, and allowed the Empire to disguise oppression behind the generals' nationalities, even more so behind the individual nations.

In this turmoil the Albanians and Serbs found themselves, through a quirk of history, in contrasting situations: the Albanians among the most favoured nations, the Serbs among the most oppressed and despised. In exploiting the Albanian thirst for glory, a thirst typical of all ancient Balkan peoples, the Turkish Empire contrived to lure them with the offer of high office. It was Albanian generals who, to the misfortune of their people, led the campaigns of conquest in Hungary and Poland, laid siege to Vienna, repressed so many rebellions with an iron fist. Albanian governors and viziers ruled over vast tracts of the Empire, and often the entire Empire when they achieved the post of prime minister. These personal achievements the Albanian people paid for in the meantime, and they were later to pay for them all the more, for the jealousy and often the anger which this situation excited was directed at the people as a whole and not simply at the Albanian vassals and generals thus identified with the occupying power; this was to prove a disaster for their small population.

The hour of vengeance struck in 1913 when, as a reward for Sarajevo, half of Albania was handed over to the Serbs and then, after the Great War, the kingdom of the Serbs, Croatians and Slovenians was confirmed in possession of it. The Albanians, the erstwhile masters of the Empire, found themselves finally at the mercy of their old Slav enemies; they were strangers, segregated, orphaned, in a state that was soon to be called Yugoslavia, that is, the country of the southern Slavs. A harsher fate could not be imagined, for the Slavs, the erstwhile oppressed nation, were not going to be long in taking revenge for offences that went back centuries. They let the Albanians know that their time had come and gone, and that, as the only non-Slav population in a Slav kingdom, they would have to bend their necks and suffer terror, or else leave the country. This strategy was borne out by the plan of that criminal and academician Cubrilović. As if this were not enough, the Germans, during the Second World War, made overtures to the Albanians: they gave them a place in the family of top nations and, wishing them to play in the Third Reich the very role they had played in the Ottoman Empire, annexed Kosovo to Albania. The mere fact that this merger was the work of Hitler was considered by the Slav victors to be a decisive argument against the Albanians.

What exactly is Kosovo? To whom does it belong now, to whom did it belong before? In other words, is it Albania's, and has it always been, as the Albanians maintain? Or has it been the cradle of the Serbs, as these claim, and consequently is it to be considered Serb, for all that today it is Albanians who are living there?

At first sight the question may look complex. In fact it is extremely simple. Both sides agree that the demographic argument, which is fundamental in determining the ownership of a nation, is absolutely in favour of the Albanians, who make up more than ninety per cent of the population of Kosovo. The quarrel therefore turns on the historical rights that each side claims to possess. The Albanians, who do not rest content with the demographic argument, assert that historically too Kosovo is Albanian land and the Serbs are nothing more than footling occupiers. As for the Serbs, they argue the opposite case: Kosovo is Serbian, it was the Serb cradle from the start, but the Albanian element by dint of sheer pressure has established a dominant position.

To arrive at the truth it is necessary to keep before our eyes the main outlines of Balkan history. Every serious historian, fron antiquity to our own day, considers that the most ancient peoples of the peninsula are the Greeks and the Albanians. "The oldest Balkan peoples are undoubtedly the Greeks and the Illyro-Albanians," writes M.G. Castellan in his recent *History of the Balkans*. And every serious historian, including the Serb ones, admit that the southern Slavs, and thus the Serbs, arrived in the Balkans in about the seventh or eighth centuries A.D.

The Albanian thesis rests on a simple question: who inhabited Kosovo before the Serbs arrived? It is not, after all, to be thought that this plain, one of the most fertile in the Balkans, was left uninhabited. The Greeks make no such claim. Kosovo is an extension of present-day Albania. The most elementary logic leads therefore to the conclusion that it was settled in early times by the same people living there today, that is, the Albanians. What happened after the Slav invasion? The Albanians say that after the bloody battles Kosovo became a place where the two peoples lived side by side, each one gaining the upper hand as the fortunes of history dictated. The Serbs, in keeping with the thesis whereby Kosovo was uninhabited before their arrival, say they were the first to settle in this plain and to make it their cradle. According to the Serbs, the Albanians remembered one fine day (better late than never!) that facing their mountains there was a very fertile plain, and that is when they flung themselves into it to drive out the Slavs. Such a thesis seems absurd, of course, to the Albanians, for the simple reason that Kosovo is clearly visible from their mountains: their inhabitants, however stupid they might have been, would have noted its existence from the outset.

It is well known that the sensational, and if possible the bloody, often helps to fill the lacunae of history. To lend veracity to their thesis the Serbs have made use of the battle of Kosovo. They bring it to bear each time other arguments fail them. But before they could make use of this battle, they needed to refine on it quite considerably, and they ended up with a fundamental travesty. The greatest travesty, when it comes to battles, is in changing their participants, but that is precisely what the Serb nationalists have done with the famous battle of 1389. Every historian in the world, and that includes the Serb ones, at least until lately, asserts that the battle was fought between the Turkish Empire and the army mustered by all the Balkan princes. To demonstrate that Kosovo is theirs the Serbs claim to have been the only people to have fought in the battle. But the Ottoman chronicles of this war, later historians and every text that merits credence do not limit themselves to giving the nationality of the members of the Balkan alliance, Serbs, Bosnians, Albanians and Walachians (some add Hungarians and Croatians), they also give the names of the coalition leaders. It is true that Prince Lazarus was elected generalissimo, but, of the five commanders of this army, a huge one for the Balkans of the day, only Lazarus was a Serb; Trvko was Bosnian, Mircea a Walachian, and two were Albanians, George Balsha and Dimeter Jonima.

It is difficult to find a battle more tragic in its consequences. For all the Balkan peoples it was a mortal blow, after which they slid into the abyss one after the other. And the blood spilt on that fateful

June day seems not to have sufficed; the spectres born of this battle continue to be exploited, so that further bloodshed, a new genocide, is to be predicted. It is the battle of Kosovo which today lies at the root of Serbian chauvinism. It serves as an argument for the Serbs, a justification for their reign of terror, for their massacres – principally of Albanians. In fact it amounts all over again to a curse on the Balkans.

What actually took place on the plain of Kosovo on 15 June 1389? There are two versions: in the Serb version their army alone confronted the massive Ottoman contingents in a struggle so terrible that the two leaders, the Serbian Prince and the Turkish Sultan, both perished on the spot. The Serbs were defeated but the battle placed an obstacle in the way of the Turkish advance on Europe. In a word, the Serbs saved Christendom from the rage of Islam. The version given by everyone else is that a Balkan coalition of equals confronted the Turkish army. The fight was undoubtedly terrible, but the two leaders' deaths did not take place on the battlefield and had nothing heroic about them: Sultan Murad was assassinated after the battle in dubious circumstances, while Prince Lazarus was captured and executed by the Turks. The Turkish victory was complete, as also was the Balkan defeat. But that evening the Council of Viziers placed on the Sultan's vacant throne not his legitimate heir, his eldest son Jakûb Çelebi, but the man's younger brother, Bâyezîd Yïldrïrïm. Moreover the viziers had Jakûb assassinated, which reinforced the idea that the murder of the Sultan was the result of some sort of palace revolution. The battle of Kosovo lasted ten hours but, as a victory never impeded the march of the conqueror, it did nothing to restrain the Turkish pressure; on the contrary, it accelerated it. If the Turks subsequently slowed down their assault on Europe, it was not on account of the batle of Kosovo but because they were attacked from the rear by a terrifying monster, Tamburlaine.

That is the truth about the battle of Kosovo. After six centuries its ghost haunts every area in which the tragedy and the massacres in the Balkans continue: in the plains of Croatia, of Bosnia and, of course, in those of Kosovo, where it takes root and means to return to complete the vicious circle.

The battle of Kosovo, the first occasion when the Balkan people made common cause against an invader, should have been the symbol of their fraternity. It should have been their first monument, a sublime point of reference, out of which light and peace should later have emerged. In the hands of cynical manipulators, however, what comes out of it today is the very opposite, it is mourning, it is venom. Once the Balkan peoples find the strength and wisdom to divert the course of history into positive channels, a great light will fill the sky of the peninsula; in the last resort that sky too is a part of the European firmament.

The works of Rexhep Qosja – not only the present novel, written many years ago in difficult conditions, but the whole of his work – constitute a prophetic warning of the apocalypse that threatens the Balkans today. It is a warning as dignified as it is poignant. It is devoid of hatred, of nationalistic hysteria. Rather it possesses that austere yet unfailingly heroic tone which great tragedies inspire. He has demonstrated not only his high intellectual worth but the way he forms part of his own culture, an integral part of the culture of the Balkan peninsula in which for the first time human repentance was made manifest. And more than ever the Balkans stand in need of this repentance.

Ismail Kadare, Paris 1993

Translated by Guido Waldman
from the French version by Christian Gut

ANNA MARIA ORTESE

The Involuntary City

One of the sights of Naples, after the statutory visits to the Scavi, the Zolfatara and, time permitting, the Cratere, is III and IV Granili; it's in the coastal zone linking the port with the outer suburbs towards Vesuvius. It is a building with a frontage of some 300 metres, a depth of some fifteen to twenty, and a height a good deal greater than that. Someone coming upon it unexpectedly, on getting off one of those little trams used mainly by working folk, would take it for a hill or a bald mountain riddled with termites, which swarm all over it noiselessly and, it would seem, without purpose. The walls had once been a dark red which still shows here and there amid the great swathes of ochre and swabs of an equivocal green. I was able to count 174 openings on the façade alone, of a breadth and height wholly out of keeping with modern taste, and most of them barred, a few small terraces and, at the back of the building, eight wastepipes located at the third-floor level, which dribbled their sluggish waters down the silent wall. There are four floors including a ground floor half sunk into the earth and protected by a ditch, and they comprise 348 rooms all of equal size and height, distributed with perfect regularity to the right and left of four corridors, one per floor, their cumulative length being 1,200 metres. Each corridor is lit by no more than twenty-eight bulbs, each one of barely fifteen watts. Each corridor is between seven and eight metres wide, so the word corridor serves rather to designate four typical urban streets superimposed on each other like the decks on a bus, and with no access whatever to daylight. On the ground floor and the two above in particular, the sunlight is represented by those twenty-eight bulbs, which shine feebly day and night.

On the two sides of each corridor there are eighty-six doors opening on to private living quarters, forty-three to the right, forty-three to the left, plus one for a lavatory, all distinguished by a sequence of numbers running from one to 348. Each of these rooms accommodates between one and five families, with an average of three families per room. The total population of the building is 3,000, made up of 570 families, with an average of six persons per family. When three, four or five families share quarters, they achieve a density of twenty-five or thirty persons to a room.

Supplying a few statistics as summary as this about the structure and population of this quarter of Naples, one is aware that one has not really said anything. Every day, in a thousand offices dedicated to the purpose in every city and country of the globe, perfect machines are aligning numbers and statistics to measure and evaluate to a nicety the economic, political and moral life of every single community or nation as it is born, prospers and decays. Other data, layer upon layer of data, positively astronomical, are concerned with the life and nature of ancient civilizations, their governance, triumphs, civic structure and demise; or, skipping every area of historical interest that lies closest to our hearts, they turn to consider the life or probability of life in the planets shining out there in space. III and IV Granili is one of the most intriguing phenomena in a world, like that of southern Italy, which time is abandoning for dead; rather than being uncovered in the simplistic figures of some obscure reporter, it needs to be scrupulously examined in all its deformities and grotesque horrors by teams of doctors, lawyers and economists. Suitable commissions could go there to count the number of living and dead, and in both cases to scrutinize the reasons which kept them going or held them in thrall or carried them off. Because III and IV Granili is not only what may be called a temporary solution for the homeless, it is the demonstration, in clinical and legal terms, of the collapse of a race.

Drawing but the most modest conclusions, we must face the fact that a social structure has to be deeply sick if it is able without turning a hair to tolerate, as Naples does, the putrefaction of one of its limbs; for this, and nothing else, is the sign beneath which the Granili as an institution lives and germinates. It would no longer enter anyone's head to come to Naples and, after visiting these barracks of the Bourbons, to go looking for something yet more abysmal. Here the barometer no longer registers, the compass goes mad. The men you come upon cannot do you any harm; they are ghosts from a life in which there used to be wind and sun, they retain practically no memory of these blessings. They slither or scramble or totter, that is how they move. They speak very little, they are no longer Neapolitan, nor anything else. A ccommission made up of priests and American researchers boldly crossed the threshold

of that dreary edifice not many days ago and turned back smartly
with incoherent words and looks.

I had noted on a box of matches, which I later needed for another
purpose, the name of Signora Antonia Lo Savio. With no other
address, one morning this November I crossed the threshold of
the main entrance which opens on the right-hand side of III and IV
Granili. The concierge was sitting behind a large black pot in which
some clothes were boiling. She looked me up and down coolly,
then told me that she did not know anyone of that name and I'd
have to go and ask on the first floor; I was tempted to put the whole
thing off to another day. It was a violent temptation, like the feeling of
sickness at the prospect of an operation. Behind me on the forecourt
some dozen boys were at play throwing stones at each other, and
uttering scarcely a word; some of them had stopped playing when
they saw me and silently drew near. Ahead of me I saw the ground-
floor corridor, 300 metres long as I have said, but at that moment
its length seemed to me beyond measure. At the middle and towards
the end of this conduit there was a vague movement of shadows,
like dust particles in a light-beam; an occasional little flame glinted;
from behind one of those doors there came an obstinate, raucous
lament. Gusts of a pungent odour, a latrine smell for the most
part, kept wafting down to the entrance, mixed with the yet more
dispiriting smell of damp. There seemed no way to penetrate ten
metres into that tunnel without passing out. After a few steps I saw
a little light seep through on the right, and discovered one of those
stairways with very broad steps and risers not more than a finger's
breadth in height, which once upon a time had allowed horses
stabled on the ground floor to reach the first floor with their loads.
Perhaps it felt less cold than I had feared, but the darkness was
almost total. I risked stumbling, and struck a match, but put it out at
once: there were a few tiny lights inside which reddish filaments
kept twisting and wavering. By this faint glow the first-floor corridor
could be made out.

At the end of this thoroughfare someone was roasting coffee,
because the odour of urine and damp was now mixed with the more
agreeable aroma of roasted coffee beans. The smoke made the eyes
water, though, and placed a rosier halo round the pin-sized lights.
I passed a group of boys playing ring-a-ring-a-roses; I didn't notice
them until I was almost on top of them; they were holding hands at
arm's length, and had their tousled heads thrown back, and displayed

an eagerness such a game would not normally occasion. I grazed
tufts of hair that were hard to the touch, as though set with glue,
and arms that felt cold. Eventually I saw the woman who was roasting
coffee, seated at the threshold of her home. Inside all was in disorder
beneath a lurid light produced by an unexpected ray of sunshine
that came through the window giving onto the rear of the building,
to illuminate a scene of pots, rags, mattresses. There was blood
too. The woman, a swarthy, wizened creature, was sitting on a cane-
bottomed chair which had lost all its cane, and evinced a sort of
pride as she kept turning the wooden handle of the metal cylinder,
from whose opening a cloud of smoke floated up to isolate her
head. Standing around her three or four girls, in black frocks open
on white chests, followed the dance of the beans in the cylinder,
a concentrated look in their sparkling eyes. Seeing me they stood
aside and the woman stopped making the cylinder jump on the fire
whose light for a moment almost faded out. The name Antonia Lo
Savio left them silent. I realized later, in the course of subsequent
visits, that this silence, rather than betokening perplexity or indeci-
sion, betrayed curiosity and a more sinister albeit fleeting sentiment:
the desire to involve this stranger, who was evidently more at home
in the light, for a moment in the darkness wherein they held the
upper hand. At least many of these people played the game, during
my visits, of not answering or of sending me off to places from which
I'd not easily find my way back. I was about to continue on my way,
forcing myself to look calm, when one of the girls turned towards
a door, and said hurriedly without looking at me: "Look. There."

A little woman, bloated like a dying bird, was combing her black
hair in front of a fragment of mirror as she held a few hairpins
between her teeth; her hair fell across a hunchback, and she had a
lemon-hued face dominated by a big pointed nose that hooked over
on to a hare-lip. At the sight of me she smiled and said: "One minute."
I was so overjoyed to see such a smile in such a place, I had to stop
for a moment to ask myself whether or not I ought to be addressing
her as Signora. She was no more than an oversized louse, but what
grace and goodness animated her tiny eyes! "Signora," I said, quickly
approaching her, and I mentioned the name of Dr De Luca, director
of the clinic for the poor of Granili, who had put her forward with
a view to her showing me round a little. "One minute . . . if you
don't mind," she repeated, continuing to smile and comb her hair,
and I realized then that beneath the rattle of catarrh she had a soft
voice. I think it must have been this unconscious awareness that

somewhat restored my courage. I leant my back against the door, waiting for this creature to finish her grooming, and meanwhile I glanced at the group round the coffee pot. The smoke had thinned out, and in that sudden greyness those females looked even paler. With a silent, scornful laugh they muttered a few words in which the name of Lo Savio stood out, and I was angered by what I presumed to be the reason for so much hostility. As this Lo Savio woman was coming to the end of her combing, there in her doorway, taking her time over it as though it were May and she were a young lass with her mind on her beloved, a little boy approached, hands in pockets, hair rigid, a cocky, baleful look in his eye. He continued, with an imperceptible hesitation, towards the middle of the room and went to sit on the planks of the bed. (In all this great building I never saw a made-up bed, only mattresses spread out or piled up, at the most with a blanket thrown on top.) Once seated, he swung his thin legs and began a toneless song: "There was once a queen, and her hair was all in ringlets." He broke off a moment to turn to her: "D'you have a wee bit of bread?" and from the slight formality with which he put his question, in Neapolitan dialect of course, I gathered that they were not related. While she made him some answer, with the last hairpin in her mouth, I went over to the little boy and asked him his name. "Luigino," he answered. I put some more questions to him, but he made no answer. His entire face reflected an ambiguous, scornful smile which contrasted strangely with the dead, absent look in his eyes. I felt uncomfortable, as if his mysterious, mature smile, no longer that of a child but of a grown man, and a man accustomed to dealing only with prostitutes, expressed a judgement, a ruthless assessment of my own person; and I moved a few steps away from him. Now the woman brought him the bread, which he began to eat. "This poor lad," she was telling me, "has no mother or father. He's been living here next door since '46 with a girl cousin of mine. What's more, he's blind."

The boy remained silent a moment, and in that moment the hands which held the bread slid down to his knees. Somehow or other he was observing me. "I see a little bit; I see shadow looking down at me. You going, missus?"

I said yes and a moment later I set out with Antonia Lo Savio.

"I'd come with you, but I'm waiting for a friend." He said this in a new tone of voice: the false bravado he needed to cling to died away to be replaced by a sort of numb pity, something warm and tender. He had momentarily lifted his head off the pallet, and now settled back again, and resumed his song: "And a boat arrived at the beach." He sang in a little quavering, unmodulated voice that was probably intended each morning to lull him back to sleep.

As I set out with my guide I was searching my foggy mind for an excuse that would enable me to abandon this place at once and get back to the square, the first bus or tram stop. I felt as if the moment I was outside I'd scream and run to throw my arms round the first people I met. I looked at my guide and kept catching her eye. Besides, I didn't know where else to look. By the light of the few lamps I saw her better: queen of the house of the dead, with her squashed face, her horrible bloated body, offspring as she was in her turn of profoundly damaged creatures, she still managed to retain about her something regal – the assurance with which she moved and spoke, and another thing, too, the brightest gleam in the depths of her little piggy eyes, wherein one might detect not only an awareness of evil in all its pervasiveness, but also a certain entirely human satisfaction in standing up to it. Behind that lamentable exterior hopes existed. Noticing my difficulty in keeping step with her, she hastened to brush my elbow with her hand, but without holding it. This persistent humility that was part and parcel of an unflagging courage, this dignity in keeping her distance from a person she considered to be out of harm's reach, imposed on me a measure of calm, and I told myself that I had no right to betray any weakness. We were walking along the first-floor corridor, towards the stairway of the horses, on our way to the ground floor which, according to my guide, was the most important thing. In a few words she explained to me what lay behind the aversion she inspired in a good part of the female population here: it had started when she had decided to devote herself to the clinic, for she was suspected of getting in the Director's good books and deriving tangible benefits from her activities, such as medicines, which she allegedly resold, and community care parcels and the like. "For the last six months I've neglected my home and everything," she confessed to me simply. "I do my hair, and down I go. Because this is no place to live, you see, this is a place of sorrows. Wherever you go, the very walls keep wailing."

It was not the walls, of course, it was the wind that forced its way through the big doors, but it certainly seemed as if the whole great building were constantly shuddering, however imperceptibly, as if an interior landslide were taking place, an agonizing dissolution of all the quasi-human material that went to make it. Now I could see the dripping, decaying walls, all flaking and mottled with dark patches.

We met two children chasing each other up the stairs with obscene gestures. A woman was coming down from the second floor, carrying a green bottle wrapped in a headscarf as if it were a baby, and pressing her other hand to her cheek, from which a sort of bubo protruded, a reddish fungus, perhaps the result of the damp. Suddenly we heard singing; it was the most peculiar, weary voice and it was singing a hymn in praise of the goodness of existence. "That's the maestro," said my companion, "a saintly man, a real gent. He's had asthma for twenty-five years and can't work any more. But whenever he feels better he can't stop talking about God."

I thought the door she pushed open was that of the asthmatic. We were on the ground floor, and the darkness and silence were that much more intense than on the first, broken only by the vague off-white luminosity in the distance, 300 metres off, where the corridor ended, and by the succession of barely discernible lamps strung along the ceiling like so many fireflies. On either side, doors, doors, doors, but made of planks, metal sheeting, sometimes even of strips of cardboard or faded curtains.

"May we come in?"

"Please do."

A strange room. At the back a large, stoutly built woman, dressed in black, stood behind a table, dragging on a cigarette butt. On the table stood an empty bottle and a wooden spoon. Behind the woman, like a stage curtain, there was an enormous window all nailed up with planks criss-crossed with battens, to keep out the smallest chink of light or breath of air. This room, 258B, was pervaded by a persistent odour of faeces collected in concealed pots; we were to come across the same thing in practically every one of these rooms. These pots must have been put away behind partitions, made of wrapping paper or strips of blanket, which divided the room, no more than a metre off the floor, into two or three dwellings. The woman, who had a squint, shot a dark, cross-eyed look at my hands and, seeing that they were empty, displayed her disappointment. The ladies of the Neapolitan aristocracy send the odd parcel from time to time, so the stranger who arrives empty-handed will be considered only as an enemy or a fool. It took me a while to realize this.

"This lady," said my guide, "has come to see how you are. She may be able to help you. So go on, my girl, tell your story."

That evil cross-eyed look fell on me again; it ran down my neck like some viscous liquid. Then, conquering the weight and fatigue of that enormous mound of flesh encasing her, Maria De Angelis spoke in a plangent, disagreeable voice, as if it were choked with disgust but also furred up with a heavy lethargy. "Turn round . . ." she said.

At the foot of a mattress laid on the floor there were some crusts of bread, and in the midst of them, barely moving, like dusty fluff, three long sewer rats were nibbling. The voice of the woman was so matter-of-fact in its weary disgust, and the scene so peaceful, and those three animals seemed so certain of their right to be there nibbling those bits of bread, that I had a sensation of dreaming, or at least looking at a picture, a horribly realistic one, which had so impressed me as to make me take the image for the reality. I knew that those creatures would soon go back into their hole, as indeed after a moment they did, but now the whole room was plagued with them, and the woman in black too, and my companion and myself, I felt that we all now partook of their shadowy nature. Meanwhile a young man came out from behind a curtain, straightening his tie; he was dressed for a social occasion, and his face was a mass of pustules, and his skin, beneath these brown spots, was of a greenish pallor. He was holding a violin, barely touching it with his old man's fingers.

"My son, a street musician," said his mother by way of introduction.

"Do you make a living?"

"Depends."

"Do you have other children?" I asked the mother.

"Seven, with this one. Antonio, shoeshine boy, Giuseppe, a porter, this one, a musician, one mentally handicapped, the rest unemployed."

"And your husband?"

She made no answer.

As we were leaving, a youth dressed more or less as a woman, with a shawl over his shoulders and a frail look about him, greeted me, bowing almost to the floor. "Oh mum," I heard him telling the woman as he came in, "I've seen a hut by the sea, it had lemon verbena, wish we could rent it." He said other confused words, then went back to the door with a preoccupied air, pulling faces.

Maestro Cutolo's place was a few metres further on, opposite that of the lunatic, and I realized what made the good man sing. This room, unlike the others, gave access to the sunshine. A benefactor who had wanted to remain anonymous had made him a present of it, by having panes of glass fitted to the tall window. Flooded with pale winter light, the big room had a clean and somehow cheerful look about it, an impression that was not contradicted even afterwards. Sitting on

the floor in the sun two of the prettiest children were playing; they
had dark slanted eyes and serious smiles, and almost nothing on.
Signor Cutolo, who opened the door to us, was in his underpants,
and apologized profusely for this. Our visit had proved an agreeable
surprise, and he had not had time to get himself ready. He was still
a youngish man, about forty years of age, of medium height, but so
willowy as to seem an adolescent. He had fair hair, blue eyes, and
his face was creased and flooded by a smile in the depths of which,
as at the bottom of shallow water, floated an unrelenting sadness.
"I am happy," he at once declared to us, "because my heart is full of
holy obedience to the will of God."

"D'you feel better today?" asked my guide. "We've just been hearing
you singing."

"Thanks to the holy mercy of God towards one of His poor
servants, yes." He replied affably, but was panting.

As I looked at him it seemed to me that his face reminded me of
another, like an old picture on which a new one had been superimposed. All of a sudden I lit upon the man he had been twenty years
earlier, when the present writer was living in the port area of Naples,
a place teeming with traffic, banners, sails, cargoes, the exhilaration
of money. He, Cutolo, was a clerk in the Compagnia di Navigazione
Garibaldi, on the second floor of the same building. He kept running
into church whenever he could, came of a good family, held a diploma
in accountancy.

"What on earth are you doing here?"

"My house was destroyed in the war. My father died, I was left
to take care of my mother and two sisters. It was the Lord's holy will
that this sacrifice should not last for long. God called my mother, one
sister married a soldier and is now at Avellino; another lives at Sezione
Avvocata with a widow. I, thanks be to God, now have a little place
of my own, my children, a good wife, I've nothing to complain about.
The clinic gives me my medicines."

"What does your wife do?"

"She's a maid, with a devout family."

He looked at me and smiled, hollow-eyed from the effort of
breathing.

"The way I get through medicines! Sometimes I feel ashamed at
taking so much advantage of Doctor De Luca's kindness."

He called the children who came slowly, and he held them
tightly beside him, with a flash of unspeakable pride. They had almost
nothing on, and their beautiful faces, their eyes radiated health but

also sadness. I imagined their mother, a robust peasant woman, a housemaid.

"For the Holy Year I should have liked another, but my wife did not obey," he said with a gentle hint of vanity. "She denied herself to the Creator Spirit who gives life to the world."

The two brothers gazed with pensive faces, now at me, now at him, chewing their blackened fingernails.

"I do so love children, there'd be so much to do here," Cutolo went on, looking wistfully at the door. "In this building there'll be at least 800 of these little rascals, but they don't know anything about holy obedience, I'm afraid they've not been properly brought up. Sometimes I call them in, I'd like to teach them the principles of our holy religion, some little song, you know, that would be just the thing to give them a little polish. But they refuse, they always refuse."

While he was talking, the heads of some individuals aged between seven and ten peeped round the open doorway. Some dozen highly attentive eyes, some of them red and half shut, others full of animal voracity, rolled in the depths of their sockets. One of them with unusual strength and intelligence in his features clutched something in his hand. Suddenly one of the Cutolo brothers started yelling and hopping about like a mad thing, holding a foot in his hand: "Ow mum, ow mum!" He had been hit by a stone, and at the same time, those four or five figures disappeared as silently as they had come.

After a moment's hesitation, perhaps of mortification, the father set himself to comforting his son and exhorted him to forgive those rascals who had not had the advantage of a Christian education. I went through the door and saw them; they had stopped in the darkness, some twenty metres further down, all out of breath, like the maestro, and their eyes betrayed the same look of ineffable joy.

Although I had seen nothing but these few things, it was getting late. In the city and elsewhere, all over the world, this was the time when people returned home. Here too, in this land of night, people were coming home, groping their way from the end of the corridor, gutter-snipes, beggars, street musicians, faceless men and women. In certain apartments cooking was in progress; smoke, bluish and substantial as a body, was escaping from doorways, in some rooms one could see yellow flames, the darkened faces of people bent over a bowl held on their lap. In other rooms, however, all was at a standstill, as if here life had petrified; men still in bed would turn over beneath

grey blankets, women would be intent on combing their hair with a
sort of spellbound lethargy, as if they had no idea of what, after this,
was to keep them occupied all day. The whole ground floor, and the
first floor to which we climbed, was in this state of hopeless inertia.
There was nothing to hope for, nobody.

On the second and third floors, my guide explained to me, life
did take on a more human aspect, it recovered a rhythm that might
up to a point resemble that of a normal city. The women in the
morning made the beds, swept and dusted, combed their hair and
the children's; many of the children would have set off with proper
black overalls and blue ties to a convent school. Some of the men
had work. They had bought radios, and at the third-floor level had
knocked together the pipework to act as a garbage discharge which
afflicted the residents on the lower floors as it released its stench and
splashed their windows.

As we climbed to this floor, enjoying a little daylight which started
to filter down the stairwell, and breathing a less oppressive air, a
group of children caught up with us on their way back from school –
boys and girls in black smocks, all plaits and satchels. From an
open door a radio was broadcasting popular tunes. We heard a clear
male voice, that of the Radio Roma announcer, saying: "And now,
dear listeners . . ." and a moment later a singer was warbling the
opening notes of "Passione". As in the rest of Naples, so here too
the radio was kept on full blast, a little through a love of noise characteristic of this population, but also through the entirely bourgeois
pleasure of being able to demonstrate one's affluence to one's neighbours, and one's ability to afford the luxury of a powerful radio set.

We did not go into any of these dwellings; the families in residence
were normal enough, the kind one would find on the top floors of
the old buildings in the city centre. Many of the windows had glass
and, in the absence of this, electric lights hung from the ceiling which
were considerably more powerful than those available to us on the
lower floors. It was light enough here to see clearly and, my companion told me, on the third floor it was positively dazzling, there were
even bedside lamps, and the beds had sheets, there were wardrobes
with proper clothes-hangers, one might see polished tables with
centre-pieces, artificial flowers, portraits and, beneath the wall clock,
the occasional sofa. Some of the men in the family had well-paid
jobs, they were on salaries, bank clerks or shop assistants, good
folk who had salvaged their self-respect and peace of mind, people
who had lost their homes because the building had collapsed or they

had been evicted and, not being able to find anywhere else straight-away, had come to make do at the Granili, without in the process compromising their standards, the fruit of a respected tradition. They avoided practically all contact with the denizens of the lower floors, and viewed their abject situation with a severity not unmixed with pity – but mixed also with complacency at their own prosperity, which they attributed to a life of virtue and over whose durability they entertained no doubts. Owing to entirely fortuitous circum-stances, purely casual and unforeseen, and that would soon come to an end, like a period out of work, or an illness, it would sometimes happen that these good citizens found it necessary to surrender their homes for some small consideration to some luckier family man, and they would have to adapt themselves to mucking in with their families on a lower floor, in the serene assurance of being able before long to return to the third floor, or even to leave the Granili altogether. That man, that family never did return to the top of the well, nor did they ever haul themselves out of it, for all that it had seemed such an easy thing to do at the start. The children, once so neat-looking and carefree, became covered in insects down in the dark and their faces became ever paler and more joyless; the girls shacked up with married men, the men fell ill. No one ever got back upstairs from down below. It was no smooth climb back up those stairs, on the face of it so easy and gently graded. There was something down there which beckoned, and whoever started on the way down was lost, but realized this only at the end.

"Excuse me, Signora mia!" A sort of *maîtresse* was standing before the door of one of these apartments in her dressing-gown, with a small cup in her hand and a smile in her blue eyes. "I could use a pinch or two of salt. I've just put on the pasta and realise I'm out of it."

A couple of twenty-year-olds were coming in, discussing a match.

A pensioner sat on a chair outside his front door reading *Il Mattino*.

Limpid voices of children could be heard shrilling round a pot of soup.

In another room two girls, lanky as fillies, in sky-blue sweaters and with make-up on their faces, were busy reading an illustrated weekly in front of the radio.

"Stronger than a chain . . ." shouted the radio, as in every quarter of Naples (that vortex of monarchists and wheeler-dealers), it being Sunday towards one o'clock, the old, familiar smell of meat and tomato sauce pervaded the whole place, through the tidied, polished rooms, full of relatives and youngsters back from Mass.

We were, or rather I was, in that state of mind halfway between distress and consolation that one feels after leaving a penal establishment and getting back to the light, the air and in some way the blessings of human freedom, some sort of standard of living, when our attention was attracted by a noise that vaguely suggested anguish; it wavered between sorrow and a sort of agonized relief – it was hard to discern just what it betokened. The sound, it seemed like that of footsteps and weeping, came from one of the lower floors and floated up the stairs to which we had in the meantime returned. The jovial voice of the Radio Roma announcer was not sufficient to drown it out, nor the relatively serene atmosphere of the second floor. After a moment's reflection my companion had quickly started back downstairs, without paying further attention to me, and I followed. On the first floor, night returning, those noises and voices were more clearly audible: footsteps of men and women, not many but assuredly a good number, who walked carrying some object, and tranquil voices that bewailed or consoled. The woman passed us whose face was covered in fungus; she was speaking slowly with a fat woman. She was saying: "Day's coming for that poor creature, he's going to see God!" and the other nodded peaceably, wiping her eyes with a rag. Other people had appeared, motionless at their front doors, commenting on the event in their dialect: "No more playtime for him." On the ground floor we discovered at last what it was all about. They were bearing off one Antonio Esposito, aged seven, nicknamed Scarpetella, who had died half-an-hour ago through causes unknown, while he was playing with some of his fellows. Suddenly he had put his hand to his heart and sat down in a corner. Now they were carrying him to the mortuary for the autopsy and the parents and friends were taking the occasion to improvise a funeral. And it was, understandably, the simplest funeral one had ever seen. The corpse was not even in a coffin but in its mother's arms; all sallow as she was, she looked a cross between a vixen and a dustbin. The child was half-wrapped in a blanket, the corners dangling this way and that, along with those spindly arms. He was a fair-haired boy with a delicate face, the lips slightly open in a look of surprise which not even the bandage round his chin had succeeded in reducing. His calm and his joy, characteristic in those who have left this life, were as if underlined by a trail of mucus arrested beneath his right nostril, which conjured up an image of relaxation and silence that would never again be disturbed. Behind him walked the father, who was carrying the boy's shoes, as a result of who knows what mental aberration before the sudden disaster. He was talking with the priest who was walking beside him, a fat, apathetic man, and forcing himself to a calm that was only superficial to judge from the way he was clutching the lapels of his jacket at his neck, across his bare chest. God had chastised them; the previous year, too, one child had died this way. Then, after the blow occasioned by Vincenzina, their peace was quite at an end. This one looked healthy enough, in the pink of condition. Following behind the parents came five or six youths looking dazed, all children of the vixen and brothers of the dead boy; they were flanked by a group of little women who were praying out aloud, and this, along with the sobs some of the brothers put on for the occasion, had been the ludicrous noise which had struck me.

Equally ludicrous was the composure of the man and the woman, in a place like Naples, where people were for ever on stage. All the doors, as on the first floor, were now open, but there was not a word, not the least comment of sympathy such as the common people tend to come out with. We also saw Signor Cutolo with his children clutched to either side; his look was ecstatic. "What a beautiful creature!" he exclaimed as he saw us. "God in His infinite goodness has wanted to deliver him from all occasions of evil in this life, calling him to Himself. Let us praise His infinite wisdom. Now that little imp Scarpetella is climbing trees in heaven."

He had not finished speaking when a horrible cry resounded beneath those darkened vaults, an extended wail suddenly truncated, as if the person emitting it couldn't get it out. At the same time a girl of about twenty, spangled and adorned with fripperies, came running down from the opening of the corridor where there was a little light. She tore herself free of the two men accompanying her, who appeared hesitant, and ran to the group and merged with it for a moment. The funeral procession stopped, as they do when some devout person wants to place a money offering on the Madonna's garment. "What is it? You're mad! You have no heart!" That is all we heard.

"Be off !" a very harsh voice shouted after a moment. It was the mother who, after a first moment of stupor, was trying to snatch the corpse from the girl's embrace. But she clung to it like someone possessed; almost falling on her knees, whether from weakness or otherwise, she tried to drag the body to herself, and as the boy's face eluded her, for the mother tried to cover it, she embraced the dirty, bare legs and the bare feet.

"Shameless hussy! She's a shameless hussy," the father was now telling the priest. "She left home without giving us another moment's thought. We asked her help in our need, and she sent word that she no longer had any parents. Now she's feeling sorry for her poor brother."

"Scarpetè!" young Vincenzina was meanwhile calling in a cry that was a compound of tenderness and terror. "Stop playing around! Wake up! You'd be calling me morning, noon and night, even when I was asleep. I don't have anyone, my love." And here a great sob.

Now the vixen was looking at her elder daughter with a glint, an indefinable smile in her bright eyes, a smile at once inane and bitter. "He always ran about clippety-clop with his little shoes," she explained to those around her. "Now where is he? He'd been playing hide-and-seek."

"Have mercy," said the priest listlessly. "God will have mercy on your poor Antonio who at this hour stands before Him with his little sins." He bent over to whisper something in the girl's ear, and she at once looked up with an expression of rapture while she continued to hug the rigid package to her breast. She placed this with a kiss in the arms of the woman and rummaged, all blushing but no longer weeping, in her shiny leather handbag which had slipped to the ground, took out a large pink banknote and handed it to the mother. She smiled; the father, too, was touched and bowed his head. Someone adjusted the bandage on the child, whose chin was drooping. Then the procession, with the sad prayers which had made such an impression on us, resumed its tranquil and apparently painful journey towards the grey arch of light that announced the exit.

After this I knew nothing and saw nothing at all precisely. Signora Lo Savio escorted me from door to door throughout the ground and first floors, then back to the ground floor, where we had overlooked one or two families. Nobody spoke about the bereavement, and I realized that down there no possibility for emotion survived. There was only darkness, that was all. Silence, fleeting memories of another, sweeter life, nothing else. Not even my escort had anything to say. She would politely open a door: "May we come in?" Someone would answer: "Come in," or else there was no answer at all, in which case she would go in, looking round with her sharp little eyes. At once eight, ten, fifteen people would come out of the shadows, some getting out of bed, like dead men in a reverie, others briefly showed a surly head above a wooden partition. Women, who no longer had anything feminine about them beyond a petticoat and hair that looked more like an incrustation of dust than hair, would approach in silence, pushing their children before them, as if that wretched brood might afford them protection and courage. The men, for their part, would hang back, as if ashamed. One or two of them would fix his gaze on my shoes, my hands, not daring to raise his eyes to my face. In many families, as in that of the De Angelis, there would be one person purported to be mentally handicapped. "What work do you do?" I would ask, and he would hesitate, attempt a smile, and say: "I'm a mental case." "You see!" the women would cry in evident triumph, "Jesus Christ wants to try us. Anyone who is good to us, may Christ reward them!" and they would watch my companion and me, anxiously awaiting some indication of parcels. I would look especially at the boys, and realized that they too might just drop dead as they ran, like Scarpetella. These children retained nothing of childhood apart from their years. For the rest, they were little men and women, already wise to everything, the beginning and end of things; they were already eroded by vice, idleness, poverty beyond endurance, sick in body and crazed in mind; their grins, at once crafty and despairing, spoke of depravity or lunacy. Nine out of ten of them, my guide told me, either had TB or were on the way to getting it, or they had rickets or syphilis, like their mothers and fathers. They were usually witnesses of their parents' couplings and imitated these at their play. Hereabouts there are no other games, anyway, apart from stone-throwing. "There's a creature I want to show you," she said.

She led me towards the end of the corridor, from where it was possible to see that twilight had fallen on Naples, by the little greenish light that penetrated a crack. There was a door whence proceeded not a sound, not a voice. My guide barely knocked then went in without awaiting an answer, like someone who'd made herself at home there.

It was a vast room, clean and deserted, something between a cave and a temple. Were it not for a minuscule lamp, whose light set high up was more of an annoyance than a blessing, that place would have reminded one of some abandoned ancient ruin. Stronger and more depressing than elsewhere was the smell of damp, filtered by matter in decay. A woman still in her youth came towards us. She wore an ecstatic expression.

"How's your Nunzia?" she was asked.

"Come this way."

She led us to a cradle made out of a Coca-Cola crate, which looked small and wretched against one of the usual portentous windows hermetically boarded up. In that cot, devoid of bed-linen, on a very small cushion, under a man's jacket, a hard dirt-encrusted thing, there lay a newborn girl with a strangely sweet and adult-looking face: a delicate face, as pale as could be, lit by a pair of eyes that reflected the blue of evening, soft intelligent eyes which moved hither and thither observing everything with an attention beyond the grasp of a baby a few months old. Her eyes rested on us, on me, climbed up to my forehead, turned to seek her mother as though with a question. The mother lifted the jacket with one hand, and we saw a little body the length of a few palms, perfectly skeletal: the bones were pencil-thin, the feet all shrivelled up, tiny as birds' feet. On contact with the cold air the little girl slowly hunched herself up. The mother dropped the jacket-blanket.

I had not been mistaken when I felt, on sight of her, that Nunzia Faiella had known about life for quite some time, and saw and under-stood everything, even without being able to speak.

"This little creature is two years old," my companion told me in a whisper. "Because of her innards, she has stopped growing . . . Darling Nunzia . . ." she called tenderly.

Hearing these words, the little thing gave a weak smile.

"I took her out once . . . to the doctor," the girl said, in her gruff, masculine voice, wavering between ecstasy and resignation (and thus I understood that Nunzia Faiella had only once in all her life seen the sunlight, maybe a pale winter sun). "She looked at the air . . . the sun . . . she was fascinated."

Now too Nunzia Faiella was fascinated: her soft eyes gazed from time to time at the high ceiling, the greenish walls, they withdrew and kept returning continually to the gleam of the electric light, which perhaps reminded her of something. There was in them not sadness and not even pain, but a sense of an expectation, of a penalty worked off in silence, as if life were confined to this expectation, of something that could come from beyond those immense walls, from that high blind window, from that darkness, that stench, that reek of death.

"Nunzia," my companion called again, bending over the crate and speaking affectionately to the little creature, "what are you doing? D'you want to leave your mummy? D'you want to go and spend Christmas with Baby Jesus?"

Then something happened that I would never have expected. The little girl turned to look at her mother, with a hesitant smile which turned suddenly into a grimace, then she broke into a wail which seemed to come from inside a piece of furniture, so weak was it, stifled, ethereal, like someone weeping inwardly with no further strength nor hope of being heard.

As I left the room I was violently knocked into by two women who had heard about the arrival of a group of journalists; they were running to make a complaint about an outrage they had been enduring for some time. One of the two ground-floor toilets had been closed on purpose, they said, and they, who were neighbours, had to go 300 metres every day to empty the chamber pots at the far end of the corridor, where the clinic was. From rage they passed immediately to tears. They were two tigresses who had endured so much in their lives that they gave voice to human laments. They started talking about their unemployed menfolk, bereft of underwear or shirts or shoes, of everything, about the children who made their lives a misery with their disobedience. They wept and clung to us, they wanted to show us where they lived. Impossible not to accommodate their wish.

In the home of one of them, Dr De Luca's assistant, a sloppily dressed young man with a cold, bored air, had come to make a call on an old man whose end seemed near and who was uncle of one of the two women, Assuntina. The room was full of people, ghosts who seemed to be sniffing the air. I did not see the dying man, who was hidden by the crowd and the doctor, but my attention was attracted by another person, I couldn't call him a man, who stood behind the doctor and tapped him on the shoulder from time to time. He was a creature of indefinable age, wasted by illness, a weird creature with something at once meek and alarming about him. His eyes were shielded by big glasses, and one lens looked thicker than the other. He had a fringe of grey hair which slipped behind the glasses frame, giving the pupils a greater element of ambiguity. While his right hand tapped the doctor, he used his left hand to keep scratching his chest, as if from a nervous tic, while trying to open his shirt.

Finally the doctor turned round.

"What d'you want?" he asked rudely.

"Bi . . . bi . . . bismuth."

"Come to the clinic later on."

"Speak proper!" said a little woman harshly, coming out from behind a curtain. She reminded one of those elongated bitches full of teats which solemnly drag themselves with a dejected air from dustbin to dustbin. Her hair still had an auburn tinge but her face was earthen, her eyes dead, her mouth toothless. Her narrow childlike shoulders contrasted with the great curve of her belly on her stumpy legs. She wore a ring on her finger.

"The d-doc . . . tor un . . . un . . . derstands," said the sick man meekly.

A minute later the doctor had left, and the ghosts had returned to their holes, in this case the four areas into which the vast room was partitioned by means of crates, blankets, old bed-sheets stretched across two poles, and even sheets of newspaper, the whole place lit by an oil-lamp. Assuntina's uncle wore a rigid, concentrated smile as the woman gave him his medicine. Right behind where he lay, where there was a partition, I now became aware of the sound of anxious, suffocated breathing. I craned my neck a fraction and saw the syphilitic and his wife at the foot of another bed. He was sitting on the edge, she was on her knees in front of him, and with her tongue stuck out was moistening one of his hands. The poor man's glasses had fallen off, he was gazing up like a blind man, and was shaking from head to foot.

Night was falling in the Granili, and the involuntary city was getting ready to draw on such goods as it possessed, in a fever that lasted until the following morning, the time for the laments to start up again, the wonder, the mourning, the inert horror of living.

From Naples is not Washed by the Sea
Translated from the Italian by Guido Waldman

JONATHAN RABAN

Seagoing

In maritime law, a ship is a detached fragment of the society under whose flag it sails; a wandering chunk of Britain – or Liberia, or Panama. However far it travels overseas, it is an ark containing the laws and customs of its home port. Here is the happy paradox of seagoing: nowhere on earth can you be as exposed to and alone with wild nature as at sea, yet aboard a boat you never leave the culture of the land.

Cruise-ship passengers know this. A mile offshore, the ship skirts the coast of an alarming and exotic country, famed for its unpronounceable language, its foul drinking water, its bloody political coups and casual thievery. High on C Deck, a steward bears gin-and-tonics on a silver tray; the tourists, snug in their temperature-controlled, four-star world of comfort and deference, see the dangerous coast slide past like a movie. They're home and abroad in the same breath.

On an autumn Atlantic crossing in 1988, in a British cargo ship, we ran into a declining hurricane in mid-ocean. For 24 hours the ship was hove to, going nowhere, while the sea boiled around us like milk, and the wave-trains thundered. In the officers' mess, the floor rolled through 75 degrees of arc, and tropical fish spilled onto the carpet from their tank beside the bar.

"Bit of a windy day we've got today," the captain said, from behind his pre-luncheon glass of dry sherry, and the two junior deck officers, stumbling crazily up the sudden hill towards the framed portrait of the Queen and Prince Philip, tried as best they could to nod vigorously and smile, as junior officers must when spoken to by their captain. The radio officer landed, from a considerable height, in my lap. "Oh, pardon! Whoops! Do please excuse me!" he said.

Had the *Atlantic Conveyor* been registered in excitable Panama, the scene might have been different, but we were flying the Red Ensign; and the more the ocean tossed us about like bugs in a bucket, the harder we all worked to maintain the old-fashioned prim civilities of our little floating England. Every student of the British class system, its minuscule distinctions of rank and precedence, its strangulated politenesses, its style of poker-faced reticence, should get a berth aboard a Liverpool-registered merchant ship in a severe storm.

The last case of cannibalism to be tried in Britain came to hinge on this conflict between the culture of the ship and the untamed nature of the sea. In 1884, the yacht *Mignonette*, on passage from Tollesbury in Essex to Sydney, Australia, met heavy weather in the South Atlantic. Caught by an enormous breaking wave, the yacht foundered, and her professional crew (who were delivering the boat to its new Australian owner) took to the thirteen-foot dinghy, where they drifted for three weeks on the empty ocean under a hot and cloudless sky. On the twenty-fourth day of their ordeal, the four emaciated mariners cast lots. The cabin boy, Richard Parker, seventeen years old, drew the short straw, and the captain slit his throat with a penknife. The survivors dined gratefully on the boy's remains.

A German ship eventually picked them up and took them back to Falmouth, England. Their trial in London was a sensation of the day. The first line of the defence was that there was no case to answer: the *Mignonette*, a registered British ship, had sunk, and the killing of the cabin boy had taken place in an unflagged open boat on the high seas. The law of the land, argued the defence, had no jurisdiction over the men's conduct in a dinghy in international waters. On the ocean, 1,000 miles from the nearest coast, the law of the wild prevailed.

Unfortunately for the men (and for those of us who would like to get up to mischief in dinghies beyond the twelve-mile limit), this reading of the law ran counter to a section of the British Merchant Shipping Act of 1854, which held that a British seaman was subject to English law whether he was on or off his ship – and the dinghy, flag or no flag, was, legally speaking, an integral part of its parent yacht. The captain and mate of the *Mignonette* were found guilty of murder, sentenced to death, then granted a royal pardon. The sympathy of the court (and British public opinion) was with them, but a guilty verdict was required to prove that the long arm of the law can extend far out to sea.

The ocean itself is a wilderness, beyond the reach of the morality and customs of the land. But a boat is like an embassy in a foreign country. So long as you are aboard a boat, you remain a social creature, a citizen, answerable to the conventions of society. You might as well sally forth alone across the trackless ocean in a clapboard cottage with a white picket fence and a mailbox.

* * *

I am now readying my own boat for a sea-trip (I can't quite call it a voyage) from Seattle to Juneau, Alaska, and I'm living day to day on the slippery interface between the nature and culture of the thing. My boat, a thirty-four-foot ketch, is Swedish-built and American-registered; like its owner, it is a native of one country, resident in another, and not quite a citizen of either. I never fly a flag, except under official duress, preferring to think of the boat as an independent republic; liberal-democratic in temper, easygoing in its manners, bookish in its daily conversation. My slovenly Utopia.

On a wall of the saloon, between the fire-extinguisher and the VHF radio-telephone, is mounted a 1773 cartoon of George III – Farmer George, the obese, rubber-lipped, mad king of England . . . our gentlest, most generous monarch, who lost the American colonies and was in the habit of putting grave constitutional questions to the wise shrubs in his garden. Every British ship has its royal portrait. George III seems the right king for me. His erratic captaincy of the ship of state is an apt emblem for my own often fumbling command of my vessel.

The real heart of my boat is its library. There are few sea-books in it – the inevitable coastal pilots, tidal atlases, and one or two grim volumes with titles like *The 12-Volt Bible*, but when I'm galebound on the dank and gloomy Northwest coast, I'm in no mood to read Conrad or Melville. At anchor in a lightless British Columbian inlet, where black cedars crowd round the ruins of a bankrupt salmon cannery, and the rain falls like ink, I shall pine for brilliance and laughter, for rooms full of voices. So, on the long shelf in the saloon, overhung by the gimballed oil-lamp, are *Lolita* and *Madame Bovary*, the novels of Evelyn Waugh (all of them), Dickens's *Great Expectations*, Trollope's *The Way We Live Now*, Thackeray's *Vanity Fair*, Byron's *Don Juan*. There are books by friends and acquaintants, like Paul Theroux, Richard Ford, Cees Nooteboom, Ian McEwan, Martin Amis. I rejoice in the thought that my eye might lift from a page of Waugh (let it be Julia Stitch, in bed, at the beginning of *Scoop*) to the sight of a black bear snuffling in the driftwood at the water's edge: nature outside the boat, society within, and just an inch of planking between the world of the one and the world of the other. The essence of being afloat is feeling the eggshell containment of an orderly domestic life suspended over the deep. The continuous slight motion of the boat, swinging to its anchor on the changing tide, is a reminder of how fragile is our tenure here – aloft with a novel, coffee-cup close at hand, while the sea yawns underfoot and the bear prowls through its dripping wilderness on shore.

I love the subtlety and richness of all the variations on the theme of society and solitude that can be experienced when travelling by sea. It is like living inside a metaphor for the strange voyage of a human soul on its journey through life.

Out on the open sea, with a breaking swell and the wind a notch too high for comfort, you are the loneliest fool in the world. You are trying to follow the vain hypothesis of a compass-course. It's marked on the chart, 347 degrees Magnetic; a neat pencil-line bisecting the white space of the ocean. The absurd particularity of that number now seems to sneer at you from the chart as the boat blunders and wallows through the water, its hull resounding like a bass drum to the impact of each new ribbed and lumpish wave. The bow charges downhill on a bearing of 015 degrees. Ten seconds later, it's doing 330 degrees, up a potholed slope. Abandoning the helm to the autopilot, which at least will steer no worse, if little better, than you do, you go below.

Slub . . . thunk. Dickens, Thackeray, Trollope and the rest are lurching drunkenly in line along the bookshelves. Two oranges and an apple are chasing each other up and down the floor. Your morning coffee has turned into a jagged brown stain on the oatmeal settee. The glass decanter has smashed in the sink. The door of the closet is flying open and shut, as if a malevolent jack-in-a-box were larking among your laundered shirts. A dollop of green sea obscures the view from your living-room window. Your precious, contrived, miniature civilization appears to be falling to pieces around your ears, and you cannot remember what madness impelled you to be out here in the first place.

Then you hear voices. For a moment, you fear that you're losing your wits, then realize that the voices are coming from the VHF set: a captain, calling for a harbour pilot; or a fisherman chatting to his wife in the suburbs. It is, after all, just a dull morning at sea, with the invisible community of the sea going about its daily business. You turn up the volume on the radio and climb the four steps to the doghouse, and regain control of the wheel. Three or four miles off, a grey, slabsided bulk-carrier shows for a few seconds, before being blotted out by a cresting wave; and you find yourself watching the ship with a mixture of pleasure at finding a companion and rising anxiety at encountering a dangerous intruder.

Loosening the sails to steer clear of the big stranger on your patch, you quickly recover your taste for solitude – and the waves themselves seem to lose their snarling and vindictive expressions. In the society of the sea, it is the duty of every member to keep his distance from all the others. To be alone is to be safe. It's no coincidence that those two most English of attitudes, being "standoffish" and "keeping aloof", are nautical terms that have long since passed into the general currency of the language. Standing-off is what a ship does to avoid the dangers of the coast; aloof is a-luff, or luffing up your sails, head to wind, to stay clear of another vessel. The jargon of the sea is full of nouns and verbs to describe the multitude of ways in which a ship can keep itself to itself. The ocean is, in general, a sociable and considerate place, where people (professional mariners, at least) treat each other with remarkable courtesy. But this civility is based on distance and formal good manners. Always signal your intentions clearly. Always know when to give way and when to hold your course. If people on land behaved like ships at sea, they'd look like characters in an Italian opera, or members of the Japanese imperial court.

I've never crossed an ocean under my own steam – never, really, more than nibbled at the ocean's edge. The longest open-sea crossing that I've made so far was from Fishguard in Wales to Falmouth in Cornwall; 200 miles, 35 hours; a day, a night, and most of the next day, with a dream-harrowed sleep (full of colllisions, groundings, swampings and founderings) at the end of the trip. Simple cowardice is one reason for my failure to tackle an ocean; my passion for arrivals is another, just as powerful as my timidity. When the light begins to fail, and the sea turns black, I yearn to make landfall – to pick out the winking entrance buoys and find my way into a strange port. The intricate, heart-stopping business of coastal pilotage is for me the great reward for spending a day jouncing about in the waves offshore.

Dusk is a good time (though just before dawn is best), when lights stand out but the shape of the land is still clearly visible. You bring one shadowy headland into line with another, then find the lazy flash of the fairway buoy, timing it against your watch to check its ID. Cautiously standing-off, you wait until the pinpricks of light ahead resolve themselves into a narrow, winding lane, into which you thread the boat, moving under engine, at half-speed.

The most satisfying harbours are those that are fringed with a maze of shifting sandbars, like the entrance to the Somme estuary in northern France, or the approach to Wexford in Ireland, where buoyed channels take one on bafflingly serpentine routes into town.

Each channel represents a pooling of knowledge by the local pilots and fishermen, and is a path whose broad outline has been trodden for hundreds of years. But sandbars alter their positions after every gale, and the buoys are never exactly in the right places. As so often at sea, you are at once in good and experienced company, and entirely on your own.

Inching warily from buoy to buoy, you watch the shivering needle on the depth-sounder. It is your blind-man's stick, with which you have to tap-tap your way, feeling for deep water as you go. Twelve feet. Ten feet. Eight feet – and you've lost your channel. Nine feet. Ten feet – and you breathe again. Now you're inside the line of breakers, in a broad, lakelike sea, with the lights of the town silvering the water in the distance. In a moment of inattention, the bow of the boat suddenly climbs as the keel scrapes sand, but it settles back, the buoy slides past, and the floating town drifts slowly towards you, taking you in.

Anyone who has struggled into a harbour out of a bad sea will understand why the words "heaven" and "haven" are closely cognate. A dismal slate-roofed town (visit the Methodist chapel and the fish-and-chip shop) is paradise itself when you find shelter there after a day of being cold and frightened aboard a lurching boat. You'd willingly kneel to kiss the stones of the dock, you are so full of gratitude for the fact of Dulltown's existence. Its people are so friendly! so attractive! Its Methodist chapel is, as Methodist chapels go, a very cathedral! Its fish and chips are, without doubt, the best fish and chips in the world!

Few travellers have ever felt this way about Dulltown. You are privileged. Your means of arrival have revealed to you a place hidden from the mass of humanity – Dulltown Haven . . . Dulltown as Heaven. For a writer, such an epiphany is pure gift – and it will save you from the addled cynicism that is the usual curse of travelling.

Yet we were, a few moments ago, on the Somme estuary and the mouth of the River Slaney, and neither St Valery nor Wexford are in the least like Dulltown. They are beautiful and complicated places even if you reach them dully, by car. The miracle of coming into them by sea is the way that, as soon as your boat is attached to the dock by a trapeze of ropes, it instantly becomes part of the architecture and skyline of the town. You belong to the daily working fabric of the community as no ordinary visitor can possibly aspire to do. Your neighbours (at least in places unspoiled by yachting marinas) are fishermen, longshoremen, local boat-owners; and the more difficult the harbour approach, the more nearly will you be accepted as a resident. In the more remote communities, your patience and skill as a navigator (you wouldn't be there if you were a complete buffoon) is an automatic ticket of entry to society.

For a day, or two, or three, or as long as the weather outside remains discouraging, you settle into dockside life. You go visiting in the afternoons, clambering over decks that are slick with fish-scales. You work on your boat. You learn a dozen names. In the evenings, you go with your new neighbours to the bar across the street, where (if you are a writer) you try to listen harder than you drink. You hear things that no one would dream of telling you, had you come here by car.

Then, at five o'clock one morning, in the final hour of the flood tide, you untie the damp ropes in the dark, and steal away from the place without saying goodbye. You leave behind a small gap, like a missing tooth, in the shape of the town as you will come to remember it.

At the fairway buoy, the sea is oily calm, with curlicues of mist rising from the water. The fading remains of a big swell make the surface of the sea bulge and contract, like a fat man breathing. Visibility is down to a mile, maybe less. A moderate westerly is forecast.

Ahead lies the open sea, and a day like a blank slate. But some things are certain. There will be – as now – moments of wonder and elation such as rarely visit you on land. There will be the building magnetic power of the unknown port across the water. There'll be at least one serious cause for alarm, and at least one unpleasant surprise.

You kill the engine, and let the boat drift on the tide, waiting for enough wind to hoist the sails. The town you left is now hidden in haze. Alone in a circle of diffuse light, you float in silence. In time, the sea and the day will begin to impose their own narrative order on your life; but for now, you are a character as yet unformed, awaiting the sequence of events that will define you.

Bon voyage!

JOSÉ SARAMAGO

Nobel Lecture 1998

How the Character became the Teacher and the Author His Apprentice

The wisest man I ever knew could neither read nor write. At four o'clock in the morning, when in France the promise of a new day was still on its way, he would rise from his bed and go out into the fields, taking with him to pasture the half-dozen pigs on whose fecundity he and his wife depended for a living. My maternal grandparents scraped by on the little they had, breeding pigs which, once weaned, would be sold to neighbours in the village of Azinhaga, in the province of Ribatejo. My grandparents' names were Jerónimo Melrinho and Josefa Caixinha, and both were illiterate.

On winter nights, when it was cold enough to freeze the water in the jugs inside the house, they would go to the pigsties to fetch in the smallest of the piglets and carry them to their bed. Under the coarse blankets, their human warmth saved the creatures from icy cold and certain death. Although they were good people, they were not driven to do this by the finer feelings of a compassionate heart. What concerned them, quite plainly and unsentimentally, was protecting their livelihood, as would anyone who, in the struggle to survive, has learned to bother only with the essentials.

I often helped my grandfather Jerónimo in his work as a herdsman, I often dug the earth in the yard by the house and chopped wood for the fire, I often had to turn the great iron wheel of the pump that brought up the water from the village well, and I would then carry the water home on my shoulder, and often, behind the backs of the men guarding the wheatfields, I would leave the house at dawn with my grandfather, armed with a rake, a sheet and some string, to gather up from among the stubble the loose straw that could be used as bedding for the livestock. And sometimes, on hot summer nights, after supper, my grandfather would say to me: "José, tonight we'll go and sleep underneath the fig tree." There were two other fig trees, but as far as everyone in the house was concerned, that particular fig tree, doubtless because it was the biggest, the oldest and had always been there, was *the* fig tree. (A kind of antonomasia, a learned term that I would only meet and understand years later . . .) In the peace of the night, among the high branches, a star would appear and then, slowly, hide itself behind a leaf, and, if I looked in another direction, there, like a river flowing silently across the concave sky, would be the opalescent light of the Milky Way, or the Road to Santiago as we villagers still called it. For as long as I remained awake, the night would be alive with the stories my grandfather would tell me: legends, ghosts, marvels, remarkable events, deaths that happened long ago, fights involving sticks and stones, the words of our ancestors, a tireless murmur of memories that simultaneously kept me wide awake and gently lulled me to sleep. I never knew if he stopped speaking as soon as he realised I had fallen asleep, or if he went on talking so as not to leave unanswered the question I always asked him in the long pauses he deliberately left in his stories: "And then what happened?" Perhaps he repeated the stories to himself so as not to forget them or simply in order to embellish them further with new adventures.

Needless to say, at that age and at that time, I imagined my grandfather Jerónimo to be master of all the knowledge in the world. When, at first light, I would be woken by birdsong, he was no longer there, but had gone off to the fields with his pigs, leaving me to sleep. Then I would get up, fold my blanket and, barefoot (I went barefoot in the village until I was fourteen), with bits of straw still clinging to my hair, I would walk from the orchard to the part where the pigsties were, next to the house. My grandmother, who was always up even before my grandfather, would place a large bowl of coffee and some bread in front of me and ask if I had slept well. If I told her of some bad dream provoked by grandfather's stories, she would always console me by saying: "Don't worry, dreams aren't real." I thought then that, although my grandmother was a very wise woman, she was not on the same high level as my grandfather, who, when he lay down beneath the fig tree with his grandson José beside him, was capable of setting the whole universe in motion with just two words.

It was only years later, when my grandfather had left this world and I was a grown man, that I realised that my grandmother did, in fact, believe in dreams. What other interpretation could I give to the words she spoke one night while sitting at the door of her humble house, where, by then, she was living alone. Gazing up at the stars, large and small, she said: "The world is so beautiful, it makes me sad to think I have to die." She did not say she was afraid to die, but sad to die, as if the life of unrelenting hard work that had been hers was, at the very last, blessed with one final, supreme farewell, the consolation of beauty revealed. She was sitting at the door of a house unlike any other, I believe, for in it lived people who could sleep with pigs as if they were their own children, people who were sad to leave life simply because the world was so beautiful, people, by which I mean my grandfather Jerónimo, herdsman and teller of tales, who, when he sensed that death was coming for him, went out to say goodbye to the trees in his orchard, embracing each of them in turn and weeping because he knew he would never see them again.

Many years later, when I first wrote about my grandfather Jerónimo and my grandmother Josefa (I should have mentioned that, in the opinion of everyone who knew her when she was young, she had been a woman of rare beauty), I became aware that I was transforming the ordinary people they had been into literary characters, and that this was probably a way of not forgetting them, drawing and re-drawing their faces with the ever-changing pencil of memory, colouring in and illuminating the monotony of their dull, narrow, day-to-day lives, like someone recreating, on the unstable map of memory, the supernatural unreality of the country where he has chosen to go and live.

It was this same attitude of mind which, when I wrote about the fascinating and enigmatic figure of a great-grandfather who was a Berber, would lead me to describe in more or less these words an old photograph of my parents (taken almost eighty years ago now): "They are both standing up, young and beautiful, facing the photographer, with a look of solemn seriousness on their faces which is, perhaps, just fear of the camera, at the very moment when the lens is about to fix the image of both of them, an image they will never again have, because the following day will, implacably, be another day . . . My mother is resting her right elbow on a tall column and is holding a flower in her left hand which hangs by her side. My father has his arm about my mother, and his calloused hand, as it rests on her shoulder, looks like a wing. They are standing shyly on a rug bearing a pattern of leaves and branches. The cloth that serves as a false backdrop to the portrait is painted with vague, incongruous neoclassical structures." And I concluded: "The day had to come when I would speak of these things. None of it is of any importance, except to me. A Berber great-grandfather from North Africa, a grandfather who was a keeper of pigs, a marvellously beautiful grandmother, my grave, handsome parents, a flower in a photograph – what other genealogy do I need? what better tree to lean on?"

I wrote those words almost thirty years ago, with the sole intention of reconstructing and recording moments from the lives of the people who engendered me and were closest to me, believing that no further explanation would be needed to make it clear where I come from and of what kind of stuff I was made, both the person I started out as and the person I gradually became. I was wrong, though, for biology does not determine everything and, as for genetics, judging by the circuitous route it chose to take, its ways must be mysterious indeed. My genealogical tree (forgive my presumption in describing thus such a thin-sapped specimen) lacked not only the branches that time and successive encounters with life had broken off from the main trunk, but also lacked someone who could help its roots penetrate down to the deepest subterranean layers, who could appreciate the consistency and savour of its fruits, who could broaden and strengthen its crown and make of it a haven for migrant birds and a shelter for nests.

In painting my parents and my grandparents in literary colours, transforming them from the flesh-and-blood people they had been into characters, and so once more, albeit in a different way, into the builders of my life, I was unwittingly tracing a pathway for the other characters I would invent, the truly literary characters, who would create and bring the materials and tools which, in the end, whether of fine quality or poor, whether adequate or inadequate, whether put to good use or bad, whether too little or too much, would make of me the person I am today: the creator of those characters, but, at the same time, their creature. In a sense, one could even say that, letter by letter, word by word, page by page, book by book, the characters I created gradually rooted themselves in the man I was. Indeed, without them, I doubt I would be the person I am today, and without them, my life might have been nothing but a vague sketch, a promise which, like so many other lives, was never more than a promise, the existence of someone I might have been but never, in fact, became.

Now I can see clearly who my teachers were in life, those who taught me most about the hard art of living, those dozens of characters out of novels and plays whom I can see parading before me now, those men and women made of paper and ink, those people whom I believed I was guiding in accordance with my needs as a narrator and who were obeying my will as writer, like marionettes whose actions could have no more effect on me than their weight as I held them and the tension of the strings as I moved them. The first of these teachers was, without a doubt, a mediocre portrait painter whom I called H., the protagonist of a story entitled *Manual of Painting and Calligraphy*, which, I believe, I could reasonably call a double initiation (his initiation, but also, in a way, mine); he taught me to have the basic honesty to recognise and respect, without resentment or frustration, my own limitations: since I had neither the ability nor the desire to venture beyond my own little plot of land, I chose to dig deep down to the roots, to my roots, but also the world's roots, if I can be permitted such a grand ambition. It is not of course for me to judge the results of my efforts, but one thing I think is clear: all my work, from that moment on, has remained true to that aim and that principle.

Then came the men and women of Alentejo, the same band of men and women bound to the earth to which my grandfather Jerónimo and my grandmother Josefa belonged, simple peasants forced to hire out their physical strength in exchange for a wage and working conditions that could only be described as appalling, scraping a living, a life, which we cultivated, civilized folk, or so we like to think, describe as precious, sacred or sublime, depending on the occasion. These were ordinary people such as I myself had known, people deceived by a Church that connived with and benefited from the power of the State and the large landowners, people constantly watched by the police, people who, time after time, became the innocent victims of the arbitrary decisions of a false justice. Through my novel entitled *Raised from the Ground* pass three generations of a family of peasants, the Mau-Tempo family (the Badweathers), from the beginning of the century up to the 1974 Revolution that overthrew the dictatorship, and it was with those men and women raised from the ground, real people whom I subsequently fictionalised, that I learned to be patient, learned to trust and surrender myself to time, which is constantly building and destroying us only to rebuild and destroy us all over again. Those men and women made a virtue out of their harsh experiences and adopted a naturally stoical attitude towards life, something I am not entirely sure I have ever fully assimilated. When I consider, though, that the lesson I received more than twenty years ago remains intact in my memory and that I hear it in my head every day like an insistent summons, I have still not lost hope that I may yet move closer to emulating the great examples of human dignity I met on the immense Alentejo plains. Time will tell.

And what lessons could I learn from a Portuguese poet living in the sixteenth century, who wrote the *Rimas* and, in *The Lusiads*, set down the nation's glories, shipwrecks and blighted hopes, and who was a poetic genius and the greatest of Portugal's writers, however that might grieve Fernando Pessoa, that self-proclaimed Super-Camões of Portuguese literature? Certainly no lesson made to my measure, none I could possibly learn, except the simple lesson that the man, Luís Vaz de Camões, could offer me in his extreme humanity, for example, the proud humility of an author who goes round knocking at every door in search of someone willing to publish the book he has written, and having to endure the disdain of ignorant noblemen, the scornful indifference of a king and his company of powerful men, and the contempt with which the world has always received poets, visionaries and madmen. At least once in their lives, all authors have been or will have to be Luís de Camões, even if they did not write the poem "Sôbolos rios". Caught between the gentlemen at court and the censors of the Inquisition, between old love affairs and the chagrin of premature old age, between the pain of writing and the joy of having written, this was the ailing man, who had returned impoverished from India, where so many had gone to get rich, the soldier, blind in one eye and sick at heart, the penniless seducer who would never again cause the hearts of the palace ladies to flutter, this was the man I placed on stage in the play called *What will I do with this book?*, which ends with another question, the really important one, the one to which we will probably never find an adequate answer: "What will *you* do with this book?" The proud humility of carrying a masterpiece under one's arm and being unjustly rejected by the world. The proud, stubborn humility of wanting to know what use will the books we write today be tomorrow, and wondering how long the reassuring reasons we are offered or that we offer to ourselves can possibly last. There is no worse self-deceit than that of allowing others to deceive you . . .

Next comes a man who lost his left hand in the war and a woman who came into the world with the mysterious ability to see what lies beneath other people's skin. His name is Baltasar Mateus, nicknamed Sete-Sois (Seven Suns), and she is known as Blimunda and, later, as Sete-Luas (Seven Moons), because it is written that where there is a sun, there must always be a moon, and that only their joint, harmonious presence will, through love, make the Earth habitable. Here too is a Jesuit priest, one Bartolomeu, who invented a machine capable of rising into the air and flying on no other fuel than the human will, which, it is said, can do anything, but which, up until now, either could not or did not choose to be the sun and the moon of simple kindness or, still more simply, of respect.

Three mad creatures living in eighteenth-century Portugal, a time and a country in which superstition and the fires of the Inquisition flourished, in which the vanity and megalomania of a king brought about the construction of a monastery, a palace and a basilica that would amaze the outside world, in the unlikely event that the outside world had eyes to look at Portugal, eyes like Blimunda's that could see what was hidden. And here come a multitude of thousands and thousands of men with grimy, calloused hands, their bodies exhausted from having built, year after year, stone upon stone, the implacable monastery walls, the vast palace rooms, the columns and pilasters, the tall belfries and the dome of the basilica suspended over the void. The sounds we can hear come from the harpsichord of Domenico Scarlatti, who does not know whether to laugh or cry . . . This is the story of *Baltasar and Blimunda*, a book in which the apprentice author, thanks to lessons he had been learning since his childhood days with his grandparents, Jerónimo and Josefa, managed to write these words not entirely devoid of poetry: "Apart from the talk of women, it is dreams that fix the world in its orbit. It is dreams that weave it a crown of moons, which is why the sky is the only glory inside men's minds, if, that is, men's minds are not their one and only glory." So be it.

The adolescent already knew something about poetry, gleaned from books read while he was at technical college in Lisbon being trained for the trade he practised at the start of his working life: maintenance fitter. He had good teachers in the art of poetry too, during the long evenings he spent in public libraries, reading at random books found by chance or in catalogues, unguided, with no one to advise him, feeling the same creative amazement as the seafarer who invents each newly discovered land. It was in the library of the technical college that *The Year of the Death of Ricardo Reis* began to be written. There the apprentice fitter (he was seventeen then) came across a magazine – *Atena* was the title – which contained poems signed with that name, Ricardo Reis, and, the apprentice, knowing little of his country's literary cartography, naturally assumed that such a poet existed in Portugal. It was not long, though, before he found out that the poet behind those poems was, in fact, Fernando Nogueira Pessoa, who signed poems with the names of non-existent poets born out of his imagination and which he called "heteronyms", a word that did not appear in the dictionaries of the time, which was why it took the apprentice so long to find out what the word meant. He learned many of Ricardo Reis's poems by heart ("In order to be great, be whole/Put everything you are into even your slightest action"), but, despite his youth and inexperience, he could not accept that such a superior mind could have written, quite without remorse, this cruel line: "The wise man contents himself with the world as spectacle". Long, long afterwards, the apprentice, now grey-haired and grown a little wiser in his own wisdoms, decided to write a novel that would show the poet who wrote those odes something of the spectacle of the world as it was in 1936, the year he chose for Ricardo Reis to live out his last days: the occupation of the Rhineland by the Nazi army, Franco's war against the Spanish Republic, the creation by Salazar of the Portuguese fascist militia. It was as if he were saying to him: "This, my serenely bitter, elegantly sceptical poet, is the world as spectacle. Enjoy it, savour it, contemplate it, since you prefer to take your wisdom sitting down."

The Year of the Death of Ricardo Reis ended with these melancholy words: "Here where the sea ends and the earth waits." There would be no more discoveries for Portugal, however, its only destiny an endless wait for unimaginable futures: the same old *fado* music, the familiar sense of *saudade*, and little more . . . It was then that it occurred to the apprentice that there was perhaps a way of relaunching those ships, for example, by setting out to sea on the land itself. The novel I wrote next – *The Stone Raft* – was the product of Portugal's collective resentment of Europe's longstanding disdain for it (or to be more precise, the product of my own feelings of resentment), for in that novel the whole of the Iberian Peninsula physically breaks away from the rest of Europe and is transformed into a vast, floating island, heading south without the aid of oars, sails or propellers, "a mass of stone and earth, covered with towns, villages, rivers, woods, factories, tangled forests, ploughed fields, with all its inhabitants and all its animals", en route to a new utopia: the cultural encounter of the peninsular peoples with those on the other side of the Atlantic, presenting a challenge – such was the daring of my strategy – to the suffocating influence of the United States on the countries of Latin America.

From a doubly utopian view, this political fiction could be seen as a far more generous and humane metaphor: the whole of Europe travelling south, in order to correct the world's imbalance, as some recompense for Europe's colonial excesses, both then and now. It was a vision of an ethical Europe. The characters in *The Stone Raft* – two women, three men and a dog – travel tirelessly across the Iberian

Peninsula, while the Peninsula itself ploughs south across the ocean. The world is changing, and they know they must look inside themselves for the new people they will become (and that includes the dog, who is no ordinary dog), and that is all they need.

The apprentice then recalled that he had, in his time, worked as a proofreader, revising texts, and that while in *The Stone Raft* he had, so to speak, revised the future, it wouldn't be a bad idea to do the same with the past, inventing a novel that would be entitled *A History of the Siege of Lisbon*, in which a proofreader working on a history book of the same name, and weary of its relentlessly unsurprising nature, decides to replace a positive with a negative, thus subverting the authority of so-called "historical truths". Raimundo Silva, for that is the proofreader's name, is a perfectly ordinary man, whose only distinguishing feature is his belief that all things have their visible and their invisible side and that we cannot claim truly to know them until we have looked at them from all angles. This is precisely the subject of a conversation he has with the historian. "I would remind you that proofreaders are serious people and have seen a great deal of literature and life, My book, I would remind you, is a history book, That, it is true, is how it would be described according to the traditional classification of genres, however, since it is not my intention to point up other contradictions, in my humble opinion, anything that is not life is literature, What, history too, Especially history, no offence, And what about painting and music, Music has resisted from the moment it was born, always blowing hot and cold, it tries to free itself from the word, out of envy I suppose, but it always comes to heel in the end, And painting, Oh well, painting is nothing more than literature performed with brushstrokes, You're not forgetting, I hope, that mankind began painting long before we knew how to write, You know the saying, if you haven't got a dog, then go hunting with a cat, or, in other words, if you don't know how to write, then paint or draw, that's what children do, What you're saying, in other words, is that literature already existed before it was born, Exactly, just as, in other words, man was already man before man existed . . . It seems to me that you missed your vocation, you should have been a philosopher or a historian, you certainly have the talent and the temperament those arts require, I lack the necessary training, sir, and what can a poor man do without training, I was lucky to come into the world with my genes intact, though, if I may put it like this, in a raw state, and I never advanced beyond elementary school, You could present yourself as an autodidact, the fruit of your own worthy efforts, there's no shame in that, society used to be proud of its autodidacts, Not any more, progress put a stop to that, people are suspicious of the self-taught, only writers of poetry and diverting stories are allowed to be autodidacts, but creative writing's never really been my forte, Well, then, be a philosopher, Ah, I see you are a very subtle humorist, a master of irony, I'm beginning to wonder how you ever came to be a historian, history being such a deep and serious science, That's because I save my irony for real life, It has always seemed to me that history is not real life, but literature, plain and simple, But history was real life when it could not yet be called history . . . So you believe history is real life, I do, yes, That history was real life, I mean, Absolutely, What would we would do if the all-erasing *deleatur* did not exist, sighed the proofreader." Needless to say, it was with Raimundo Silva that the apprentice learned to doubt. And about time too.

Now, it was probably that apprenticeship in doubt that led him, two years later, to write *The Gospel According to Jesus Christ*. It is true, as he himself has said, that the title was the result of an optical illusion, but it would be legitimate to ask ourselves if it was not the proofreader's serene example, which, in the intervening period, had been preparing the ground from which the new novel would spring. It was not a case this time of trying to look behind the pages of the New Testament for contradictions, but of shining an oblique light on the surface of its pages, the way one might light a painting in order to emphasise the contours, marks, obscure depressions. That was how the apprentice, surrounded now by evangelical characters, read, as if for the first time, the description of the Massacre of the Innocents, and, having read it, was at a loss to understand it.

He did not understand how there could already be martyrs to a religion that would have to wait another thirty years for its founder to utter the first words about it, he did not understand why the one person who could have saved the lives of the children of Bethlehem did not do so, he did not understand Joseph's complete lack of any sense of responsibility, remorse, guilt, or even curiosity, on his return from Egypt with his family. Nor could one argue, in his defence, that it was necessary for the children of Bethlehem to die in order for Jesus's life to be saved: plain common sense, which should preside over all things, whether human or divine, reminds us that God would not send his Son to Earth, especially a Son charged with redeeming humanity's sins, in order for him to die at the age of two with his throat slit by one of Herod's soldiers. In that *Gospel*, written by the apprentice with the respect that all great dramas deserve, Joseph is conscious of his guilt, he accepts his feelings of remorse as punishment for his failure to act and allows himself to be led almost unresisting to his death, as if that were the only way for him to clear his debts with the world. The apprentice's *Gospel* is not, therefore, another edifying tale of fortunate people and of gods, but the story of a few human beings subject to a power against which they struggle but which they cannot defeat. Jesus, who inherits the sandals that his father wore to walk the dusty roads of the world, also inherits the tragic sense of responsibility and guilt that will never leave him, not even when, as he hangs on the cross, he lifts up his voice to say: "Men, forgive him for he knows not what he does," doubtless referring to the God who brought him there, but perhaps also remembering, in his final agony, his real father, who had humanly engendered him in flesh and blood. As you see, the apprentice had come a long way when, in his heretical *Gospel*, he wrote the last words of the dialogue in the temple between Jesus and the scribe: "Guilt is a wolf that eats the son having first devoured the father, said the scribe, That wolf you speak of has already eaten my father, said Jesus, Then all that's left is for it to devour you, And you, in your life, were you eaten or devoured, Not only eaten and devoured, replied the scribe, I was vomited up again."

If the Emperor Charles the Great had not built a monastery in northern Germany, if that monastery had not given rise to the city of Münster, if Münster had not decided to mark the twelve hundredth anniversary of its founding with an opera about the horrific war fought between Anabaptists and Catholics in the sixteenth century, the apprentice would never have written a play called *In Nomine Dei*. Once again, with only the small light of reason to guide him, the apprentice had to plunge into the obscure labyrinth of religious beliefs, which so easily lead human beings to kill and be killed. And what he saw again was the awful mask of intolerance, an intolerance which, in Münster, reached crazed, paroxysmal heights, an intolerance that was an insult to the very cause that both parties claimed to be defending. For it was not a war fought in the name of two opposing gods, but a war fought in the name of the same god. Blinded by their own beliefs, the Anabaptists and Catholics of Münster were incapable of understanding what should have been evident to all: on the Day of Final Judgement, when they stood before God to receive the prize or punishment that their actions on Earth deserved, God, assuming his decisions are ruled by something resembling human logic, would have to receive them all into Paradise, for the simple reason that they all believed in him. The terrible carnage in Münster taught the apprentice that, contrary to what they promised, religions never served to bring people closer to each other, and that the religious war is the most absurd of all wars, bearing in mind that God, even if he wanted to, cannot declare war on himself.

Blind. The apprentice thought: "We are blind," and sat down to write *Blindness* to remind anyone who read it that, when we debase life, we pervert our reason, that the dignity of human beings is abused every day by those in power, that the universal lie has replaced multiple truths, that man loses his self-respect when he loses respect for his fellow man.

Then, as if trying to exorcise the monsters engendered by the blindness of reason, the apprentice set out to write the simplest of all stories about a person who goes in search of another person simply because he realises that life has nothing more important to ask of a human being. The book is called *All the Names*. Although not written down, all our names are there. The names of the living and the names of the dead.

I will finish here. The voice that read these words is only the echo of the collective voices of my characters. If truth be told, theirs is the only voice I have. Forgive me if this, which is everything to me, has seemed little to you.

Translated from the Portuguese by Margaret Jull Costa

Reproduced by courtesy of The Nobel Foundation, Stockholm

JOSÉ SARAMAGO

From Poem to Novel,
from Novel to Poem

Everyone knows the story of the youth with a natural gift who, without ever having studied fine arts or learned any particular craft and without any tools other than a penknife, could immediately transform a piece of rough wood into the most beautifully carved bear known throughout the history of sculpture, if art historians were ever interested in such simple peasant skills. The neighbours never failed to marvel at his speed and craftsmanship and, when questioned, the youth would say:

"It isn't difficult. I pick up a piece of wood and look at it until I can see the bear. Then it's simply a question of cutting away the rest."

With these words our naïve sculptor taught us two valuable lessons at the same time: the lesson of modesty, and that of generosity. Without guile or deception, he revealed the secret of his craft and showed us how to set about creating a bear: to look where no bear exists and make it appear simply by staring at it.

But, alas, there is no greater perversity than that of the naïve. This kind-hearted youth, so willing to explain how he did it, did not say a single word about how it is done. The bear is there for all to see, but between the bear and our hands there is a solid wall made of wood, with the toughest knots, awkward grains and treacherous flaws in the fibre. It is all too obvious that it will require much skill and artistry to forge a path and transform it into an avenue we may gaze upon with satisfaction. Art, after all, is not easy; and the youth who carved bears was amusing himself at our expense.

Yet only a foolhardy man would be prepared to swear that inside each piece of wood there is no bear awaiting us. There is and always has been. Even though we may not see it clearly, we are at least capable of divining it and can intuitively sense its presence. We can see the bear in the distance like a slow, flickering light, a star somehow incapable of illuminating itself.

And all of a sudden, I discover that this is not a bear after all, but a theme, my theme to be precise: "From Poem to Novel, from Novel to Poem". I think I can make it out and perceive its outlines, transform it into something clear and precise, convince myself that I need only stretch out my hand, but just as I am about to exclaim in triumph: "Ladies and Gentlemen, behold the bear", I realize the whole thing has been an illusion and mockery, and all I have to show is what you can see here, a severed trunk, a stump, a gnarled root. And once again the light starts flickering, like a plea from the heart: "Get me out of here."

I said: "From Poem to Novel" – and this route, this journey through space and time and different worlds, from the Homeric poems to Marcel Proust or James Joyce, passing through the *Tales of A Thousand and One Nights*, the Indian epics, the parables of Holy Scripture and the *Song of Songs*, through the Milesian fables and *The Golden Ass*, through the *chansons de geste*, the romances of Roland and the quest of the Holy Grail, Alexander, and Robin Hood, through the *Roman de la rose* and the *Roman de Renart*, through Gargantua, the *Decameron*, *Amadis of Gaul*, and *Don Quixote*, as through *Gulliver's Travels* and *Robinson Crusoe*, *Werther* and *Tom Jones*, through *Ivanhoe*, *Cinq-Mars*, and *The Three Musketeers*, through *Notre Dame de Paris* and the *Comédie humaine*, *Dead Souls* and *War and Peace*, through *The Brothers Karamazov*, *The Charterhouse of Parma* and *The Magic Mountain*. So far, our route is clear; it began one day with a loud cry in the shade of a tree or inside a cave, in an encampment of nomads under the stars, in a public square or in the market-place, then someone began to write and thereafter someone wrote about what had just been written, forever repeating, forever modifying, and so on and so forth, arranging the words in silence for a reading that was carried out in silence.

No matter the almost certain mismatch between the actual facts and this lyrical evocation of the progression from narratives intoned in chant to a neatly ordered text written in conformity with rules, precepts and norms, and, inevitably, with systems of conventions, notwithstanding the inescapable fact that they are transitory and therefore replaceable by other systems, which are in turn condemned to disappear when their time comes. The vision I have just evoked simply serves to illustrate, as persuasively as I can, the first part of the title I have given to this brief exposition, "From Poem to Novel", and for the purposes I have in mind this title is as well or ill-suited as any other. Any problems will arise later. Or rather, now.

I say: "From Novel to Poem" – and at this point I should demonstrate, or at least propose as a plausible hypothesis, that the literary genre we refer to as the novel, having moved in one direction as far as it can go, like an imaginary pendulum, is now swinging back the way it came, perhaps repeating all those moments already experienced before returning to rudimentary verse, where it will recommence its familiar journey, leaping several centuries or millennia ahead into the future.

I am not entirely devoid of common sense. I know that dynamics and kinetics belong to a different field of knowledge, and if literature infinitely repeats itself, as we stated earlier, it is also infinitely varied, as we also stated earlier. But here one cannot help recalling a certain Pierre Menard who wrote a *Don Quixote* literally identical to that of Cervantes, as Borges informs us in his *Fictions*, and who, having repeated word for word the work of the immortal "One-handed Man of Lepanto" (so called to avoid repeating his name, and a fate spared Camoens, for no one to this day has ever dared call him the "One-eyed Man of Ceuta"), often says quite different things, just as there are different ways of understanding them in this twentieth century in which we find ourselves and in that sixteenth century which we cannot recover. Yet this example shows us that, in the end, any exact repetition is impossible; therefore, as the pendulum swings all the way back on its return journey, retracing an identical path, it leaves something of itself behind, akin to a coincidental alternative, if such a crude contradiction in terms is permissible.

Of course, I have only myself to blame for ending up in this blind alley from which there is no easy exit. In fact, if the novel is not allowed to travel in reverse, if Pierre Menard, when he painstakingly made a faithful copy of *Don Quixote*, ended up writing another book, how shall we get back to the poem, that much desired poem, and if we should get there, which poem would we recite nowadays, even if the words and music were to be the same? The *Homeridae* no longer have any place in this world; time, of all things, is the one thing we cannot change. What will be left for us to do then? How shall we invent this new poem to which I am committed by the second half of my title? And with what justification shall I propose or, if this is my real intention, announce the coming of new eras, in terms of who must live and practise this new literature? Is there any sense in reviving Homer today or in trying to write a Homeric epic? Given their nature, these questions and the order in which they are presented are anything but innocent. They finally allow me to move from the general to the particular, by penetrating the only universe of which I can legitimately speak with any deep knowledge, that is to say, my own tiny universe, the kind of novel I write and its whys and wherefores.

First, let us take time, if such a thing is conceivable. Not the time in which we find ourselves, nor that other time when the author was writing his book, but a time confined and enclosed within the novel, and which is not the few hours or days it takes to read it, nor a temporal reference implicit in the fictional discourse, much less a time made explicit outside the novel, as, for example, in the title of novels like *One Hundred Years of Solitude* or *Twenty-Four Hours in the Life of a Woman*.

The time I am speaking of is a poetic time, comprised of rhythms and moments of suspense, a time at once linear and labyrinthine, uncertain and inconstant; a time with its own laws, a flood of words carrying a duration which in turn brings an ebb and flow like that of a tide between two continents. This, I repeat, is poetic time which pertains to recitation and poetry, a time that exploits all the expressive possibilities of tempo, beat, and coloratura, a time that can be florid or syllabic, long, short, or instantaneous. It is my ambition that the fictions I invent should live with this concept of time, conscious as I am of trying to get increasingly closer to the structure of a poem which succeeds in being expansive while remaining physically coherent.

Musicians and musicologists argue that it is impossible to compose a symphony today, just as it would be impossible, in my opinion, to carve a Corinthian capital nowadays according to classical precepts. Obviously anyone endowed with enough skill will succeed in disproving any such categoric statement by actually composing a symphony or carving a capital. But this achievement would be unlikely to convince us that the artist was responding to some genuine need, either for the sake of his own creativity or for the sake of our enjoyment. Now, who can tell whether we might not have to face up to the grave responsibility of passing a similar sentence on the novel, by affirming, for example, that it, too, has been impossible in its paradigmatic form, as it were, which has lasted up to the present day, with only the slightest variation, rarely radical, and always assimilated and integrated into the subject matter, which allows us, by the grace of God and the blessing of publishers, to go on writing novels as if we were composing symphonies in imitation of Brahms or carving Corinthian capitals.

But this same novel which I appear to be condemning possibly contains in itself, and in its different and various transformations today, the only possibility of changing its literary classification (I deliberately say classification rather than genre), capable of absorbing, like some vast, stormy, and sonorous sea, the torrential tributaries of poetry, drama, essay, as well as those of science and philosophy, thus becoming the expression of knowledge and wisdom, of a cosmic vision, like the poems of classical antiquity in their time.

I may be mistaken, if one takes into account the growing and to all appearances irreversible specialization of man, which has become almost microscopic. But it is not inconceivable that this specialization, because of some predetermined mechanisms or compensatory impulses, and perhaps as an instinctive condition of survival and psychological equilibrium, may lead us to seek a new exaltation of the general as opposed to the apparent safeguards of the particular. Perhaps in a literary context, for here we are only discussing literature, the novel might restore that supreme exaltation, the lofty and ecstatic poem of a humanity which has so far been unable to reconcile itself with its own countenance.

And this brings me to my conclusion. Wielding my blunt penknife, I trimmed and cut into the piece of wood I brought before you. I assure you that I could see that bear before; I saw it quite clearly, and I swear to you that I can still see it even now. But I am not sure – my fault, of course – that you can see it. The carving I have made is probably a platypus, that awkward mammal with a duck's bill which looks as if it were made from loose bits of other animals, a disproportionate and fantastic creature – although not as fantastic as man. The person we become when we write or read novels. Interminably.

Translated from the Portuguese by Giovanni Pontiero

ADRIAAN VAN DIS

Stolen Languages

In the discussion concerning the threatening clash of cultures, in which the cultures of the poor South become entrenched or take up verbal arms against the arrogance of the rich North, the translator can play a useful and sobering role. Especially in a period in which many population groups wish to retain their own identity, even if they have no idea as to what or who they really are, there is a need for negotiators capable of providing a platform for the smaller languages and finding a way of enriching the larger languages with the culture of smaller, exotic ones, or vice versa.

The translator as a builder of bridges between rich and poor worlds. A few years ago I spent a few months on the island of Gorée, an old slave island off the coast of Dakar. Gorée. A beautiful name and old Dutch, not that any of the inhabitants would know. Literally it means Goede ree, Goede rede: Good roadstead, Bonne rade. Poor translations because we miss the echo of the homonym: Good reason, Bon raison. In Dutch, *rede* also means reason.

The Dutch bought the island from the Portuguese and had good reason to do so: Gorée was a safe haven for Dutch slave traders. A place where tens of thousands of West African slaves were dragged on board for the Americas. And regardless of later changes in owner-ship, the French, the English and then again the French, the Dutch remained in charge of transport.

The Dutch have always excelled at transport. Take a look at the canal houses and warehouses in Amsterdam. Here and there above the doors on the Herengracht, you can still see the negro heads.

French is the official language of Senegal, and in the towns and on Gorée, so close to Dakar, a stranger can get by with French alone. Inland it's another story. Eighty per cent of the population speak Wolof, other indigenous languages are Serere, Diola, Mandingue and Sorcé, and there is also Pulaar, the language of the old desert people, the Peul. Pulaar is a kind of lingua franca for West Africa in the same way that Swahili is for East Africa. Senegal has a flourishing modern culture which, especially when it comes to film, enjoys considerable respect in Western Africa. Sembene Ousmane is Senegal's greatest cineast and at the same time a famous writer whose books, like *Xala* and *Les bouts de bois de Dieu* – *God's Little Bits of Wood* – are translated in several languages. Like all important writers in French-speaking Africa, Ousmane writes in French.

I lived on Gorée to work, and quietly cloistered in an old slave house I was one of the few white noses on an island whose population numbers some 700.

My presence there aroused curiosity: what was I doing every day? Writing.

Aha. So I can read one of your books?

Well, perhaps. I don't know. A few have been translated into French.

Translated? Didn't I write in French?

No. I didn't speak it well enough.

English then?

No. I wrote in Dutch.

Was that a language?

Yes. *C'est le Wolof des Pays Bas*. The Wolof of the Netherlands. My mother tongue.

But who can read it? And why didn't I write in French?

Which is pretty much what passed for conversation several times a day, there not being much else to do on an island where curiosity is almost a career.

Each time I said I wrote in Dutch the islanders laughed sharply. The head teacher, the male nurse at the dispensary, the guide in the Museum of Slavery; all educated people who knew what a book was but nonetheless found it difficult to take me seriously. Because nobody – but nobody – wrote in their mother tongue. The head teacher, who taught me French for an hour every day, said that in Wolof it was impossible to write a real book: the poverty of the language was truly prohibitive. No, anybody who had anything to say said it in French. Or in English.

And I said to him: go to the baobab tree in the big square where the women tell each other stories. Turn on the radio and listen to Yousou N'Dour who has hits in the European hit parades. Or head inland and listen to the *griots* relating the history of West Africa in heroic song. Ssst . . . can you hear the fishermen chanting and the mothers in the courtyards singing nursery rhymes for their children? All in Wolof.

The head teacher spoke fair French, but an African novel in French was too much. I noticed it when we were reading a book by the Congolese writer Henri Lopez and I had to look up more than the occasional word in a dictionary. French is a language taught in primary school but still a second language. For the first six or seven years children speak an African language, and both outside and within the family the spoken language is an indigenous one.

French in the Francophone countries, or English or Portuguese in other ex-colonies, is the language of intellectual exchange. Few writers, if any, publish in their mother tongue. Although every Senegalese learns French in primary school, research has shown that less than ten per cent of the population actually have a good command of it, while more than seventy per cent can neither read nor write. Which also counts for the rest of Africa. Nothing is as easy as teaching a village to read and write. The reading bus arrives, everyone gathers under a tree and A is for Apple, B is for Bear and C is for Cat. But actually nothing is easier than forgetting. The caravan moves on and nobody gets to see another letter. Ever. And within a year the art of reading and writing belongs to a dark and distant past.

The readers of an African author are therefore to be found in the city and especially abroad, and the majority of writers have their readers in London or Paris. They are writers who have exchanged the sounds and melodies and rhythms of their youth for a language forced upon them by the colonizer.

Which is not to cry shame or to say that this excrescence of imperialism should immediately be eradicated. In many cases there is no alternative to affording a welcome to the language of the colonizer. Someone once told me that in Cameroon there are 131 different languages, that one hillside does not understand the other. Thank God for French. But there are also a number of languages shared by millions: Yoreba in Nigeria, Kikuju in Kenya, Tshiluba in Zaire, Shona in Zimbabwe, Tonga and Dingaan in Mozambique and Xhosa or Zulu in South Africa. The Bible has been translated into all these languages, and one might be forgiven for thinking that if it is good enough for the Book of Books then it is good enough for a novel. After all, where else can you find more murder, manslaughter, love and adultery? Nonetheless, the writers in these countries use French, English or Portuguese, and nothing could be more natural for them than to write in a borrowed language. And this is not only the case in Africa: writers in Asia and Latin America have also opted for the language of the colonizer.

One could be of the opinion that the Africans are one step ahead, that they have distanced themselves from claustrophobic nationalism and chosen a common language, that in that sense they are further than the Europeans. Wishful thinking! It is erroneous to perceive Africa as a blueprint for progressive unity as long as the individual states are not unified and the inhabitants do not even know who they are. One has to find oneself, before achieving unity with others. A denial of individuality only breeds a tribal, "my people first" mentality.

In the period following independence, the great example for young African writers was Joseph Conrad. A Pole who wrote in English and an important figure in world literature. If he could do it why couldn't they? Certainly it was true that Conrad's talent was such that it towered above his unconventional English, but what Conrad did was extraordinary: he created his own English, with its own idiom, which, native speakers have assured me, is sometimes clumsy, has awkward rhythms and a lot of vague adjectives. Still, African writers such as Chinua Achebe, Wole Soyinka, James Ngugi and Ben Okri write a very personal English coloured by Africa, proving that it is possible to write great literature in a foreign language. So why should one complain?

In the first place because the peoples of Africa are denied literature in their own languages. If one wants to fight illiteracy one has to provide books. However, in the absence of a significant literature in one's own language the intellectual shame felt for the mother tongue is unlikely to disappear. How is it possible to develop an interest in foreign literature if one has already disclaimed the language and culture of one's birth? It was this that Soyinka and Ngugi discovered in the mid-Seventies when they decided to write from then on in their mother tongues, respectively Yoruba and Kikuju. James Ngugi even exchanged his English name for an indigenous one: Ngugi wa'Thiongo. Both writers also exchanged an international readership of thousands for a national one of no more than a few hundred. A courageous step, which, if I am not mistaken, Soyinka quickly retraced. Ngugi wa'Thiongo now writes in Kilukyu and then translates it into English.

Strangely enough, it is the Africans themselves who offer the most resistance to attempts to stimulate literature in the mother tongue. In Senegal, a group of American linguists are involved in a project to publish stories in Wolof, but the Senegalese intellectuals sneer at it. At school, they were taught that the fables of La Fontaine were superior, that the lively African fables were no match for the French ones.

This, you may argue, is their choice. Africa is independent, so let the African people find their own solution.

The problem, however, lies deeper. Over the past few years it has been possible to witness a growing sense of displeasure among African youth (and in this case by African I refer to the whole of the Third World). They feel themselves forgotten and neglected. They feel that the voice of Africa is unheard and they seek solace in a black nationalism that rejects the mighty white world. There is an emotional craving for a great, mythical African past, and teaching in the universities is increasingly used as a therapeutic instrument for breeding self-respect. Africa is painted as the mother of western civilization, brought to Europe by way of an ancient Egypt ruled by exclusively black pharaohs. Beethoven and Pushkin, so the Afrocentrists teach, were Afro-Europeans. It was African seamen and not Columbus who discovered America, and the Atlantic Ocean was originally called the Ethiopian Ocean. All this wisdom was taught at the University of Dakar, but I have also heard it in Harare and Maputo, where my concern about the validity of the theories was dismissed as being ethnocentric or racist.

To make matters worse, these theories did not even originate in the continent of Africa. They come instead from the United States, where militant black professors have successfully gained the attention of groups of young blacks in search of identity. The traditionally underprivileged now see the melting pot as a Eurocentrist tool for suppression. In his book *The Disuniting of America, Reflections on a Multicultural Society*, Arthur M. Schlessinger gives countless examples of the Afrocentrism which has deluged American universities. White skin, for example, is proof of "genetic inferiority". This cult of ethnicity is not only to be found in Africa and America. It is also to be found in the Magreb, where the poor and chanceless search for solace in fundamentalism, and among the young migrants in Europe who find themselves crushed under the arrogance of western culture.

All this is, of course, understandable. Confronted daily with the technological and economic superiority of the West, there is a desire to restore equilibrium, self-esteem and a "feeling of pride". But it also remains a dangerous lunacy which disturbs the dialogue and results in a situation in which the West is increasingly confronted by a Third World unwilling to tow the line on international agreements on human rights and the environment.

What does all this have to do with translation? Everything. By showing respect for other cultures, remaining open to languages with a centuries-old oral history, we can shed our arrogance without, of course, denying our own values – I am not advocating a form of cultural relativism. The translator is not just building a bridge from one language to another, he is also a herald, broadcasting the words of a small language into the wider world, enriching a small country with the literature of a large one. The translator can put a country back on the map, rescue a civilization from isolation, and help it rediscover its pride and identity.

In Holland we are tempted to speak with disdain of such matters. We are scared of chauvinism that we would ideally just like to be ignored. This, however, is an attitude born of arrogance rather than humility: we believe ourselves to be so internationally oriented that we no longer need our own sense of country.

With our European drive and energy we had a Minister of Education who seriously advocated English as the teaching language at our universities. There was a Professor of Dutch at the University of Limburg who wanted to scrap Dutch. As far as he was concerned, English was destined to become our language in the future. Dutch as the Wolof of the delta. In the science departments of our universities it is a must to write papers and theses in English, and I know several young Dutch writers who, high in their student garrets, are trying to write their First Work in English. One of our greatest Dutch writers, Gerard Reve, tried it in the Sixties with *The Acrobat and Other Stories*. This was not the wildest of successes on foreign shores, though: it was full of mistakes.

Personally I shudder to think of writing in a language other than my own. Even if the number of Dutch speakers was reduced to 1,500, I'd still "go Dutch". What was good enough for Isaac Bashevis Singer, who wrote for the Yiddish paper *Forverts* in New York (with only a handful of readers), is good enough for me. How could I write without the sights and smells of my first language? Without the rhythm and the strange outdated words of my father, who only arrived in the Netherlands when he was 31? He came from old colonial Indonesian stock and invariably placed the wrong emphasis on each and every word. That is where my inspiration lies: in the melody, sounds and mythology of the Indonesian Dutchmen. I can speak English, but it remains for me an amputated language. The "foreign language" that half and whole intellectuals on the "continent" now speak has little to do with the English spoken in Great Britain. It is not even the neo-Latin of our time. It is a sloppy heap of words scraped together from soap operas, pop songs and hot Spanish holidays.

Thanks to a translator, I can read the Albanian Ismail Kadare, in my opinion one of the great European writers of our time, and thanks to Kadare I have a better understanding of what is happening in the Balkans, however historic his novels. Kadare speaks French, lives in Paris and Tirana, writes his letters in French and speaks fluent Russian. But for his magnificent stories he chooses his tiny mother tongue.

Writers from Estonia, Latvia and Lithuania, having lived for so long in the shadow of imperialist Russia, are also struggling to be heard. They too need translators to tell the world that theirs are independent, obstinate countries, with their own past and their own, rich culture. The Germans, having discovered that Dutch tomatoes are red and watery, have recently realized that Dutch writers (like Cees Nooteboom, Harry Mulisch and Margriet de Moor) taste better. And while the Dutch take tremendous pleasure in ridiculing what little they have, we positively glowed with pride in the recognition we received as *Schwerpunkt* at the Frankfurt Book Fair in 1993. Our literature seemed at last to be worth something and, thanks to translators, we even achieved greater recognition at home. On the one hand translators contribute to a country's national identity, on the other they help to combat a suffocating nationalism by introducing strange literatures and cultures.

This is also the case in the Third World. People there have had their languages stolen, together with their belief, their history and their pride. If we do not want them to slide into indifference, hate and fundamentalism, we shall have to ensure recognition of their own language and culture. As Nadine Gordimer stated so clearly in her essay "Turning the Page" (*Leopard II*, 1993), if Africa wants to develop a literary culture, it will have to reach an African audience that can read prose, poetry and non-fiction in its mother tongue. How can twentieth-century African literature hope to succeed if publishers of the African languages remain restricted to textbooks, pamphlets and religious tracts? "We writers cannot speak of an African literature unless writing in African languages becomes the major component of the literature of the continent. Without this we cannot speak of an African literature. It must be the basis of the cultural cross currents that will both buffet and stimulate that literature." If African democracy is to have a chance of survival, it needs to be rooted in its own culture, and that is a problem to be addressed and solved by the inhabitants themselves. Those in the Third World blessed with a better education are perfectly bilingual. It should not be difficult for them to return their best authors – so celebrated abroad – to the mother tongue.

The more translations into the mother tongue, the richer the culture, but there are many, many peoples in the world unable to experience this. Publishing, printing and distribution of books are not a normal part of development aid. In the whole of Africa south of the Sahara there are far too few newspapers published in indigenous languages. (Exactly how many is hard to establish. Twenty? Thirty? Whatever the precise figure, the number is very low.) This situation is encouraged and maintained by dictatorships ruled by the principle "the less they know the better off they are", while politicians in need of votes suddenly display a surprising vocation for the local language. An Africa where the people have no voice of their own is a breeding ground for populist resentment; it is then that tribal thinking rears its ugly head and creates a situation conceivable not only in Africa but also in Europe, in what was formerly the Soviet Union and in Asia.

It is the job of translators and publishers to give oppressed and threatened cultures their languages back.

Translated from the Dutch by Charlie Murphy

CLAUDIO MAGRIS

Caffè San Marco

The masks are up on high, above the black inlaid wood counter that comes from the renowned Cante workshop – at least it was renowned once. But prestigious signs and fame last a bit longer at the Caffè San Marco, even the fame of those whose only qualification for being remembered is the simple, but not inconsiderable, fact of having spent years at those little marble tables with their cast-iron legs that flow into a pedestal sitting on lion's paws, and of having given forth every now and then on the correct pressure of the beer and on the universe.

The San Marco is a Noah's Ark, where there's room for everyone – no one takes precedence, no one is excluded – for every couple seeking shelter in a downpour and even for the partnerless. By the way, I've never understood that story about the Flood, observed Mr Schönhut, *shammes* at the Israelite Temple next door, so someone recalls. The rain was beating against the window-panes and in the Public Gardens at the end of Via Battisti, immediately to the left as one leaves the café, the big trees were crashing, soaked heavy in the wind under an iron sky. If it was for the sins of the world, said Mr Schönhut, He might as well have finished it off for once and all, why destroy and then start again? It's not as if things have gone better since; in fact there's been no end to blood and cruelty, and yet never another Flood ... nay, there was even the promise not to eradicate life on earth.

Why so much pity for the murderers who came after and none for those before, all drowned like rats? He should have known that together with every being – man or beast – evil entered the Ark. Those He felt compassion for carried within themselves the germs every epidemic of hatred and pain that was destined to break out right up to the end of time. And Mr Schönhut drank his beer, confident that the thing went no further, because he could say whatever he liked about the God of Israel, he could really let rip, because it all remained in the family. But for others to say these things would have been indelicate and even, at certain times, strictly below the belt.

Your hair's a mess, go to the washroom and sort yourself out, that's what the old lady said to him, severely, on that occasion. To reach the washroom whoever is in the room where the bar is has to pass under the masks, beneath those eyes that peep out avid and frightened. The background behind those faces is black, a darkness in which Carnival lights up scarlet lips and cheeks; a nose projects lewd and curving, the very hook for grabbing someone standing below and dragging him or her into that dark party. It seems that those faces, or some of them, are the work of Pietro Lucano – the attribution is uncertain, despite the work of scholars who devote as much patience to the San Marco as to an ancient temple. In the church of the Sacred Heart – not too far from the café, just across the Public Gardens or back up Via Marconi which runs alongside the park – this painter was responsible for the two angels in the apse that hold up two circles of fire: two acrobats of eternity whose skirts the artist was obliged by the Jesuit fathers to lengthen almost to their ankles, so as not to leave their androgynous legs in view.

There are those who maintain that some of the masks are by Timmel, who was perhaps responsible for a mask (female) in another room. The hypothesis barely holds up: undoubtedly at that time, towards the end of the thirties this "favourite of the road", as the roving painter loved to define himself – he was born in Vienna and came to Trieste to achieve his self-destruction – undoubtedly he contrived some bearable evenings in the cafés to provide himself an hour or two's distraction from the impossibility of living. He would make a gift of some little masterpiece to one or other of the rich Trieste merchants, patrons for whom an artist was a dancing bear and could be tripped up, in exchange for generous drinking sessions that allowed him to get through an evening and which gradually sent him to the bottom altogether.

Timmel reinvented his own childhood. The meningitis he'd had as a child, he recounted, was a base lie invented by his parents out of their hatred for him, and while his mind and his memory were unravelling he was writing the *Magic Notebook,* a mixture of striking lyrical epiphanies and verbal sob-stuff verging on aphasia and rendered crazed by amnesia, which he called nostalgia – the desire to cancel out all the names and signs that enmesh the individual in the world. The wayfaring rebel, fated to end his days in the madhouse, was trying even before reaching that utmost refuge, to escape from the tentacles of reality by closeting himself in an empty, dizzy inertia, "sitting to one side idle and uninterested", arms crossed, immobile and content just to feel himself rotating together with the planet in its vacuum. He sought passivity and welcomed Fascism, which liberated him from the weight of responsibility and spared him the frustration of pursuing liberty without being able to find it, rather it thrust him back into the submission of infancy: "To achieve beatitude requires absolute dependence."

The route through the café and its L-shaped structure, even if only to satisfy what Principal Lunardis could never bring himself to define as anything other than an impulsion, is not straight. Chessplayers love the café – it resembles a chess-board and one moves between its tables like a knight, making a series of right angles and often finding oneself, as in a game of snakes and ladders, back at square one . . . back at that table where one had studied for the German literature exam and now, many years later, one wrote or responded to yet another interview about Trieste, its *Mitteleuropa* culture and its decline, while not far away one son is correcting his degree dissertation and another, in the end-room, is playing cards.

People come and go from the café and behind them the doors continue to swing; a slight breath of air makes the stagnant smoke waver. The swinging loses some of its strength each time, a shorter heartbeat. Strips of luminous dust float in the smoke, serpentine coils that unroll slowly, feeble garlands round the necks of the shipwrecked holding on to their tables. The smoke envelops things in a soft and opaque blanket, a cocoon in which the chrysalis would like to shut itself up indefinitely, sparing itself the pain of being a butterfly. But the scribbling pen bursts the cocoon and frees the butterfly, which flutters its wings in fear.

Above the French windows the fruit bowls and the bottles of champagne gleam. A red marbled lampshade is an iridescent jellyfish. Up high the chandeliers glow and sway like moons in water. History states that the San Marco opened on 3 January, 1914 – despite resistance put up by a consortium of Trieste café owners, who in an attempt to obstruct it turned in vain to the Royal Imperial author-ities – and immediately it became a meeting place for irredentist youth and a workshop for the production of false passports for anti-Austrian patriots who wanted to escape to Italy. "Those youngsters had an easy time," grumbled Mr Pichler, ex-Oberleutnant on the Galicia front during the 1916 massacres. "They had great fun with that traffic in cutting and pasting photographs, it was like taking down one of those masks and putting it on, without thinking that those masks can pull you into the darkness and make you disappear, as then happened to many of them and us, in Galicia or on the Carso . . . and don't let's exaggerate with the famous destruction of the café on 23 May, 1915 by the Austrian pigs . . . yes, the pigs, that's the right name for those desk officers and the scum that came after them – of course it was a terrible business, such a beautiful café all smashed up and broken . . . but Austria, on the whole, was a civilized country. De Frieskene, the governor, even apologised during the war to an irredentist like Silvio Benco for having to keep him under special surveillance, on orders from above. If the Empire existed today everything would still be the same, the world would still be a Caffè San Marco, and don't you think that's something, if you take a look out there?"

The San Marco is a real café – the outskirts of History stamped with the conservative loyalty and the liberal pluralism of its patrons. Those places where just one tribe sets up camp are pseudocafés – never mind whether they are frequented by respectable people, youth most-likely-to, alternative lifestyles or *à la page* intellectuals. All endogamies are suffocating; colleges too, and university campuses, exclusive clubs, master classes, political meetings and cultural symposia, they are all a negation of life, which is a sea port.

Variety triumphs, vital and florid, at the San Marco. Old long-haul captains, students revising for exams and planning amorous manoeuvres, chessplayers oblivious to what goes on around them, German tourists curious about the small plaques commemorating small and large literary triumphs whose begetters used to frequent those tables, silent newspaper readers, joyous groups predisposed towards Bavarian beer or *verduzzo* wine, spirited old men inveighing against the iniquity of the times, know-it-all commentators, misunderstood geniuses, the odd imbecile yuppie, corks that pop like a military salute, especially when Doctor Bradaschia, already under suspicion because of miscellaneous vaunted credits – including his degree – and in trouble with the law, brazenly offers drinks to all within reach, peremptorily instructing the waiter to put it on his account.

"Basically, I was in love with her, but I didn't like her, while she liked me, but she wasn't in love with me," says Mr Palich, born in Lussino, summing up a tormented marital romance. The café is a buzz of voices, a disconnected and uniform choir, apart from a few exclamations at a table of chessplayers, or, in the evening, Mr Plinio's piano – sometimes rock, more often popular music from the years between the wars, *Love is the sweetest thing* . . . fate advances stepping to a danceable kitsch.

But what do you mean "for the money"? As if someone like old Weber would let himself be ripped off. In fact she was the one with the money, not he and she knew well enough that he had almost nothing to leave her. For the likes of you and me maybe a little apartment in New York would be a fortune, but for someone like her it wouldn't even register. He wanted to marry her – his cousin Ettore said so too. They hadn't been speaking for almost fifty years because of that business over the family tomb in Gorizia, and anyway when Ettore heard that the old man, who in fact was two years younger than him, had only a few months left to live, he got on the plane and went to see him in New York. Almost before inviting Ettore to sit down he told him there was big news, that he was getting married the following week – yes, because, he said, he'd done almost everything in life except get married, and he didn't want to make his exit without having tried marriage as well. He emphasized marriage, a proper marriage, it was impossible to die without having been married; everyone's capable of living together, even you, which is saying a lot, he added, giving his cousin a glass of Luxardo maraschino. And so, explained Ettore, having crossed the ocean I had to sample that maraschino which used to turn my stomach when I was a young man, in Zara. Anyway, he died peacefully – now that I've filled in the last box in the questionnaire, as he put it – and I have to admit that he wasn't a trial to anybody, not even during the last days, and here was a man who had always been a royal pain . . . marriage evidently did him good.

Voices rise, they blend, they fade, one hears them at one's shoulder, moving down to the end of the room, the noise of the undertow. The sound waves drift away like circles of smoke, but somewhere continue in existence. They are always there, the world is full of voices, a new Marconi might be able to invent a device capable of picking them all up, an infinite chatter over which death has no dominion; immortal and immaterial souls are stray ultrasounds in the universe. That's according to Juan Octavio Prenz, who listened to the murmuring at those tables and turned it into a novel in his *Fable of Innocent Honest, the Beheaded*, a grotesque and surreal story that is ravelled and unravelled by voices that are crossed, are superimposed, are separated and are lost.

Prenz was born in Buenos Aires but his roots were in the hinterland of Croatian Istria. He taught in Italian and wrote in Spanish. He taught and wandered in the most diverse countries this side and that side of the ocean. Perhaps he settled in Trieste because the city reminded him of the cemetery of boats and figureheads at Ensenada de Barragán, between Buenos Aires and La Plata, which only lives on now in a slender volume of his poems. He sits in the Caffè San Marco still feeling the gaze of the figureheads on him – worn by wind and water, and dumbstruck at the approach of catastrophes that no one else can see yet. He leafs through the translation of one of his collections. One poem is dedicated to Diana Teruggi, who was his assistant at the University of Buenos Aires. One day, in the time of the generals, the girl disappeared for ever. Once again poetry speaks of absence, of something or someone who is not here any more. It's not much, a poem. A little card left in an empty place. Poets know this and don't give it too much weight, but they give even less weight to the world that celebrates or ignores them. Prenz pulls his pipe from a pocket, smiles at his two daughters sitting at another table, chats with a Senegalese who's going round the tables selling junk, buys a cigarette lighter from him. Chatting is better than writing. The Senegalese moves on, Prenz sucks on his pipe and makes a start.

It's not bad, filling up sheets of paper under the sniggering masks and amidst the indifference of the people sitting around. That good-natured indifference balances the latent delirium of omnipotence that exists in writing – purporting to sort out the world with a few pieces of paper and to hold forth on life and death. Thus the pen is dipped, willingly or otherwise, into ink diluted with humility and irony. The café is a place for writing. One is alone, with paper and pen and at most two or three books, hanging onto the table like a shipwreck survivor tossed by the waves. A few centimetres of wood separate the sailor from the abyss that might swallow him up, the tiniest flaw and the huge black waters break ruinously, pulling him down. The pen is a lance that wounds and heals; it pierces the floating wood and leaves it to the mercy of the waves, but it also plugs the wood and renders it capable of sailing once again and keeping to a course.

Keep a hold on the wood, fear not – a shipwreck can also be salvation. How does the old story go? Fear knocks at the door, faith opens; there's no one there. But who teaches you to go and open? For some time you've done nothing but close doors, it's become a habit; for a while you hold your breath, but then anxiety grabs your heart again and the instinct is to bolt everything, even the windows, without realizing that this way there's no air and as you suffocate, the migraine batters your temples; eventually all you hear is the sound of your own headache.

Scribble, free the demons, bridle them, often simply presume to ape them. In the San Marco the demons have been relegated up on high, overturning the traditional scenario, because the café, with its floral decor and its Viennese Secessionist style reminds us that it can be alright down here: a waiting room in which it's pleasant to wait, to put off leaving. The manager, Mr Gino, and the waiters, who come to the table with one glass after another – sometimes off their own bat offering, but not to everyone, salmon canapés with a special *prosecco* – are angels of a lower order, but they are trustworthy, enough at any rate to keep an eye on things so that these exiles from the earthly paradise feel at home in this clandestine Eden and no snake tries to tempt them away with false promises.

The café is a Platonic academy, said Hermann Bahr at the beginning of the century – the man who also said that he liked being in Trieste because here he had the impression of being nowhere. Nothing is taught in this academy, but sociability and how to break spells are learned. One may chat, tell stories, but preaching, making political speeches, giving lessons are against the rules. All, at their respective tables, are close to and distant from the person next to them. Love your neighbour as you love yourself, or bear your neighbour's mania for biting his nails just as he endures some habit of yours that is even more unpleasant. At these tables it is not possible to found a school, draw up ranks, mobilize followers and emulators, recruit disciples. In this the place of disenchantment – in which how the show ends is common knowledge but where no one tires of watching nor chafes at the actors' blunders – there is no room for false prophets who seduce those vaguely anxious for a facile and instant redemption, misleading them with empty promises.

Out there, the false Messiahs have an easy time of it, as they drag their followers blinded by mirages of salvation down roads they cannot travel and thus setting them off towards destruction. The prophets of drugs, men who can control their own habit without being overborne by it, seduce helpless disciples into following them on the road along which they will destroy themselves. Someone, in a drawing room, proclaims that revolutions are made with rifles, knowing well that this is an innocuous metaphor while leaving other simple souls to take them literally and end up having to pay the penalty. Among the newspapers on their long sticks an illustrated magazine displays the face of Edie Sedgwick, the beautiful and vulnerable American model who believed in the testament of disorder preached with order and method by that tribal guru Andy Warhol. She let herself be convinced to seek not pleasure, but an undefinable sense of life in those feverish sexual transgressions, those ingenuous group rites and those drugs that led her, with painful banality, to unhappiness and death.

In the San Marco no one has any illusions that the original sin was never committed and that life is virginal and innocent; for this reason it's difficult to pass off anything phoney on its patrons, any ticket to the Promised Land. To write is to know that one is not in the Promised Land and that one will never reach it, but it also means continuing doggedly in that direction, through the wilderness. Sitting in the café, you're on a journey; as in a train, a hotel, on the road, you've got very little with you and you cannot in your vanity grace that nothing with your personal mark, you are nobody. In that familiar anonymity you can dissimulate, rid yourself of the ego as if it were a shell. The world is a cavity of uncertainty into which writing penetrates in obstinate bewilderment. To write, take a break, chat, play at cards; laughter at the next table, a woman's profile, as incontrovertible as Fate, the wine in the glass, time the colour of gold. The hours flow . . . amiable, carefree, almost happy.

The owners and the ex-owners of the café – almost a list of the sovereigns of ancient dynasties. Marco Lovrinovich of Fontane d'Orsera near Parenzo, who started restaurants and wine houses much as others write poems or paint landscapes, opened the café on 3 January, 1914 on the site where The Trifolium Central Dairy had once stood, complete with cowshed. Officially Lovrinovich said he had named it San Marco in his own honour, but he took every opportunity to repeat the image of the Venetian lion, the irredentist Italian symbol even in the decoration on the chairs. Perhaps he was convinced, deep down, that the winged lion was indeed a tribute to his Christian name. You don't reach the age of ninety-four, as he did, without being intimately convinced that the world revolves around you.

And yet some died young and alone among his tables, devastated by the imbalance between their spirit and the world, which was definitely not tailor-made for them – for example that youngster who was always a bit sweaty, the one who went round like a hunted animal; his eyes forever spoke his awareness of being already caught between the tiger's jaws. He use to come every afternoon with so many sheets of paper which he filled one after another and always carried with him, until one day he came no more; he'd thrown himself into the courtyard the previous evening.

The cafés are also a sort of hospice for those whose hearts suffer need and café-owners like Lovrinovich are benefactors too, offering a temporary refuge from the elements, like the founders of shelters for the homeless. And why shouldn't they earn something on the side, even patriotic glory as Lovrinovich did following the devastation of the San Marco and his detention in the Austrian punishment camp in Liebenau, near Graz, where the Austrians sent him because he'd infected both eyes with trachoma to avoid being sent to fight against Italy.

Among the various owners the Stock sisters stand out, minute and relentless. And then there are also memories of a seasoned barwoman with lank blonde hair; they still talk about the occasion when an enormous drunk, to whom she'd denied one final whisky, threatened her with a little demonstration, lifting up the coffee machine – a massive weight – from the bar as if it were a twig, then dropping it with an almighty clang. Meanwhile the nearest regulars, among them one intently writing at his usual table, alas all too close to the bar, looked around in fright, hoping that someone else might nobly step forward to prevent the slaughter of the woman. Finally the enraged giant lunged at her just as she pulled a hatchet from a drawer and jumped at him, ready to plant the thing in his neck and the dutiful customer, who had stood up from his paper-strewn table and had been moving as slowly as possible towards the furious colossus, was only too glad to tackle the barwoman, firmly seizing and twisting the wrist that brandished the hatchet, and thus saving the impulsive youngster's life.

It might be one of the few places in Trieste where there are plenty of young people to be seen, but the San Marco suggests a rejuvenated existence, it seems to imprint on the faces of its habitués the same seasoned and decorous robustness that a little restoration periodically confers on the decor. The Triestine Mephistopheles is a prudent, bourgeois demon; his rejuvenation of the friezes when they are about to crumble away and of the walls cracked like a wrinkled face, provides a noble, vigorous middle age – not the tempestuous and improvident youth of a Faust that spells Marguerite's ruin, but the charm of the teacher who in bed concludes the seduction of the pupil begun austerely in the classroom, a little misunderstanding soon to be dissipated.

So far as the structure is concerned, the rejuvenative function tends to be carried out by the Generali insurance company, which restores to the cafés and public buildings of Trieste the ordered and mysterious beauty of the florid bourgeois city it once was. The portrait of the writer who spends much of his life at the San Marco, receiving mail and visitors who ask him about that flourishing, lost city that once was – a city which he only knows about second-hand, through other people's gossip and nostalgia – the portrait, by Valerio Cugia, hangs on the left-hand wall as one enters, in front of the board with the plaques dedicated to the illustrious patrons. The portrait could justifiably be replaced by the old nineteenth-century portrait of Masino Levi, insurance director, which hangs in the foyer of the Politeama Rossetti theatre, next to the Public Gardens: waistcoat, paper in one hand, goose quill in the other, a discrete and elusive Jewish smile on his lips. A Mephistopheles insurer of lives and guarantor, with a policy to boot, of a healthy middle age for which it's worth signing and handing over one's soul.

Indeed that middle age – or post-middle age – offers good possibilities for success, delayed yet sweet. On certain evenings the sun lights up the broad, gilded coffee leaves that surround the medallions on the walls; the light as it moves sinks the mirror behind the table into a lake of shadow enclosed by shining borders, the last rays of a distant sun that gleams and sets over the sea. A nostalgia for marine clarity reflects on the half-submerged faces in the dark waters of the mirror, the insidious call of real life. But one is quick to shut it up, if it is too insistent. When, in a certain period, assiduous regulars who also attend the adjacent synagogue stop coming and disappear one after another from their usual tables, then almost no one, not even those who up until recently loved to chat with the people who came out of the Temple and into the café for refreshment, almost no one asks indiscreet questions about their absence.

In the café the air is veiled, a protection against remoteness; no gust blows the horizon open and the red of the evening is the wine in one's glass. Mr Crepaz, for example, certainly does not regret his youth; in fact just now he's busy touching it up, like an unsuccessful painting that's not beyond repair. As a young man things never went well for him with women. Oh, nothing dramatic – simply nothing happened, or very little, ever since he was a youngster, since the time

when they all used to meet up at the summer cinema in the Public
Garden, just a few hundred metres from the San Marco. The girls
were kind, pleased if he was there too, but when the dark white-
capped sea of the *Bounty* appeared on the screen, bright spray and
black waves, a black as deep as the night so that it seemed blue,
and there was freshness and darkness around them and noises among
the leaves, the girls' eyes shone and tender laughter in the shadow
was the promise of happiness, and he felt that none of this was for
him. He felt it in the awkwardness of his body which was a barrier
between himself and those tanned arms that, all right, they were
flung about his neck at the moment of going home, but it was
nothing to compare to what happened with the others, even just
the clasp of a hand in the dark.

It had been more or less always that way, at any rate often; those
beauties opened up like flowers in water, and in vain he'd passed
them by, the art of placing a hand on another's had remained an
unknown initiation. Until once, many years later, he had seen Laura
again – beautiful in her ageing, which was already clear in the lines
in her face and the abundance of her breasts; suddenly she had looked
at him differently and everything had loosened up, it had become
so easy. "You were so immature," Clara, said to him months later, in
bed. They used to sit together at school and then, as now, she would
throw her black hair into his face like a wave, although now it had
the odd streak of white.

And so his life had changed. Not that he'd become a womanizer,
anything but. He was faithful, he was only interested in the women
he'd desired in vain in his youth and he wanted to square things
up. He was methodical in his research; the girls had left him behind,
but he had caught up on more than one of them. Slowly things
reverted to a new order, a new balance. He was making up for that
day of useless heartbreak at the seaside with Maria, the unbridgeable
distance he'd felt then as he have her his hand to help her up on
to the rock. He made revisions to that lunch when Luisa, with that
sidelong, teasing glance of hers, had eyes only for Giorgio, while
now her soft, plump fingers, so practised in awakening desire, were
only for him.

Little by little he retraced his path backwards, back to that little girl
in the white socks in the cycling area in the Public Garden, the one
who'd ordered him sulkily to sort her wheel our for her and then had
shot off without so much as a glance. But now, she was an odalisque,
a woman with avid, imperious lips who would have inspired envy

in the fine daughter she'd had all those years ago by one of the lucky ones, a rival who in the meantime had been removed from the scene with a divorce.

And then there were the ladies he'd pined for in an even more distant time, his mother's friends and his friends' mothers, elegant and perfumed women who always picked up and cuddled the other children, kissing and stroking them on the cheek or putting a chocolate in their mouths, even pushing it through their lips with a finger, the nail varnished. Indeed there was even a rumour – but it's easy to exaggerate in the café – that he recently had gone to bed with Mrs Tauber, perhaps the doyenne of her line, who some fifty years previously had been a real beauty; even now she still had the pert little nose that was his by rights. Anyway, gentleman as he was, he said nothing because they all knew her and she sometimes still came to the café with the few surviving friends of her own sex.

Giorgio Voghera has for years sat at a table on the bottom right, as one comes in. He is an acknowledged leader and purported author of *Secret,* a distasteful and charming masterpiece, its subject, renunciation seen in its heartless geometry, a book written against life that serves to highlight all of life's seductive qualities. Next to Voghera sit mild-mannered ladies, cousins who are also writers of some merit, undemanding friends, aspiring writers who cling to past literary glory, journalists who every two or three months come up with the same questions on Trieste, students looking for dissertation topics, the odd scholar from far away perhaps sniffing out a future banquet of unpublished works. Piero Kern, expert in oral literature and a protected specimen of the grand Triestine cosmopolitan bourgeoisie now in danger of extinction, if it ever existed, tells of a robbery in a Rio de Janeiro travel agency; he is highly critical of the robbers' lack of professionalism, but even more so of the unseemly behaviour of a fat American, a fellow victim.

Voghera listens good-humouredly, patient and distrait, letting his own words and others' slide into the great indifference of the universe. Those watery sky-blue eyes have seen the other side of life, its underside, and their glance roves meekly among the tables. "Basically, I'm optimistic," he loves to repeat, "because things always end up working out worse than my gloomy predictions." He's been through historic catastrophes and personal hells, skirted abysses into which he cannot have found it easy to avoid being swallowed, especially as a young man.

It's not easy being in the desert, outside of and far away from the Promised Land. It's not just the big sand storms in the desert, the strong wind that stuns and sweeps one away; there are even more venomous dangers – the grains that stick everywhere and take the air away from one's skin, the dryness that desiccates the body and dries up the soul's sap. Perhaps as a young man, before he reached this state of indulgence for his own and others' shortcomings, Voghera must have been fairly unbearable – an irritable teacher who found life slapdash and in need of correction and failed it. But his syntax is clear and smooth, doggedly honest, like Ariadne's Thread running through the labyrinth without getting tangled and implacably weaving the image of a random, painful, grotesque reality.

In this prose Voghera writes out his kaleidoscope, celebrating the useless virtues of a white-collar universe – methodical precision and assiduous effort dedicated to nothing. He describes the process of ethical reverse selection that inevitable brings the worst onto the bridge of society and history. He reviews the sciences that venture into the meanders of the soul, those like psychoanalysis that reveal tortuous truths that soon become banalities, cruel misunderstandings in the comedy of existence. He re-evokes the years of exile and the war in Palestine, a war that for him was above all a solemn labour of patience. He gazes with disenchantment and compassion on the world, as though viewing it from another planet; the contemplation of chaos does away with trust and illusion but not with good manners, a pure style and that melancholy nineteenth-century respect that is one manifestation of goodness.

"I know, I know that everyone has so much to do in this world," Voghera murmurs, as though he himself does not belong to it. Often, despite the aches and pains and the years, and there are many of them by now, he goes to visit a venerable and despotic authoress, forgotten by everyone; she keeps him for hours, hassling him and tearing him apart because he's the only victim she has left. "Well, what am I to say?" he explains, almost apologetically, "I know what loneliness is, to be alone and forgotten . . . and then she was kind to my parents, once, although in truth . . . well, it doesn't matter. But above all it's because if I don't call on her she she phones me up and bends my ear relentlessly, which is much more tiring." Every now and then, at night, in the Jewish rest home where he lives, an addled old woman from a neighbouring room makes a mistake, comes in and sits on his bed, for hours sometimes. "Even if it had happened fifty years ago," he says, "it wouldn't have made any difference . . ."

God continues to inflict sores on Job and Voghera keeps the record. *Our Lady Death,* a questionable but unforgettable book, is the diary of the bereavements he's been through: his father, his mother, Aunt Letizia, Uncle Giuseppe, Aunt Olga, his friend Paolo, his cousin Cecilia. Jewish Trieste, to which he bears witness and of which he is perhaps the last chronicler, exits from the stage. One by one the bit players disappear, in the final hours of his many characters, whose agony also includes the bureaucratic processes to be gone through, the emergency hospital admissions, the vesical haemorrhages, the smells of old age and illness, the red tape for hospital in-patients, the arteriosclerosis, the tyrannical manias of the ill and the egoism of their carers, the wiles, the pains and the great detachment of those who suffer and die.

The archivist of the end neglects no detail of the disintegration, nor of the squalor that accompanies it – the vomit choking the breath, and the rude arrogance of the switchboard operator at the emergency unit. He's like a beast of burden, beneath his pack and the blows – he absorbs it all, patient and helpless, but he lifts his eyes and repeats: "Now mind, because I'm noting it all down." Those hospital admissions and those deaths pursuing one another from chapter to chapter produce in the end an involuntarily comic result, just like any exaggerated sequence of tragedies that initially awakes compassion but then, beyond a certain point, provokes hilarity in the observer. This irresistible comic quality of tribulations brings out the extreme weakness of the human condition, which under an overload of misery is robbed even of its decorum, exposed to ridicule and reduced to waste and refuse.

In a certain sense Voghera rewrites the Book of Job, but with himself taking the part of Job's first sons and daughters, who, during their father's trials, perish in the ruins of the house, demolished like the flocks by the wind in the desert, and in the happy ending they are replaced just like the flocks and the camels, so that their memory will not disturb Job's late and happy years. Job is protagonist of a terrible story, but one which is set in motion in order to make him stand out; from his point of view, from the perspective of a man to whom the Lord and his Opponent dedicate much attention, it is easier to acknowledge that life, despite its tragedies, has a sense. Nobody wonders, even, whether and how Job's first children, crushed under the rubble, accepted their fate as mere extras brought in to glorify Job. If one identifies with them, with their nameless destiny, it's more difficult to praise the order of things.

Voghera adopts the point of view of those creatures who have been demolished, overlooked, the viewpoint of the stone which the builders rejected, mindful and perhaps mistrustful of the Lord's promise to use it as the cornerstone of His house. His objective and fastidious prose is a great memorial to the vanquished. But something blocks and dilutes, the watery gaze clouds over, the goodness darkens, perhaps becomes polluted. Whether or not he is the author of the splendid *Secret,* it anyway couldn't have been easy to be its protagonist, the bitter hero of a mania and an inhibition, which in stories are transformed into magic, into love's abandonment, but in real life leave scars that rarely heal – all the more so if the author of that great book was (as he maintains without letting anyone know what it is he really wants us to believe) his father, Guido Voghera, in an improper, almost incestuous profanation of the deep and heartbreaking unhappiness of his son.

His crystalline style and his preferred topics – love's enchantment, life's failure – sometimes seem to come from a page of *Secret,* but often they are weakened and watered down in mere fastidious verbiage; straightforward, charming simplicity slides away into banality, and humility dissolves into a questionable submissiveness. Perhaps anyway Voghera is a plaster saint, a man who had to master the lessons of life's meanness and perhaps did not mind doing so. When his writing is praised he retires shyly and blushes, saying that the true writers in his family are his father, his uncle and his cousin. But in the myopic eyes as they look past his interlocutor, there is perhaps a glint of malice, if he gets the impression you might just end up believing him.

Doctor Velicogna sits near the counter where the newspapers are; he's not interested in reading them because they all say the same things, but he likes to hold them, the stick in his left hand while he leafs through with his right. The world is there, in his hands, threatening disasters with enormous black headlines, but one has the sense of keeping it at bay. Doctor Velicogna has a theory, founded on personal experience, about the best ways of saving a marriage: mine, for example, he blethers in front of his beer – draught, naturally, bottled beer's not for him because pressure and temperature are crucial and the head has to be just right, not that stuff that comes out when you take the cap off, which looks like a syrup shaken before use – mine was saved thanks to that stunt of spending the whole night out, a couple of times; that way I opened my eyes and I understood. Even the most irreproachable can find himself, without quite knowing how, caught up in some little affair and to begin with it's not even unpleasant. But often, almost from the start, she asks you to stay over at her place for the night and, who knows, maybe it seems more decorous and besides, despite all the complications and the manoeuvres to be set in motion, how do you say no? I at all events always felt surprised and grateful if a woman was attracted to me and it seemed all wrong not to be kind.

It's true that kindness and courtesy pay, continues Doctor Velicogna, still holding the newspaper stick. Thanks to that kindness the whole show soon came apart; soon enough, anyway, before anyone got hurt. Because after a while, in bed, what are you supposed to do? It's not your woman, the one who goes with you through all the business and the strife of living – she's the one you never tire of, never tire of simply being close to her and doing nothing, just feeling her shoulder and her breath.

Now when you're with another woman – she might even be a better woman and warrant all the respect in the world – after a while you're lying there and you don't even have the courage to get up and go and read a book – all right, you can go to the bathroom and stay in there a while, but only once, at the most twice. You can sleep a bit, but even falling asleep too quickly doesn't do, it's not polite. And so I used to lie in bed, hoping she'd fall asleep. When I heard the first trams I was relieved and the Municipal Transport Authority shot up in my esteem as their pre-dawn heralds announced the imminent end of my embarrassment. A couple more hours and leaving would no longer be a discourtesy, indeed it was a duty, a delicate gesture given that they, too, had to go out to work.

That's how I understood that sleeping together – not just sleeping, but being close together in the dark, living even, and I don't mean anything special but just chatting, sharing a few laughs, a few anxieties, going to the cinema or to the sea for the last swim at the end of October, on the rocks between Barcola and Miramare – you can only do that with the woman of your life. And I understood all that because I stayed over and slept with another woman and the next morning it was all over without a word spoken. Otherwise I would have carried on for who knows how long and with who knows what complications, songs and dances, mix-ups and upsets for everyone. I'll have to tell all this to Father Guido, he might come today as well, he likes his beer and the Sacred Heart church is just down the road. He might be able to work it up into a fine topic for a sermon on marriage. On the supremacy of marriage, I mean. And perhaps he could spare a thought for those fine girls – one or two at most, for someone like me that's more than enough – who lead us back onto the straight and narrow and to the knowledge of ourselves. For them, too, it was a good thing not to have me hanging around any more.

At the table of Voghera and cousins, the memoirs of his uncle, Giuseppe Fano, are doing the rounds in typescript. He'd starting writing them just before he died, in 1972, at the age of ninety-one. He could have recounted an active, colourful life in this work: already a merchant before the Great War, he'd then taken on the leadership of an Italian committee for aid to Jewish emigrants and in this role he had carried out an epic job, with imperturbable calm and stolid fidelity to his daily habits, chartering ships for voyages to Palestine, collecting donations with persistent tenacity and organizing services, helping refugees from all over the world, doing all he could for others and trying, whenever possible, to stay in bed with his skullcap on his head in order to save his strength and reach old age.

The memoirs carry barely more than an echo of these risky and charitable deeds; what chiefly comes across is the worry about punctiliously recovering the energy so generously expended in the doing of them. The protagonists of the memoirs are colds and draughts, which bothered Fano more than any other disaster, to the point where he wore, even in summer, several pull-overs one on top of another, and Saba used to tell him that it took an iron constitution like his to bear the measures he took to protect it, measures that would have given anyone else pneumonia. So as not to abandon those who needed him, he'd stayed in Trieste even during the German occupation, despite the risk of being deported; one September or October day while going round the Nazi-controlled city in a fur greatcoat that made him look as though he'd just come out of a Polish ghetto, he observed with relief, in German, that luckily the cold of the past few days had relented. The entire Third Reich was completely powerless to make him budge from his habits; Hitler could make him risk death, but not a cold.

With his Central European discretion, Fano almost never speaks of himself, in his memoirs, but of others; he, the narrative I, is simply the connecting thread. He does not permit himself to alter nor to colour events unduly and neither does he evaluate them subjectively, but depicts the world as it is, with God's eye, which sees everything and its opposite. He does not select things, neither does he eliminate incoherent data, because he claims no right to establish hierarchies of importance or the authority of the demiurge who sets reality aside or corrects it. He admires, venerates Saba and recounts how in Milan in 1914 the poet begged him, when he had to return to Trieste, "To take the fate of his mother and his aunt to heart, and to make sure that his aunt's will was in his favour, thus avoiding the loss of the little nest-egg she had. Back in Trieste I kept the promise scrupulously and visited the dear old ladies if not every day, at least three times a week . . . I took the aunt to the solicitor and she, willingly, happily, made out her will in favour of her nephew."

In Fano's testimony there is no trace of derision, no debunking. The comedy, never provoked, never repressed, is born out of faithfulness to reality, which brings out the foolishness, the incoherence but also the picaresque adventure of life, the family epic lived day by day with loved ones. The details, entertaining or embarrassing, are recorded with an entomologist's precision. During his adolescence when his father suggested cold showers for quenching the fires of puberty, Fano naturally heeded the advice: "I got up warm from my bed, and went into the freezing kitchen. To the water tap I applied a rubber hose that terminated in a cone-shaped funnel with holes (like a rose on a watering can) . . . This treatment was useless for my neurosis, but it strengthened my lungs and protected me from colds."

The size of his family is suggested indirectly by some marginalia: "I can't remember which newborn it was, but Mother was exhausted and Father . . ." Order is defended punctiliously: a distant relative is one of the first young women to receive educational qualifications in nineteenth-century Trieste; when she turns to an aunt who was most involved with numerous charity committees and specialized in aid for prostitutes and their rehabilitation in society, hoping that this aunt, thanks to her contacts, might find her a job, the latter regretfully replies that she would be only too pleased to but she cannot, "because we only help whores", and if one starts mixing things up there's no telling how it all might end.

The nineteenth-century positivist intelligence is too honest to attempt any synthesis of the random multiplicity of what is real – this would be too presumptuous. "Compromise as much as you like, but for God's sake no syntheses!", warned Guido Voghera, presumed anonymous author of *Secret*. Objects exist and they demand loyalty, even at the cost of ridiculousness. For Fano there are no data to be removed because they are incoherent or contradictory in relation to the picture one wants to offer or because they are at variance with an image – even one's own – that is now accepted. Fano does not even worry about the coherence of his memoirs, which he dictated from his bed, sometimes renarrating entire episodes that he had forgotten he had already recounted; he would repeat them once more in his pages because, when the typist told him she had already set them down, he told her not to give it a thought, since it was none of her business, and to keep going.

Every life, like Fano's pages, repeats itself many times, in its passions, in its acts and in its whims. His autobiography has the coherence of its fragmentary nature, there is no pretence at a conclusion and it interrupts itself in homage to reality, which remains unfinished and inconclusive. So be it even for the pen that means to recount it all and snaps in two while it attends to this heroic-comic task. Whatever happens, respect for others, even for things, remains paramount. "May I have your revered telephone number?" Fano would ask if he thought he might need to call someone.

In the medallions on the walls – accredited to illustrious artists but not always confirmed, certainly to Napoleone Cozzi (climber, decorator, writer and irredentist) possibly to Ugo Flumiani, painter of foam-flecked waters – the nudes represent the rivers which "from the Italian peninsula, from Friuli, from Istria and from Dalmatia flow into the Adriatic, into the sea of Saint Mark". That apotheosis of Mare Nostrum, of Our Sea, which was supposed to be Italic on both shores, is toned down in the amber glaze of the decor, an evening of gold verging on russet. The estuary looks like a highly decorated exit leading into a larger room. In the aisle near Via Battisti, the characters in the *Offerers* by Giuseppe Barison – who also painted the allegories of Electricity and Geography in the railway station café – parade with gifts in their arms, to propitiate unknown gods; a red glow illuminates the greys, the ochre, the brown of the figures. Flumiani's seascapes and lagoon paintings, in the wing nearest the synagogue, are bright; sails and water, sand and mud, too, gleam in the sparkle of the midday sun. Oh to leave the ark, to plunge and disappear into that water gilded by the sunset; even just to paddle in the lagoon, to squeeze and splatter the mud that glitters with nuggets.

"Your hair's a mess, go to the washroom and sort yourself out." With the authority that normally derives from a physical intimacy, the old lady that time brooked no nonsense. Since then, whenever he goes to the washroom, he feels as though he's obeying that injunction, the conclusion of their vapid dialogue. "Well done, what a worker . . . bravo!" she had said to him when once she was left sitting alone at the table next to his. Perhaps the compliments were a peace offering after her tirade against modern times and the youth of today, which had developed out of her chat with her friend and now, seeing that he had stopped writing and was looking around vacantly, she wanted to repair the damage. "Bravo! . . . what a worker!" He sketched an embarrassed smile. "And what's your area of interest?" "Well . . . let's see . . . German literature." "Splendid . . . the most beautiful literature, most interesting, most spiritual . . . bravo!" With each reply his smile became progressively more inane. "But you're already wearing a wedding ring, and you being so young . . . how old are you? Really, I'd never have guessed. You look much younger . . . well done, you've done the right thing, marriage is the most important thing. No children yet though, I imagine. Yes? Congratulations! That's really important. One? Oh . . . two! You really are very lucky . . . the right number. Boy and a girl? Oh . . . two boys. The best thing. You'll see what it means to them, in life, to have a brother . . . Glad you married so young?"

The affirmative response to this last question, that involuntary final touch to the portrait of perfection – husband, father, worker and what's more young and replete – was followed by a long silence, which he had turned to account by starting to write again until, after a few minutes, she leaned over him and, crossing that distance between two faces and two bodies that is only ever crossed under special circumstances, whispered angrily because of the single blemish on the general perfection: "Your hair's a mess, go to the washroom and sort yourself out!"

Such an authoritative tone, which usually comes from a bed, demands to be obeyed. The washroom is at the end on the right. On the walls a Siamese dancer closes her unfathomable eyes, the sinuous art nouveau lines curve the cruel eyebrows and shameless legs of female figures, a wave finishes in the vortex of the void like Mr Plinio's waltz, music for a backstage exit. The coffee leaf is repeated in a vegetal proliferation, and the grimace on a Harlequin's face bespeaks a raw, nameless pain.

Some paintings have been recovered after being painted over for decency's sake, so say the scholars of restoration. But it's difficult, for all one might try, to find anything indecent in them. Anyway it doesn't hurt to repaint, to cover, to close the hatches. Perhaps writing is covering up too, an accomplished coat of paint applied to one's own life, so that it assumes a mantle of magnanimity thanks to the skilful display of faults under a pretence of hiding them in a tone of candid self-accusation that makes them seem big-hearted, while the real filth remains below. All saints, that's what writers are; yes . . . daredevils, prodigal sons, full of lusty sins shown off with meretricious shame, but still large, beautiful souls. Is it possible that among us there is not a single pig, no truly shabby, mean-spirited swine?

The washroom is cramped, a reddish trickle runs under the urinals, it clots in lumps, glass from a shattered bottle on the beach. Now and then a jet of clear water comes down. Get washed, a change of underwear. In the face at the mirror something comes undone, as though whatever it was that had held it together up to that moment has started to work loose. The hair is dirty, tangled serpents on a Gorgon's head that emerges from the depths of Hades. There's someone smiling on a scrap of newspaper. The washroom is the antechamber before Judgement, an indefinite wait, eternity is the dribble that runs along the urinals. Back to the café, kill time, read the newspapers. A quick rinse has made the face presentable, but the hair's all sweaty. Go to the washroom and sort oneself out. To plunge into the sea, even just to wash one's hands in the shallow, tepid water of the lagoon, to put one's face into the drinking fountain in the nearby Public Garden, as one used to do back then after having run, or in the snow that was so white it seemed blue, and in the small spring in that clearing in the wood where the deer used to go to drink, or in the holy-water stoup in the Sacred Heart church, in Via del Ronco – so fresh. Indeed, it is all so close by, little more than a stone's throw. For those who want to stretch their legs and take a little tour of the world, the San Marco is in an excellent position. Central, an estate agent would say. To reach the church in Via del Ronco, going through the Garden and all the other necessary places, takes only a few minutes.

From Microcosms
Translated from the Italian by Iain Halliday

For Erwin Glikes

Erwin was no stranger to publishing awards – his work was acknowledged repeatedly by different parts of the American publishing industry – but this great honour is something other; he would have been moved to his core by it, and humbled, because to be claimed by Jerusalem is truly to be chosen, and nothing on his scale of values would have measured higher than this.

It is a prize that celebrates not just a body of work, but a man and a life, that recognizes something much deeper than mere success – it recognizes a spirit. In this gathering of so many people who loved him, that's what I would like to talk about today; what made him who he really was. The name Erwin Glikes is so synonymous with American publishing and a part of American intellectual life over the last quarter-century – those initials E.A.G. in their characteristic scrawl on so many manuscripts and editorial critiques, so many notes and memos and contracts, cited in so may dedications – that the message they contained went unheard. But if you listen to his name spoken in the language of his birth – Erwin Arno Glükes – it tells you volumes about the values to which he was born, and what he made of them.

Erwin is a name that resonates in Germany's idea of itself, for Meister Erwin was one of its creative colossi, the architectural genius of the Middle Ages who built Strasbourg cathedral and who symbolizes the very essence of the Gothic, which runs so deep in the German mind that Germany claims it as the embodiment of the Germanic soul: to read Goethe on Meister Erwin is to experience an extraordinary moment in a culture's rediscovery of its past.

Arno again is a talismanic name. Not since the ancient Romans has a country called its children by the names of its great rivers, no matter how redolent of power and history these rivers might be – but the German reverence for Italy and its civilization was such that they took the name of Florence's river Arno as an act of homage. To give a boy the names Erwin and Arno was therefore to proclaim

that he too belonged to Germany's highest cultural tradition. But
Erwin's last name in its original German form was *Glükes*, for his
parents were Frankfurt Jews, and all the love and confidence they
placed in a German culture in which they believed they shared was
about to be shattered.

After the Book Fair last year, I took a trip which Erwin and I had
wanted so much to make since the Wall came down, but time did
not allow. Instead, I made it with very dear friends. We headed east
from Frankfurt in a journey that was as much about mythology as
it was about geography. And at the centre was Weimar . . . in the
morning of that day, the three of us walked through that exquisite
tiny city to Goethe's house, which in its magnificent simplicity is so
exactly as it was on the day he died that it delivers a sense of the
man as powerful as a shock. After exploring the first rooms, we
came up a narrow, turning stair into a little upstairs hall, where
there was an open doorway. As you moved into it and turned your
head, you were looking down the length of Goethe's library. It's
a narrow room, perhaps thirty feet long in my recollection, with a
plain, scrubbed floor and with the light falling in from his beloved
garden through two windows at the other end. The jolt comes
from its arrangement – the books do not line the walls within the
protective custody of grand book-cases, as was the fashion of the
time and indeed the tradition of libraries since the Renaissance, but
are crammed into stacks and bays from floor to ceiling, more than
5,000 of them, many still with Goethe's homemade paper dustcovers
on them and his scraps of notes and markers sticking out. There's
a little handwritten tally near the door which gives his count of
the volumes in each area of his interest – aesthetics, art, economics,
education, engineering, freemasonry, geography, geology, history,
law, mathematics, medicine, mineralogy, mythology, philosophy,
psychology, theatre, theology – and of course all world literature.
From astrology to phrenology, it's all there, ranging across German,
English, Italian, Latin, Greek and Hebrew. It is like viewing a
brain-scan of the last universal mind. As I stood rooted in the doorway, I suddenly felt with absolute clarity that Erwin was at my
shoulder, then he moved past me into the room. As he turned to
look back, the sense of his delight was overpowering – it was as if
we had brought his mind home.

Some time later, when I'd caught my breath, we left the house
and explored some more, and then following in Goethe's footsteps,

took the road that leads out of Weimar and up the hill. The distance
to the top is about eight kilometres – five miles; on the crest are beautiful beech-woods and it was a favourite destination of the Weimar
citizenry on their Sunday outings. Just over the crest of the hill was
a great oak tree, famous to lovers of literature, because it was where
Goethe used to rest from the walk and read poetry to his platonic
love, Charlotte von Stein. A picture of the tree still hangs where
he set it, above his desk; he wrote poems to it. The tree survived –
only its surroundings changed. From 1937 to 1944, when it was
mercifully destroyed by lightning, it stood right in front of the
entrance to the Commandant's office in the centre of Buchenwald.
For Buchenwald means Beechwood. Just as classical Weimar is tiny,
Buchenwald – though it spread beyond its perimeters – is tiny.
Part of the horror when you stand inside the main gate is that you
can see all four corners of the original camp, its north and south
and east and west – it is a child's garden of evil. I had not understood until that day what *mental* cruelty is also bound up in the
invention of barbed wire. It makes a prison without walls. You can
see through it, even reach through it (if not electrocuted) to the
air and life and sun and green of the beech trees on the other side.
It is indeed an obscene play on the word "en*light*enment". Inside
that perimeter fence – nothing. Nothing now moves, nothing stirs,
nothing grows. Even the weeds die in the broken, black, bituminous
stone underfoot that stretches like a desert. Those eight short
kilometres from Goethe's house to Goethe's oak are the distance
from Germany's crowning glory to its degradation. And it was those
three things – an understanding of what was at the bottom of the
hill, an understanding of what was at the top of the hill, and how
short the distance was between them – that shaped Erwin's character,
his mind and his life.

He was one of the lucky ones. In the Thirties his parents had left
Frankfurt for Belgium, where he was born. They fled on the day of
the German invasion, reaching Marseilles, where they lived – if that
is the word – for almost three years of suffocating danger while
they tried to rescue other relatives and friends out of the Occupied
Zone and waited – and waited – for the visas from America that
would save them. Erwin's uncle and grandfather were rounded up
by the French and sent to Auschwitz. Erwin remembered standing
in a little tin sink being washed by his mother when there was a
crashing at the door; it was the sound of his father's manacled hands

as he was taken away to one of the prison ships in the harbour from which forced labour was sent to the camps. Erwin's mother collected all the money and valuables they had and sent Erwin's nurse – an orphaned Jewish girl they'd brought with them from Belgium, with deceptive blonde pigtails – to the boat. Miraculously, and incredibly bravely, she bribed him off again. There are Erwin's stories from that time that became famous among his friends. There are others he would tell almost no one. When we were talking about this time once, long ago, I asked him what the idea of home meant to him as a little child. He was quiet for a while, then he said "home is what you lose". For the rest of his life, those lessons remained. Love was survival. Loyalty was survival. He gave both prodigally. He demanded both absolutely.

Finally the relatives in America stopped wringing their hands and saying "*Gott wird helfen*" (God will help) and got to their local congressman instead. It was another lesson Erwin never forgot. A private addendum was hitched on to a bill in Washington that nobody cared about anyway. Visas materialized. They got out. Erwin was five years old when they reached New York. I have a photograph of them, taken on one of the centre dividers on Broadway: two loving, frail, exhausted people each clutching one hand of a tiny boy in a cap and jacket and flannel shorts who is laughing and trying to tear free so that he can go play in the traffic. That never changed either! He loved America, as George Will has said, almost immoderately. That was, of course, because the alternative was burned into his mind. Even friends and authors who knew Erwin's story did not, I think, grasp the degree to which the duality remained vivid in him at all times. German was his mother tongue. Growing up, he spoke English outside, but *Hausdeutsch* at home. His parents never saw Germany again. However, after a brilliant undergraduate career at Columbia, Erwin turned down a fellowship to Cambridge to go and do graduate work at Tübingen instead, and to make his peace – and theirs – with Germany. It was a time that influenced him profoundly in his thinking about the cultural and the political, and about power. But it too had its price. The night before his boat docked on the homeward journey to New York, his father died waiting for him. I think that some of the conversations they never had were played out in his publishing.

The European Erwin was always inside the American Erwin. Many of our great private running jokes and serial games were conducted in German – he was a lethal mimic, and wickedly funny in both languages. More importantly, however, English was certainly the language in which he construed his life, but whenever he dropped into German (he did this frequently, but, as in his childhood, when he was "home" – i.e. when we were on our own) it was always by way of ironic or philosophical commentary on the main action. I suspect that he talked to himself silently in German in public too. Many survivors of the Holocaust refuse ever to speak or read German again – it is true of Erwin's relatives who escaped from Germany to Palestine in the Thirties. For Erwin, the effect was also powerful, but it was different. German was both the language of danger and the language of closest family: it was also a mirror that held his past, a navigational device, an internal instrument that kept him on course and preserved his clearsightedness.

He mastered his early childhood intellectually, devoid of self-pity, but drawing from it an unsparing instinct for reality which he brought to bear in his manhood on political posturing and the delusionary games of society. When we got to know each other, I marvelled at his calm, and the rich use to which he had put his experience. It was not until we took our first trip together that I learned my lesson. We were in a huge airport, in a hurry, with the full complement of luggage/visas/passports/currency/check-in etc to accomplish. Seeing him started on one part, I switched without thinking into my own airport drill, raced off to deal with the rest, came back happily with it all done – to be met with utter, white-lipped, focused rage at my disappearance. Stricken, I suddenly saw the modern harmless chaos of a huge check-in hall dissolve into another chaos of men and women and bundles and lost children, and I was looking straight into 1942, face to face not only with his earlier self but also his parents' terror, overmastered by will and iron control and the rules of survival – stand still, be calm, stay quiet, do not ever move from my sight, STAY TOGETHER. It was like touching magma. His equilibrium reasserted itself over the next minutes, and it came to me that he was unaware of the full force of his own emotion. Nothing in real life that he went through – public attacks, struggles, dangers – ever evoked that response in him. To my shame, there were other occasions down the years when I forgot, when I wasn't paying enough attention, or I was tired, and my feet would start to take me through my own checklists on our journeys – and each time the same crack would suddenly yawn open for a dreadful moment. It taught me, as nothing could have, the price of his remarkable collectedness as a human being.

* * *

It was the upheavals of 1968 that decided his life, when politics and hysteria invaded the academy, and the academy – as so often in history – foundered. Columbia, where he was teaching English and Comparative Literature, began to eviscerate itself in a frenzy of self-righteous assaults on academic freedom. Appalling in itself, it was enough to save Erwin from becoming a professor, catapulting him into publishing instead. The complicated transactions between culture and politics, between moral philosophy, the power of ideas and the power of the state, were his field and his passion. Publishing in America has been increasingly self-reflexive in the last quarter-century, particularly in its mental geography; I think it is true to say that the only publisher who taught himself Washington, who was at home in real politics as he was on the campuses of the great universities, was Erwin. In part, that was because, inoculated by Camelot, he was immune to the general expectation (which was a Kennedy spore) that literary and academic intellectuals, as representatives of the national public mind whose constituency was the book, should share in, or ever wholly assume, the political power exercised by elected officials. Erwin remembered 1848's Parliament of Fools, and he thought this pure hubris. There could be signal exceptions – he revered Daniel Patrick Moynihan's combination of the two roles – but in general, no. Conversely, he knew in his bones that politics must not be all-pervasive, that indeed one of the first conditions of freedom is to set the limits to politics, and that books are one of the means by which we discover where that line gets drawn. The officious state found no champion in Erwin: he was considered the most formidably analytic and effective chairman of the Freedom to Read Committee of the Association of American Publishers that that organization has ever had.

Understanding Washington's political structure allowed him to touch contemporary life at many more points than New York publishing could offer. Finding his way to the one place where he could bring the centre of gravity of his working life as close as possible to the political centre of gravity of the nation, while remaining unseduced by it, and retaining the most generously broad and rich conception of what American nationhood should mean, was his life's journey. To find that way required not only intelligence and immense fortitude, but also a kind of native balance, an intuitive clarity of judgement that was rooted in his childhood. The enormous powers of absorption that he brought to an understanding of the world were complemented, as is well known, by a spirit of unyielding scepticism. His tenure in publishing can be expressed by the series of literary and intellectual and political temptations which he resisted. His interest in a lot of what went on in America was polemical. When he did indulge his own intellectual passion, it was always with a tempering judiciousness; he watched, he learned, as changes presented themselves he always *grew*. As a result, he never seriously repeated himself as a publisher, which was part of his extraordinary success. His famous image of the role of the publisher was as the gatekeeper of the culture. It is an image both more modest and more formidable than most publishers would conjure with, for an awful lot of publishing these days is distinguished by being indefatigably unimaginative, let alone serious.

But this most serious of publishers was also, and often, the least serious of men. He could talk annihilatingly; he overflowed with wit and surprises. While he always knew what was expected of him, he was as capable of ignoring it as doing it, and a vast amount of fun in life came from the former. He was the most enchanting and constant of companions who could, if he chose, enjoy anything, and could also seduce you into believing that you would enjoy it with him (provided you did what he wanted!). Since I'm not unequipped with the same will, we spent a lot of time ambushing each other for our greater entertainment. He was a magnificent tease, particularly when thwarted, and it was my fate to thwart him quite often in the exercise of one of the activities he loved most: namely, explaining things. Erwin was the emperor of explainers, which was mostly wonderful, but sometimes not, and on those occasions – particularly when the size of the thing being explained was in inverse ratio to the elaborations of its dissection, or when all I wanted to do was enjoy it – I was a recalcitrant explainee. You mutinied against Erwin at your peril. If I stifled his explanations, he invoked mine.

The field of revenge was often the opera, which he came to love for many reasons, not least its opportunities for strategic retaliation. As any opera fan knows, it is the art form most resistant to rational analysis – the last thing you want to have to do is explain it. We usually came flying into our seats with mere minutes to spare. Erwin, to my initial amazement (until I caught on) seemed uncharacteristically happy not to plunge right into reading the programme. The lights would go down, the orchestra would start up, and he would go straight into his Act One, Scene One recuperative doze, along with half the men in the audience. This was so entirely predictable that I failed initially to detect the danger. Things were well on their way, musically speaking, the first time he struck. His eyes opened, and there he was, raring to go. A glance at the stage and "Who's the dragon?" he whispered conversationally. I explained as quietly as I could. "Why's he . . . ?" I'd tell him that too. Faint stirrings in front of us. "But what happened before . . . ?" I'd have to tell him. Stirrings now becoming shiftings in the next row. There's a famous line in Ring Lardner that goes "'Shut up,' I explained." I tried it. No dice. By this time the shiftings had turned to glowerings. Have you ever tried to explain Act One of *The Magic Flute* in one desperate sentence? Let alone *Turandot*. Erwin would be in seventh heaven, while I silently battled to formulate thunderbolts in twelve words or less. The benchmark for this sort of thing is, of course, Anna Russell's glorious potted version of *The Ring*, in which she takes the entire sexual catastrophe underlying *Götterdämmerung,* and settles its hash with "She's the only woman Siegfried's ever met who isn't his aunt." Freud couldn't do better, and neither could I, but gradually, over time, I must have boiled down quite a lot of the operatic repertoire to similar sound-bites. Anything too demented would leave him shaking with laughter, which didn't endear us to our neighbours either, so I was sometimes a wreck by the first interval. After that the torment usually subsided, unless I had racked up a particularly bolshevik week, in which case the teasing went on all night.

Not that Erwin was a stranger to recreational bolshevism himself. To see him at weekends was to watch everything that he was most serious about during the week go into complete and exact reverse. He loved the country, couldn't wait to get there every Friday, was beatific with pleasure until Sunday evening – and his desire not to learn about it was total. Present Erwin with an idea, particularly a bad or sloppy one, and his drive to get to the root of it was unyielding. Present Erwin with a dandelion, or any vegetable foe, and he absolutely, truly, deeply, didn't want to know that it had a root at all. He would happily slice the tops off things in any of his rare bursts of gardening enthusiasm, then be outraged when they sprouted again. He longed for a garden. As I got it started, he was brainlessly happy. "Flowers!" he said triumphantly when they all came up in the spring. I got him a bench, the first of many around the place, so that he could sit out under a big crab-apple tree in the middle of it all as I crawled around doing what one does – but rather than discover what the flowers were up to, he preferred to read the labels. Show him ideological Armageddon, and he was on his horse; show him insect Armageddon, and he looked fascinated while advancing backwards indoors. Show him me and my mother, on her visits, when the really useful things got done and large holes dug, and he would be quite horrified, standing on the edge of whatever mayhem we were making and saying hopefully: "Aren't you tired? Shouldn't you stop now?"

Funniest of all, show Erwin an author at weekends and he went straight to sleep. Publishers, as we all know to our cost, are constantly on call. No matter how much came up to the country with us on Fridays in the editorial bags, more tended to spew itself out of the fax machine on Saturday mornings – usually from those authors we all know and love so well who, suddenly delivering a mere eight years late on their contracts, want you to be sure to read it by 5.30 latest. Every Saturday afternoon after lunch, Erwin would announce that he had to work now, round up a pile of paper, and retreat. The only interesting question then became not what happened next, but where it took place. I would slowly start to count down from ten under my breath, and usually before I hit zero the sound of a distant snore would work its way through to me. The great thing about wooden houses is that they act as sounding boards; by standing still and listening, I could work out where he was, and over time I learned to deduce from that what he was feeling, for he chose his napping spots by mood. There were sleep-in-my-big-desk-chair moods (good); sleep-in-the-library moods (reorganizing problems); sleep-on-various-guest-beds (restless); sleep-on-Carol's-study-sofa (territorial); and sleep-in-the-porch-hammock (absolutely terrific). If truth be told – and maybe authors should know it as a fact of life – publishers all over the world tend to spend their weekends in some form of this benign rebellion. The work gets done at other times, before dawn or after midnight; most of us colonize one end of the night or the other. But no matter what the venue, by 4.30 or 5.00 he'd reappear in a trail of books, to rights with the world and hopeful of tea. Tea meant cake and that – as any of you who spent time time with him knew – was one of his life's other passions. A walk, to Erwin, in the true old European fashion, meant the shortest, gentle distance between you and a good cake-and-coffee shop. Rain, which to the British as least is merely a condition in which other things happen, to Erwin was an absolute which triggered an immediate urge to summon up everything arkwise by twos and retreat into shelter with a comforting slice of something until it was over. One of the reasons that he took to Scotland like a homing pigeon was probably not just that Edinburgh spelled Adam Smith and David Hume and Locke and the whole Scottish Enlightenment which animated America's Founding fathers and featured so large in Erwin's moral philosophy – it spelled pudding too. Scots don't mess around much with new-fangled notions: they bake, and they make puddings as central heating, and they do it all to be eaten with absolute certainty at set times of day. Erwin thought this was heaven, and obliged with alacrity. My mother could even get him to go on walks that involved both hills *and* rain, sure in the knowledge that there would be scones and shortbread and chocolate cake at the end of the circuit. This even consoled him for the deprivation of another passion on these visits. To much of Edinburgh, politics is bad manners, and if you can't agree, you always talk about something else, like the weather. This to Erwin was absolutely unbelievable. He managed it only by keeping up his sugar count and arguing back at the evening newscasters on television when nobody else was in earshot.

But no matter how much he loved the interludes, what he loved most was being out there in the roar of the traffic. He respected ivory towers, but had no desire to live in one himself. Instead, he took his particular inner quiet – Erwin could *always* hear himself think – and went into the world to publish intellectual books with a speed, an accuracy of aim and a ferocious skill that left many more overtly commercial publishers winded and clutching their stamina. He had little patience for wilful stupidity, but endless kindness for stumbling learners until such time as they should know better. Sloppiness and facile thinking bored him to distraction – and when bored, he could be savage – but he was an extraordinary teacher, and his alumni loved him. The fact that he published the lists that he did and consistently earned one of the highest percentage profit margins of any trade publisher in America is a confounding rebuke to an entire school of self-excuse dedicated to the proposition that one cannot make money doing serious books, as if this very failure were proof of distinction. Erwin's publishing was formed in a more demanding school than that. He grew up in the culture of that great library at the bottom of the hill in Weimar, and it was his genius as a publisher to mobilize the market-place in order to ensure the widest possible expression and debate of those ideas and values that would guarantee the continuity of that enlightened culture in a vigorous democracy. It was a large ambition – but this was a large man.

Memorial address, Jerusalem Town Hall, 13 March 1995

ROBERT MORT

Burmese Journey
(*1990–96*)

1. Executive members of the National League for Democracy (NLD) in the gardens of Daw Aung San Suu Kyi's house – known as The Compound – in October 1996. Back row (*left to right*): U Tin Oo, Daw Aung San Suu Kyi, U Kyi Maung. Front row (*left to right*): U Nyant W ai, U Hla Pe, U Aung Shwe, U Than Tun, U Soe Myint. The NLD is regarded as the main opposition movement in Burma. Some of its members are ex-military men, with an understanding of how the present military junta operates.

2. Daw Aung San Suu Kyi seated on the steps of her Rangoon home with her aunts. In Burma, as in most of South-East Asia, women hold a pre-eminent position in the community. It is often said, not entirely in jest, that if one wants to do business in Burma, one speaks to the wives of the generals first.

3. These three men work in an ice factory using methods that have not changed since the nineteenth century. During the night the ice sets into hard, four-foot high blocks. At about four in the morning, they extract the ice from its casing and pack it onto trucks before distributing it to restaurants and markets around Rangoon.

4. With great humility and patience, these Christian nuns from the town of Bassein (Pathein) administer to the needs of the Catholic congregation, which includes feeding and educating the many orphans in Burma.

5. A group of Pa'o tribesmen who live in one of the many villages by the mountains that surround the town of Kalaw, where a garrison is permanently based. The Pa'o have to contend with the vagaries of the seasons as well as with the unwanted attentions of the military authorities who assume that because the P'ao produce so much tea they will not object to some of it being confiscated.

6. Danu tribesmen at the Konlon monastery, near Pindaya. A proud, industrious people, they are treated with contempt by the Burmese military authorities because of their agricultural success in the Shan State. Being subjected to forced labour and having their hard-earned money taken away has only strengthened their resolve.

7. A line of monks is prevented from continuing down Windermere Road to University Avenue. Not 500 metres from where this photograph was taken is the modest home of Daw Aung San Suu Kyi. Windermere Road has been closed since December 1996 and access is strictly controlled.

8. The Venerable Te Za Niya is one of the most important and influential monks in modern Burma. According to legend he was born blind, but having lived in a cave near a monastery for several years, he emerged with his eyesight intact. He is regarded as a saint, with healing powers and able to grant wishes.

9. Catholic priest Father Angelo arrived in Burma from a small village near Rome in the early 1930s. He has come under intense pressure from the military authorities for his lifelong protest against the maltreatment of the Christian Burmese.

10. U Myient Thein was the Chief Justice of Burma after the withdrawal of the British in 1948. He presided over the trial of the assassins of Burma's first president, Bogyoke Aung San, Aung San Suu Kyi's father. From 1962–68 he was one of eight high-profile political prisoners incarcerated by the present dictator General Ne Win. He died in 1994.

11. A rice miller at a factory on the outskirts of Bassein. Poverty continues in the rural areas in part because the best rice is taken by force to feed the army, as well as to prop up the crippled export economy.

12. A hospice for the mentally and physically handicapped outside Taunggyi, the capital of the Shan State. So calm was the atmosphere there that one could almost forget the madness beyond its walls.

13. A Buddhist monk in the town of Bassein (Pathein). Westerners are often surprised to see Buddhist monks smoking. They also wrestle, kickbox and play football, activities not obviously conducive to a life of contemplation.

14. A building site in Mandalay. It is not uncommon to see Burmese women performing heavy labour.

15. A boy carries on his head the shavings from a timber mill in Mandalay. Responsibility begins early in Burma, and children often have to work hard to help feed themselves and their families.

16. A boy from the Pa'o tribe. Although a primitive people, the P'ao are by no means naïve. They understand the modern world and are only too aware of the difficulties imposed on them by the military administration. Underlying their steely resolve is the conviction that they have the right to choose their own destiny.

POETRY

GESUALDO BUFALINO

To My River Íppari

Ancient Íppari, bone-white gravel-bed,
it was to you I confided my childhood,
the day's bad deeds I told you daily,
and as in your crevices snakes are sleeping
all my born days are waiting upon me
and under your runnel of water lies
embedded, the boulder of my heart.

Ancient Íppari, river of wind,
one of these summers I hope to see you.

How many sands of time have run
between your riverbanks of quick light,
how many the voiceless, treacherous tresses
dangling on windowsills that I forget not!
Ah blind-man's-buff of eyes and gauzes,
and ah, my darkling pot-of-basil,
the buried utterance of my love!

Ancient Íppari, O stricken river,
suffer me to hear your voice once more.

When I went away the roads were red
but along black roads shall I travel home;
the very last breath to pass my lips
from far far off will attempt your name.
O but to reach your estuary
of sluggish mudflats, doleful reeds,
where the measureless sea comes searching for you . . .

Ancient Íppari, gypsy river,
there where you die let us die together.

From Bitter Honey
Translated from the Italian by Patrick Creagh

ERNST JANDL

still life

I have laid my ball-pen which writes
red or blue on the matchbox.
That is thrilling as the fire engine
compared with the sheet of paper beside it.

I succeeded in that after trying
to have a magnificent thought.
(In the process a sheet of paper
died of a rash of ugly blue letters.)

to remember

Young and imprisoned
behind barbed wire
on a patch of clay
for a hundred men
at night, on his way
from tent to latrine
he began to remember
the visibility of stars.

Young and returned
to his home town,
on a wooden patch
for seven persons,
at night, asleep
between hunger and cold
he began to remember
the fruitfulness of far places.

asleep

He came across a tree.
He built his house beneath it.
Out of the tree he cut
himself a stick.
The stick became his lance.
The lance became his rifle.
The rifle became a gun.
The gun became a bomb.
The bomb hit his house and ripped
up the tree by the roots.
He stood there wondering
but he didn't wake up.

*Translated from the German by
Michael Hamburger*

Three Poems

Suspended

I dreamt
I dreamt I was wanted
I dreamt of the moon waning
I dreamt
of the tenderness I deserve
I dreamt of the lost word coming to me
of it hovering within me
and flowing forth as an alphabet of tears
I dreamt of myself
I dreamt of an ice-cold loneliness
I dreamt that space was pushing at the bounds of
    its firmament
and the candle flickering
on its wick
released a blue incandescence that refused to fade
I dreamt of myself
I dreamt of a strange child
turning his back on the world
suspended beneath the foliage of my voice I drank from
    the waters
around my body shadows gathered
embracing me

the house had begun
to wake him at night
he could hear a loathsome rasping sob
breaking off yet returning again
the walls

the grain of the wood on the floor
the chairs
they had all intruded upon him
in a feverish trance-like state
and shown him their wrists
made him conscious that he
had been wandering about in a murder
that he had been lodging in something that
had been knocked to the ground
and all the time lived under observation
enveloped in the gaze
of a lacerated and exhausted body

you never knew
that after you left I stayed
by the impression on the ground where you'd lain
I drew my hand
over the flattened grass and it was
as if I needed and cherished your absence more
than I needed and cherished you
it was as if nothing should be allowed to return
if you had come back
had you intruded
you would have halted the advance of my grief
and you will never know how tenderly and fiercely I
talked to your shadow on the grass
it was as if I was already mourning you
as if I was trying to come to terms with
what awaits us all
and that the price for our human insight
is a feeling of abandonment
which from the very first precludes and destroys
    any belief
in the permanence of love

All poems from The Lost Word
Translated from the Swedish by Tom Geddes

PAUL DURCAN

The Bloomsday Murders, 16 June 1997

*A nation? says Bloom. A nation is the same
people living in the same place.*
Ulysses, Bodley Head edition, 1960, p. 489

Not even you, Gerry Adams, deserve to be murdered:
You whose friends at noon murdered my two young men,
David Johnston and John Graham;
You who in the afternoon came on TV
In a bookshop on Bloomsday signing books,
Sporting a trendy union shirt.
(We vain authors do not wear collars and ties.)

Instead of the bleeding corpses of David and John
We were treated to you gazing up into camera
In bewilderment fibbing like a spoilt child:
"Their deaths diminish us all."
You with your paterfamilias beard,
Your Fidel Castro street-cred,
Your Parnell martyr-gaze,
Your Lincoln gravitas.
O Gerry Adams, you're a wicked boy.

Only on Sunday evening in sunlight
I met David and John up the park
Patrolling the young mums with prams.
"Going to write a poem about us, Paul?"
How they laughed! How they saluted!
How they turned their backs! Their silver spines!

Had I known it, would I have told them?
That for next Sunday's newspaper I'd compose a poem
How you, Gerry Adams, not caring to see,
Saw two angels in their silver spines shot.

I am a citizen of the nation of Ireland –
The same people living in the same place.
I hope the Protestants never leave our shores.
I am a Jew and my name is Bloom.
You, Gerry Adams, do not sign books in my name.
May God forgive me – lock, stock, and barrel.

ALEKSANDR PUSHKIN

The Bronze Horseman

INTRODUCTION

By the shore of the deserted waves
He stood, engrossed in lofty thoughts,
And peered into the distance. Before
Him the river surged in spate; a
Frail craft all on its own sped along.
Amidst the mossy, miry banks
Huts, here and there, appeared all black,
The shelter of some wretched Finn;
And forest, which had never known
The rays of the sun, shrouded in mist,
Was murmurous with sound.
And thus he mused:
From now on we shall threaten the Swede,
And here a city we shall found
To spite our overweening neighbour.
Here it has been ordained by nature
To cut a window into Europe,
And gain a firm foothold by the sea.
Ships of many flags will visit us,
Over seas they've never known
And we shall revel in abundance.

A hundred years have passed, and the
Young city, pearl and wonder of the North,
Has risen up in pride and splendour
From gloomy forests and marshy swamps,
Where once the Finnish fisherman,
Woeful progeny of nature,
Alone by low-lying shores would
Cast his ancient net into unknown
Waters and where now by busy banks

Vast shapely palaces and towers
Are crowded; and throngs of ships,
From the very ends of the earth,
Come hying to the wealthy quays;
The Neva is clad in granite;
Bridges hang above the waters;
Her islands now are covered
With gardens dark with greenery,
And ancient Moscow has grown dim
Before the younger capital,
Like a dowager enrobed in purple
Before a new-crowned empress.

I love thee, creation of Peter,
I love thy stern and graceful view,
The imperious flow of the Neva,
Thy embankments clothed in granite,
Thy wrought-iron gates in tracery,
The translucent dark, the moonless shine,
When in my chamber I am writing,
And without a lantern reading,
And the vast buildings all asleep
On the deserted streets are clear
And bright the spire of Admiralty,
And without allowing the murk of night
To mount into the gold of heaven,
One dawn hastens to suceed another,
With hardly half an hour of night.
I love the windless air and frost
Of thy cruel winter season,
The dash of sledges by the broad Neva,
The cheeks of girls, brighter than roses,
The brilliance, noise of balls and chatter,
And the hiss of foaming goblets,
And the blue flame of the punch
At the bachelors' hour of feasting.
I love the military liveliness
On the playing fields of Mars,
The monotonous magnificence
Of the mounted troops and infantry,
The tatters of those trophy banners,

Waving in their orderly array,
The lustre of those brazen helmets,
Shot through from side to side in battle.
I love thee, city filled with soldiers,
The smoke and thunder of thy forts,
When the northern empress bestows
A son upon the royal house,
Or Russia celebrates once again,
When victory is won against
The enemy, or breaking through its
Dark blue ice, the Neva bears it out
To sea, exalting at the scent of spring.

Show off your beauty, Peter's city,
And stand unshakeable, like Russia!
And may the conquered elements
Be completely reconciled to you;
May the Finnish waves quite forget
Their enmity and ancient feud,
And with futile hatred no more
Disturb the perpetual sleep of Peter!

It was a terrible moment,
Fresh is my recollection of it . . .
My friends for you I shall begin
My tale of it and narrative.
My story will be sorrowful.

PART ONE

Above gloom-laden Petrograd
November breathed its autumnal cold.
Swashing with its noisy waves
Against its graceful parapets
The river tossed itself about, like
A sick man in his uneasy bed.
Already it was late and dark;
The rain beat in fury at the window,
And the wind blew with a dismal whine.
At that moment from a visit

To his home came young Yevgeny . . .
From now on our hero we shall
Call by this name. On the ear
It falls most pleasantly; and indeed
Long since my pen to it has been inclined.
Of his surname we have no need,
Although in times of yore, maybe,
It was resplendent and in the writing
Of Karamzin rang out in the
Country's legends; but nowadays
It is forgotten by society
And gossip. Our hero lives in
Kolomna; somewhere is employed,
Avoids the famous and doesn't grieve
Either for the near and dear departed,
Or for old times, quite forgotten.

And thus, Yevgeny home returned,
Flung off his coat, undressed, lay down.
For long he could not fall asleep,
A prey to various reflections.
About what were his thoughts? That he
Was poor, that by his labour
For himself he must ensure both
Independence and his honour;
That God might grant him in addition
Both brains and money. That, indeed,
There are such idle lucky folk,
Lazybones of little wisdom,
Who lead a life of slothful ease!
That he was serving but two years;
His thoughts ran on: the ugly weather
Was not abating; the river
Was rising higher, the bridges
Already had been swung no doubt;
And he must be parted from
Parasha for some two days or three.
Here Yevgeny heaved a heartfelt sigh
And fell adreaming, like a poet:
Should he get married? Why ever not?
Naturally, it is a burden,

But after all, he's young and healthy,
Prepared to work, both night and day;
Somehow or other he would make
A humble, simple shelter, in which
He would set at ease Parasha.
Perhaps a year or two will pass –
I shall get some modest job – and
To Parasha I shall entrust
The running of our home and
Bringing up the kids . . .
And we shall live thus to the grave,
Both hand in hand we shall end our days,
And our grandchildren will bury us . . .

Thus it was he dreamed. And sorrowful
He was that night and wished that
The wind would howl less drearily,
That the rain would beat less angrily
Against the window . . .
    His sleepy eyes
At length he closed. And soon the mist
Of the stormy night grows clearer
And the pale break of day dawns . . .
A terrible day!
    All night the Neva
Strained towards the sea, against the storm,
But could not overcome their raging fury . . .
And no longer could it struggle . . .
By morning above its banks
Throngs of people jostled each other,
Revelling at the towering of
Spray and foam of waters now enraged.
But the strength of the winds from the gulf
Drove back the blocked Neva and it
Turned furious, tempestuous,
And plunged the islands into flood,
The weather grew more violent still,
The Neva swelled up and roared,
Bubbling like a cauldron, swirling,
And of a sudden, like a frenzied beast,
Flung itself upon the city.

All fled before it; round about
All was of a sudden empty – the waters
Flowed into subterranean cellars,
The canals surged against the gratings,
And Petropolis became afloat, deep
Like Triton, plunged waist-high in water.

A siege! Attack! Malicious waves,
Like thieves, climb through the windows. Boats
Ram and smash the glass panes with their poops;
Trays under soaking coverings,
Broken pieces of huts and beams and roofs,
The goods of thrifty traders,
The chattels of beggars, pale of face,
Bridges torn away by storm,
Coffins from the sodden churchyard
Float down the streets!

   The people
Perceive God's wrath and wait their doom.
Alas! All is lost: where will they find
Both food and shelter? In that grim year
The late Emperor still ruled with glory
Over Russia. Onto the balcony
He stepped, both saddened and bemused
And spake: "No Tsar can command
The elements of God." In thought he sat
And gazed and gazed with eyes of sorrow
At the terrible disaster.
Whole squares were turned to lakes,
Broad rivers flooded into streets.
The palace seemed a forlorn island.
The Tsar gave voice and from end to end,
By streets both near and far his generals
Set off on their perilous journeys,
Through raging waters to save the folk,
Struck dumb with fear, from drowning,
And secure their homes, their houses.

Then on Tsar Peter's square, just where
A new house towers on the corner,

And where, high above the entrance steps,
Two lions stand guard, with paws upraised,
As though alive, Yevgeny sits
Astride one of these beasts of marble,
Quite motionless, without his hat,
As pale as death, hands clasped across his breast.
He, poor man, was scared to death,
Not for himself. He did not hear
The greedy rollers rising high,
Splashing against the soles of his shoes,
And the rain which lashed against his face,
And the turbulent, howling wind,
Which snatched his hat from off his head.
His gaze was fixed in desperation
Upon one spot. The waves, like mountains,
Reared up from the indignant deep
In anger; and there the storm raged,
There shattered fragments floated by . . .
Oh God! Oh God! There alas! Right
By the waves almost at the very gulf
There hove in sight an unpainted fence,
A willow and an ancient little house;
There they were, widow and daughter,
His Parasha, his only dream . . .
Or maybe it was a vision? Or
All our life is but an idle dream,
Sent from Heaven to mock us here on earth?
And he, as though under some spell,
As though rooted to the marble,
Cannot dismount! Round about him
Lies water and nothing more!
On his impregnable high cliff,
With his back turned towards Yevgeny,
The idol sits, with hand outstretched,
Astride his steed of bronze,
Above the turbulent Neva.

PART TWO

But now, quite sated with destruction,
And wearied by her stormy
Insolence, the Neva stole back,
Admiring her own boisterousness,
And carelessly left all her booty.
Thus does some bandit burst into
A village with his gang of cutthroats,
Smashing and slaying, plundering
And pillaging to wails, gritting of teeth,
Violence, curses, howls, alarms! . . .
And loaded down with all their plunder,
The robbers, fearing hot pursuit,
Make their weary way in haste for home,
Dropping their plunder on the way.

Meantime the water had abated
And the roadway lay revealed and
My Yevgeny, with sinking heart,
Torn by hope and fear and longing,
Hastens to the chastened river.
But the waves topped up by triumph
In their victory yet seethed in fury,
As though a fire beneath them smouldered.
And still the waves were wrapped in foam
And heavy was the breathing of the river,
Like a horse come galloping from battle.
Yevgeny gazes and sees a boat;
He runs towards it, as if he's found them;
And hails a boatman without work.
And the ferryman, quite unconcerned,
For a mere ten copecks gladly
Carries him through that perilous sea.
For long the skilful boatman grappled
With the stormy waters; hour by hour
The ark with its daring crew seemed
About to sink beneath the wave-troughs –
But finally it reached the shore. The luckless
Yevgeny runs through familiar streets

To a familiar spot. He gazes
But knows it not. The sight was terrible!
A pile of rubble heaped before him;
Some buildings abandoned, some torn down,
Some houses all awry, some destroyed,
Others shifted by the waves; all around
Lie scattered bodies, like a battlefield.
Quite heedless, tormented to exhaustion,
Yevgeny runs headlong to the spot,
Where fate awaits him with unknown news,
As though enclosed in a sealed letter.
And now he runs through the town's outskirts,
And here's the gulf, the house is near . . .
But what is this? . . .
    He came to a halt,
Went back a little and returned.
He looks . . . he walks . . . he looks again.
Here's the spot where their house stood;
Here's the willow. The gates were here–
Torn down, it's clear. Where then's the house?
And filled with sombre suffering,
He keeps walking round and round the place,
Talks to himself aloud, and then
Suddenly strikes with his hand his face,
And bursts into a guffaw.
    The mist of night
Descends upon the frightened town;
But for long the townsmen could not sleep,
And amongst themselves debated
About the day just past.
    A ray of morn
Flashed forth through the pale and weary clouds
Above the peaceful capital
And already found no traces
Of yesterday's catastrophe;
Royal purple concealed the evil.
All had returned to former order.
Already through the empty streets,
With cold insensibility, people
Were wandering. Official folk,
Emerging from their refuge of the night,

Were on their way to work. The bold pedlar,
Not losing heart, was opening up
His cellar, plundered by the river,
Hoping to make good his heavy loss
Out of the pockets of his neighbour.
From courtyards boats were carried.
  Count
Khvostov, a poet beloved in Heaven,
Already sang in immortal verse
Of the disaster on the river banks.

But my poor, my poor Yevgeny . . .
Alas! His mind was quite confused and
Could not withstand those shocks of terror.
The riotous roar of the Neva
And the noise of wind resounded
In his ears. Hideous thoughts ran through
His mind. In silence he wandered on.
A kind of nightmare racked him.
A week passed by, a month went by,
But he did not return to his home.
As time ran out Yevgeny's landlord
Rented the deserted dwelling
To an impoverished poet.
Yevgeny still did not come to claim
His property. He was soon a stranger
To the world. The livelong day he tramped,
And on the quay he slept; he ate
Morsels proffered from a window.
His worn-out clothes were frayed and rotten.
Malicious boys threw stones at him.
Quite often he felt the coachman's
Lashes, because he never could
Make out the road; it seems he didn't
See it. He felt deafened by the noise
Of his inner agitation.
Thus he dragged out his miserable existence,
Neither wild beast, nor man was he,
Neither one, nor t'other, nor denizen
Of earth, nor a dead phantom . . .
  Once

He was sleeping on the river quay,
Summer days were turning towards autumn;
A stormy wind was blowing. Gloomy waves
Plashed against the quay, stirring foam
And breaking on the smooth steps,
Like a suppliant ignored
At a judge's door. Our poor Yevgeny
Woke up. It was dismal: rain pelted,
The wind howled in desolation,
And afar off in the dark of night
A watchman challenged it with cries . . .
Yevgeny leapt up; recalled the horror,
The horror of the past; hastened
To his feet; went off to wander,
And suddenly he stopped and began
Quietly to stare about him,
With a wild fear upon his face.
He found himself beneath the pillars
Of the great house. And on the steps,
With paws uplifted, as though alive,
Stood like sentinels two lions,
And in the dark of the Empyrean,
Above th'embattled crag sat
The idol upright, with his hand outstretched,
Astride upon his steed of bronze.
Yevgeny shuddered. His thoughts grew clear
In terror. He recognized the spot
Where the waters of the flood had gambolled
Where the rapacious waves had seethed,
Rebelliously, maliciously
About him, and the lions, the square
And him who, motionless, reared up
His brazen head amidst the gloom,
Him, whose fateful will had founded
The city beside the sea . . .
Terrible to behold in the encircling mist!
What thoughts were graven on his brow!
What strength lay hidden in his frame!
What the fire breathed in his steed!
Where are you galloping to, proud horse,
And where will you lower your hooves?

O mighty potentate, lord of fate!
Was it not thus above the void,
With your iron curb, held on high,
You made Russia rear upon her haunches?
About the base of the idol's statue
Poor mad Yevgeny circled round
And cast frenzied glances at the
Face of the lord of half the world.
His breast felt cramped. His forehead
Leaned against the chilly grating,
Over his eyes a mist came creeping,
A flame ran coursing through his heart,
His blood was seething. Gloom assailed him.
As he stood before the haughty idol,
With teeth clenched and hands clasped,
As though possessed by dark forces,
He whispered in a fit of hatred, trembling:
"All right, builder of these myriad marvels,
Just you wait! . . ." And of a sudden, headlong,
Took to his heels. It seemed to him
That the menacing emperor
In an instant, aflame with anger,
Slowly turned his visage to Yevgeny . . .
And through the empty square he ran
And heard behind him, like the rolling
Roar of thunder, the heavy ringing clonk
Of a galloping horse's hoof,
Reverberating on roadway.
And there, illumined by the pale moon,
With arm outstretched on high,
Headlong rode the Bronze Horseman
On his clanging, galloping steed;
And all night long our poor madman,
Whichever way he tried to turn,
Was pursued by the bronze Horseman,
Galloping, with heavy thump of hooves.

And from that time forward, whenever
It chanced he passed by the square,
Confusion was writ upon his face.
To his heart he would in haste

Clasp his hand, as though to ease
The torments of his soul, he would take off
His shabby cap, not raise his troubled gaze,
But pass by some other way. Near the
Shore a little island could be seen.
Sometimes a fisherman would land
With nets and a belated catch,
And prepare his meagre supper
Or of a Sunday some official in a boat
Would come to visit the desert isle.
Not a blade of grass grew there. The flood,
In its sport, had carried thither
The dilapidated ancient little house.
It remained above the water,
Like some black bush. Last spring some boat
Had carried it away. The house was empty
And all in ruins. On the threshold
They found my mad Yevgeny
And on the spot his poor cold body
They buried and left it to God's mercy.

Translated from the Russian by Peter Norman

STORIES

JAMES SALTER

My Lord You

There were crumpled napkins on the table, wine glasses still with dark remnant in them, coffee stains, and plates with bits of hardened Brie. Beyond the bluish windows the garden lay motionless beneath the birdsong of summer morning. Daylight had come. It had been a success except for one thing: Brennan.

They had sat around first, drinking in the twilight, and then gone inside. The kitchen had a large round table, fireplace, and shelves with ingredients of every kind. Deems was well known as a cook. So was his somewhat unknowable girlfriend, Irene, who had a mysterious smile though they never cooked together. That night it was Deem's turn. He served caviare, brought out in a white jar such as make-up comes in. It was Sevruga, to be eaten from small silver spoons. "The only way," Deems muttered in profile. He seldom looked at anyone. "Antique silver spoons," Ardis heard him mistakenly say in his low voice, as if it might not have been noticed. She was noticing everything, however. Though they had known Deems for a while, she and her husband had never been to the house. In the dining room, when they all went in to dinner, she took in the pictures, books, and shelves of objects including one of perfect, gleaming shells. It was foreign in a way, like anyone else's house, but half-familiar.

There'd been some mix-up about the seating that Irene tried vainly to adjust amid the conversation before the meal began. Outside, darkness had come, deep and green. The men were talking about camps they had gone to as boys in piny Maine and about Soros, the financier. Far more interesting was a comment Ardis heard Irene make, in what context she did not know. "I think there's such a thing as sleeping with one man too many."

"Did you say 'such a thing' or 'no such thing'?" she heard herself ask.

Irene merely smiled. I must ask her later, Ardis thought. The food was excellent. There was cold soup, duck, and a salad of young vegetables. The coffee had been served and Ardis was distractedly play-ing with melted wax from the candles when a voice burst out loudly behind her, "I'm late. Who's this? Are these the beautiful people?"

It was a drunken man in a jacket and dirty white trousers with blood on them, which had come from nicking his lip while shaving two hours before. His hair was damp, his face arrogant. It was the face of a Regency duke, intimidating, spoiled. The irrational flickered from him. "Do you have anything to drink here? What is this, wine? Very sorry I'm late. I've just had seven cognacs and said goodbye to my wife. Deems, you know what that's like. You're my only friend, do you know that? The only one."

"There's some dinner in there, if you like," Deems said, gesturing towards the kitchen.

"No dinner. I've had dinner. I'll just have something to drink. Deems, you're my friend, but I'll tell you something, you'll become my enemy. You know what Oscar Wilde said – my favourite writer, my favourite in all the world. Anyone can choose his friends, but only the wise man can choose his enemies." He stared intently at Deems. It was like the grip of a madman, a kind of fury. His mouth had an expression of determination. When he went into the kitchen they could hear him among the bottles. He returned with a dangerous glassful and looked around boldly.

"Where is Beatrice?" Deems asked.

"Who?"

"Beatrice, your wife."

"Gone," Brennan said. He searched for a chair.

"To visit her father?" Irene asked.

"What makes you think that?" Brennan said menacingly. To Ardis's alarm he sat down next to her.

"He's been in the hospital, hasn't he?"

"Who knows where he's been," Brennan said darkly. "He's a swine. Lucre, gain. He's a slum owner, a criminal. I would hang him myself. In the fashion of Gomez, the dictator, whose daughters are probably wealthy women."

He discovered Ardis and said to her, as if imitating someone, perhaps someone he assumed her to be, "'N 'at funny? 'N 'at wonderful?"

To her relief he turned away. "I'm their only hope," he said to Irene. "I'm living on their money and it's ruinous, the end of me." He held out his glass and asked mildly, "Can I have just a tiny bit of ice? I adore my wife." To Ardis he confided, "Do you know how we met? Unimaginable. She was walking by on the beach. I was unprepared. I saw the ventral, then the dorsal, I imagined the rest. Bang! We came together like planets, Endless fornication. Sometimes I just lie silent and observe her. *The black panther lies under his rose-tree,*" he recited. *"J'ai eu pitié des autres . . . "*

He stared at her.

"What is that?" she asked tentatively.

". . . *but that the child walk in peace in her basilica,*" he intoned.

"Is it Wilde?"

"You can't guess? Pound. The sole genius of the century. No. not the sole. I am another: a drunk, a failure, and a great genius. Who are you?" he said. "Another little housewife?"

She felt the blood leave her face and stood to busy herself clearing the table. His hand was on her arm. "Don't go. I know who you are, another priceless woman meant to languish. Beautiful figure," he said as she managed to free herself, "pretty shoes."

As she carried come plates into the kitchen she could hear him saying, "Don't go to many of these parties. Not invited."

"Can't imagine why," someone murmured.

"But Deems is my friend, my very closest friend."

"Who is he?" Ardis asked Irene in the kitchen.

"Oh, he's a poet. He's married to a Venezuelan woman and she runs off. He's not always this bad."

They had quietened him down in the other room. Ardis could see her husband nervously pushing his glasses up on his nose with one finger. Deems, in a polo shirt and with rumpled hair, was trying to guide Brennan towards the back door. Brennan kept stopping to talk. For a moment he would seem reformed. "I want to tell you something," he said. "I went past the school, the one on the street there. There was a poster. The First Annual Miss Fuck Contest. I'm serious. This is a fact."

"No, no," Deems said.

"It's been held, I don't know when. Question is, are they coming to their senses finally or losing them? A tiny bit more," he begged; his glass was empty. His mind doubled back, "Seriously, what do you think of that?"

In the light of the kitchen he seemed merely dishevelled, like a journalist who has been working hard all night. The unsettling thing was the absence of reason in him, his glare. One nostril was smaller than the other. He was used to being ungovernable. Ardis hoped he would not notice her again. His forehead had two gleaming places, like nascent horns. Were men drawn to you when they knew they were frightening you?

She could feel his eyes. There was silence. She could feel him standing there like a menacing beggar. "What are you, another bourgeois? I know I've been drinking. Come and have dinner," he said. "I've ordered something wonderful for us. Vichyssoise. Lobster. S. G. Always on the menu like that, *selon grosseur*." He was talking in an easy way, as if they were in the casino together, chips piled high before them, as if it were a shrewd discussion of what to bet on and her breasts in the dark T-shirt were a thing of indifference to him. He calmly reached out and touched one. "I have money," he said. His hand remained where it was, cupping her. She was too stunned to move. "Do you want me to do more of that?"

"No," she managed to say.

His hand slipped down to her hip. Deems had taken an arm and was drawing him away. "Ssh," Brennan whispered to her, "don't say anything. The two of us. Like an oar going into the water, gliding."

"We have to go," Deems insisted.

"What are you doing? Is this another of your ruses?" Brennan cried. "Deems, I shall end up destroying you yet!" As he was herded to the door, he continued. Deems was the only man he didn't loathe, he said. He wanted them all to come to his house, he had everything. He had a phonograph, whisky! He had a gold watch!

At last he was outside. He walked unsteadily across the finely cut grass and got into his car, the side of which was dented in. He backed away in great lurches.

"He's headed for Cato's," Deems guessed. "I ought to call and warn them."

"They won't serve him. He owes them money," Irene said.

"Who told you that?"

"The bartender. Are you all right?" she asked Ardis.

"Yes. Is he actually married?"

"He's been married three or four times," Deems said.

Later they started dancing, some of the women together. Irene pulled Deems on to the floor. He came unresisting. He danced quite well. She was moving her arms sinuously and singing. "Very nice," he said. "Have you ever entertained?"

She smiled at him. "I do my best," she said.

At the end she put her hand on Ardis's arm and said again, "I'm so embarrassed at what happened."

"It was nothing. I'm all right."

"I should have taken him and thrown him out," her husband said on the way home. "Ezra Pound. Do you know about Ezra Pound?"

"No."

"He was traitor. He broadcast for the enemy during the war. They should have shot him."

"What happened to him?"

"They gave him a poetry prize."

They were going down a long empty stretch where on a corner, half hidden in trees, a small house stood, the gypsy house. Ardis thought of it as, a simple house with a water pump in the yard and occasionally in the daytime a girl in blue shorts, very brief, and high heels, hanging clothes on a line. Tonight there was a light on in the window. One light near the sea. She was driving with Warren and he was talking. "The best thing is to just forget about tonight."

"Yes," she said. "It was nothing."

Brennan went through a fence on Hull Lane and up on to somebody's lawn at about 2:00 that morning. He had missed the curve where the road bent left, probably because his headlights weren't on, the police thought.

She took the book and went over to a window that looked out on the garden behind the library. She read a bit of one thing or another and came to a poem some lines of which had been underlined, with pencilled notes in the margin. It was "The River-Merchant's Wife", she had never heard of it. Outside, the summer burned, white as chalk.

> *At fourteen I married My Lord you,* she read.
> *I never laughed, being bashful . . . .*

There were three old men, one of them almost blind, it appeared, reading newspapers in the cold room. The thick glasses of the nearly blind man cast white moons onto his cheeks.

> *The leaves fall early this autumn, in wind.*
> *The paired butterflies are already yellow with August*
> *Over the grass in the West garden;*
> *They hurt me. I grow older.*

She had read poems and perhaps marked them like this, but that was in school. Of the things she had been taught she remembered only a few. There had been one My Lord though she did not marry him. She'd been twenty-one, her first year in the city. She remembered the building of dark brown brick on Fifty-eighth Street, the afternoons with their slitted light, her clothes in a chair or fallen to the floor, and the damp, mindless repetition, to it, or him, or who knew what: oh, God, oh, God, oh, God. The traffic outside so faint, so far away . . .

She'd called him several times over the years, believing that love never died, dreaming foolishly of seeing him again, of his returning, in the way of old songs. To hurry, to almost run down the noontime street again, the sound of her heels on the sidewalk. To see the door of the apartment open . . .

> *If you are coming down the narrows of the river Kiang,*
> *Please let me know beforehand,*
> *And I will come out to meet you*
>   *As far as Chô-fu-Sa*

There she sat by the window with her young face that had a weariness in it, a slight distaste for things, even, one might imagine, for oneself. After a while she went to the desk. "Do you happen to have anything by Michael Brennan?" she asked.

"Michael Brennan," the woman said. "We've had them, but he takes them away because unworthy people read them, he says. I don't think there're any now. Perhaps when he comes back from the city."

"He lives in the city?"

"He lives just down the road. We had all of his books at one time. Do you know him?"

She would have liked to ask more but she shook her head. "No," she said. "I've just heard the name."

"He's a poet," the woman said.

On the beach she sat by herself. It was nearly empty. In her bathing suit she lay back with the sun on her face and knees. It was hot and the sea calm. She preferred to lie up by the dunes with the waves bursting, to listen while they crashed like the final chords of a symphony except they went on and on. There was nothing as fine as that.

She came out of the ocean and dried herself like the gypsy girl, ankles caked with sand. She could feel the sun burnishing her shoulders. Hair wet, deep in the emptiness of days, she walked her bicycle up to the road, the dirt velvety beneath her feet.

She did not go home the usual way. There little traffic. The noon was bottle-green, large houses among the trees and wide farmland, like a memory, behind. She knew the house and saw it far off, her heart beating strangely. When she stopped, it was casually, with the bike tilting to one side and she half-seated on it as if taking a rest. How beautiful a lone woman is, in a white summer shirt and bare legs. Pretending to adjust the bicycle's chain she looked at the house, its tall windows, water stains high on the roof. There was a gardener's shed, abandoned, saplings growing in the path that led to it. The long driveway, the sea porch, everything was empty.

Walking slowly, aware of how brazen she was, she went towards the house. Her urge was to look in the windows, no more than that. Still, despite the silence, the complete stillness, it was forbidden.

She walked farther. Suddenly something rose from the side porch. She was unable to utter a sound or move.

It was a huge dog, a dog higher than her waist, that came towards her, yellow-eyed. She had always been afraid of dogs, the Alsatian that had unexpectedly turned on her college room-mate and torn off a piece of her scalp. The size of this one, its lowered head and slow, deliberate stride.

Do not show fear, she knew that. Carefully she moved the bicycle so that it was between them. The dog stopped a few feet away, its eyes directly on her, the sun along its back. She did not know what to expect, a sudden short rush. "Good boy," she said. It was all she could think of. "Good boy."

Moving cautiously, she began wheeling the bicycle towards the road, turning her head away slightly so as to appear unworried. Her legs felt naked, the bare calves. They would be ripped open as if by a scythe. The dog was following her, its shoulders moving smoothly, like a kind of machine. Somehow finding the courage, she tried to ride. The front wheel wavered. The dog, high as the handlebars, came nearer. "No," she cried. "No!" After a moment or two, obediently, he slowed or veered off. He was gone.

She rode as if freed, as if flying through blocks of sunlight and high, solemn tunnels of trees. And then she saw him again. He was following – not exactly following, since he was some distance ahead. He seemed to float along in the fields, which were burning in the midday sun, on fire. She turned onto her own road. There he came. He fell in behind her. She could hear the clatter of his nails like falling stones. She looked back. He was trotting awkwardly, like a big man running in the rain. A line of spittle trailed from his jaw. When she reached her house he had disappeared.

That night in a cotton robe she was preparing for bed, cleaning her face, the bathroom door ajar. She brushed her hair with many rapid strokes. "Tired"? her husband asked as she emerged. It was his way of introducing the subject.

"No," she said.

So there they were in the summer night with the far-off sound of the sea. Among the things her husband admired that Ardis possessed was extraordinary skin, luminous and smooth, a skin so pure that to touch it would make one tremble. "Wait," she whispered, "not so fast."

Afterwards he lay back without a word, already falling into deepest sleep, much too soon. She touched his shoulder. She heard something outside the window.

"Did you hear that?"

"No, what?" he said drowsily.

She waited. There was nothing. It had seemed faint, like a sigh.

The next morning she said, "Oh!" There, just beneath the trees, the dog lay. She could see his ears – they were small ears dashed with white. "What is it?" her husband asked.

"Nothing," she said. "A dog. It followed me yesterday."

"From where?" he said, coming to see.

"Down the road. I think it might be that man's. Brennan's."

"Brennan?"

"I passed his house," she said, "and afterwards it was following me."

"What were you doing at Brennan's?"

"Nothing. I was passing. He's not even there."

"What do you mean, he's not there?"

"I don't know." She felt confused. "Somebody said that."

He went to the door and opened it. The dog – it was a deerhound – had been lying with its forelegs stretched out in front like a sphinx, its haunches round and high. Awkwardly it rose and after a moment moved, reluctantly it seemed, wandering slowly across the fields, never looking back.

In the evening they went to a party on Mecox Road. Far out towards Montauk, winds were sweeping the coast. The waves exploded in clouds of spray. Ardis was talking to a woman not much older than herself, whose husband had just died of a brain tumour at the age of forty. He had diagnosed it himself, the woman said. He'd been sitting in a theatre when he suddenly realized he couldn't see the wall just to his right. At the funeral, she said, there had been two women she did not recognize and who did not come to the reception afterwards. "Of course, he was a surgeon," she said, "and they're drawn to surgeons like flies. But I never suspected. I suppose I'm the world's greatest fool."

The trees streamed past in the dark as they drove home. Their house rose in the brilliant headlights. She thought she had caught sight of

something and, oddly, found herself hoping that he had not. She was
nervous as they walked across the grass. The stars were numberless.
They would open the door and go inside, where all was familiar, even
serene. After a while they would prepare for bed while the wind
seized the corners of the house and the dark leaves thrashed each
other. They would turn out the lights. All that was outside would be
left in wildness, in the glory of the wind.

It was true. He was there. He was lying on his side, his whitish coat
ruffled. In the morning light she approached slowly. When he raised
his head his eyes were hazel and gold. He was not that young, she
saw, but his power was that he was unbowed. She spoke in a natural
voice. "Come," she said. She took a few steps. At first he did not
move. She glanced back again. He was following.

It was still early. As they reached the road a car passed, drab and
sun-faded. A girl was in the back seat, head fallen wearily. Being
driven home, Ardis thought, after the exhausting night. She felt an
inexplicable envy.

It was warm but the true heat had not risen. Several times she
waited while he drank from puddles at the edge of the road, standing
in them as he did, his large, wet toenails gleaming like ivory.

Suddenly from a porch rushed another dog, barking fiercely. The
great hound turned, teeth bared white. She held her breath, afraid of
the sight of one of them limp and bleeding, but violent as it sounded
they kept a distance between them. After a few snaps it was over. He
came along less steadily, strands of wet hair near his mouth.

At the house he went on to the porch and stood waiting. It was
plain he wanted to go inside. He had returned. He must be starving,
she thought. She looked around to see if there was anyone in sight.
A chair she had not noticed before was out on the grass, but the
house was still as ever, not even the curtains breathing. With a hand
that seemed not even hers she tried the door. It was unlocked.

The hallway was dim. Beyond it was a living room in disorder,
couch cushions rumpled, glasses on the tables, papers, shoes. In the
dining room there were piles of books. It was the house of an artist,
abundance, disregard.

There was a large desk in the bedroom, in the middle of which,
among paper clips and letters, a space had been cleared. Here were
sheets of paper written in an almost illegible hand, incomplete lines
and words that omitted certain vowels. *Deth of fathr*, she read, then
indecipherable things and something that seemed to be *carrges sent*

empty, and at the bottom, set apart, two words, *anew, anew.* In a different hand was the page of a letter, *I deeply love you. I admire you. I love you and admire you.* She could not read any more. She was too uneasy. There were things she did not want to know. In a hammered silver frame was the photograph of a woman, face darkened by shadow, leaning against a wall, the unseen white of a villa somewhere behind. Through the slatted blinds one could hear the soft clack of palm fronds, the birds high above, in the villa where he had found her, where her youth had been bold as a declaration of war. No, that was not it. He had met her on a beach, they had gone to the villa. What is powerful is a glimpse of truer life. She read the slanting inscription in Spanish, *Tus besos me destierran.* She put the picture down. A photograph was sacrosanct, you were excluded from it, always. So that was the wife. *Tus besos,* your kisses.

She wandered, nearly dreaming, into the large bathroom that looked out on the garden. As she entered, her heart almost stopped – she caught sight of someone in the mirror. It took a second before she realized it was herself and as she looked more closely, a not wholly recognizable, even an illicit self, in soft, grainy light. She understood then, she accepted the fate that meant she was to be found here, that Brennan would be returning and discover her, having stopped for the mail or bread. Out of nowhere she would hear the paralyzing sound of footsteps or a car. Still, she continued to look at herself. She was in the house of the poet, the demon. She had entered forbidden rooms. *Tus besos . . .* the words had not died. At that moment the dog came to the door, stood there, and then fell to the floor, his knowing eyes on her, like an intimate friend. She turned to him. All she had never done seemed at hand.

Deliberately, without thinking, she began to remove her clothes. She went no further than the waist. She was dazzled by what she was doing. There in the silence with the sunlight outside she stood slender and half-naked, the missing image of herself, of all women. The dog's eyes were raised to her as if in reverence. He was unbetraying, a companion like no other. She remembered certain figures ahead of her at school. Kit Vining, Nan Boudreau. Legendary faces and reputations. She had longed to be like them but never seemed to have the chance. She leaned forward to stroke the beautiful head. "You're a big fellow." The words seemed authentic, more authentic than anything she had said for a long time." A very big fellow." His long tail stirred and with faint sound brushed the floor. She kneeled and stroked his head again and again.

There was the crack of gravel beneath the tyres of a car. It brought her abruptly to her senses. Hurriedly, almost in panic, she dressed and made her way to the kitchen. She would run along the porch if necessary and then from tree to tree. She opened the door and listened. Nothing. As she was going quickly down the back steps, by the side of the house she saw her husband. "Thank God," she said.

They approached each other slowly. He glanced at the house.

"I brought the car. Is anyone here?"

There was a moment's pause.

"No, no one." She felt her face stiffen, as if she were telling a lie.

"What were you doing?" he asked.

"I was in the kitchen," she said. "I was trying to find something to feed him."

"Did you find it?"

"Yes, no," she said.

He stood looking at her and finally said, "Let's go."

As they backed out, she caught sight of the dog just lying down in the shade, sprawled, disconsolate. She felt the nakedness beneath her clothes, the satisfaction. They turned onto the road.

"Somebody's got to feed him," she said as they drove. She was looking out at the houses and fields. Warren said nothing. He was driving faster. She turned back to look. For a moment she thought she saw him following, far behind.

Late that day she went shopping and came home about 5:00. The wind, which had arisen anew, blew the door shut with a bang. "Warren?"

"Did you see him?" he said.

"Yes."

He had come back. He was out there where the land went up slightly. "I'm going to call the animal shelter," she said.

"They won't do anything. He's not a stray."

"I can't stand it. I'm calling someone," she said.

"Why don't you call the police? Maybe they'll shoot him."

"Why don't you do it?" she said coldly. "Borrow someone's gun. He's driving me crazy."

It remained light until past 9:00, and in the last of it, with the clouds a deeper blue than the sky, she went out quietly, far across the grass. Her husband watched from the window. She was carrying a white bowl. She could see him very clearly, the grey of his muzzle there in the muted grass and when she was close the clear, tan eyes. In an almost ceremonial way she knelt down. The wind was blowing her hair. She seemed almost a mad person there in the fading light. "Here. Drink something," she said. His gaze, somehow reproachful, drifted away. He was like a fugitive sleeping on his coat. His eyes were nearly closed.

My life has meant nothing, she thought. She wanted above all else not to confess that.

They ate dinner in silence. Her husband did not look at her. Her face annoyed him, he did not know why. She could be good-looking but there were times when she was not. Her face was like a series of photographs, some of which ought to have been thrown away. Tonight it was like that.

"The sea broke through into Sag Pond today," she said dully.

"Did it?"

"They thought some little girl had drowned. The fire trucks were there. It turned out she had just strayed off." After a pause. "We have to do something," she said.

"Whatever happens is going to happen," he told her.

"This is different," she said. She suddenly left the room. She felt close to tears.

Her husband's business was essentially one of giving advice. He had a life that served other lives, helped them come to agreements, end marriages, defend themselves against former friends. He was accomplished at it. Its language and techniques were part of him. He lived amid disturbance and self-interest but always protected from it. In his files were letters, memorandums, secrets of careers. One thing he had seen: how near men could be to disaster no matter how secure they seemed. He had seen events turn, one ruinous thing following another. It could happen without warning. Sometimes they were able to save themselves, but there was a point at which they could not. He sometimes wondered about himself – when the blow came and the beams began to give and come apart, what would happen? She was calling Brennan's house again. There was never an answer.

During the night the wind blew itself out. In the morning at first light, Warren could feel the stillness. He lay in bed without moving. His wife's back was turned towards him. He could feel her denial.

He rose and went to the window. The dog was there, he could see its shape. He knew little of animals and nothing of nature but he could tell what had happened. It was lying in a different way.

"What is it?" she asked. She had come up beside him. It seemed she stood there for a long time. "He's dead." She started for the door. He held her by the arm.

"Let me go," she said.

"Ardis . . ."

She began to weep. "Let me go."

"Leave him alone!" he called after her. "Let him be!"

She ran quickly across the grass in her nightgown. The ground was wet. As she came closer she paused to calm herself, to find courage. She regretted only one thing – she had not said goodbye.

She took a step or two forward. She could sense the heavy, limp weight of him, a weight that would disperse, become something else, the sinews fading, the bones becoming light. She longed to do what she had never done, embrace him. At that moment he raised his head.

"Warren!" she cried, turning towards the house. "Warren!"

As if the shouts distressed him, the dog was rising to his feet. He moved wearily off. Hands pressed to her mouth she stared at the place where he had been, where the grass was flattened slightly. All night again. Again all night. When she looked, he was some distance off. She ran after him. Warren could see her. She seemed free. She seemed like another woman, a younger woman, the kind one saw in the dusty fields by the sea, in a bikini, stealing potatoes in bare feet.

She did not see him again. She went many times past the house, occasionally seeing Brennan's car there, but never a sign of the dog, or along the road or off in the fields.

One night in Cato's at the end of August, she saw Brennan himself at the bar. His arm was in a sling, from what sort of accident she could not guess. He was talking intently to the bartender, the same fierce eloquence, and though the restaurant was crowded, the stools next to him were empty. He was alone. The dog was not outside, nor in his car, nor part of his life any more – gone, lost, living elsewhere, his name perhaps to be written in a line someday though in truth he was forgotten, but not by her.

LUDMILLA ULITSKAYA

Genele – The "Handbag" Lady

By temperament aunty Genele was a public servant but somehow life refused to present her with major challenges. So, for want of anything better, she busied herself with relatively minor problems, in particular, the neatness of the rather spacious communal gardens of the court-yard's north-west corner. In fact she was quite capable of looking after the entire square but she preferred to take on a smaller section where perfection was more easily attainable. Aunty Genele simply loved perfection.

No sooner had the slush begun to dry, than dragging her boots through the puddles camouflaged by the remains of the winter rubbish, she would plod over to her observation post, an unpainted bench near a ramshackle fountain where she would sit herself down to await transgressors.

The pre-anniversary [Mayday] spring-cleaning had not yet begun and the paths were littered with faded sweet wrappers, swollen fag-ends and small artefacts left over from hasty, vagrant love-making.

It was still the dead season; visitors rarely ventured into the square but Genele would start her vigil early, taking up her position a day or two before the arrival of the first visitor.

The first to arrive this time was a man with a briefcase who sat down nearby, lit a cigarette and threw the match over his shoulder. Genele's whole being quickened, like a hunting hound, and, smiling sweetly, she fired her first shot.

"Citizen, the refuse bin is only two steps away, is it really too much to ask?"

The citizen, his eyes preoccupied and distracted, threw her a baffled look.

"Sorry, did you say something?"

"Yes," Genele rapped out officiously, "the refuse bin is two steps away and you have to go and throw your match straight onto the ground!"

He unexpectedly burst out laughing, stood up, picked up the

match, which gleamed white among the darkened grey rubbish, and threw it into the bin.

The old lady turned away in disappointment: this prey was not the real thing at all! The man finished his cigarette and left after properly disposing of his fag-end.

"And so you should!" she muttered scornfully in his wake, fully convinced that, without her supervision, the next match would be sure to miss the bin.

Next, three puffed-up, bedraggled pigeons arrived on the scene. They looked hungover. Genele pulled out of her shopping-bag a jar of soaked bread contributed by her neighbours – she herself never had any bread left over. Kneading the bread, she divided it evenly into three portions. But the stupid birds had no concept of fair play or perhaps they were inveterate collectivists. Jostling each other, all three of them threw themselves onto the nearest portion and greedily pecked it up, without even noticing the other two.

Genele tried to attract their attention to the rest of the food but, as always, failed to make herself understood.

At last lunch time arrived and as a sickly sun peeped out, she dragged herself home on her crooked, bony little legs. She was in a splendid mood. The interim between the seasons had ended and she felt a certain spiritual uplift. Besides, after lunch was the time assigned to the fulfilment of her principal duty in life – the visit to relatives. She would visit them by rota: sister Marusya, niece Vera, niece Galya, grandniece Tamara and nephew Victor represented one cycle; the other was headed by brother Naum who lived with his unmarried and somewhat "not all there" son, Grigory. Then followed nephew Aleksandr and niece Raya. There were also two childless sisters, Motya and Nyusya, and the circuit of relatives was completed by Anna Markovna, a rather distant relation but in Genele's eyes worthy of visits.

As there was a considerable number of relations, Genele would usually turn up at the same house no more than once a month. This arrangement satisfied everyone as they realized that she fulfilled the function of a kind of cement, preventing the family's complete disintegration.

Small, neatly dressed, with white curly hair, she would enter the house and make a statement which at first sounded like a compliment, something like:

"Marusya, last time you looked so wonderful . . ."

She was a genius in this department; she would never say any unpleasant word to anyone, nothing but compliments, but somehow they were always slightly double-edged . . .

"Oh, if only you knew what a son Shura has! A star pupil, nothing but A's! But of course standards in schools these days aren't what they used to be, are they!"

"Oh Galya, what a tasty pie! If only you knew the cabbage pie Raya bakes – simply scrumptious," she would exclaim, finishing the pie Galya had baked.

She would enter the house laden with small shopping bags, with her left elbow firmly clasping to her side a large handbag from which she was never separated. The selfsame handbag that earned her the nickname "Handbag Lady".

This handbag had been brought over from Switzerland before the First World War by a well-to-do aunt who studied dentistry in Zurich. Originally it was dark brown with a rich lilac nuance and a silky sheen. With the passing years it started to darken, turned almost black, and then, together with its mistress, began to go grey and gradually acquired an indescribably exquisite yellowish-grey tinge. The handbag had come into and gone out of fashion several times. On the back of it was a deep seam, sewn by the meticulous hand of its mistress – once in 1944 the bag had undergone a bandit's knifing and had suffered the consequences. On its lock coiled the limp, plant-like lines of a moribund style and the skinny, knotted fingers of its mistress seemed to interweave with this motif. The worn-out skin of both bag and mistress could have originated from one and the same extinct beast.

Genele never opened her precious handbag in the presence of others but from her numerous shopping bags she would produce a home-made offering – cabbage Provençal, which she had prepared according to some preposterous recipe comprising seventeen ingredients among which some rather odd things were to be found: parsley root, raisins and lemon zest.

Some of the relatives considered this illustrious cabbage to be utter poison but nobody would have dreamt of refusing the offering which was usually presented in a mysterious and emotional manner.

Everybody knew that Genele's pension consisted of a ludicrously meagre sum but she never complained of being short of money. On the contrary, she behaved with the dignity of a wealthy relative. She coached her nieces and subsequently their daughters in the fine points of domestic lore, regarding herself a pundit in this lofty genre.

"One has to buy in small quantities but the very best," she would enlighten her foolish nieces. On one occasion she gave Galya, her favourite, an unforgettable lesson on how to shop at the market. It was on a Sunday, towards the end of trading, approximately one hour before closure, the Genele took her to the Tishinsky market.

"First of all you have to go around and give everything the once over. Make a mental note of who has the best produce. On your second round you already know where the best stuff is and this time it's the price that counts. And then, on your third round you buy, this way you will never go wrong."

And Genele, her eyes blazing, flew around the market, sizing things ups, disparaging the goods, enthusing over the weather, heartily greeting a stout Ukrainian woman who was rushing to catch a train; she even found the time to call a gloomy, long-faced Oriental fellow "crazy out of his head!" She gesticulated; fingered the parsley; in passing explained to Galya that one always has to choose carrots with rounded tips; squeezed a tired-looking aubergine; sniffed with her sharp nose the "peempled" – as she called them – gherkins; found fault with the pickling brine; rubbed between her thumb and index finger a drop of honey and whispered to her niece:

"If the honey's pure it's completely absorbed without a trace, if there's a trace then it's not pure!"

From a simple old granny from the Moscow district she bought, for half the already reduced price, carrots, beetroot and two parsnips. Into the bargain she managed to get the last twisted courgette which she thrust into her bag, deeming it a well-deserved commission on the purchases paid for by Galya.

"I need 150 grams," she demanded from a saleswoman but the latter, unaccustomed to dealing in such small quantities, tossed from her knife on to the scales a thin slice of cottage cheese which weighed almost 300.

"Why so much? I need 150! Surely you can give me as much as I need and no more?" she insisted. But the phlegmatic saleswoman was already wrapping the cottage cheese in white paper and she growled:

"What do I care, this isn't going to ruin me."

And Genele, giving Galya a triumphant look, pontificated in a whisper:

"So, you get it! You have to have brains! Brains! I could tell at a glance that to put the cottage cheese back would be too much trouble for her, she's so lazy. And anyway, it's impossible to weigh out 150 grams, it always comes out more."

By now Galya's pale face was covered in red, nervous blotches.

She begged to leave but Genele was in full flight. She wanted to display her talent in all its glory and, in her excitement, she was even trying to beat down the officially fixed price of the goulash in the market's delicatessen kiosk.

All her life Galya would remember with horror that outing. She would reminisce about it to her daughters. Her auntie's pronouncements on that market day would enter the annals of family jokes. At the mention of carrots, a member of the household would be sure to ask: "with rounded tips?" and gherkins were referred to as either "peempled" or not "peempled" at all.

Genele lived in utmost poverty. However, she would have been surprised if anyone had hinted to her that this was so, because she lived exactly as she wanted to. Among the multitude of people forced to live constricted lives, bound by all kinds of ties, she was so independently solitary that she considered even her visits to her relatives as a gift bestowed on people in need of her company, her advice and her homilies.

She bore her penury with the self-denying joy of a nun. The cleanliness in her eleven-square-metre, elongated room was festive if daunting: the white starched cloth lay so stiffly on her little table with its well-waxed legs, her bedspread was so clinically white, the severe covers on her two white chairs were so officially welcoming . . .

In her proud poverty she strictly adhered to her guiding principle: to buy the very best. And so, sparing no effort, every other day she would set off to the Filipovskaya bakery and would buy there the best kalatch [fancy white bread] in the world; this would suffice for two days. Then she would pop into Yeliseevsky's and buy 100 grams of Swiss cheese. As for the cheese, she suspected that better cheeses do exist but here in Russia the very best to be had was this Swiss cheese from Yeliseevsky's.

The rest of her diet consisted of buckwheat and millet kasha about which she would modestly claim that no one could prepare them more deliciously than her. Indeed, this was not far from the truth. She would pep up her kasha with vegetable oil from the market and her lunch was completed with a quarter of an apple or an onion, or a small carrot with a rounded tip.

Once a year, at Passover, she would buy a chicken. Actually, this chicken was her Passover. On the day of the purchase, she would get up at the crack of dawn and slowly and carefully prepare herself, stuffing a black twisted rope and a pile of newspapers into a strong, silk net bag. Leaving the house at five in the morning, she took the first tram from Pokrovka to Tsvetnoy Boulevard and arrived at the Central Market about twenty minutes before opening time. For a long time, sometimes as much as two hours, she would await her "own" vendor, a one-eyed, swarthy Jew who earned his living by an enterprise rarely encountered in our days – the trade in live, clucking merchandise. It seemed that, like Genele, the vendor too had his whimsical life precepts. Thus, he didn't like to display more than one chicken at a time on his counter. Genele, for her part, observing her own precepts, could not buy even the most magnificent chicken until she had thoroughly plucked at all the others.

She would wait for the old man to start unhurriedly unstitching a thick grey rag, sewn on to a big oval basket into which he would plunge his hand and, without looking, pull out by its tied-up legs the first chicken he found. Leaning on the counter, Genele would drawl out in the indifferent voice of a chance passer-by:

"Well well, you decided to make an appearance . . . That you call a chicken?"

One-eyed didn't deign to answer.

With her left elbow clasping her antiquated handbag closer to her side, Genele would begin to tackle the chicken. Her manipulations recalled nothing so much as a thorough medical examination. She peered into the chicken's stunned eyes, opened its beak, examined its throat, prodded its breast and backside. Spreading its wings, she appeared to be piercing its bird's soul with her X-ray glare. Then she nonchalantly pushed it aside.

"And that's all you've got?" she asked him scornfully.

One-eyed silently delved into the basket and extracted another . . .

"What on earth is that meant to be, remove it at once!" Genele exclaimed, offended. And the vendor, pursing his thin lips would seize yet another from beneath the counter.

Trembling at the enormity of the responsibility and the fear of making an irrevocable mistake, it was as if she was choosing a bride for her only son. She remembered her inexplicable partiality for black speckled hens and endeavoured to maintain her objectivity so that this partiality would not distort the precision of her choice. After all, the "chosen one" could just as well be a white or a rusty brown hen.

This importunate buyer inspired in the old man irritation, mixed with a growing respect. He also knew a thing or two about chickens – the choicest, most esteemed Passover chickens raised on pure grain. He realized that the old woman would indeed select the very best and he tried to figure out which one she would pick. He remembered her from years back and knew that she wouldn't make a mistake.

At last the "chosen one" was singled out. Prolonged haggling followed. Genele took some new money out of her cherished bag and the "tsar's bride", retaining her unnatural upside-down position, was transferred into the hands of Genele, who wrapped her in quantities of newspaper, then in a clean, white cloth, then in a net bag and finally, in a shopping bag.

After all these procedures, Genele went to the ritual slaughterer in Malahovka and waited in a queue of two dozen of her co-religionists near a small shed at the back of a solid, two-storey house. Here, she handed over her mute victim to a small, fat Jew in a skull cap and waited for the slaughterer to intone a short prayer of forgiveness over the chicken and to set free its foolish bird's soul, which was said to reside in the small quantity of blood that the final shudders of the heart cause to drip onto the zinc tray.

However, at this point, all analogies came to an end, superseded by her culinary activities. One single chicken in her skilled hands turned into a multitude of delicacies: consommé with matzoh dumplings known as "kneidlech", stuffed chicken neck, balls made out of chicken mince, chicken liver pâté and even chicken in aspic. How did she manage all this? She managed . . . In the midst of all this "chicken" business, she also concocted some "gefilte fish" [stuffed fish] and even some little pastry nuts, boiled in honey.

All this was then packed into jars and saucepans. Those things that had to be kept warm were bundled up. Everything was wrapped and wedged with rolled-up newspapers to keep it upright. Then Genele would take it all to her brother Naum to celebrate Passover. Her brother would supply a bottle of Cahor wine.

He was a twice-widowed utter failure. After the death of his first wife, who died young, he remarried, hoping that his new wife would bring up his young children, but she soon fell prey to a perniciously lingering cancer and took years to die. Meanwhile, far from her being of use to the family, Naum's remaining strength was expended on useless pity for her. His ill-fortune even extended to his children, especially his son Grigory, who was born bright and healthy but then sustained a powerful electric shock which left him permanently feeble-minded.

To this woebegone home, Genele would bring her Passover offerings. Seated at the festive table, having listened to Naum's perfunctory reading of the well-known story of the exodus from Egypt, she would unhurriedly relish that wise universal order which encompasses all the hustle and bustle; the dignified festive meal; the one and only God with his emissary Angel, like a postman, calling at the houses of the children of the chosen people; and the feeble-minded Grigory, smiling joyfully, his entire face glistening with chicken fat.

And so, on the very day we are talking about, Genele, her three bags filled with Passover goodies, came out of her house intending to go to Naum's, but set out in the wrong direction. She reached the corner, looked around for the tram stop, and failed to find it. She didn't recognize the junction which had been familiar to her almost from childhood.

"My God! However did I come to be in this strange city!" she thought in horror, and still clutching her brown handbag, without releasing her tenacious grip on her precious net bags, she started falling slowly to the ground.

Thus, together with her net bags and handbag, the ambulance brought her to the emergency ward of the former Yekaterininsky hospital at the Petrovsky gate.

Something terrible had happened to Genele: the whole of the simple, solid and rationally constructed world had lost its internal connections and become unrecognizable. She saw the iris of the greenish speckled eye of the doctor who was bending over her, the collar of his white gown sparkling with excess starch, the stubble that had grown on his swarthy cheek during his twenty-four-hour shift, the tiny bubbles on the white painted wall, the side of the little medicine cabinet, and the window frame, but all these details were fragmented and just wouldn't form into a whole picture.

Genele kept trying to think it through and to formulate the elusive thought in words, but she couldn't. She was left with the feeling that her little self had gone astray, had got lost and that she had to rush somewhere on a matter of great urgency. They took away her bags and the fingers of her left hand kept moving because she had the sensation that something was missing.

Humiliated and robbed, little Genele was lying on the narrow couch with a feeling of tormenting bewilderment. She didn't hear the questions she was asked. An elderly nurse opened her brown handbag and rummaged in it with her long-fingered hand. Genele's glance fell onto the bag and tears ran slowly down her cheeks.

The nurse pulled out of the bag a little jar of cream wrapped in dark paper, a bunch of small keys and a worn passport. Genele was identified.

They put her into a cubicle in the neurological department. Her anxiety was growing. Poor Genele couldn't make anything out; it was as if, at one fell swoop, she had forgotten her entire life. When the orderly brought her water, it took her some time to remember how to swallow. She took a sip and gasped in agony. The experienced orderly tapped her throat and she swallowed it instantly.

In their office, two doctors were discussing precisely which part of her brain had been affected. One maintained that there had been a haemorrhage in the brain stem while the other claimed that there had been no haemorrhage at all but that there was a severe vascular spasm, causing the failure of blood circulation in the brain.

While the young doctors discussed this medical dilemma, Genele's head began to clear a little. The tormented reshuffling of disjointed pictures both inside and outside began to slow down and from it emerged one single image, accompanied by the word associated with it. It was "handbag". Not any old handbag but that very handbag, the brown one. In a rather loud voice she uttered the words:

"Handbag! Handbag!"

And her eyes were beseeching.

"Didn't I say it was a spasm," one of the doctors said triumphantly. "She still has some speech!"

She shouted this one word which was still left to her, into the depth of the night. She tried to jump up, she tried to run, she tossed and turned. They restrained her with a net so that she wouldn't fall out of bed and hurt herself.

She felt as if she already had the handbag in her hands and didn't want to relinquish it and kept shouting: Handbag! Handbag!

And she knew that the louder she shouted, the more this leather scrap with the coiled motif on its lock would belong to her.

But a familiar voice, gentle and sad, kept saying to her:

"Don't, don't, let it be!"

Yet Genele wouldn't surrender till the end. And that is how she died, her left arm contorted, her fingers bent, clutching the invisible lock.

In the morning, her grieving nieces, Galya and Raya, and her old brother Naum, in short, wide trousers, collected from the hospital her belongings, listed by inventory. Galya took the brown handbag and the small sum of money in it, which was noted as a separate item. Naum took the Passover delicacies, which had reached him belatedly.

Later, when he unwrapped all these packages at home, he found in the thermos some consommé which was still warm; the rest of the food, prepared by Genele's own hands, would be placed on the memorial table, and this last supper would be a gross infringement of the Jewish tradition because, from time immemorial, far from gorging oneself on delicious food, it was customary to maintain a strict fast after the funeral of a dear one.

Raya went round to all kinds of doleful offices to fill in the requisite forms, while Galya went to the cemetery at Vostryakovo, to find out which papers were needed in order to place the late Genele next to her sisters, brothers and parents.

In the evening, niece Galya went to Naum. Raya had arrived earlier. A small lamp, which he used to light on the anniversaries of the death of relations, was burning in the room. They sat around the rickety table. With a happy smile, Grigory went to put the kettle one. When he'd left the room, Naum solemnly turned to his nieces, addressing in particular the clever and somewhat pedantic Galya:

"My children! Genele has died. She didn't suffer. May she rest in peace. Go to her place before the neighbours steal everything from her room and before the house management seals it up, and make a thorough search."

"What is there to search for, uncle Naum?" asked Raya, perplexed.

"First of all, a will . . ."

Raya shrugged her shoulders but Naum continued sternly:

"And secondly, some diamond earrings, belong to our grand-mother, fell into Genele's hands. And such huge diamonds!" He formed a ring the size of a walnut, with his thumb and index finger.

"What diamonds, uncle Naum, are you hallucinating?" Galya exclaimed in astonishment. "We've always been paupers!"

"But that's what happened. There were earrings. Of Spanish crafts-manship. Out of this world!" Naum kissed his finger tips (Russian gesture of appreciation). "I swear on my life! Grandma was dying in Genele's room. And Genele was a shrewd girl; she just appropriated them. When her sisters asked her about them, she said: "I haven't got a clue! I looked after grandma, I fed her, did her washing. This I know. But where the diamonds are, I don't know!, Well, now do you understand me!" Naum insisted. "Search amongst her underwear, her stockings. Oh, you know where women hide things. What do I know . . ."

Galya looked glumly out of the dark window, she stood up.

"I'm going, uncle Naum. Sasha is on a business trip, the children are on their own . . ."

And she left.

Late into the evening, Galya busied herself with endless household tasks which she performed precisely, mechanically and mindlessly.

Then she sat down, took hold of old Genele's handbag and looked at it sadly. She opened it. Inside, she found some old recipes, a bunch of small keys and a little jar for cream, wrapped in parchment. She unwrapped the parchment. In the little jar was something that looked like vaseline covered with a thick layer of oxide.

"Poor little Genele!" commiserated Galya, emptying on to a newspaper all the bits and pieces from the handbag. "There must be something I can do for her now! No, there's nothing . . . "

And suddenly, it came to her. She swept all the old trash back into the handbag.

Now she knew how to please Genele: at the funeral, she would secretly slip this very handbag into the coffin . . .

And that's how it happened: the grey smoke from the chimney of the Donskoy crematorium dispersed, and Genele, frail and translucent, set off along the celestial path with her fussy gait, hugging to her left side the shadow of the handbag in which were preserved for eternity the shadows of the diamonds, now forever saved from the authorities and her relatives.

Translated from the Russian by Sylva Rubashova and Eve Cozzin

On the Death of Ken Saro-Wiwa

I

I decided to give up the ghost the moment I was brought into the interrogation room at the Government Reservation Area in Port Harcourt from the torture room where I had been left for thirty-five days and found out that my interrogator was to be a famous detective from the Federal Investigation and Intelligence Bureau, Lagos whom I shall call Mr X.

I was to be interrogated, I was told, in connection with the brutal murder of my friends and in-laws on May 21 1994 somewhere in my Ogoni land. The day after the murder, the Military Administrator of Rivers State, Lt.-Col. Dauda Musa Komo, had announced to a stunned world that he already knew the perpetrators of the murder, and had ordered their arrest with immediate effect. Having done the detective work, constituted a court and condemned the criminals, it was obvious that any investigations to be done would only be a façade behind which Komo would hide in order to complete his true assignment in Rivers State: the pacification of the oil-producing state starting with the glorious people of Ogoni. The crime of the Ogoni people was their demand for rents and royalties for the oil found on their land; that their environment not be destroyed by oil exploitation and that they not be treated as slaves in Nigeria.

The demands were very offensive to the multi-national oil company, Shell, which had already taken 900 million barrels of oil out of Ogoni and put nothing back, and to the cabal which rules Nigeria and had usurped and enjoyed Ogoni oil royalties since 1958. Together, these powerful two had decided to teach the Ogoni people a lesson they would not be alive to forget: genocide.

As founder and president of the Movement for the Survival of the Ogoni People (MOSOP) and having argued at national and international forums that the ecological degradation of Ogoni since 1958 was genocidal in intent and that the Nigerian constitution itself condemned groups such as the Ogoni to extinction, I knew that I was a marked man. Already, Shell had decided at top-level meetings in Rotterdam and London on February 19 1993 that I should be closely monitored by the giant company worldwide. Predictably, from April 3 1993, I began to be followed and was arrested by men from Nigeria's dreaded State Security Service (SSS). Ibrahim Babangida, the Monster of Minna, even signed a death decree aimed especially at me. And there is more into which I shall not go here.

My arrest on June 21 1993 is already history. I was ostensibly arrested for election offences which took place in Ogoni on that historic date, June 12. Well, I was nowhere near Ogoni on that date. I was in Lagos and had been there since June 4. Which shows either that the Nigerian police and SSS are very great institutions or I am.

To cut a long story short, the famous detective, Mr X, whom I referred to earlier, was put in charge of the case. He bundled me at midnight into a van, drove me from Port Harcourt to Lagos, interrogated me, bundled me into the van, drove me to Owerri, dumped me there for three weeks without food or water, returned, interrogated me, bundled me into a van and drove me to a magistrate's court in Port Harcourt.

There, a formidable lady magistrate whom I shall call Mrs Y was waiting with a huge pen and a huge book. And I was charged, by Mr X, not with any election offence, but with "sedition and unlawful assembly". The formidable lady magistrate wrote formidably into her formidable book and then ordered that I be remanded in prison custody. Then she announced with a smile that she would be going on leave for two months and would see me thereafter.

I was marched to Port Harcourt Prison, fell ill there, was transferred to the University of Port Harcourt Teaching Hospital. At midnight on the day I went into hospital, the famous detective, Mr X, came like a thief in the night to drag me out of my sick bed to transfer me to either Enugu Prison or the cemetery. The matron of the hospital saved me from the famous detective that night.

One week later, the famous detective turned up with a letter from Vice President Augustus Aikhomu, granting me bail. And that was the last I heard of that particular case.

I learnt a lesson from that case. It was that Mr X, famous detective that he is, always detects whatever his superiors order him to detect. Therefore, when I saw him in late June 1994, ready to interrogate me in a case over which His Excellency, Lt.-Col. Dauda Musa Komo had already pronounced judgement, I knew I had to give up the ghost. I had been advised to do so by the ghost himself.

2

I should tell you how I met the ghost. Lt.-Col. Komo, that great detective, administrator, military officer and judge, having already known me as a member of his appointed murder squad, since I refused to perform, condemned me to death by torture.

And who else to fulfil this glorious task but that great invention of his, the Rivers State Internal Security Task Force. In Nigeria, a Force uses force. A Task is a task and has not only to be done, but to be created. Thus a Security Task Force must first create insecurity, this insecurity rapidly develops into a Task, against which force must be used to secure security.

The success of a Task Force leads to promotions and, if you know Nigeria, you will know that a Task Force spends money which no one accounts for. Because the maintenance of security, as everyone knows, is an expensive operation, a very expensive operation.

Now, the master-stroke of Lt.-Col. Komo was that he found to head his famous Task Force a man after his heart, a former classmate who bragged about ways of murdering people and that he was duty bound to use his entire repertoire on his immediate target, the Ogoni people. The successful use of his entire repertoire would earn both men promotion to the rank of General of the Nigerian Army. And as is well known, Nigerian Generals are always multi-millionaires.

Some of Nigeria's greatest intellectuals and men of conscience have publicly doubted the sanity of the famous Task Force Commander, but that is neither here nor there. The important thing is that he is obeying "orders from above". And in Nigeria "orders from above" are a divine injunction and where they decree murder, murder there must be. Where they decree genocide, genocide must take place. The beauty of it all being that "above" is anonymous. Who has ever seen God?

The Task Force Commander knew his onions. He seized me from my bed at midnight, his men having broken into my house by force of arms. He had me beaten black and blue, then he manacled me and threw me into a torture chamber in a secret location with instructions that I must remain incommunicado and be stunned to death. For good measure, he took pictures of me in chains with both video and still cameras to show his masters that he was "doing his job", so he said through the lenses. And I have it on good authority that the images were and are a great source of joy to Lt.-Col. Komo. He shows them still to his family, to visitors and to the public as evidence of his great success as an officer and a gentleman trained, for God's sake, in Sandhurst and Georgetown University. Give a good thing to an African and he'll spoil it!

Physical torture did not kill me. Nor did mental torture. Then, one night, the ghost arrived. Tall and gangly, dressed in ragged Nigerian Army camouflage uniform, his bones shooting out of holes in the uniform, his brown teeth as huge as tusks projecting from enormous lips, he came to me, automatic weapon slung over his shoulder, a little drum, an Ogoni drum called "Ekoni" in his hand. He sounded the drum, Ken-ti-mo, Ken-ti-mo, Ken-ti-mo!

The familiar sound of the little drum woke me up. At the sight of the ghost, I laughed. Annoyed by my laughter, he dropped the drum and laid hold of his automatic weapon. He pointed it at me at close range. I did not flinch. He cocked the weapon and fingered the trigger. I did not bat an eyelid.

"Who are you?" I asked.

"I'm General Jeno Saidu."

"Sounds like genocide to me," I said.

"You should know."

"What do you want?" I asked.

"I'm here to finish you," replied he, in a gruff voice.

"General, stop swaggering. You don't impress me."

"You will be impressed. I've finished all your Ogoni people – men, women and children. Once I deal with you, my task is done."

"Go ahead," I challenged him.

"You are not afraid to die?"

"No."

"Why not?"

"I'm prepared to go with all my people whom you confess to having already murdered."

"Yes, I worked hard on them. I made short work of them. All five hundred thousand of them. You are the last man."

"So, go ahead."

General Jeno Saidu, the ghost, shot into the ceiling. I laughed.

"Why did you shoot into the ceiling and not into my chest?"

"You're still not afraid?"

"No, General."

"And why not?"

"Because I have what is greater than your weapon." Whereupon, I said after the English poet, Blake:

> I will not cease from mental fight
> Nor shall my pen sleep in my hand
> Till we have built a new Ogoni
> In Niger delta's wealthy land.

Then I drew my pen from under my pillow. The General's weapon fell from his hand, his tusks from his mouth and he slumped to his knees.

3

Yes, the moment I drew my pen from under my pillow General Jeno Saidu became as meek as a lamb. He lost his swagger which I thought he would, and became my confidence. From which I drew the lesson, if I did not know it beforehand, that these Generals are strong only if they have an automatic weapon in their hands. Without that, they are as dumb as pap and sit much the same wherever you place them and will then become civil and human.

General Jeno Saidu, ghost as he was, asked me to sheath my pen and he would tell me a thing or two about my torture and the death he had inflicted on Ogoni men, women and children.

I put my pen back underneath my pillow. The ghost sighed with relief and made a seat for himself beside me on the bed. He reeked of human blood and I had to hold up my nose. "Sorry about the smell," says he. "There's nothing I can do about it. All the soap in the world, all the deodorants in the market will not wash it off me. I've murdered too many Ogoni people in the past month. I don't mean to hurt you, Ken, if I may call you by that endearing name which all my victims cried as they went to their death. No, I don't mean to hurt you. I did what I did on orders. Orders is orders, I must tell you. Even as a General, orders is orders. I tell the truth.

"I was told to shoot into the air, drive your people into the forest, the bushes and marshes, dispose of them there, to destroy all evidence of death, then return to their rickety towns and burn as many of them down as I could. Thereafter, I was to visit my power on all goats, chickens, yams and plantains. That, my dear Ken, is what we call a scorched earth policy.

"I did what I had to do, man. Orders is orders. My last task was to come and finish you off. I confess that I missed my way coming to the secret location where you are held. The description given me was not exact. I went past the Imo River and crossing a river always has a dampening effect on me. It forces me to think, for a while at least. And it was no different this night.

"And you know, I realized that in all those villages we went to, there was not a single gun. I mean, it's really sweet to annihilate a powerful enemy, or one who at least answers you back. But to be ordered to annihilate babies and pregnant mothers sleeping in their beds. That is madness. And what is it that can make anyone so mad?

"In Nigeria, it is money. Your country is money-mad, Ken. There is nothing people will not do for money. And you who sit on rich deposits of oil and gas are doomed. I hear the famous jingle, 'We are one' on your Radio Rivers every day. And I laugh to think anyone believes it. You know, we soldiers, we use deception as a tool of war. So also propaganda. So we organize prayers for peace while we murder, loot and burn. We are after the oil and gas, Ken. And anything above that oil which lies in the depth of the land is due for extermination.

"And don't think we are the only ones who need the money. The Europeans and Americans need it even more. And after all, they are the ones whose brains and money bring the oil and gas from the earth to the surface. They are the ones who buy the oil and gas and then pay you some money. Their only friend is he who allows them to take the oil away as cheaply as possible. Therefore, a man like you, Ken, who dares to ask them to pay a bit more money, take care of the people on the land, put back something, wash their trousers or whatever, you are a mortuary candidate. Worms' meat.

"I have to tell you the truth. I go all over this country unseen. I am General Jeno Saidu. Unless I reveal myself, you never know. But I am in all councils of dangerous men to take orders. I know the origin of your present ordeal.

"No, don't speak. You know those in-laws and friends of yours who met their sad end a month or so ago. They suffered a fate that was meant for you. You should have died shortly after at that same spot. But you are a lucky man. You probably have a mission. That bag of bones they took to Government House. That man who told the world that you incited the youths whereas you were in your car all the way under escort and spoke to no one till you got to Port Harcourt long before I and my men did what we were ordered to do, that man, I say, is a paid agent. And he was well rehearsed to say all he said. I think we will still have to invent more lies if you do not die by torture.

"As to your present ordeal, the origin lies in that gas pipeline which is supposed to go through the heart of Ogoni to the German

Aluminium Smelter plant in Akwa Ibom State. You remember that guy from the Italian company Saipem who tried to offer you inducement for you to allow them to start constructing the pipeline? And you know Shell has already awarded a $500 million contract to those who are to design the pipeline to deliver the gas which they believe is theirs. You dared, through MOSOP, to ask the Ogoni people to resist the construction of the pipeline until an Environmental Impact Assessment Study has been completed to determine what harm the pipeline would do to the Ogoni people.

"Environmental Impact Studies are only good for white people in their country. The headquarters of the three companies I have mentioned have asked their employees in Nigeria why the project is being delayed. And the answer is Ken Saro-Wiwa and MOSOP. These impediments have to be removed and any other Ogoni people who stand in the way. I swear to you, that is the game plan. I know. I was at the meeting where the decisions were taken. And I have my orders.

"And if you do not believe me, if you do not believe the torture through which you have been put, the denial to you of medical treatment, of a lawyer's attention, of your family's love, if you do not believe the chains on your legs, then wait until they take you for interrogation. If the detective is not the same man who detects what he is asked to detect, then you can give me up. But before you do so, write your story. Write it fast. Goodbye."

He spoke and disappeared as only a ghost can and I woke up with a start from my sleep. The rest of the story you already know.

4

When the news came that Ken Saro-Wiwa had given up the ghost in the offices of the State Investigation and Intelligence Bureau in Port Harcourt, there was a flurry in newspaper houses in Lagos as in many other places in Nigeria and abroad. I was hurriedly despatched to cover the story.

I found, on arrival in Port Harcourt, that the funny little man had given up the ghost a few days after this interrogation by men of the Federal Investigation and Intelligence Bureau from Lagos, leaving behind an epitaph to be put on his gravestone, and a hurriedly written note explaining why he had decided to give up the ghost.

His presence in the office of the State Investigation and Intelligence Bureau is explained by the fact that he was refused accommodation in the dingy, dank, smelly guardroom where men in police custody were normally kept. Senior police officers who knew their onions and had information of the plot against the man decided that they would not have his blood on their hands. Eventually, they found him a place in an office where he bathed, ate and slept – for three nights running – and was able to write his story as advised by the ghost.

There was great jubilation at Government House, Port Harcourt, the headquarters of the notorious Rivers State Internal Security Task Force. Champagne bottles popped endlessly. Military buffoons gleamed. Boots shone. The Commander of the Task Force shook hands with the Military Administrator. The former knew that he would soon be promoted to the rank of General. The latter knew that his position was secure and he would soon be nominated to Nigeria's highest ranking body, the Provisional Ruling Council. The Task Force had successfully completed the genocide of the Ogoni people.

All that was left was to dispose of Mr Saro-Wiwa's corpse. There was a debate as to how best to carry out this Task. In the first place, there were none of his relatives alive, all Ogoni people, men, women and children having fallen to the gallant troops led by the deadly ghost, General Jeno Saidu. The telephone to his house and office had been cut to deprive his family of sustenance and ruin his business. His poor family had fled to London before they could be murdered. This knotty problem was solved when it was decided that it was a Task and therefore the Internal Security Task Force should be assigned the responsibility.

Next was where he should be buried. This question was quickly settled. The entire Ogoni territory had become a cemetery. The five hundred thousand Ogoni people had all been buried. Ken Saro-Wiwa would cap the mass burial ceremony.

So, as is usual in Nigeria, a contract was awarded for the burial of the little man. The officer who won the contract for supplying the coffin, to maximize his profit from the deal, decided to hire a carpenter to make it. He gave the coffin-maker precise instructions. The coffin had to be no more than five feet long and one foot wide. The shocked carpenter succeeded in making the coffin to specification. But, being a Nigerian, and therefore innumerate, he actually made it two inches shorter either way. This also saved money.

Poor Ken was squashed into this contraption. And being used to protesting injustice, his corpse squeaked and screamed. The officer who had won the contract for putting Ken in the coffin ran for his dear life. So the Military Administrator had to do the job himself.

He duly cancelled this aspect of the contract and demoted the officer for cowardice.

Then the soldiers who were to act as pallbearers refused to do the job alleging that they had not been paid their Ration Cash Allowance (RCA) for exterminating the Ogoni people. The Commander of the Task Force paid the money on the spot, and the bier was borne through Port Harcourt to show all the residents and other Nigerians what it costs to demand an end to environmental degradation and pollution by oil companies and social justice for the poor and oppressed.

When the funeral procession got to Ogoni territory, it was no surprise to find Shell, Saipem, Ferrostaal, Chevron, and a gaggle of industrial oil contractors from Europe and America. This helped to give the burial of the little man a well-deserved international flavour since he had made it a point to complain to the international community about the dehumanization and denigration of the Ogoni people and other peoples of the Niger delta.

Shell and Chevron, who have oil mining leases covering the whole of Ogoni territory, chose the exact spot where the funny little man was to be buried. Care had to be taken, they said, because all of Ogoni land was a huge oil well and now that human beings, flora, fauna and all had been disposed of, oil exploitation could go on without let or hindrance or protests about ecological war, double standards, hypocrisy, acid rain, gas flaring and all.

The right size of hole was dug – tiny and narrow, no more than five foot by one. And the coffin was lowered, and wait for it, stood upright – to save space. Which fulfilled Ken's prophecy in his epitaph which was duly laid on the grave:

> Here stands the funny little sweet
> The Nigerians loved to cheat
> So much so that e'en in death
> They denied him six feet of earth.

As the procession made to go, a message flashed across the sky like lightning: "Congratulations, congratulations to the Internal Security Task Force. Your success has won for Nigeria unanimous election to Permanent Membership of the United Nations Security Council."

And Ken Saro-Wiwa laughed in his grave.

STARLING LAWRENCE

The Crown of Light

For most of the year he could not see the house at all; it was hidden
from the farm, first by the shoulder of the hill, and then by the rows
of hardwood trees along the drive, so that even in the far corner of
the field, as he turned the tractor up out of the wet swale and onto
that curious little hump, the smell of fresh hay so strong it almost
choked him, he would look up, as if out of a mirror or a photograph
taken from his own bedroom window long ago, and see nothing
but a far curtain of green, oblique, as the trees followed the course of
the drive up that sloping lawn below the terraces. He could measure
his life against the height of those trees.

But in the fall, when the season turned and the sharp drafts of
arctic air stripped the leaves from the trees and brought the stars
close, he might catch a glimpse of the house when he least expected
it. The last time had been a couple of years ago early in the morning
when he had been out beyond the field hunting a pheasant that he
had been listening to, catching out of the corner of his eye for a
couple of weeks. "What about a pheasant, Cat?" he had said to her
one day, catching her off guard so that the eyes stared at him almost
cross-eyed through the thick lenses. "Been a long time," he went on,
as if he had more to say. "Been a long time." He would shoot the
pheasant, then, and they would eat it together, as long as he could
keep the damn dogs away from it while it hung. He knew just where
it was, as if it had been walking that slow, thrusting walk through
his mind, and the only thing that surprised him as he threw up the
old over-and-under 16 to meet the racketing pheasant rising above
the alders was to see the house there glowing in the distance through
the curtain wall of bare twigs, with the morning sun just catching
it. He did not miss the bird, but his timing was put off, and instead
of swinging up past the flurry of red and gold feathers to the head
shot, he was slow, then hurried and got it full in the breast and guts.
He would have to hang this one carefully, or the meat would spoil.

It had been cold now for weeks, cold so that you saw your breath like those locomotives as used to be, and when the weather got so he usually stayed near the barns if he went out at all, or climbed in his pick-up and went on over to town, to the garage to see how the boys were getting on. He knew them all pretty well, even the young ones, some of whom he recognized as kids who might have used the straight stretch of road in front of his farm to test out a new carburettor or a set of mag wheels. Back a while he'd used the grease pit or the fancy arc welder when the back-hoe or the tractor needed repairs. In exchange he'd give them a little advice on how to nurse some old machinery through another season. Look at a side hitch mower, these boys, and think they was looking at a space ship. But mostly now it was for the company he went, and it was warm in there, so warm he couldn't stay long without he started sweating in his big coat, or he took it off altogether. Stay a while, they'd say. Don't you ever feel like working no more?

When it got cold enough that he knew the ground was solid in the low places beyond the field, he took the wire down off a section of the fence so he could cut a couple of the pines that had been killed by the beaver and snake them out with the tractor. Big pines, they were, older by a sight than he was, and it was a shame to cut them at all, a shame to cut anything, or kill a pheasant either, if it came to that. But the beaver had found a way to get at that culvert again, no stopping them without shooting them or dynamiting the dam, and he had just got too tired of all that to go on with it. Let them do it, if that's what they wanted, even if it meant that the water backed up nearer the edge of his field each year and killed the pines, one by one. Well, he needed the wood anyway. Might be dry enough next spring to patch the holes that the cow had kicked in the side of the barn.

It was hard, awkward work in the frozen swamp, and he had hated cutting the wire on the fence. Any wire was best left alone once you got a fence the way you wanted it, but here there was no other way in. He would need help with the restringing, though. Couldn't pull like that no more.

After the operation, the doctor had told him what to expect, told him that muscle doesn't grow back, and he would just have to get used to certain things. He had nodded politely. But even though he couldn't move his arm too good without that pad of muscle in his right breast, he was sure his strength would come back: it had to. Got it all, the doctor said, that was the good news.

Maybe he could do it himself after all: rig some kind of extension handle to the fencing tool to give him the leverage he would need, take a quick twist around the post and staple the son of a bitch off. It might work, but probably not. Be an ugly job if he managed it, and no telling what sort of trouble he might find once he got at it. The post didn't feel all that solid to him when he cut the wire and dragged it back, as if maybe worms or rot had got into it down below. If it broke he'd have a hell of a time setting a new one by himself, and if he lived long enough, why he'd have to find a way to replace this whole line down here, set in the wet soil as it was. How long would that be, he wondered. He thought of stone walls running off into forests of pine where once there were pastures. Wouldn't want to leave anything behind to embarrass himself.

He had cut both of the trees, and they had fallen the way he had wanted them to, being nothing much to hang up on down here, as long as they didn't kick back on you, and the undergrowth of alders cushioned their fall and muffled the noise of it. Fine straight trees down here in this deep soil, without all that branching and strangeness you got when they grew on rocks. Sweet boards in them, he judged, and he might get two twelves and maybe an eight out of the larger one. He worked deliberately with the saw, taking the limbs close to the trunk and keeping his eye out for the sprung ones that could kick the saw out of your hands like a mule or break a rib. He thought when he started that he might get the whole job done in one afternoon, but if he went slow and positioned himself just so to make the cuts on the limbs without reaching and swinging the saw about as he once would have done, then the pain between his ribs stayed in that little pocket where he could almost ignore it. He knew, then, as soon as he saw how he would have to go about the limbs, that he could not finish the job before the early darkness dropped out of the sky, and the short twilight – with the shadows working about him in the fallen limbs – was no time to be fooling with a saw. Several times, too, he was surprised to find himself not working but standing there with the saw idling in his hands or resting on the trunk of the pine, just like that fool boy he had once fired for mooning about when he should have been cutting firewood. Most expensive damn firewood he ever put up, and the boy's face came back to him several times that winter as he opened the doors of the stove and fed the wood in, piece by precious piece. In love he'd been, said so himself, and took no offence at being fired, and no money neither.

He was not tired, not working fast enough to need to stop, but he did stop, and stood there remembering things that he had not thought of in years. The first time it was the beavers, must have got to thinking on them because they had killed the tree he was cutting, when it should have stood twenty feet higher and lived eighty a hundred years longer. It was his father who had planted the tree, or maybe it had seeded itself in the old pasture, and the funny thing was his father had always wanted to see the beaver, talked about it in a funny, kind of mystical way along with the other creatures of the forest that had vanished or just gone off elsewhere when all the land was cut over for charcoal a hundred years and more ago. He wished his father was alive again to work on this tree with him, so's he could know that the beaver had come back at long last, as all the pastures and most of the fields dissolved back into the forest they had once been. But he'd died in, what was it? 1952 maybe, and here he was older than his father had been when he died, and never once thought about it until this very day. Books, the man had, shelf upon shelf of books, and that was all his pleasure. Even had a book about the damned beaver, and the Indians out west or some such nonsense, though it was exciting enough at the time. He remembered listening as his father read to them, him and his brother, out on the porch where they slept in the summer, and him trying to keep awake till the end of the chapter when he would know if the Indian boy had killed the bear in his den. Where were those books now? Must be his sister over in Avon had them. Never cared enough about them himself, but he wished he could show his father this tree that he had planted and that the beaver he never saw had now killed.

The next time it was when the saw stalled in his hand, pinched in a careless cut on the wrong side of a limb not three inches through. Careful he should be, out here alone. And instead of freeing the saw he let the silence close in on him like the parted waters in the hymn, and thought on the men who had cut the forest back then, not with a saw like the one caught in a tree before him, but long two-handled saws and big clumsy axes that a man would have trouble swinging properly today, unless he practised at it. Raggies, they were called, and the old man who had worked this farm for his father claimed to have been one in his youth, said he had stayed up on the mountain for weeks on end, living on whisky and raw eggs, he said, and cutting two cords a day, each man. Cut and split for a dollar and a quarter a day, cash money. And as if that wasn't work enough to kill a man outright, they also had to tend the big fires night and day, when all that wood was laid up like a puzzle and covered with earth and leaves to burn down into the charcoal. And the raggies walked on top of that great mound of smouldering wood, pushing long poles down into the pile to let a breath of air in just to keep the fire going right. And if the stack had been built wrong, or the air got in too strong, why, a pillar of fire might come up out of the pile, or the raggy just disappeared down into a fiery hole and that was that. Made a whisky omelette out of him, old Bob would say, slapping his knee. That was always the last line of old Bob's stories about the raggies. Got so that any talk of the raggies made him think of the whisky omelette, and Bob slapping his knee, then blowing his nose, kind of loud. But the idea of the great hidden fire with a mind of its own made him think now of the fire between his ribs, and he remembered the pale fleshy cheeks and chin of the doctor when he told him that he must call him if the pain returned. He hadn't liked the man much, let alone the hospital, and all he had wondered, looking at that face, was whether the man had ever spent a day out of doors in his life. Not cutting wood or shovelling dirt or even working – just outside, walking around, or even sitting still with the sun on him. Couldn't live without that, himself, and so he hadn't called the doctor when the pain came back, hadn't even told Cat, which he now knew was a problem, something he had to think on and find a way. He'd had a dream not long ago, in which the doctor wanted him to come back to the hospital, just for a while. He could see the doctor in there beckoning to him through the big glass window, but he wouldn't go, not even with Cat telling him otherwise. You come out here, he said, loud as he could, but the doctor paid him no mind.

Whether he had planned it so or not, he had been working through the late afternoon with his back to the sun. Maybe it was easier on his eyes that way, or maybe that was just the way the trees wanted to fall. When he had finished packing the saw and the fuel can and the wedges under the tarp – no use in carrying it all back to the barn only to carry it out here again tomorrow – it was dark so he could scarcely see the tools in his hand. But up there beyond the slanting edge of the hill was a purple glow, not even purple, but lilac, or some colour like that, the kind they wrote about in old books of fairy stories, paler down near the black shape of the hill, and growing deeper and richer as it rose up there to the first stars. The house was outlined against this luminous colour, black so your eye didn't go right to it, but only gradually came to recognize the strange bite out of the lilac sky. And a light went on, a single light in what must have been the kitchen, and he thought that they too must have been looking at the sky, or perhaps at its reflection spread out there on the black ice of the lake.

Driving the tractor home over the dark rough field, he caught another glance of that light, winking now through the tree trunks, and wondered about those people up there, sitting around a table that was probably more familiar to him than it ever would be to them. Why, he could walk blindfolded through the whole damn house, and never hit a stick of furniture. Well, they might have changed it all around anyway. The jolt of the tractor in a deep rut caught him unawares, and before he could catch himself, steady his body against the shock of it, the pain bloomed in his side, in a deeper place.

"Ah, Christ," he muttered aloud. He tried to think how many years it had been since he had been in the house to see it for himself, but could remember only one spring afternoon he had spent as a boy, staring out of the attic windows wishing the rain would stop. Anyway, whatever the number, it had been years and years, the visits to his brother growing less and less frequent, even though it was just up the road from the farm, his farm, and a pleasant enough walk on a summer evening. The woman, his brother's wife, had just stared at him all the while, never offering him so much as a drink of water, always looking at his boots and overalls as if he had stepped straight from some swamp, some Goddamn swamp, instead of Cat's kitchen, which was clean enough to please any Christian. He was sorry now that he had sworn, even if he hadn't spoken the words, for he knew that Cat would not like it.

Well, the woman was gone now, locked up the house the day after his brother died and instructed her lawyers in Wilmington to sell it, which they did with never so much as a letter or a word to him or his sister. So the table in the kitchen was probably still there, unless the new people – not so new, come to think on it – had moved things around. They can live there, he thought, but they ought to leave things be. And the only regret he felt now was for those evenings on the porch with his brother, sometimes a little glass of whisky, sitting out there where his rough clothes wouldn't be a bother to the woman, where she wouldn't set foot until he was gone, no matter how hot it was inside the house. That had been a good time, except he could tell that it made his brother uneasy, as if he was having to choose between them. Maybe if he had changed his pants and shoes it would all have been different, but he didn't see why a man had to wear Sunday clothes just to visit with his own brother. So after a while, a pretty long while, he stopped going altogether, and would run into his brother from time to time in the hardware store, as if by accident, and they would sit there a while, hanging their butts on the wide tables full of brass screws and stove bolts, with old Joe

Carroll giving them the eye, as if they was scaring any customers out of there, then maybe they'd have lunch in the Collins Diner. He'd asked Cat once if maybe they could go up together, if maybe that would make the woman – her name had gone clean out of his head – feel better about him, about them. But she had set him straight, and without too many words: "I don't like her, and she don't like me, so what's the good in it? She don't even like him, let alone you." That was Cat, through and through, and a good thing the woman never gave Cat's shoes or dress that insolent, travelling stare that seemed to take a good two breaths to make it to the floor and back up to your face. And then he died, and that was that. These folks must have been here ten or twelve years now, and he knew them just about well enough to wave back, and no more. Doctor or something, he was. Probably good enough people, in their own way, and he held nothing against them; but he thought again of that view of the lilac sky and how from that porch you had an unobstructed view of the sun coursing down over the far range of hills that ran clear up into Massachusetts. He imagined that turning on that kitchen light must have spoiled their view of it, or maybe they weren't even watching.

He had a sick heifer in the barn next to the tractor shed, and he spent a few minutes there putting the purple salve on the udder and making sure she had fresh hay. There it was, the heavy, rich smell of summer grasses around him as he broke a bale and forked it over the top of the stall. If you put your hand to it you could feel the fine, papery flowers of the alfalfa, so purple when it was cut, and he imagined sometimes that he could smell that purple flower in it, or the pink ragged robin that had crept into the grasses in the wet corner of the meadow, for the one made good hay, and the other did not. The cows knew that much, and you could understand them if you took the time to watch and to listen. He listened now for the breathing of the heifer, while in his mind he saw the hay with all its flowers going down in wide rows under a hot sun, and he thought that she would be all right and he would not have to call the vet again, which was a relief. Seemed the man was afraid of animals, for he wouldn't go near one without he had a twitch on one ear, that cruel chained stick that could take the ear right off if he twisted hard enough, and the animals knew it. Twitch Pepe they called him up at the garage, and laughed about it. Not a bad man, for all that, but he should have chosen another line of work. He turned off the light and was swallowed into the darkness of the early night that held no hint of twilight beyond the hill.

When he finally came to the house, Cat was waiting downstairs for him, wiping her hands slowly on her apron, as she always did. She looked slow and ponderous in those heavy boots – maybe she was just coming out to meet him in the barn, to see if he was all right – but years ago she could dance, by God, he remembered that, how she could dance. There was one night, over at Denby's . . .

"You see something funny, you with that smile on your face?"

"No, ma'am, didn't even know I was smiling. I was just thinking."

"I guess you were, and I guess I was thinking I should drag you back in here by the neck before you froze for good." Now what the hell did she mean, for good? He told her then about the cow and about the lilac sky and the house black against it on the edge of the hill, and as he did so he saw her cocking her head a bit, as if trying to get a better look at his face.

"You," she said, "you who never looked at a sunset in your life?" And so he tried again to put into words how he felt, looking at that sight from such a distance, yet feeling himself there, inside the picture he was looking at.

"You're right," he said at last, "it's stuff I ain't thought about in thirty years, or maybe never. But when that light went on, the kitchen light, I realized that I was thinking about something I wasn't seeing, something I would have seen if I'd been sitting in that kitchen, or something I'd seen a long time ago. Well, you know, you can't see anything too good out a window if the light's on, and maybe nothing at all at that time of day, and so that lake and the lilac sky was more real to me than it was to them, because they wasn't paying any mind to it at all. Not that there's anything wrong with them, they're just . . ."

"How would you know, one way or the other? You don't even know their names."

"That ain't true, of course I know their names." That was one thing you had to get used to about Cat, she being given to bald statements like that, and before he knew it, she had gotten the rise out of him. Got it out of other people too, so not everybody could get along with her. You were the only man who would have me, she told him once, though that wasn't true neither. At least he never believed it, though it had kind of stuck in his mind, and maybe he'd been meaning to ask her about that. Maybe the truth was the other way around, maybe she was the only woman who would have him, and if that hadn't been true before, it was sure as God true now.

"Did you make my dinner, or am I supposed to do that too? I get hungry in a cold like this."

They went on up the stairs, he following the slow sway of her haunches, thinking there was a time when I couldn't keep my hands off her, when something as everyday as walking behind her or seeing her bent over the child would be enough to set him off. She is still the same woman, he thought, smiling to himself and glad she couldn't see it, and I am still the same man.

It was an awkward arrangement, having the kitchen like this on the second floor, and he often wished he didn't have those stairs ahead of him when he came in from a long day mowing or bucking wood. Well, that was one thing he'd often said he'd get around to, and never had, putting the kitchen where it ought to be, downstairs. But the food was all ready for him, set out on the table in the pots with the heavy iron lids. And there were candles on the table, burning a little low, so no wonder she was going to drag him out'n that barn.

They ate: she quickly, as she always did, perhaps out of annoyance with the food she had fussed over, stirred, and smelled all that afternoon with the windows shut tight against the sudden cold of November, so that he still had half a plateful of food when he heard her fork clattering on empty china.

"You don't eat like a hungry man, or maybe it's the cooking?" He smiled at her and did not answer, eating a little faster now not to keep her waiting. She needed no compliments on her cooking, and he never could keep up with her anyway. "I like to taste what I eat" is what he would have said, if his mouth weren't full.

But there was something about this evening that conspired against him, or with him: he was tired from the long day in the cold, and the sudden warmth of the kitchen made him drowsy; in the uncertain light, the unfamiliar light of the candles, his eyes played tricks on him, and he had to look close to get his fork on what he wanted. Like working with that chainsaw in the falling dark, he thought, and might have said it too, but you had to be careful how you made jokes in Cat's kitchen, and he remembered that he'd already joshed her about the food being ready. Leave well enough alone. The candle, burning low and guttering, made a terrible mess of wax on the table, but Cat didn't seem to mind or notice, looking at him, his face, as she was. Funny having another person watch you while you eat . . . must look kind of like a fool. The light played on the sugar bowl and the bright square of his napkin, but the pitted, grimy surfaces of those black pots devoured it. How many times had he heard her call out to him not to soap them pots? Seemed almost like something you could set your watch to.

"Now what the . . . what is that?" He thrust the yellow thing, bitten in half, close to the candle, where the light shone through it and around it, so he couldn't get a good look.

"Don't tell me you never ate a parsnip before, Thomas Waters, because I know for a fact that you have."

"I never ate a parsnip before, and I'm telling you that, at least not if I knew it. The doctor tell you to do that?"

"No, they was on sale down to the Finast, and I don't need advice from him nor you on my cooking. Ask me, they taste all right." It wasn't true that she took no advice from the doctor, though he'd leave it be. He hadn't had a good fat piece of meat in so long he couldn't remember, and strange vegetables, like this damn parsnip, bobbed to the top of the stew, often as not. He ate the parsnip for show, then put his fork down.

"The mail come?"

"The mail always comes. Maybe this is a love letter you're waiting for?" She liked to do that to him sometimes, though when he got a letter once from . . . Jesus, he couldn't remember her name . . . anyway when he got that letter she didn't see anything funny in it. And the poor woman was only trying to raise money for some charity. Showed the letter to Cat, just to put her mind easy, and she'd said to tell her that he hadn't got nothing for her any more. What was her name? Known her when he was still living up at the old house, with his parents, and she from Darien or some fancy place like that along the water. His father liked her pretty well, and his mother always favoured her over Cat. They'd spent a couple of long summer evenings on that porch up there, sitting side by side on the swinging couch, barely touching each other until they could hear for certain that his parents had gone to bed. Had they watched the sun go down? Well, he remembered the colour of her dress, and the feel of it slipping off her shoulder, and Cat could like as not put a name to her was he foolish enough to ask her. Probably knew the colour of her dress, too, and the name of her perfume. Hadn't thought about that girl in years. What a crazy thing to remember now, all this time later, when the girl was a woman, an old woman older than Cat maybe, and he, well, maybe remembering was all he was good for.

"I was thinking of that insurance letter. It's about that time of year." He hoped Cat wouldn't make anything out of it, wished he could have got at the mail himself so they didn't have to talk about the damned insurance, and he could just pay it and not think any more on it.

"I have it," she said.

"Well either you pay it or give it to me," he said, a little quicker than he'd meant. "It's something that's got to be done, or we lose the value in it, after all these years."

"Value," Cat snorted. "There's only one way to collect on that value, and it don't look like no bargain to me." They had a little quarrel about the life insurance every time it came due, and this year was no different, except that Cat seemed to look through him now to that little burning place that had made him put down his fork. She was superstitious, that's what it was, and the insurance, or talk about it, was like an omen, a feeling she could not be talked out of any more than he could make her walk left out of the driveway at night when they took a turn before going to bed, because there was the elm, no more than a grassy stump now, where Billy Taylor got himself killed, drunk, 35 years ago. Made her flesh crawl, she said. Maybe she had the second sight.

"It's sense, Cat, and you know it, so just fetch me the damned papers." She wouldn't argue against that, and the envelope, unopened, was produced from the drawer right in the table where they sat, right under that pot of parsnip stew, as he figured it. "What was you going to do with this thing and I hadn't asked?" In the time it took her to make no answer, he was thinking about his mother, about the look on her face the first time he misused a word like that in front of her, said was when it should have been were or ain't when it should have been something else. "I taught you better than that," was all she would say, a kind of lost look on her face. That was Cat's triumph, though she wasn't even in the room at the time, over his mother, over that girl from Darien, over all those people who live on top of hills.

He had signed the paper and written out the cheque, a fearful amount of money it seemed, with a kind of satisfaction, a private triumph, in spite of that hard look on Cat's face: as far as she was concerned, this was asking for trouble, whether or not it made good sense. She didn't put much trust in good sense.

"You'll want to mail that in town tomorrow," he said, but she made no move to take it, pointed instead to the corner of the counter. The letter lay in his hand gathering weight: paper and ink and his own meaning threaded through the difficult words but not said, not caught exactly in any of them, like a love letter that way. Had he ever written a letter to Cat in all the years he had known her? Likely not, and certainly not that kind of letter. How she would have laughed. But maybe somebody else had written such letters to her and she hadn't laughed, and maybe she had them still, tied in a piece of yarn in the bottom of some sewing basket where she knew he'd never look. It was only a part of her he knew, loved, though no doubt the rest was good too, even if it had nothing to do with him. And this thing he held in his hand was a love letter from him to a woman he would never know.

After the washing-up, after he'd bitten his tongue not to answer back when she told him again how to wash the pot, like he was that moonstruck boy who couldn't even split a piece of kindling for being mad in love, after he'd dried his hands and sat down again in his own chair, she surprised him. She'd been restless, wandering about the big room that was the kitchen and dining room and living room to them, moving the picture of Ethan from one table to another and the ashtray full of paper clips and junk a little nearer the phone. As if they had guests coming, or someone was going to photograph the place. And when he was sitting down, comfortable for the first time in twelve or maybe fourteen hours, she passed her hand over his hair, pulling the heavy fall of it back from his forehead in a gesture between rough and tender. Cat wasn't much for tender gestures, then or now. "You talk a pretty good old man's game, common sense and all that, but I see a lot of the boy in you yet." He looked up at her, having no answer to a thought like that, and wondered if he could see the girl in her, the girl he had brought to this house long ago with nobody's blessing, had chased naked through the darkened rooms that first night. He had ridden her on his tractor out to that far wet corner of the field to show her the pink blush of ragged robin and the curling purple spires of alfalfa – she standing on the hitch bar and sweating with fright, her arms wrapped so tight around him that it hurt – before he cut and baled the hay, had bedded her on that flat part of the barn roof, the longest night of the young summer it was, had conceived a child with her, quarrelled with her, grown old with her. "Maybe," he said. "Maybe."

The moon came out late that night, low, but bright as a story book, and flooded in the window where he had forgot to pull the shade, so eager had they been. He should be asleep, he knew, he who never had a sleepless night, and on this of all nights, when Cat had so thoroughly taken the boy out of him. Asleep nothing . . . he should be dead. He smiled into the darkness, felt the clean ache in his hands from holding her, the flow of blood in the muscles of his back, the sword-point in his ribs there, always there. Cat was asleep, her back turned to him, and in this light she might be anybody, might be old or young. Wouldn't know what to do with a young one, he thought.

He eased his feet over the side of the bed, rearranged the quilt to keep the chill off her, and made his way to the bathroom. He did not turn on the light, but stood by the little window naked, with a glass of water in his hand that he never got around to drinking. Across the road to the meadow his gaze wandered, seeing each frozen blade of grass, every shadow of trunk and branch in the carpet of hoar frost. Snow, there should be snow any day now. He remembered winters as cold as this one, and as if he were indeed standing out in that field, his thoughts turned up the hill to the house outlined there against a strange, bright sky. My mind is playing tricks on me, he thought. There was the field, with the moon now setting beyond the beaver swamp, here the window in front of him misting with his breath. And yet there was something more.

He dressed as quietly as he could, grateful that he had left his boots downstairs. The dog at the foot of the bed looked at him once, but he made no sign to it, thinking ahead to the sound of its claws on the steep wooden treads. It would stay there with Cat, who slept on, her slow, regular breathing almost like a sound of summer.

Though he had put on all the clothes he could find without rummaging in drawers or opening the closet, the shock of cold air at the door made him catch his breath. He would be walking for a good ten minutes before the heat would creep up the inside of his down vest, to balance this penetrating cold, this enemy.

He grew accustomed to the ghostliness of objects, saw the shining field ahead of him between the old maples, marked the luminous sky above the hill that rose to his right. He wondered if maybe the house up there was on fire, if maybe he should call the fire department just on the chance. No . . . it was the wrong colour, it was . . . he couldn't put a name to it, maybe like a rotten log glowing by the side of a swamp.

Along the field he went, by the road, with the frost making it slippery but marking it for him as well, a path that he could follow without thought while his mind wandered elsewhere. The moon was gone now, but the light falling through the leafless branches illuminated old memories and forgotten things: in that stand of trees, steep above the road on the rocky hillside, he had found a well or a cistern. A boy he was then, and he wondered at the fitting of the rocks, how they embraced each other. He looked for a cellar hole and found none, only this cunningly made thing, half-buried in the leaves, to hold a few barrels of the ground seep. The mystery of it, who had made it and why, stayed with him, was awakened again now. In a clearing further up the hillside, where the glacier had cut a curious groove in the rock and left a view out over the little valley, he had found what he knew to be an arrowhead, a broken thing, its shape barely recognizable, but carefully chipped out of a kind of rock he had never seen before. Like black glass, it was. He had told no one about it, and he had lost it; one day it was simply and without explanation no longer in his pocket. He wished he hadn't lost it, but was glad it had been his, even for a while. It was still his, wherever it was.

At the end of the field, where the road bent to the left, he carried on up the winding driveway towards the old house, towards that glowing in the sky. He was warmer now, except for his gloveless hands. He put them in the pockets of his coat to shield them from the frost, but found that the free swinging of his arms as he climbed the long incline was more important to him. He would have cold hands. He climbed faster, eager to get there, drawn by the idea of the light and a stirring of memory; and though it was the middle of the night, and dark, dark here under the trees, he felt so awake, so alive, so powerful that he confused this time with his waking hours. He would never sleep again.

And there below the drive, on a bare little rise he could just see, or thought he saw, was the Blackman's camp, the site of an old lean-to abandoned by a black squatter, perhaps a raggy, years before his own lifetime, but still there, still marked by a presence that sent a chill through him. His father had seen him once as a young man, though the Blackman spent most of his nights and days inside the hovel, drinking vanilla extract. And when he himself was a boy, the rise, always bare of trees, was still littered with those curious little bottles in varying shades of green, along with rusted remains of cooking implements that thrust up like teeth or daggers out of the ground. He had never known so much as the man's name, but his father's tales and his own imagination had provided an image of a huge, square, silent man wearing a hat and an ancient suit of grey worsted wool, and in his rambles through the woods that had been the province of the raggies or the dairy farmers so long ago, he had expected to see the Blackman sitting on some jut of a stone wall, staring at him. It had never happened, but it might yet, might yet. What was impossible on such a night?

The end of the long slow climb was in sight, up ahead where the woods opened like a railway tunnel to the sloping grass below the house. The light above the line of the hill was not moonlight, but colder still, and pulsing, sometimes with a reddish cast. He felt the hair rise on his forearms, as if he were surrounded now by presences summoned by this light. The Blackman was near, seated on a wall, his thighs shaped like the stones themselves, eyes fixed on the firmament. His father too walked somewhere in these familiar woods, drawn from his chilly Swedenborgian paradise to comment on the miraculous return of the beaver, and to explain the phenomenon of the northern lights. Had he waited for them there would have been others: farmers, settlers, Indians, anyone who had known this land, or had worked on it, or had died on it. Hallowed ground, the phrase came back to him.

But he hurried on, drawn by curiosity and by the reverberation of that other phrase that had come to him unbidden: the northern lights. He had been very small, light enough for his father to hold him effortlessly against his hip in the savage cold of another night with the unearthly light pulsing above them, veils of strange colours that shimmered among the bright stars from a point up near the top of the heavens down almost to the far horizon of hills. His father had scared him at first, reaching down to pick him up blankets and all out of a dream, and he thought the house must be on fire. But the only fire was in the sky, and his father kept repeating the phrase *Something you will never forget* as they made their way clumsily up the steep stairway to the attic and the bare porch with a white railing where he played in the summer and threw pebbles at the peonies below. He had been almost warm at first, though his father let drop a corner of the quilt in his eagerness to explain the veils of light, impressing on him the grave physical complexity of this event and the privilege of witnessing it. Was it like a mirage? Yes, in a way, though this was no optical illusion but the visible effect of a vast discharge of electrical energy from the sun to the poles of the earth, exciting the gases and ice crystals of the atmosphere and . . . and he had fallen back asleep, in spite of the cold, wondering what God might have to do with this brightness unfurled above him.

It was not as he remembered it, the shape of the hilltop as he emerged from the trees, nor the sky, for there were no veils or streamers now but midway between the zenith and dark hills a crown of light, red and white, around a dark centre. He made his way up the old terraces and the frosted grasses sang out beneath his boots. Ahead of him the house was darker than the sky, and now he could make out the old lines of it, subtracting in his mind the row of dormer

windows along the ridge of that attic and the unfamiliar block there –
a dining room or new kitchen? – that crouched in his mother's
herb garden, a place of low stone walls where the bees came all
summer long to the thyme and savory and thickets of mint.

He began, too, to find familiar shapes in the shrubs and trees
that flanked the house and spilled down the gentle slope to where
he stood. The maple loomed beyond the house, its trunk impossibly
huge, but the branches, wired together even then, were fewer now.
Untended hedges soared above the line of his eye, and there, by the
rock that had been a cliff to his childhood stood a single Japanese
maple, where once there had been two, a red one and a green one.
It was the first tree he had ever climbed, for it was possible to step
off the top of the rock, a dizzying height of some four feet, and into
the twisted crown of the tree, where he hung onto the tough little
branches and peered out above the flat dome of feathered green leaves.

In the red tree, now gone, he had found the girl from Darien,
who had vanished from the porch into the brilliant moonlight, into
the June night with its sound of frogs and the smell of cut grass as
strong as the perfume on his hands. *Catch me*, she had said, in a harsh
whisper as she rearranged the ruined straps of her dress, and she
was gone. No noise betrayed her as he walked barefoot in the dew
of the terraces, but the blood hummed in his ears. He began to
wonder if she had gone all the way down to the lake, had in his mind
the idea of a pale, graceful form arcing out of darkness towards the
bright surface of the water, when there, practically beside him, he
saw her dress under the shadows of that red tree. He held his breath,
waiting for her to move or speak, and was surprised by her laughter
floating down to him from above, for she had hung her dress on
a branch to climb naked into the tree. Now the smooth bark beneath
his hand, now the smoother warmth of her calf, downless, fluted with
muscle and braced against his weight, at last the familiar shape of
her shoulder, where the fine bones came together. When she pressed
against him the heat of her was like a shock. She took the clothes
off him then, almost fell out of the tree as she fumbled with both
hands at the buttons of his fly. "How do . . . " he began to ask, until
she put her hand over his mouth and showed him exactly how it could
be done. She was laughing when he finished, a nearly soundless
hysterical laughter that made it dangerous for them to get down out
of the tree. He was on the point of getting angry with her, but when
he saw the comical disarray of his clothes scattered on the grass, he
too began to laugh. Then she gathered up his clothes, made a rough

bed of them under the tree, and showed him again how it could be done. They fell asleep, to be awakened by the impossibly loud night song of an oven bird, perhaps singing for love himself. The grass was soaking now, and the cooler air of the night slid down the slope past them, pulling at their bare bodies like an undertow.

He listened now for that laughter, muffled yet echoing, looked, as he had then, for a light to pierce the dark shape of the house. The only sound, loud enough to wake a dog he thought, was that of his boots on the hard ground. What sort of people, he wondered, would live in a house out here without a dog?

The night was still, but so cold that he knew he must not stand long without moving, for the frost attacked his feet now as well as his hands, seeping through the soles of his boots, and he began to feel tired. The sight of the lake below him as he rounded the corner of the hill took his breath away, erased all notions of cold and fatigue: the fan of light stretched away before him, almost beneath his feet, mirroring the celestial event, bringing it to earth, to his lake, out of the high cold heaven. *Something you will never forget*, he repeated aloud, stumbling, almost falling down the hill, and said it again as he took his first step out onto the black ice.

There was no way of telling how thick it was this early in the season without taking an auger and cutting through, as he used to do when the cold didn't bother him so and he would spend whole days of the winter fishing through the ice on some pond in the woods, or right here, fifty steps along the shore where there was a good drop off and a long dead tree, slanting down into the greenish-black water that the fish seemed to favour. No way of telling, he thought, and though he was reassured by the groaning and the sharp answering crack of the ice expanding in the cold and thickening beneath him, still he knew this was a damn fool thing he was doing, for there were springs in this water running all year long. He should go back, he thought. What if Cat should wake and find him gone? What would be the first explanation that would come to her mind? He thought of his mother waking to find his father dead in the bed beside her, his hands folded on his breast, and then of Mrs Healey, who found a note on the breakfast table from Mr Healey, saying he was sorry that he just couldn't live that way any more, and was leaving for Mexico. Would she please forgive him? She may have forgiven him, but likely not, as three days later, when her sister was out doing the shopping, she hung herself. Put the rope on one side of the beam, as the town clerk, who was also the coroner, explained it, and herself on the other. Cat had surprised him by her reaction, a short and derisive laugh, when she heard the news about Mrs Healey, whom she had never thought much of anyway. No danger of Cat doing anything foolish, he thought, smiling to himself, but he wished he could spare her that moment of waking alone, her first glimpse of the years to come, the silence. And if he came back from this night wouldn't he have something to tell her, something she wouldn't dare doubt him on?

Halfway out on the ice towards the middle of the pond he still thought he would turn back, wanted a sign, some combination of chill and fatigue and fear to tell him that enough was enough. But he was stubborn, once he started something, and he was drawn by the mystery of the lights, which made him think about God now the same as it had back then, the first time. Perhaps he was now in the hand of God: he was no longer cold, or at least he did not care so long as he was moving, and he was not tired; instead of fear he felt a kind of joy, fierce and serene, as if he were entering a battle, like the soldiers of the Lord who triumphed whether they lived or died. I have lived, he said, I have lived, and drew a deep breath, and did not mind that the dark feather brushed his side. Beneath his feet, on that surface that was both a window and a mirror, he saw the flickering boreal colours, smiled at the suggestion of familiar hues: the ragged robin and the white clover and other grasses of the field as they fell beneath the sidebar of his tractor. He would know them anywhere, just as you could break the bale of hay in the middle of winter and see again the colours in the meadow. And ahead of him now, but not beyond his reach, the brightest image of all, the hollow crown of light with its centre of perfect darkness.

JAVIER MARÍAS

Lord Rendall's Song

For Julia Altares
who has not yet discovered me

"Lord Rendall's Song" was first published in my anthology *Cuentos únicos* (Ediciones Siruela, Madrid, 1989) in apocryphal form, that is, attributed to the English writer James Denham and purportedly translated by me. For that reason I also include here the biographical note that accompanied Denham's story, since some of the facts in it contribute, tacitly, to the story itself which would otherwise remain incomplete.

James Ryan Denham (1911–1943), born in London and educated at Cambridge, was one of the ill-starred talents of the Second World War. The son of a well-to-do family, he embarked on a diplomatic career that took him to Burma and India (1934–37). His known literary work is scant and hard to come by, consisting of five books all published in private editions and all now unobtainable, since it would seem he never considered this activity to be anything more than a hobby. He was a friend of both Malcolm Lowry, whom he had met at university, and of the famous art collector Edward James, and he himself came to own a fine collection of eighteenth- and nineteenth-century French paintings.

His last book, *How to Kill* (1943), from which this story, "Lord Rendall's Song", is taken, was the only one he tried to publish in a commercial edition; however, at the time, when the country was still at war, he was unable to find a publisher willing to accept it, partly because of the depressing effect it was felt the book might have on soldiers and civilian population alike and partly because of the oddly erotic under-tone present in some of the stories. Before that, Denham had published a book of poetry, *Vanishings* (1932), another volume of short stories, *Knives and Landscapes* (1934), a short novel, *The*

Night-Face (1938) and *Gentle Men and Women* (1939), a series of sketches of famous people, amongst them Chaplin, Cocteau, the dancer Tilly Losch and the pianist Dinu Lipatti. Denham died when he was thirty-two years old, killed in action in North Africa.

Although the story translated here (a vertiginous *mise en abîme*) is self-explanatory, it might be useful to know that the popular English song "Lord Rendall" consists of a dialogue between the young Lord Rendall and his mother after the former has been poisoned by his lover. To his mother's final question, "What will you leave your sweetheart, Lord Rendall, my son?", he replies: "A rope to hang her, mother, a rope to hang her."

I wanted to give Janet a surprise and so I did not tell her exactly when I would be home. Four years, I thought, is such a long time that a few more days of uncertainty will not make any difference. Getting a letter on Monday informing her that I would be arriving on Wednesday would be far less exciting than finding me there on the doorstep when she opened the front door on Wednesday itself. I had left war and imprisonment far behind me now, and so quickly had they been left behind that I was already beginning to forget them. I would gladly have forgotten it all instantly so that I could do my best to ensure that my life with Janet and our son would be unaffected by my sufferings, so that I could pick up my life again just as if I had never gone away, as if my time at the front – along with the orders and the fighting and the lice, the mutilations, hunger and death – had never existed. Nor the terror and the torments of the German prisoner-of-war camp. She knew I was alive, she had been notified to that effect, she knew that I had been taken prisoner and was therefore alive and would come home. She must have been waiting daily for some word of my return. I would give her a surprise, not a fright, and that would be a good thing. I would knock at the door and she would open it, drying her hands on her apron, and there I would be, dressed in civilian clothes at last, looking rather ill and thin, but nonetheless smiling and longing to embrace and to kiss her. I would take her in my arms, untie her apron, and she would bury her face in my shoulder and weep. I would notice my jacket growing damp with her tears, very different from the damp of the

punishment cell with its constant dripping or the monotonous rain
falling on our helmets during marches and in the trenches.

From the moment I made that decision not to forewarn her of my
arrival, I enjoyed the anticipation of my return so much that when
I finally found myself standing outside the house, I almost regretted
having to put an end to that sweet waiting. And that was why I first
crept round to the back of the house, hoping I might hear or see
something from the outside. I wanted to accustom myself to all the
usual, familiar sounds again, the sounds I had missed so dreadfully
all the time I had been kept from them: the clatter of pots and pans
in the kitchen, the creaking bathroom door, Janet's footsteps. And
the child's voice. The child had been one month old when I left, and
then he only used his voice to scream and shout. He would be four
years old now and would have a real voice, his own way of talking,
perhaps like his mother's, since he would have spent all that time
alone with her. His name was Martin.

I could not be sure if they were home or not. I got as far as the
back door and held my breath, eager for sounds. The first thing
I heard was a child crying and I found that odd. It was the crying of
a small child, as small as Martin had been when I left for the front.
How was that possible? I wondered if I had got the wrong house or
if Janet and the child had moved away without my knowing and
another family had moved in. The child's crying came from far off,
apparently from our bedroom. I peered in. There was the kitchen,
empty, no one there, no food. Night was falling, it was about time
Janet started preparing something for supper; perhaps she would
do so as soon as the child had calmed down. I could not wait,
however, and I walked round to the front of the house to see if I
had any better luck there. On my right was the living room
window, on my left, on the other side of the front door, our bedroom
window. I walked round the house to the right, keeping close to
the walls, half crouching so as not to be seen. Then I slowly drew
myself up until I could see into the living room with my left eye.
That was empty too, the window was closed but I could still hear
the child crying, the child who could not possibly be Martin. Janet
must be in the bedroom, calming the child down, whoever that
child was, and always assuming that the woman was Janet. I was
just about to move over to the window on the left when the living
room door opened and I saw Janet come in. Yes, it was her, I had
not got the wrong house and they had not moved away without
my knowing. She was wearing an apron, just as I had pictured her.

She always wore an apron; she said taking it off was a waste of time because, she said, she would only have to put it on again later to do something else. She looked very pretty, she hadn't changed. I saw and thought all this in a matter of seconds, because behind her, immediately behind, I saw a man follow her in. He was very tall and from my perspective his head was cut off by the upper frame of the window. He was in shirtsleeves, but still had his tie on, as if he had just come home from work and so far had only had time to take off his jacket. He seemed very much at home there. When he came in, he had walked behind Janet the way husbands in their own homes walk behind their wives. If I crouched down any lower, I would be unable to see anything, so I decided that I would wait until he sat down to get a good look at his face. He turned round for a few seconds presenting me with a close-up view of the back of his white shirt, his hands in his trouser pockets. When he moved away from the window, I could see Janet again. They did not speak. They seemed angry. It was one of those brief, tense silences that tend to follow arguments between husband and wife. Then Janet sat down on the sofa and crossed her legs. I thought it odd that she should be wearing sheer stockings and high heels when she had her apron on. She suddenly buried her face in her hands and started crying. He crouched down by her side, but not in order to console her; he just watched her crying. It was then, when he crouched down, that I saw his face. His face was *my* face. The man in shirtsleeves looked exactly like me. I do not mean that he bore an unusually close resemblance to me: his features were identical to mine, they were mine; it was like looking at myself in a mirror or, rather, like watching one of those home movies we made shortly after Martin was born. Janet's father had given us a camera so that we would have pictures of our child when he was no longer a child. Janet's father had had money before the war and I hoped that, despite any financial difficulties, Janet would have been able to film something of the years with Martin that I had lost. I even wondered if what I was seeing was, in fact, a film. Perhaps I had arrived at precisely the moment when Janet, feeling nostalgic, had chosen to sit down in the living room to watch one of those films showing scenes that took place before I went away. No, that was impossible, for what I was watching was in colour, not black and white and, besides, no one had ever filmed her and myself from that window, because what I was seeing I was seeing from the position I was occupying at that moment. The man in the room was real: if I broke the glass and reached in, I could touch him. He was crouching by the sofa and he had my eyes, my nose, my lips, my blond, curly hair, he even had the small scar at the base of his left eyebrow from the time my cousin Derek threw a stone at me when I was a child. I touched the small scar. Outside, night had fallen.

He was talking now, but I could not make out what he was saying through the closed window and Martin had stopped crying since they went into the living room. Meanwhile Janet was still sobbing and the man who looked like me was crouched down beside her, saying something to her, though I could tell from the expression on his face that his words were not consoling but mocking or even accusing. My head was in a whirl, but despite that, two or three ideas still surfaced in my mind, each more absurd than the last. I thought she must have found a man identical to me in order to take my place during my long absence. I thought that time must have been incomprehensibly altered or cancelled, that those four years really had been forgotten, erased, just as I had wished, so that I might pick up the threads of my life with Janet and the child again. The years of war and imprisonment really had not existed and I, Tom Booth, had never gone to war or been taken prisoner which was why I was here, as on any other day, arguing with Janet on my return from work. I had spent those four years with her. I, Tom Booth, had not been called up, I had stayed at home. But then, who was the "I" looking through the window, the "I" who had walked up to this house, the "I" who had just been released from a German prisoner-of-war camp? Who did all these memories belong to? Who had fought in the war? And I thought something else too, perhaps the excitement of returning home had evoked some scene from the past, a scene, perhaps the very last scene, that took place before I went away, something I had forgotten and that resurfaced now with the shock of homecoming. Perhaps, on that last day, Janet had cried because I was going away, possibly to my death, and I had treated it all as a joke. That might explain the child Martin's crying, for he was still a baby then. The fact was, however, that it was no hallucination, I was neither imagining nor remembering it, I was seeing it now. Besides, Janet had not cried before I left. She was a woman of great strength of character, she had kept smiling right up until the very last moment, she had behaved as if it were the most natural thing in the world, as if I were not really going away at all. She knew that to have done otherwise would have made everything so much more difficult for me. She would weep today when I opened the door, but this time she would weep on my shoulder, making my jacket damp with her tears.

No, I was not seeing something from the past, something I had forgotten. I knew this with absolute certainty when I saw the man, the husband, the man who was me, Tom, suddenly stand up and seize Janet round the throat, his wife, my wife, sitting there on the sofa. He seized her round the throat with both hands and I knew that he had begun to squeeze even though, again, all I could see was Tom's back, my back, the vast white shirt blocking my view of Janet who was still sitting on the sofa. Of her I could see only her outstretched arms, her arms flailing in the air and then hidden behind the shirt, perhaps in a desperate attempt to loosen the grip which was not my grip; and then, after a few short seconds, Janet's arms appeared again, on either side of the shirt of which I could see only the back, except this time they were limp, inert. Through the closed windows I could hear the child crying again. The man left the room, going off towards the left, doubtless towards the bedroom where the child was. And when he moved away, I saw Janet there dead, strangled. In the struggle her skirt had ridden up and she had lost one of her high-heeled shoes. I saw the suspenders I had tried so hard not to think about during those last four years.

I was paralysed, but I managed to think: that man who is me, that man who has not moved from Chesham during all this time, is going to kill Martin as well or else the new baby, assuming that Janet and I have had another baby during my absence. I must break the glass and go in and kill that man before he kills Martin or his own newborn child. I must stop him. I must kill myself right now. Except that I am outside the window and the danger is inside.

While I was thinking all this, the child's crying stopped, suddenly. There were none of the little whimpers you usually get as a child calms down, none of the progressive calm that overtakes children when you pick them up or rock them or sing to them. Before I went away, I used to sing Lord Rendall's song to Martin and sometimes I managed to quieten him, to stop him crying, but it took a long time, I had to sing the song to him over and over. He would go on sobbing, but his sobs would gradually diminish, until at last he fell asleep. That child, on the other hand, had fallen silent abruptly, with no transitional phase. And in the midst of the silence, without realising what I was doing, I stood up by the window and started singing Lord Rendall's song, the song I used to sing to Martin and which begins: "Where have you been all the day, Rendall, my son?", except I used to sing: "Where have you been all the day, Martin, my son?" And then, when I began singing it there next to the window, I heard the voice of the man in our bedroom join with mine to sing the second verse: "Where have you been all the day, my pretty Tom?" But the child, my child Martin or his child who bore my name, had stopped crying. And when the man and I stopped singing Lord Rendall's song, I could not help wondering which of us would be hanged.

Translated from the Spanish by Margaret Jull Costa

LUIGI MALERBA

Silvercap

For some time now an odd thing has been happening to me, easy enough to say but not so easy to explain: I have an uncomfortable relationship with my body, and I mean with all the various parts of my body. For a start I really *feel* that I have a skin, that I have an extraneous wrapping around me, like a glove pinching in to every fold and wrinkle and covering every square millimetre.

Everyone knows he has a skin, of course, but I think it seldom happens that people actually feel they are wearing it, as I do. However, it's not only the skin. I have the same problem with the rest of my body. I really believe people forget they have a liver, a spleen, a heart, and the rest of it, and only recall it to mind when they feel pain in one place or another. Of course, if someone has liver trouble he's bound, while seeking the source of his discomfort, to remember that he has a liver. I, on the other hand, am incessantly mindful of these things. I am conscious of my stomach and intestines while they are doing their digestion, of my liver while it is filtering my blood, of my heart while it is pumping away. I number my veins one by one, and the same thing goes for my muscles and bones. Some days I have to find any means of distraction whatever, because my mind can no longer keep pace with it all. It makes me feel like a sentinel put in charge of some unbelievably complex piece of technology. The human body, in short.

Some years ago I broke both an arm and a leg by crashing into a tree on my skis. Well, at the hospital they patched me up by shooting (as they called it) two steel pins into my femur and another two into my humerus. When I was discharged the surgeon was keen to reassure me, saying: "You'll see, in a week's time you'll have forgotten those pins, let alone feel them."

But on the contrary I went on feeling them, and feel them still, more than four years later. But the real surprise came when along with that purely physical feeling came the realization that the steel pins there in my body were far from being a disagreeable presence. The unusual sensitivity I have always had regarding all my bodily members was further enhanced by these two metal adjuncts.

Well, after those two smashed limbs I gave up skiing and took to racing about on motorbikes. I rode the mountain trails of the Apennines like a maniac, and everyone said to me: Take care, or one of these days you'll crack your skull. And sure enough I did. They picked me up way over the brow of a bend and hauled me into hospital with not a sign of life in me. I can tell you that mending a cracked skull is no easy business, but modern-day surgery works miracles, and four months later I left the hospital with a large chunk of skull replaced by a silver cap, a kind of silvery helmet which is now a part of my head. I have scrupulously concealed it with hair identical to my own, though I confess I would rather have left the silver in full view, and kept it polished like the old family plate. But my wife put her foot down. I am a very understanding man, so I yielded, however reluctantly, to her wish to keep it hidden.

Now and again I would have a bit of fun by making a bet with someone who didn't know my secret. Try and make a hole in my head with a pin, I'd say. I won every time. But when I explained that I had a silver skullcap I would glimpse in the look they gave me a spot of embarrassment, and who knows even of pity.

So in the early days I made bets on my silver skull. Then I dropped it, because a strange thing was taking place: little by little the metal was becoming sensitive. There's no other explanation. I'd say try and puncture my head with this pin, and the other fellow would try, and fail, but I felt something very near to pain. Rather than real pain I'd be inclined to call it "brain pain". I've heard it said that in many cases of amputation the pain remains even when the limb has been lopped off. It's called phantom pain. Mine also was this same kind of pain.

Another thing that interests me in this field, though my own sight is as right as rain, is the matter of the glass eye. I don't have to tell you that no one can see through a glass eye, its presence in the socket is purely for aesthetic reasons. All the same, a friend of mine who has worn one for many years tells me that from time to time he places a hand over his good eye and simply with his glass one still manages to discern images vaguely corresponding to what he would really be seeing. He doesn't claim that he actually sees through it, but that he can form mental pictures of what the glass eye is "looking at". This shows that a material normally considered inert, as glass is, from being in contact with the human body at a certain point acquires a sensitivity of its own; it succeeds in communicating with the nervous system and transmitting its impulses. These are phenomena which official science refuses to take into consideration. Every time I've tried to talk about it to a doctor I've met with utter bafflement. I've resigned myself to never getting it across.

I have less than no shame in confessing that I love metals in general, and am proud of my steel, my silver, and the gold with which many of my teeth are crowned. Mine is a genuine avowal to metallurgy. When the dentist asks me whether I want my teeth crowned with porcelain or synthetic resin I invariably reply: gold. Except for my front teeth I have insisted that all repairs, fillings, bridges, crowns and so forth should be made of gold.

Plastics interest me less. They come in handy for rebuilding valves in the heart, reconstructing the circuits of veins and arteries, remodelling joints, replacing lengths of intestine, and are the last word for artificial arms and legs. I'm told that lots of people learn to live with them with no problem at all, but they're of no interest to me. I am interested solely in metals.

I have often tried to come up with a sort of philosophical reason for this dedication to metals, and have eventually arrived at a very simple notion, perhaps all too simple, and it is this. The world is a very hard place full of hard things, the tree that smashed my arm and my leg, the stone that cracked my skull, but also the walls of houses, and furniture, floors, cars, trains, streets and their pavements, and ice. All these things are hard, as the mountains are hard, and hard is the whole crust of the earth. Mankind, on the other hand, is soft, is yielding. This notion nagged at me constantly, and my thoughts always returned to my metals.

When I say I take pleasure in having certain parts of my body made of metal, nobody understands what I'm talking about. That's natural enough. To understand it you have first of all to undergo the same experience, but even that is not enough. You have to *live* it with what I call physical sensibility, and what I call physical sensibility is that particular bodily perception that you have a natural disposition for, but which can be perfected by practice. This type of sensitivity enables you to concentrate, now here now there, on a specific area of your body, but in the course of time this can become widespread and automatic. When I left hospital with my silver cap I felt a slight itching on the metal, but the odd thing was that I took an immediate liking to it. It felt good. I instantly switched my attention onto that piece of metal as onto a part of my body privileged and practically in a state of grace. I'm coming on too strong of course, but this was the beginning of my yearning to have other parts of my body – many

parts! – made of metal. And just to think that before seeing me off
the surgeon described those four steel pins as "foreign bodies".

Having stated my interest in metals inserted into the human body
I must in all honesty admit certain drawbacks. For example, if I stay
too long with my head in the sun the silver, which is a formidable
heat conductor, gets baking hot and broils my brain. This is a highly
unpleasant sensation and, so they tell me, even dangerous. The doctor
told me that if I'm not careful I could go mad. I wouldn't care for that.

Living with metals naturally creates problems of equilibrium
between the metal parts and the others. There is a difficult period to
be overcome, and that is when the metal parts are more than one,
scattered here and there and not yet co-ordinated among themselves.
I confess that to begin with I had some moments of bewilderment
and organizational uncertainty in my cohabitation with metals, but
we have to take account of the fact that my experiences were traumatic
and painful. A broken arm and leg and then a smashed skull. Painful
and hazardous experiences indeed. Had I decided to have a silver
skullcap inserted without being forced to it by my accident everything
would have been simpler. But as yet there are no surgeons prepared
to perform such an operation because there are no clients demanding
it, and in the absence of demand there is no supply.

The fact is that without being aware of it mankind envies machines,
especially those in which the parts can be replaced just as soon as
they are worn out or broken. This is an impulse which very few
people have admitted to themselves. We should start to promote
awareness of this repressed desire. From my own personal standpoint
I want to be quite explicit: I would like to be made from head to
foot entirely of metal. Put like that it seems like a pipe-dream, but
I believe that in the none too distant future many people will succeed
in becoming glittering machines.

Now I realize that I'm still hypocritically beating about the bush
and that the truth is that I'm dead scared of words because I have
to come straight out with it: I want to become a robot, and I do
believe that in that none too distant future many people will manage
to become robots.

At this time I must explain a few points. First of all, when I say
robot I really do mean a mechanical robot, even more intelligent than
the robots described in Asimov's stories, and to express it as precisely
as possible, a "human" robot. I have no intention of giving up on
my personal self, I intend to remain myself, come what may. If I
have to give up on being myself, then the whole thing's off. I've heard

of people who have a longing to be birds and once I met a fellow who had an urge to be a crocodile. A friend of mine sometimes thinks he's Napoleon, so I ask you what's so odd about dreaming of being a robot?

One day I sounded the matter out with my wife and (talking in general terms of course) I said: Imagine what fun to be robots all made of metal, and all those transistors and electrical circuits organizing your life and what have you. Well, she started off laughing, but when she caught on that I was serious she got mad at me. Right you are, she said, you're all patched up with metal in any case, so now all you need is an iron cock and we'll be up and away.

She has a coarse way of talking, my wife does, but from time to time she comes out with something that makes sense. For example, I confess that this detail had never occurred to me. How to solve the question of love-making for robots? But come to think of it that iron cock doesn't seem too bad an idea, even if brass, bronze or copper might be better for the job, being softer, more malleable metals, which do not rust, which slide back and forth without too much friction or disagreeable squeaks. It's no coincidence that they are used for pumps and our bathroom taps. But I had to put a stop to this conversation about cocks and metals, because divorce is always lurking round the corner.

However, I haven't given up working at my idea, or dwelling on my dream. If it is the case that nature produces analogies, then mankind, being part of nature, must begin to produce something analogous to himself, albeit simpler and above all harder. Simplicity and hardness: that is what entices me most about robots as opposed to the human body. Metals are solid, unbreakable, resistant to heat and cold. All the organs of the human body are soft and perishable, and it only takes a longish pin to slay the heftiest man on earth.

I broke an arm and a leg and got my four steel rivets. Then I smashed my skull and was given my silver skullcap. But it's not enough and I'm not satisfied. I know that I am fragile and perishable in a world of hard, stony, hostile, bruising things, things that can slice you to the bone. Even the Bible says that the flesh is weak, and weak not only in a metaphorical sense, but really and truly so. And it goes on to say that it falls to dust as soon as winking. But I don't want to fall to dust. I want to be made of metal, a shining metal machine I want to be, to match up to all the hardness of this world.

Translated from the Italian by Patrick Creagh

JULIAN MAZOR

The Lost Cause

Walter Desmond had been a banker. Banking for him had held but one drawback, the problem of foreclosure when the debt could not be paid. He'd done all within his power to delay that awful time, given extensions, refinanced the loan, anything to save the man his property; and if all efforts failed, he'd state his own distress at how things had turned out and tell the man, whether coloured or white, farmer or merchant, that he hoped he'd soon be on his feet again. He had hated to foreclose; and no one had ever left him untouched by his kindness and goodwill. "Don't you worry. You'll be all right, just have some faith now," he'd say to each one, meaning every word. But when the economy went bad and stores closed on the main street of town and people left to find work elsewhere, he sold his interest in the bank and retired to his house on the hill. Not long after that, his wife died.

"I just don't *believe* you, Walter," Rose Lee had said. "I can't believe what comes out of your mouth. You are outrageous in your views."

"Well, honey, I don't know what's so hard to believe. My views are nothing but moderate," he'd replied.

They were from Virginia, of the same background, but had long differed in their views of the South. Even when first married and very much in love, they were aware of their differences; but it hardly mattered then. Other things were more central to their happiness. But as time went by and the world changed, as she grew more politically aware and joined liberal groups and subscribed to left-wing publications that offended his sense of proportion, he felt their growing estrangement. The things about him that had once pleased her, his affability and charm, his way of deflecting unpleasantness with a smile and a kind word, had only come to irritate her, for she saw them as an unconscious deception to maintain the status quo and represented for her a style and way of life she had long abandoned. Their main disagreement was about the Southern past. Rose Lee'd felt it was best forgotten or remembered only with regret. "See it as a morality play, Walter, or cautionary tale. But don't dwell on it. Don't *sentimentalize* like your poor old mother, that mad heartless woman you defend day and night just because she is your mother. You are a nice man, Walter, but the Southern past is an albatross around your neck."

"Honey, we must look back with sympathy," he'd said.

"You have too *much* sympathy. You've got to break with all that – and change. One must often be ruthless to be moral."

But it was not in him to be ruthless. He feared rapid change. The change that she desired would destroy the social order and create chaos in its place. It would destroy continuity, and life would lose its meaning. Change had to come slowly; a man had to understand where he'd come from. It did no good to hate the past or to condemn those who had gone before. He preferred to look back thoughtfully and give due respect and honour. He did not wish to stand in the way of progress but rather to move forward with care and deliberation.

The word she'd loved more than any other was "new". She spoke of entering a new day, being part of a new world, newness was everything; her greatest desire was to give up the "sad old backwater ways" of their parents and the "dead hand of past generations". She favoured every kind of liberation, intellectual, emotional, political and sexual. She hated tyranny of heart, mind and soul. In that regard, she likened herself to Thomas Jefferson, though she disapproved of him for owning slaves. As for sexual matters, she desired that "the act of love be always fresh and new". Walter had tried to make allowances for her thinking, he knew she was nervous and high-strung, but he'd been upset by her insistent modernity.

"Why, you just don't have to make love in the bedroom, Walter. You can make love all over the house – there's no rule against it. You can make love on the floor, on the dining room table, for God's sake."

"Well, honey, why would we want to do that?"

It was her burden, she often thought, to have been born in the South and to have married a man like him.

At the beginning he was her project and at the end her hopeless task. "If I die first, I'm going to haunt you, Walter," she'd said with a kind of rueful affection. And after her death in the spring of 1962, she did haunt him through his memories of their life together.

It was his mother's birthday, on a cool fall afternoon.

He started out for the cemetery. It was not too far from his house, a white frame building with a gabled roof and a long porch. The house rested on a hill. Looking west from the porch, one could see farms and fields and farther off the Blue Ridge Mountains. The ground in front sloped down a good distance to a narrow winding road. Behind the house was an open field of wild grass, then an expanse of woods. A path through the woods led to the cemetery, which could also be reached by car taking the road below a quarter mile to the north and then turning right and driving on past a church, a general store and an old wood structure one wing of which had collapsed. Just past that abandoned building in a clear meadow on the edge of the woods and surrounded by a white board fence lay the cemetery.

On this day he walked through the woods.

The sky was overcast. It had rained the previous night, and the ground was soft underfoot.

He climbed over the white board fence, then stood under a tree by the graves and looked at the headstone with the name "Desmond" and at the footstones of the dead. They were all there, his mother and father and younger brother and his wife, Rose Lee. His mother and father had been dead for three years, dying a month apart. His brother, Weber, had died in a car wreck in the Shenandoah Valley ten years before the death of his parents. Walter's own footstone with his name and the year of his birth was beside his wife's. She'd been dead a little more than a year.

Rose Lee had died of a stroke while at the home of her sister, Cora, in Newport News. Walter had been in Richmond at the time.

At the funeral, Cora had said, "Rose Lee was the most unselfish person I ever knew. She was good and caring and brave – and so misunderstood."

A year before she died, he had spoken of separation. He had wished to live a more serene life. He was not blaming her, but he was worn out by contention; he needed breathing space. He thought it would be better for both of them, for he could never please her.

She'd been hurt and surprised. She could not imagine him leaving. He was such a loyal person, but then she knew it was a matter of divided loyalties, and she felt bitter.

"I know we can thank your old mother for this. Well, she'd be happy now."

"Rose Lee, I'm sorry for any wrong I might have done you."

She pushed her fists into her eyes.

"Oh, be quiet. You are tormenting me. I can hardly breathe! Oh, yes, she's happy now lying in her grave. Well, go ahead and leave me, Walter, if that's what you want!"

But he did not leave her, he discovered he did not know how to walk away for good; he could not give up the habit of their married life with its familiar rhythms, strains and opposition. He loved her in his sorrowful way, and he could not imagine life without her.

He could hear his father saying, "What does Rose Lee mean? Wasn't I good to the coloured? They are people just like us and God made them and I helped them out when I could. George Mobley worked for me for thirty years. And he was more than my employee. We were friends. George had a very refined sensibility. You know I often felt he was spiritually superior to me. He'd been deepened by suffering and travail and he had a wisdom, Walter, that I could never possess. We weren't on an equal footing to be sure. Each of us understood his place, but that helped us feel natural with each other. I knew he was a coloured man, but I still got to know him as a person. Of course we've kept the coloured down. We are not without blame. But at the same time I have loved some of those people like they were my own family. I took care of George. I took care of his medical bills, and I paid for his funeral and later helped out his wife Rayola. Don't you know I cared about them? I would have liked to uplift the whole coloured race if that was possible. Why, my own father taught this Negro Obadiah Parker how to read. Obadiah was old. His parents had been slaves in Westmoreland County. He'd come up to the house and sit in the parlour and my father taught him the alphabet, and then how to read. Don't you know he'd have lain down his life for my daddy? Sure, we did wrong, there are things that need fixing. But we could straighten it out, if given half a chance. It's all got out of hand. The white extremists and Negro agitators are wrecking the country, and I don't know where it will end. It's hard to make friends with the coloured now, not the old ones but the young ones coming up. They hardly look at you when they pass in the street or they have a scowl on their faces. It's all so sad, this passing of good feeling. You know why Obadiah loved my father? He knew he was *appreciated*. My father valued him. You don't find that in the north. I know Rose Lee means well, and if she wants to judge me, it's her right, but, Walter, here's the truth. I love my coloured friends. They have humour, they have grace, and they know how to laugh and tell a joke and see the sunny side of life. We don't need outside agitators spreading discord and confusion."

Walter remembered Calpurnia, the coloured woman who had helped raise him and Weber. He recalled his mother saying to Rose Lee, "When they were small children, they loved Callie as much as they loved me. Maybe more. I didn't resent it at all. They loved her for good reason. I loved her, too, and in her later years I did all that I could to make her life comfortable and pleasant. When she died, we were all sick with grief."

Rose Lee had shaken her head with irritation.

"What's *that* have to do with anything? I was discussing civil rights. You are not saying you'd give rights to the coloured because you loved Calpurnia. You are not saying anything. What is left unsaid is that you just miss the old ways, and want to turn back the clock."

"I implied no such thing. What's gone is gone, and I know that as well as you. I was just saying that we loved Calpurnia. My, how you twist things, Rose Lee."

Walter and Rose Lee had gone to New York in 1959 to visit her Wellesley College room-mate, Irma Braverson, and he remembered how she had pleaded with him to watch what he said.

"Don't embarrass me with your reactionary views, don't try to correct anyone or *explain* things," she'd said, but during a dinner party in their honour the discussion had gotten around to the South and the race issue, and Walter, shy at first and reluctant to speak, soon found himself talking at great length on the "complexity of this sad old problem".

"Oh, I can't believe what came out of your mouth," Rose Lee said, later. "What must they think of us now? Why must you justify all the prejudice intelligent people have against the South? It's hard enough to live down our past, and you just play into their hands. Who cares that your grandfather was a good friend to a Negro named Obadiah and how Obadiah loved him, and how your grandfather taught him to read and write? And how he said, 'Obadiah has more wisdom than I.' It was embarrassing. No, humiliating is more like it. And then you had to go on about old Calpurnia. I wanted to die."

"Rose Lee, I just tried to say that there was much mutual affection between the races. And that some lovely Negroes came out of that society of discrimination."

"What are you saying? You want to create more lovely Negroes? My God, I can't believe you wouldn't have had the sense to sort of tailor your remarks."

"I only said we have to forgive each other and move on."

"Oh, your fake old piety! Whatever do we have to forgive the Negroes for?"

"For their anger and impatience, Rose Lee – for their hysteria. We have to forgive them, as they should forgive us."

"But we were unjust to the Negroes! They don't need our forgiveness."

"We are very much together, and we are very much apart – we require a new spirit of brotherhood."

"Oh, be quiet."

Walter held up a hand.

"We must seek understanding and good will between the races."

"What does that *mean*? Nothing! You are not saying anything. God, you are just like your father. You are both *so comfortable* with yourselves. And your old mother! The thought of her has nearly ruined New York for me, as she has ruined everything else. She is a living symbol of everything that's wrong, Walter, and you are getting just like her."

His mother, Grace Desmond, had loved history and had been a member of the Daughters of the Confederacy. When he and his brother Weber were children, she had taken them to Virginia plantations and to the battlefields. She had talked often about Robert E. Lee. Once they'd gone into Westmoreland County to visit Stratford Hall, his birthplace, and she'd told them how Robert at the age of four had to leave his beloved home. "His father had lost the property due to poor investment and rash speculation. But before they left Stratford Hall Robert went into one of the rooms and said goodbye to the little angels carved on the fireplace."

And she'd taken them into that room to see the angels that he had seen when he was four.

Walter could remember almost perfectly her lecture on Lee. He had heard it so often in his youth, and later on as well.

"Robert E. Lee was the son of Henry 'Lighthorse Harry' Lee, a hero of the Revolutionary War and a friend and confidant of Washington and Lafayette. When Lafayette came to Virginia some years after the war, he paid a call on his old comrade-in-arms at his home in Alexandria. But though a great hero and loved by all, Lighthorse Harry had suffered many financial reverses. He did not have a good head for making money, and he squandered his entire estate. His life was tragic, and he died when young Robert was only twelve. Robert was his son by his second wife, Ann Carter, who grew up on the Shirley Plantation. His first wife, Lucy, died young.

"General Lee's mother devoted herself to the raising of her children, and when she later became an invalid, Robert cared for her with great tenderness until her death. Later in his life he cared for his invalided wife, Mary. She was the daughter of George Washington Curtis, the grandson of Martha Washington and the adopted son of General

Washington. Mary was not an easy person to live with. She was difficult and temperamental, and did not show General Lee the proper respect even when he commanded the forces of the Confederacy, but Robert loved her and treated her with understanding and compassion. He was a man who gracefully bore his burdens.

"Next to Lee the greatest soldier of the War Between the States was Stonewall Jackson, but he died at Chancellorsville, shot mistakenly in the dark by his own men. His left arm was amputated. He seemed to recover for a time but later died of pneumonia. His last words in delirium were, 'Let us cross over the river and rest under the shade of the trees.' When Lee heard the news he said, 'I have lost my right arm.' I do not care much for General James Longstreet. He was not a Virginian – I think he was from Georgia or South Carolina – and he did not have good manners – and he had blamed Lee for the defeat at Gettysburg. Lee had been good to Longstreet, had called him 'my old war horse', but Longstreet betrayed him. It was Longstreet who lost Gettysburg, not Lee. As you can gather, boys, James Longstreet is not in my pantheon of heroes. If Longstreet's corps had attacked at sunrise on the second day, Lee would have been victorious, and the North would have sued for peace. But Lee's orders had been disobeyed, and Longstreet did not attack until late in the afternoon. By then the opportunity was lost. For the Yankees had gained time to strengthen their centre at Cemetery Ridge. On the third day Pickett's division moved out towards that ridge in some desperate attempt to break through the Yankee lines. Oh, you know what happened there, boys. They charged right into the Yankee guns. It was heroic and futile, like the Charge of the Light Brigade. Weaknesses that could have once been exploited by rapid movement had disappeared. If only Longstreet had attacked early on the second day, there would have been no need for Pickett's Charge, and victory would have been assured. If only Jackson had lived! He would have arrived on time!"

They were all together at his mother's home.

"Why Southern boys and girls are becoming nearly as rude as Yankee children. They are losing sight of courtesy," Walter's mother said.

Rose Lee smiled.

"It's a good sign. They are not so cowed. They are thinking for themselves."

"They are not thinking at all. Children need not show disrespect to prove they are independent thinkers. But of course, Rose Lee, you mock courtesy. It had once been bred in you by your dear parents, but you went north to college and got ruined."

Rose Lee laughed.

"Mother Desmond, you are so *provincial*. You ought to travel some and get a broader view."

"I don't need a broader view, thank you. I know what I believe. I believe in *loyalty*. And I don't mean loyalty to the NAACP. Why I can't believe that you are sending them money, and acting so *moral* about it. You are just flaunting your liberal ways."

"Why, because I send them a little money? Well, I see no need to apologize. I hope it helps the coloured advance."

"It is unseemly how you push your views on my friends. It is embarrassing to me."

"What are you saying? You are more concerned about embarrassment than morality?"

"I said nothing about morality, Rose Lee, but I know it gives you pleasure to twist the meaning of my words."

"Your meaning is quite clear, and I twisted nothing."

"I will not answer you. I leave myself open to your malice and contempt."

Rose Lee shook her head.

"Lord you are so *devious*."

"I am in no way devious. You take pride in being a renegade. You are disloyal to Virginia."

"Disloyal? Last I heard Richmond had fallen. The war has been over near a hundred years."

"I dislike your tone."

"The war is over, that's all."

"Oh, yes, but think of our sorrow and loss!"

"What sorrow, what loss? This is 1959."

'The Confederacy died at Appomattox. And we have not recovered to this day."

Rose Lee shook her head.

"We are one nation, Mother Desmond. You ought to thank Mr Lincoln."

"Please don't speak of Lincoln."

"Oh, I forgot. Here I must speak only of General Lee."

"No, I prefer that you *not* speak of him, for there is something sardonic in your tone and offensive in your manner."

"Oh, forgive me. I'll go to Richmond tomorrow and *genuflect* before his monument."

"Your sarcasm is unbecoming. And you are his distant kin."

"So what. Who cares?"

"I care, Rose Lee. He doesn't deserve your scorn and mockery."

"How you go on."

"Yes, I go on. You are so unfair. All through his life he was nothing but good, a devoted son, a model cadet at West Point, a loving husband and father. And you mock this man. Yes, all through his life, at every stage, he was exemplary. He was a hero of the Mexican War. General Winfield accorded him the highest praise in his reports."

"Oh, please calm down."

"In the ordeal of surrender at Appomattox, he thought only of his men."

Rose Lee shook her head.

"Just calm down, will you. I say he was *selfish*. His daughters never married because he wished them to nurse him when he got old."

"That is slander! They never married because they were loyal to their dear father, and they could find no man to match him."

"I can't believe you, Mother Desmond. You are so blind, so naïve."

Walter's mother sighed.

"Rose Lee, you are so predictable. Everything southern is *bad* . . . I know you so well."

"I live in reality, and I won't buy your old myths. I am so sick of Robert E. Lee. I find your adoration sickening. He was no saint."

"Why must you tear him down? What pleasure can it give you?"

"I do not *romanticize*. I will not invent."

"I invent nothing. I romanticize nothing. After the war he allowed no one in his presence to speak unkindly of General Grant, that's the sort of man he was, magnanimous and good! I do not declare him to be a saint, Rose Lee. He was flesh and blood. He was human. He loved the company of pretty young women, and he had a tender correspondence with a number of them, but there was never a hint of scandal. I find it hard to accept how you slander him, your own distant kinsman. I cannot understand how you slander him and betray the cause for which he suffered. I am still affected by his life. I am consoled by his memory and the beauty of his character. Yes, he was too good to be true, but there he was, true and good, and neither envy nor spite nor the calumny of small-minded detractors can change a thing."

Rose Lee laughed.

"Oh, how *dramatic* we are today! Lee is no model for the modern age. He was tied up with duty and self-denial. He was neurotic, a depressed personality."

"Oh, how up to date we are! He was not *neurotic*, Rose Lee, not a *depressed personality*. He had lived through great tragedy and suffered from the long strain of war, but he bore it with grace and he never burdened others. And what's wrong with duty? It's a virtue, not a crime. It entails sacrifice for others. I'm in distress at your remarks. God might forgive you for them but I never will!"

"Oh, I was wondering when God would appear. Come on, Walter, I can't deal with God *and* General Lee."

Walter, standing with his father in another part of the room, walked over.

"Mama, we're leaving. Don't be upset now," he said.

"Take her out of here."

Rose Lee put on her coat.

"I'm leaving, Mother Desmond, and I will not set foot in your house ever again."

"I know you will not, for you are not welcome here."

"I would not come, even if I were welcome."

"Well, don't worry. You're not and never will be."

"Good! I'm so glad to be relieved of your tiresome company."

And three days later they were all together again at his parents' home.

His mother was speaking.

"Stop talking of the *Civil* War. This was no rebellion, Rose Lee. It was the War Between the States. We seceded, we had a right to secede, and we became a separate nation, and for this we were brutally invaded. And we defended ourselves as was *our right*. And after four years of resistance, worn down by superior numbers and materiel, we could fight no more, and we lay down our arms, our land and people in ruin."

Rose Lee sighed.

"Spare me your orations. The truth is obvious. Southern society was based on the practice of slavery, and all our problems came from that."

"Our forefathers did not invent slavery. They were born into it. Slavery was part of the time in which they lived. I do not mourn its passing. Had I lived back then, I'd have opposed that peculiar institution, as did General Lee. As you know, he believed in gradual emancipation."

Rose Lee laughed.

"I'm sure you like the *gradual* part."

"Out of concern for the slaves. He wished them prepared for freedom when it came."

"Oh, why don't you admit it. You'd love to turn back the clock. 'Oh, how nice to hear the darkies singing. Is there anything more lovely than to hear them in the dusky light? Oh, they really love us. We've been so *good* to them.'"

"Is that supposed to be funny? Well, it isn't, not one bit. I despise your sarcasm and your bitter mockery. Of course, slavery was wrong, but I want to tell you something, Rose Lee, and please don't throw a fit – many slaves *did* love their masters. Yes, there were some very nice plantations. And loyalty and affection between slave and master were not uncommon. It's possible to say that, and yet not condone slavery."

Rose Lee pushed her fists into her eyes.

"I don't believe the stuff that comes out of your mouth! You are outrageous!"

Walter walked in the room.

"I wish you ladies would stop."

He was greeted with silence. Rose Lee's face was flushed red. His mother sat grim-faced and angry.

A little later, they sit down at the dining room table.

His mother, still upset, finally breaks the silence.

"Rose Lee, you are too acerbic in your tone. You lack the gentle Virginia way."

"I do? Well, good for me!"

"You have forgotten your manners."

"Hurray! I don't aspire to be a Virginia hypocrite."

Mr Desmond raised his hand.

"Courtesy is not hypocrisy. It is a serious moral matter."

She shakes her head.

"I beg to disagree. In Virginia it's just a smokescreen to conceal our inhumanity."

He smiles at her.

"Well, I must take exception to that, Rose Lee. In Virginia courtesy is morally ingrained from birth. We are the heirs of the genteel tradition."

Rose Lee laughs.

"Oh, yes, we are of a *purer* strain. We are descendants of Cavaliers. Well, I'm sorry, but if you believe that, Father Desmond, you had best see a good doctor." She raises her arms. "I say, we are not Cavaliers. We are not even genteel. And nothing's ingrained from birth in this commonwealth but prejudice against the coloured and a sense of our own superiority."

Walter's mother sighs.

"Yes, go on and mock *everything*. It's just so like you."

Mr Desmond regards Rose Lee with a look of calm forbearance.

"We are a moderate and balanced society. After the war we acted with restraint. We had a good relationship with our former slaves. In all the Old Confederacy we had the fewest lynchings. There were states in the North that had more lynchings than Virginia."

Rose Lee laughs.

"Oh, we are truly progressive. We lynched *moderately*!"

Walter's mother shakes a finger.

"You are always *judging* someone! You can't judge all the people of the South by the barbarous actions of the ignorant."

Rose Lee smiles.

"How can you speak of the ignorance of *others*?"

"I beg your pardon."

"What about your ignorance? Look how you treat Mattie."

"I treat Mattie fine. Why she loves me to death."

"Oh, really. I say she's little more than a slave in her subservience to you."

"How insane you are!" Mrs Desmond calls to the kitchen. "Mattie, come here."

Mattie, a slim dark brown woman in her early thirties, comes out.

"Yes, Ma'am."

"Tell Miss Rose how I treat you."

"You treat me fine."

"Am I fair in my dealings? Am I good to you?"

"Yes, Ma'am."

"Has anyone ever treated you better but for your own dear mother?"

"No, Ma'am."

"Thank you. You can go, Mattie."

Mattie leaves.

"Are you satisfied?"

Rose Lee sighs.

"Well, what's she going to say? She has such *low* expectations – and she needs a job."

"I care for her and she cares for me. I would do anything for Mattie that I could."

"Why don't you have her for dinner one night? Let her sit at the table with you."

"What is the matter with you? She *serves* the dinner."

"Well, you serve it, and she could be your guest."

Walter's mother shakes her head, then calls to the kitchen again. "Mattie, come here, please."

Mattie returns to the dining room.

"Yes, Ma'am."

"Miss Rose has a wonderful idea. We are having the Waybrights over tomorrow night. Well, we are going to do things differently. I'm going to serve, and you'll sit at the table. Wear your best dress now."

Mattie smiles.

"Miss Grace, I ain't going to sit down with white folks, and you ain't going to serve."

"Well, if you don't want to, we'll do it the old way."

Mattie leaves.

Walter's mother nods at Rose Lee.

"I would not cause her such pain and embarrassment. I would not make her a figure of fun, and she understands better than you."

"Oh, she understands all right. She knows to stay in her place. Well, I *enjoy* talking to Mattie. I *like* sitting with her. I have sat with her many a time."

"That is in the kitchen. But she does not sit down at the table. On a social level we have nothing in common."

Walter's father stands up from the table. "Walter, let's leave the ladies."

They go into an adjoining room.

"Why that is so heartless of you, Mother Desmond. And *so condescending.*"

"It is nothing of the sort. It is kindness. It is reality. We would all feel uncomfortable. She could not carry on a conversation."

"Then invite the genteel coloured to sit at your table. They would not feel embarrassed, for they could speak as intelligently as you."

"I'm aware of the refined coloured, but we all seek our own kind, Rose Lee."

"God, I feel sorry for you."

"I dare say. You are such a liberal now. You think you're smarter than everyone else."

Rose Lee sighs, then shakes her head.

"If you are party to an evil then you had best separate yourself from it or you cannot call yourself a moral person."

"What evil are you talking about? If the races are unequal, is that my fault? We are not all equal, Rose Lee. Inequality is the nature of life. Some are good in art. Others in abstract thinking. Some at working with their hands."

"Lies and evasions! You just want to keep the coloured down. No, we just have to do the right thing."

"Excuse me, lady. I don't need moral instruction from you."

"You are *devoid* of morality. It's disgusting how you delude yourself from morning to night. All your sick reverence for the Confederate dead! All that putting flowers on graves!"

"I pray that I am loyal. I won't desert them to please you."

"How you obfuscate, how you *glorify* your ignorance!"

"I wish you would not shout at me."

"I will shout at you! You are *evil* !"

"Rose Lee, I have borne your enmity for many a year."

"I am just so *sick* of you."

Walter's mother nods.

"I think you are sick of yourself. If only you'd had children. It might've made you more tender."

"Why, how cruel you are. You know I can't have children – and through no fault of my own."

"Poor Walter is the last of the Desmond line."

Rose Lee half laughs, half sobs.

"God, you are crazy."

Mrs Desmond looks towards the adjoining room.

"Walter, come and get your wife. You have to live with her, I don't."

Rose Lee takes a deep breath.

"I find the atmosphere in this house *oppressive*."

"Well, then leave."

"I will, gladly."

"Good. Then do so at once."

"I am going, happily."

"Then why don't you."

Walter comes into the room.

"I wish you all would stop it."

Rose Lee begins to walk away.

"Come on Walter. Let's leave this old museum."

His mother leans forward in her chair.

"Yes, let's not keep her waiting. I feel so *sorry* for you, son."

"Mama, please. Goodnight now. Goodnight, Daddy"

He was in the cemetery with his mother. She held flowers wrapped in newspaper.

"Walter, I know she is your wife and your first loyalty is to her. But I won't endure her rudeness to Father and me."

"Mama, she means well. But she is high-strung and impatient. She can't help it."

"Don't make excuses. She is hateful." She took a deep breath and sighed. "I know you must defend her. You are too good. And she takes advantage of your kind nature."

She placed the flowers at the foot of Weber's grave.

"Poor Weber's gone but he is not forgotten," she said, nodding. "When my life is done, I hope you'll come here and visit. Maybe each year on my birthday. You could read something, Walter." He nodded vaguely. "I'd prefer something by General Lee. I'll leave word in my will on just what. But say nothing to your wife. I can do without her mockery, thank you."

"We better go, Mama," he said. He adjusted the shawl around her shoulders. As they walked away, she moved unsteadily and held on to his arm.

"I don't like the way she treats you, Walter."

"It's all right."

"No, it's not all right. She does not treat you with respect. You deserve better. Much better."

He smiled and shook his head.

"Mama, if I outlive you, I'll read whatever you like, but you'll be here a long time yet."

"You're doing what? I can't believe you. But I *know* it will give you pleasure. Are you going to sing 'Dixie', too? You are *pathetic*."

"Be kind, Rose Lee. Let's try to forgive and forget."

"*Forgive*! Is that all you can ever say? I do not wish to forgive. I will speak out. I'll not be cowed like you. You are so blind, Walter, and crippled in your devotion."

Rosa Lee shook her head.

"I want to tell you something, Mother Desmond. It was Lee who lost Gettysburg, I spoke to professors in Charlottesville and they said that Longstreet has been unfairly blamed for the defeat. Longstreet had a superior plan that would have won the battle but Lee wouldn't listen. Lee blundered, Mother Desmond. He lost the battle and the war. Of course, I'm glad he did. I would not want to live in the Confederate States of America. But I just want to say that I have it on good opinion that Longstreet was right and Lee was wrong."

"How dare you speak of matters you know nothing about. You know nothing of military history and care less. You are saying this only to provoke me. I know you so well, Rose Lee. Longstreet's views have long since been discredited."

"Only by Lee worshippers like General Jubal Early, that's what my professor friends said. Early was a malcontent, he made mistakes himself at Gettysburg, and he tried to recover his reputation by blaming Longstreet and defending Lee. No. I'm sorry to inform you that General Lee was at fault."

"What joy you take in spreading slander. I'm truly distressed by your attitude. General Lee was the greatest man of his time. Some say he was too good to be true. But his sort of greatness would always be attacked by those who feel threatened by a true man. He hated war and he did not wish it, but he was loyal to Virginia and the South. It was his duty to resist the invasion of its borders. There are those who say that he had one flaw as a military leader, that in his desire not to offend his subordinate commanders he was perhaps too lenient and patient with them, and not firm enough in his insistence that they follow his orders precisely, that he gave them room if not to overtly disobey him, then at least to frustrate his intentions. I say that this was not done out of weakness but out of the respect he accorded his brother officers. He allowed them some free play in their interpreta-tion of his orders, for he knew that in the heat and confusion of battle things changed rapidly and he relied on their judgement to respond to a changing situation. It is true that General Lee lacked ruthlessness. His good manners prevented him from wounding the feelings of others. He was the politest and most courteous of men. Of course, Rose Lee, you mock courtesy and call it a sham display. But true courtesy is not something one wears for an hour like a coat but is inherent in one's being. It arises from the deepest wellsprings of kindness and compassion, virtues that General Lee possessed in abundance but which sad to say are fast departing from our world."

Rose Lee laughed.

"Oh, how you go on. I can't believe you're real."

"Goodnight to you, Rose Lee. I don't wish to see you anytime soon."

Walter stood by a tree in the cemetery. Putting on his glasses, he removed a paper from the side pocket of his coat.

The sun came through a break in the clouds. Shading his eyes for a moment, he leaned against the tree. A breeze passed through the branches, and his mind drifted. He could hear his father. "The important thing, Walter, is to take your time. Don't be rushed. And never lose your composure." And then he heard his mother say, "A gentleman does not reveal to others the burden of his sorrow." Some sparrows landed on the ground, then quickly flew away, and Rose Lee's voice went through him. 'I hate your courtly restraint! I despise your moral confusion. Oh, I know, everything's so *complicated*. You make me tired, you really do. You dishearten me! You battle and frustrate me from morning to night! For God's sake, Walter, liberate yourself!" He bowed his head and sighed. "Rose Lee, I know I'm not perfect. I truly regret any wrong I might have done you," he thought. "Oh, be quiet, Mr Saintly!" she replied.

The sun disappeared in the clouds. Walter looked at the woods, at the road, then out toward the Blue Ridge. A small truck passed by. He heard the cawing of crows. He did not feel well. He had not for some time. Looking out at the mountains, he thought, "I'm the last of the Desmond line."

Overhead some geese flew south.

Adjusting his glasses, he took a deep breath and looked at the paper in his hand.

"Well, happy birthday, Mama," he said, and feeling life's brevity, and wondering where it all had gone, he commenced reading Lee's final order to the Army of Northern Virginia.

"After four years of arduous service marked by unsurpassed courage and fortitude, the Army of Northern Virginia has been compelled to yield to overwhelming numbers and resources.

"I need not tell the brave survivors of so many hard-fought battles who have remained steadfast to the last that I have consented to this result from no distrust of them: but feeling that valour and devotion could accomplish nothing that could compensate for the loss that must have attended the continuance of the contest, I determined to avoid the useless sacrifice of those whose past services have endeared them to their countrymen.

"By the terms of the agreement, officers and men can return to their homes and remain until exchanged. You will take with you the satisfaction that proceeds from a consciousness of duty faithfully performed; and I earnestly pray that a Merciful God will extend to you His blessing and protection.

"With an unceasing admiration of your constancy and devotion to your Country, and a grateful remembrance of your kind and generous consideration for myself, I bid you all an affectionate farewell.

"R. E. Lee"

Dinner at Natalia's

When the four cousins finally got back to their table, they were positively beat. The fiddlers had kept them dancing all night, the women in one circle, the gentlemen circling them, and not once had they gotten halfway back to their seats when some man hadn't caught them round the waist and trotted them back to the dance floor again.

"Lord!" smiled the first cousin, shoving her bangs off her forehead with the side of one hand. "That man nearly danced my legs off!" She was referring to a wiry fellow in spit-shined patent leather shoes who had been her partner all evening.

"That man!" the second cousin cried. "The man I was with could have broken my back!" and she heaved up her narrow, slightly padded bosom, arching her spine delicately and laying one hand on the small of her back.

The eldest cousin had been dragged at a loping pace all night by "Pops", smiling despite it all over his balding head, which had soon become moist and pink with perspiration. "Well it was fun," she sighed, and turned to the last cousin who had remained conspicuously silent, asking: "How about you, Natalia?" Natalia smiled pleasantly, but said nothing, so the rest lit cigarettes and blew streams of smoke evocatively into the air, called for more beer, and ran their fingertips languidly round the rims of their empty glasses while they waited for it. The fiddlers' bows had begun to rise and fall from the crests of sad arpeggios, and couples were wandering down the promenade like strollers on a deck for a waltz under the coloured lights, and Natalia had fallen into a despondent mood, so she stood up and excused herself and went to the ladies' room.

"Poor Natalia," said one cousin to the others when she had left. They all nodded sympathetically and swivelled round to watch her go. She moved with quick, long strides on bevelled heels, a curt turn of the ankle gaining the darkness. Her red hair had been swathed up and pinned in a soft chignon at the nape of her neck, and the buttons on her little red jacket rustled vacantly as she swept past the slope-shouldered men at the bar. "She is a strong and wilful woman," observed the second cousin, "but she does have her weak moments," and they all nodded, for Natalia's weak moments were a subject of constant wonder to them which they had spent many hours discussing. Mostly, they blamed them on some terrible romance with west Texas. Sometimes, when she had been drinking, she told them about this, rounding it like a lasso spun real wide: the mountains and the deep snows, and the rivers frozen along the banks. Then, circling in closer, she told them about the little towns and the children and the churches. But when that rope began pulling in tight on the centre knot, she let it drop dead around her ankle, and her foot began tapping to the fiddles, and the man there got carefully lost in the music while she finished her drink. Then she would look longingly into the darkness, and, if a sad song was played, she would leave the room. Once, she had alarmed them all by staring at the door and saying nothing as long as she could, only to sweep suddenly over the table at them and cry: "There ain't a man in this world I would want, if I could have him!" Then, acting horrified by her own words, she looked into the lights, blinking wildly. Tonight, she disappointed them by returning to the table undaunted, calling for more beer, and downing half of it at once. She had been home nearly five years, and her cousins imagined she had finally found some peace in the Carolinas where the mountains are just a blue dream on the horizon and the winters are just a shrug of snow. Still, when it came around to the last dance, no matter whose arms she was in, they always said, "Natalia's in the west, again."

Tonight, a particular man happened into the dance hall, and as soon as he came through the door, Natalia sat bolt upright as if she'd been hit by three hours of drinking whisky. Her cousins raised their eyes and looked over their shoulders in the direction of her gaze to where he stood, drawn up in a black coat and shining black boots, a stranger to them. A large onyx ring mirrored the lamplight as his hand went to his brow, catching the crown of his hat between the three middle fingers, and when he turned from the shadows, they saw his face was marred by a faded scar that gave him a stern expression.

"Who is that?" one cousin whispered, wrinkling her nose over the amber horizon of bottlenecks on the table. Natalia shook her head swiftly, lit a cigarette, shook out the flame in exaggerated arches, and turned away. But when the stranger approached her and bowed from the waist, she rose, acting very perturbed.

"I'll be right back," the second cousin murmured, dropping her handbag in the middle of the table and trotting off to the ladies' room curiously; and when she returned, she whispered his name was John Thomas, a ranch owner from El Paso, who was driving a brand-new pick-up truck. The cousins all nodded wisely. When he sold that ranch and took a job on a back-hoe and married Natalia, they were not surprised. And though the two of them rarely showed up at the dance hall after that (and when they did, the cousins all shook their heads, for in his dusty leather work boots, John Thomas seemed a little diminished), one cousin would say to the others, "John Thomas don't say too much, but just between us, I am sure he is that man come to get her, I mean, being from the panhandle and all," and they would all nod knowingly, and then sigh sadly, for though they were happy for Natalia, it was like the end of an epoch to them.

Of course, John Thomas knew better. One Sunday morning, turbulent with wet leaves, he stood in front of the oval mirror above his wife's dressing-table, working the string tie at his collar. The fingers that fashioned his thin bow were freckled over the knuckle, large and firm, ending in clean, square pink nails. He hummed, as he worked, a single note, deep in his throat, which stopped each time he leaned towards the window and looked down on the shiny street guttered with a sludge of wet black leaves.

Presently, he saw the three cousins in navy coats hurrying along, bent against the wind. At the gate, they stopped, and one cousin insisted they all walk back to admire his pale blue pick-up truck which was parked on the curb. Then another, apparently perturbed, tugged at the sleeves of her jacket, actively flicked its bib with her fingertips, and hurried them back up the walk.

John Thomas sat down on the edge of the bed and began struggling with his boots. The air in the bedroom was cool and damp, shot with musty drafts from the attic. Downstairs, sounding far away, he could hear the brisk rapping of the cousin's small fists on the panelled door. This stopped in anticipation of his wife's footfalls which sounded rapid and halting, all the way down the hall beneath him. The clatter of plates, slamming of doors, and the soft belling of women's laughter floated round him in the grey bedroom and made him feel sad. He wondered angrily how his wife could have done this to him, but he supposed he would have to show. So he stood up, pulled on the edge of his coat, and looked at himself critically in the mirror. He thought he had put on a little, but they said, when a man settled down, that happened. He sat back down on the bed, listening. The truth was, he was no good around women until he had had a few drinks.

When he walked, the sombre sounds of his own footfalls gave him courage, but halfway down the stairs he became convinced his suit had become far too small and he stepped into the foyer tugging at the tight sleeves of his coat futilely.

Natalia's cousins regarded him in silence from the dining room table.

"I swear," Beatrice piped, "I've never seen one man shut up all my cousins single-handed! If I'm not mistaken this husband of Natalia's is shy!" She at once got up and trotted towards him, taking him by the arm. "Now you are not to be shy amongst us, John Thomas, seeing as we are all family, now." Beatrice brought him straight to the table, smiling up from a round, ivory face that smelled of sweet, peppery talc.

John Thomas winced and grappled like a blind man with the back of his chair. "Where's Natalia?" he asked roundly.

Beatrice regarded him curiously. He was a man of about forty with a face tanned to agelessness through perpetual shaving and sunshine. His manners were gruff and polished; those of a man accustomed to his own solitude. Women were drawn to him as if he were some great, injured animal. She began plucking at the cotton fingertips of one glove. "Natalia's in the kitchen, yet," she told him, pointing with both hands towards the closed louvred doors from behind which could be heard the running of water. "You know we would welcome you both at Sunday services."

"Now don't you start that, Bea!" the eldest cousin, Ellen, frowned. "A man like John Thomas is set in his ways and has a right to be." Then she turned graciously to him, brushing her cheek against the pale corsage pinned to her collar. The lilies were a trifle wilted since church, but they still set off nicely her blue suit, and gave off a moist, fruity, female odour. "We were just discussing what a pretty table Natalia's dishes set, John Thomas. It was Boyd give them to you, wasn't it?" The dishes had been a wedding present.

John Thomas touched his collar and cleared his throat, trying to remember. "But they don't make half so pretty a table as the ladies round it today," he said finally, then, pleased with himself, he pointed to a large diamond ring on Ellen's hand. "And I see there is to be another wedding, shortly."

Ellen shoved her hand in her skirts. "O, this! It don't mean a thing, John Thomas! Just the leftovers of a disappointment!" And she waved the empty hand and plucked up her linen napkin, shaking the folds from it.

"I told her she would have to give it back," said the youngest cousin smartly. "But she told me to do that was in poor taste."

"I read it in *Emily Post*," Ellen snapped. "And besides, it ain't our faults if all the men in these parts manage to make jackasses of themselves before you can get them to the altar!" She lifted her chin, swaying righteously in her seat, and Beatrice, whose age, too, had begun to show, rubbed a consoling hand in her lap saying to him in a low voice: "None of us had the sense Natalia did. We should have gotten out of this town when we could. I don't care what anyone says."

John Thomas moved uneasily in his chair.

There wasn't ten years difference in the ages of Natalia's cousins. Their yellow hair had always been their secret pride, and they had boasted the fact that they had all managed to remain single, but since Natalia's matrimony, they had not felt so comfortable among themselves. Although Ellen had not lost the gold of her curls, she had come to that age that set her apart from Marguerite, who was the baby, and everything in Marguerite's giddy behaviour had suddenly got badly on her nerves. She seemed to see her own fading beauty still shining blithely in Marguerite's face, and held her in reproach for it. And when Marguerite started talking about dating both Steve Conrad and his older brother at the same time, even Beatrice, who, being in the middle, was an even-natured woman, felt crushed, and began spending an unusual amount of time brooding over her old pieces at the church where she had prevailed on the organ for the last ten years, thumbing through the brown sheaves with the strange feeling that among them she had lost, or forgotten, something.

But they had all presently come to an understanding that marriage was still not beyond them, and found themselves looking with new eyes on the familiar faces at the dance, and Natalia's success became a little light in their changed lives, and John Thomas gave them new hope.

Now he was looking over his shoulder, suddenly anxious for his wife. He thought she was being a poor hostess, leaving them all at the table with nothing to drink. At this thought, he brightened up some, and decided to ask the ladies himself what they would like; but then the toe of Natalia's shoe thrust open the kitchen door, and she backed into the dining room carrying a platter of rosy ham.

"Dinner's ready," she said blandly.

John Thomas glanced up at her. "What you been doing in there, anyway?" he mumbled impatiently, but Beatrice saw his glance had been full of quiet adoration of his wife.

Natalia was a tall, slight woman with arms spent at the shoulder and wrists with tiny bird-like bones. Her hands were marbled with grey veins except where two ovals of amber from tobacco glowed on the mound of the first and second fingers. She had large, mournful eyes, and high, crescented cheeks. Her nose turned up, and due to a slight overbite, her lips were parted in a perpetually inviting way. Of the four cousins, she was the only red-head.

Beatrice's eyes hung on her blearily a moment; then, remembering her manners, she jumped up and reached for the platter. "Now don't you look lovely, Natalia! I do believe marriage suits her, don't you, Ellen?" She made room for the platter, sat down quickly, caught her breath, and smiled brightly across the table. Should she turn thanks? Her cousins' eyes said no. "Well, pass the food!" she sang out, and picked up a plate of biscuits, taking one off the top.

John Thomas was caught holding the sliced ham, and stared down, puzzled at the direction it should take.

"Clockwise, clockwise," Beatrice whispered. "We are all so curious as to how you have taken to the south, John Thomas."

Marguerite took the biscuits from Bea. "From what Natalia's told us, it gets awfully cold in west Texas, winters. But you know, no matter how the rest of the family behaves, *we* never blamed her for taking off. Her momma always was partial to her boys."

"Well, I just never did understand that," Ellen reflected. "Natalia was always such a pretty child. You can imagine," she nodded first to John Thomas, then to his wife, "with all that red hair."

"But you got to remember," Marguerite pointed out fairly, "that her momma's heart went out her real young. We have all been told about *that*!" Then she began swinging her legs back under her chair girlishly, and talking about getting on part-time nights at the Blue Fox Bar and Grill.

John Thomas had a hard time remembering the cousins' names, except for Marguerite's. She was still quite young and he could not help admiring her. She was perched on the edge of her seat with her cheek inclined on her hands, waiting for the gravy to come around. The gathers of a pink, capped sleeve bit into the soft flesh of her arm, bringing up blood. Jack Kettle, the night manager at the Blue Fox, had told her she was the prettiest girl who had come into the place in two years, and besides, all the men knew her on sight. "That's what makes a good waitress," she was explaining, "a familiar face."

Now and then she turned back an ankle, ordering the woollen pleats over her knees with her fingers.

John Thomas leaned closer to her and said a little huskily: "I'm sure you'd make a real fine waitress, Marguerite."

"You know Ellen don't like to hear you talking about working in a place like that, Peggy," said Beatrice, tartly. This was the first time they had brought a man into the family, and she was anxious to make a good impression. John Thomas, on the other hand, was beginning to feel a little reckless, and Marguerite was giggling at him into her hands. "Look here, ladies," he suggested loudly, shoving back his chair, "Sunday or not, let me fix you all a drink – ladies' pleasure!"

"O no! We're just fine!" Beatrice assured him quickly, signifying her tumbler of ice water.

"Now you just sit right back down there, John Thomas! We don't need a thing!" said Ellen.

"Why don't I make some coffee, instead," said Natalia, and left the room.

John Thomas stood there a moment, then sat down crossly.

"Well I thought that sounded like a fine idea," Marguerite told him, producing a long white cigarette from under the table. She seemed to have taken her reprimand lightly enough, and why not? She had no doubt learnt that idle carriage from Ellen and Beatrice themselves. They had a few years on her, but he could tell they had been real party girls in their prime, too. John Thomas stuffed his hands into his coat pockets, feeling for a match.

Ellen, seeing they had him to themselves, touched her lips swiftly with her napkin and leaned earnestly over the table, interceding his search. "You see, John Thomas," she explained, "Natalia's mamma's daddy, that is, her grand-daddy, come home drunk one night and beat his wife so badly she fell on the cook-stove and hit her head and died. Well, that left eight children for Natalia's momma, being the eldest, to rear. All those children and the old man, too, to wait on! We understand the old man had red hair and a red beard, but none of us ever seen him ourselves, because when Natalia's momma was sixteen, he come out the house, set down on top of the picnic table to clean his shot-gun, took one long look at Natalia's momma, who was a woman full grown by then, spat a stream of tobacco juice across the yard, and blew his head clean off. That's right," she nodded. "*My* momma, who was just a toddler at that time, said she figured the old man simply had to have relief for what he'd done to his poor wife. And you know what else? Natalia's momma that day was wearing one of her dead momma's dresses. It was blue. So my momma always says it must have been that old blue dress done it. But I imagine Natalia's told you all about that!"

John Thomas stared at her. "She never told me no such thing." Then he turned seriously to his dinner, feeling the colour rush to his face as if by virtue of his sole masculine presence at the table, he somehow shared the guilt with that old man.

"It was because of grand-daddy Natalia's family is always carrying on about their *bad Irish blood*," Marguerite laughed, lighting her cigarette herself. "Whenever a baby with red hair turns up, they never give it a family name. That way, in years to come, if worse come to worse, they could more easily disown them. That's what they say, anyhow; that's how Natalia got her name: it's out of a book, and I don't mean the family bible! If you ask me," Marguerite raced on, "it's all the rest of them got the bad blood; Natalia just got the pretty hair! Why, Natalia told us, when she was born, her mamma saw that red hair and said to the doctor – just take that damn thing back! A course, there was no way of doing that, but even the Lord must have jumped when she said it because right soon after, she had a yellow-headed son, and then five more of them, one after another."

"Why, Natalia should know!" Ellen laughed. "She was there!"

"Well, if you ask me, it was all just jealousy. Natalia's momma never had hair like that," Marguerite declared finally.

At this point, Natalia returned from the kitchen carrying a pot of coffee. Hearing Marguerite's last words, she pursed her lips and shook her head good-naturedly, but Marguerite insisted pleasantly that it was the truth; just look how jealous Marguerite's own sisters were and all because *she* was blonde. Sweeping her yellow hair over her shoulder with casual pride, she teased: "Of course, Natalia never helped things when she run off and took up with a *Texas* man! But like I said, *we* never blamed her for that!"

"What Marguerite was meaning to say was Natalia's momma wasn't really looking for her when she come, and what was worse, she was not a boy," Beatrice tried to explain. "But that sort of thing frequently happens to young women. Of course, all that happened back in Virginia. We were poor folks then. But we didn't know it – no, we all thought we were having a good old time! Then things got real bad around nineteen forty-nine and Ellen's daddy went out to Oklahoma and started making his money in the oil fields, wild-catting. Ellen's momma was real reluctant to make the move. All the women were. But finally she said – home is where your husband is . . ."

"That's the truth," Ellen echoed.

". . . and the family packed up, lock, stock, and barrel and took the train to Oklahoma City."

"A course, we always intended to go back to Virginia," sighed Marguerite.

"We still intend to go back," Beatrice corrected her. "Ellen and I remember Virginia as if it were yesterday. A course, Marguerite don't recall. She was just a baby."

"Things ain't the same anywhere, no more," John Thomas told them. "It's all changed now."

"No. No," Beatrice assured him lightly. "Natalia's told us Virginia ain't changed a bit. She's the one of us who has travelled!"

John Thomas looked curiously at his wife. She was chewing thoughtfully and watching Beatrice speaking. Natalia was no great talker herself, and he supposed her cousins were accustomed to making up for her. She did not seem to mind; in fact, she was listening with silent interest as if she had never met the subject of the conversation.

"Must have been a while since she's been there," he said. Beatrice considered this over her coffee and then agreed that it had, in fact, been at least five years. But John Thomas was not listening to her. Suddenly, he found himself wanting very much to be alone with his wife. It seemed to him this was the first time he could remember not being alone with her in his entire life. Her inaccessibility, as she sat in the ghostly circle of her cousin's reveries, had made her marvellously desirable. Despite the intimacy of marriage, her mystery had not diminished for him. Now he watched her, and wondered what she could be thinking so deeply about. He hoped she would not return his look. He wanted to regard her with the curious and imaginative eyes of a stranger again.

Dinner had made him feel heavy and drowsy, and he began to hope the cousins would soon leave. Looking around, he was pleased to see Ellen, who seemed suddenly weary. She was licking her fingertips and folding her napkin. Now she rested her chin on one hand and brushed at the crumbs on the tablecloth with the back of her crimson nails. A pleasant silence fell over the table; the three cousins exchanged mild glances, and Beatrice took a deep breath. Then Marguerite simply blurted out: "But it was *you* Natalia carried on most about, John Thomas! She used to tell us all about you! By the time you finally showed up, we would have known you anywhere! Not another man could turn her head!"

Beatrice, who had held her breath through Marguerite's entire confession, exhaled loudly and made her own small, tardy contribution: "And you were worth every day she waited."

"What did you think, all those years?" Marguerite went on. "What made you make up your mind to come on out here, after all that time?" She poised one prong of her fork on her plate and spun it absently. "I know it's none of our business; it's just all so romantic. Just like out of a book. Just like Natalia's name. Like I said before, if any of us had the sense Natalia did, we'd have gotten out of this town too!"

John Thomas frowned. Pinching open the button of his coat, he looked to his wife for explanation. She was staring blankly into one corner of the ceiling. Suddenly she sniffed, turned her head, and said in a voice of omniscience: "Something's burning." She put her fork down noisily and strode into the kitchen.

John Thomas looked back at the cousins and said loudly: "Folks is folks anywhere. There's the good and the bad, the honest and the dishonest, same here as in the city. Only in the city, there's more of them. At least here you know who is who, and which is which."

Natalia's cousins looked at their plates and then at each other with fading smiles. "Of course, this ain't such a small place as all that!" Beatrice smiled. "I mean it ain't like this is Shallot or Chapel Hill."

"No!" Ellen agreed hastily. "It ain't a small place at all, and it is just a hop, skip, and a jump to Raleigh! But you know what they say! The grass is always greener!"

The kitchen door parted and Natalia, wiping her hands apologetically on her apron, announced dessert was ruined.

Dessert didn't matter, the cousins assured her energetically. They had eaten so much they couldn't take another bite, and besides, Beatrice pointed out, it was snowing.

John Thomas shrugged his shoulders and dropped an arm over the back of his chair so that his coat fell open. He stared darkly at his lap, and occupied himself with arranging the silver on his empty plate, trying to appear at ease. But he was wondering wildly just what sort of man Natalia had been carrying on with before, anyway, and why she had never told him a word about it. Still, he knew it did not matter what the man had been like; there was never any competing with a memory. And he supposed he could say any man who'd let a woman like Natalia get away had to be a damn fool, anyway, and then, for one horrible moment, it occurred to him that the fellow might have died, and he knew there was no winning against a dead man.

Ellen had stood up. "We hate to eat and run, Natalia, but you know the street will be nothing but ice as soon as the sun goes down." Hurrying to the closet, she began pulling out their blue coats. John Thomas shoved back his chair and started heavily across the room to help, but Ellen waved a desisting hand, arguing: "Now don't you bother, John Thomas. Remember we are just family now."

Once outside, the three cousins paused to fasten the buttons of their coats and raise their collars against the wind. John Thomas stuck at the window to watch them go. They scurried down the icy walk, watching their step, leaving three light paths in the fresh snow. When they passed from view, he shuffled round and faced the one they had left behind. Natalia was still brooding over the snowfall. It was heavier, now, in fact, the sky seemed to have turned itself inside out, showing a pale, faded lining.

John Thomas's eyes ran from the slender white fingers curled in the indentation of Natalia's waist made by one shifted hip, to the reddish chignon with its tiny black pins on her nape, and then stuck on the furry white rhomb above her collar. His mouth, twisted with derision, relaxed as he reconsidered. But at the first sound of his heel, Natalia crossed her arms and fled up the stairs.

Guilty, he concluded, closing his hands in the air, and dully regarding the dark window across which her flight had sent small sharp lights of henna dancing. Among these stood his own small, wet reflection. For a moment, he was alarmed to fancy the shrunken figure and devilish face of the old Irishman hailing him from the glass. Shoving his hands into his trouser pockets, he shuffled away. At the steps, he hollered righteously into the darkness, "Damn it, Natalia! And I give up everything for you!" Then he covered his head with his hat and hurried quietly down the hall.

The street had become a frozen desert. Confused faces blinked out from behind opaque panes, wet palms rubbing away a liquid view. Beneath all these quiet eyes, John Thomas sidled uneasily along the slippery gutter towards his truck; after a shock like this, a man deserved a drink.

Natalia observed the deluged sky calmly from her bedroom window, a look of restricted victory on her brow. After a few hours, she fell asleep.

Round about four in the morning, she awoke and found herself still alone in the dark house. She did not like to be awake when the rest of the world was sleeping.

Presently, she heard the pick-up making its way noisily back down the street, pausing and moving on. She leaned forward, inclining with care on the glass, lowering her eyes quietly until she looked down into the whorls of dark glass below. Nothing stirred on the street at that hour. Everyone in the town appeared to be sleeping. It was Monday.

The truck approached the house, paused, geared into park, and idled loudly. Then the engine shifted into a roaring reverse, and it backed down, stopping on the side of the road in front of the mailbox. In a moment, John Thomas jumped out.

Natalia saw him run a finger over the name on the mailbox as if considering the significance of it. Then he lifted his face to the windows of the house, shoved his hands into his pockets, and sauntered up to the gate. He kicked this open and then braved the sidewalk. At the stoop, he crossed the front yard and started down along the side of the house, out of sight. Though he went very quietly, his heart was crying out. Through the wet snow he trudged, between the snow-covered forsythias and altheas, beneath the crab-apple's thin branches, slipping through a hedge of boxwood. Once his hands came from his pockets and ran swiftly through his hair. Again, he slipped through the shrubs and disappeared, emerging, eventually, on the lawn, all in all like a man who is uncertain of his own whereabouts or how he got where he was. By now, he was running, his face turned up anxiously, and the brim of his hat rolled in one fist, as if he half expected something to fall off the roof and was intending to catch it in the hollow. When it was apparent that he was going to come inside, Natalia slipped across the bedroom and lay down flat on her back across the bed, staring up at the plaster ceiling.

She wondered vaguely what was in his mind and where he had been. If he only knew the whole misunderstanding had sprung up out of one small exaggeration, he might have been amused at the cousins' silly beliefs! Here they all thought she was living some dream come true, married to a mysterious stranger who is torn between his need for solitude, and his one great passion – a lover who had returned from out of her past to claim that one passion: Natalia! She lifted her eyebrows and laughed aloud, whimpered really, a small, questioning "Ha!" It was true: she *was* living a dream, and she *was* married to a stranger! Why, she had never once laid eyes on John Thomas before the night he stepped through the doors of the dance hall; she had never set foot over the Mason-Dixon line. Poor Natalia. But how could she have come, over the same dirt roads, past the tin-roofed shacks, home, to the same yellow calendars and droning

porch lights, home to the same dreary houses, her mother's reproachful looks, and her brothers' muttered demands; how could she have
come home, with her shoes walked off and her courage used up,
and told them all how she had found herself in the wide world
hopelessly lost, frightened as a bird, and longing only to go home
again? Thus: the redeeming lies.

Now, her eyes riveted upon a corner of the ceiling and moored
there until she heard John Thomas's slow footfalls starting up the
stairs; they sounded different from her father's and different from
her brothers' and yet they did not sound different at all. The door
of the room brushed open. Natalia lay quite still. John Thomas's
dark silhouette against the luminous grey light of dawn began to rise
and fall as he started to undress. He stepped out of the dark pile of
clothes he had dropped around his feet, and he sank down on the bed
with a deep sigh. Twisting around, he regarded her, thinking she was
asleep. Then he whispered her name huskily.

Natalia stirred to signify she was awake.

"I was afraid you would have left me," he said. Then he dropped his
forehead into his hands. He had been drinking. After a long moment,
he bore around on her, bowed his head, penitent, and buried his
face in her neck. "God knows that would kill me. God knows I give
up everything for you and wasn't nothing I ever had worth nothing
like you."

Trapped under his sodden weight, Natalia's breath was short. Her
eyes darted back and forth across the low ceiling, like a trapped
bird, hitting the walls, and tumbling down into darkness. Then they
flitted across the silver line his smooth shoulder made against the
window. Imperceptibly lifting her free hand from the bed, she laid
it testily on his back. His flesh trembled and contracted helplessly at
her touch. Quickly, she withdrew the hand, placing it beside her on
the bed again.

Natalia stared furiously into the ceiling, explored the soft horizon
at the top of the wall, and followed the regions of shallows and rifts
until she had turned her face to the wall, could feel its relieving
coolness on her cheeks, and breathe the moist, familiar scents trapped
in the old plaster. She truly despised weakness; that one moment
of weakness for which we must be strong; strong and mute in our
sorrows for the rest of our lives.

YI MUN-YOL

The Knife-grinder

It was still not sufficiently light for me to set off, but there was light enough to find my way around. It had started to snow again. Not the previous day's big drifting snow-flakes, but steady snow driven by an icy wind. The only good thing was that I would not have to fight against the wind as I walked.

My first intention had been to warm myself up and get something to eat in the village before setting off, but the entire place showed no signs of waking out of its deep sleep. So I resolved to leave and hoped to find something better in the next village along the way.

I went out into a strange, alien world, where the only sign of life was the sound of the wind sighing through the bare branches of the trees along the roadside. The fields, now more deeply covered than ever by the new snow, lay like a vast empty sea. The line of trees alone indicated the road, which was otherwise simply a white river of snow. Yet strangely enough, someone had been there before me, leaving a trail of footprints down the middle of the river. But those prints only attracted my attention for a moment, on account of the terrible cold that was driving me almost out of my mind.

As soon as I left the village, I began to run, and went on running. More than anything else, I had to shake off that intolerable cold. Normally I would have lit a fire with dead branches and twigs, but since everything was buried under two feet of snow, all I could do was run. Running was necessary too, in order to reach the next village as quickly as possible.

Luckily, since the snow had frozen during the night, I no longer sank in up to my knees as on the previous day. After a while, my body began to lose something of its stiffness, and my breath steamed white.

As soon as the cold vanished, though, I began to feel unbearably hungry. Not that simple hunger you feel in the stomach, but the kind of hunger that racks your whole body. I began to regret bitterly my last three days' negligence in not eating properly. In particular, the day before I had taken almost no solid food at all except breakfast. At last, unable to bear it any longer, I stopped, gasping, and swallowed a handful of snow. I felt a momentary aching pain, nothing more, then it brought back all the cold I had so painfully rid myself of.

I started to run again. Now feeling seriously threatened, I summoned up all my strength to run faster. The trees along the edge of the road rushed past me, as if I were in a speeding train. I felt I was flying, whereas in actual fact my pace was slowing and my feet were beginning to drag. I was later to realize that the eternity I thought I had covered as I ran that morning was little more than a mile in all.

Gradually, though, the sensations of cold and hunger left me, as my consciousness began to waver, and I felt an almost irresistible desire to sleep. Deep snowdrifts beckoned like plump cushions, several times I felt an urge to collapse into an eternal sleep. I was no longer capable of distinguishing where the road lay. There was nothing to be seen but a vast sea of snow, and I kept going by sheer instinct.

I don't know how long I went on like that; suddenly I vaguely heard a voice shouting: "Hey! hey! That's not the road! This way!"

I looked round, abruptly jerked out of my trance. At some point I had left the road and gone plunging off across the fields.

"This way! This way!"

Again I heard someone calling. I squinted towards where the voice was coming from. First I made out the wavering flames of a small fire. Then I saw a hovel that had probably been used as a daytime shelter the previous summer. Finally I made out the vague silhouette of a man. I came a little to my senses. Summoning up all my remaining strength, I went running in that direction. To my astonishment, I found the knife-grinder sitting there.

"It's madness in weather like this!"

He spoke quietly, at the same time making a rough cushion for me to sit on with some of the dried millet-stalks he was burning in his fire, and I collapsed forward on to it, almost embracing the flames.

"Watch out! You'll scorch your hair!"

His voice was firmer now, and as he warned me he put out a hand to restrain me. But my mind was in no state to register the sense of his words. Seized by a new attack of cold, I sucked in the heat of the fire as someone thirsty might gulp down water.

"Pull your legs back! Your clothes are on fire!"

There was obvious irritation in his tone now, as he brushed at the bottoms of my trousers that had caught in the flames.

"First, something to eat."

When I had recovered my wits sufficiently, he took a fire-blackened pan from the wooden box he always carried with him. He arranged a rough hearth at one edge of the fire and, after throwing several handfuls of snow into the pan, he began to feed the flames. He added more snow, until the pan was half full, then he took a packet of dried noodles from the box and broke them into the boiling water.

It was not until I had drained the last drop in the pan that I really came to myself. The man had been watching me all the time I was eating.

"Thank you very much."

I felt a little ashamed at not having said anything before.

"You'll have to pay for the noodles," he said, his voice quiet again. Flurried, I took my few remaining five-hundred Won notes from a pocket and held them towards him.

"Just one, and that's too much," he said, taking one note from those I was holding out. He stuffed it into his pocket, then handed me four hundred Won in change. There was a kind of dignity in his attitude that would brook no contradiction.

"And what made you set out so early in this snow?"

I was busy licking peeling skin off the roof of my mouth, the result of eating the boiling noodles too quickly, when he casually shot out his question. I remained perplexed for a moment. Would this knife-grinder be capable of understanding why I was heading for the sea? But at the same time I felt that I must not lie to him. Trying to be as frank and simple as I could, I told him where I was going and why.

"I guessed as much. People only do crazy things for crazy reasons. If you'd been a fishmonger on his way to buy fish, you'd never have set out so early in weather like this."

Then, with an expression halfway between a scornful smile and a real smile, he went on:

"It looks as though you and I are going to do exactly opposite things down there."

He seemed to have grasped my real intentions despite the rather confused explanations I had offered him. But his words troubled me strangely.

"So you're going to Taejin as well?"

"That's the harbour nearest here."

"What do you mean, do the opposite?"

"It looks as though I'm going there to kill and you to die." He spoke without the least hesitation, while I suddenly shuddered. I asked stupidly:

"Who . . . ?"

He looked at me sharply for a few seconds. There was something inquisitorial in his gaze. Then he smiled, a smile darker than before, an odd smile that might have been expressing scorn at himself or contempt of me.

"The charm of trust lies in its possibility of betrayal. But after all, you owe me your life, don't you?"

"What?"

"I mean, I want to trust you. I want to tell you my story."

I was still confused, trying to understand his words, when he suddenly asked, "How old do you think I am?"

"Umm . . . about fifty, I'd say . . ."

"That's exactly ten years older than I am. It's all on account of the nineteen years that bastard got me."

"What do you mean?"

"Let me tell you about those nineteen years."

Once again he seemed to hesitate, then made up his mind and began his story, in a low, thoughtful voice, a kind of monologue:

"In those days we dreamed dreams, big, dangerous dreams called liberty or equality. It's an age when people dream, but we were worse than most. We bought acetic acid and glycerine to mimeograph leaflets with. And we kept our knives sharp. Apart from our leader, we were all about twenty.

"Then one more artful woke up before the rest of us. He reported us while we were still giddy dreaming. The one who killed himself just before he was arrested was the luckiest of us all, I reckon. We were all arrested, tortured, and tried. Our leader was sentenced to death, and I and one other got life. The other two got ten and fifteen years.

"It was the time of the war. The only reason we survived at all was because there was absolutely nothing linking us with the North.'

His words chilled me with horror.

"It was our hatred for the one who betrayed us that kept us going through the endless years we suffered in prison. We had been much more deeply hurt by that betrayal of trust than by the shattering of our dreams or the collapse of our ideals. We swore revenge. And there was this knife to remind us of our vow. One of us made it, he learned to use a lathe in prison.

"The first of us had his sentence reduced. When he came out at the end of seven years he had this knife hidden in his coat. It was no easy job trying to find the traitor. At first he tried sincerely enough, but his sentence had been relatively short, and that helped his rehabilitation. Soon he had a job, savings, a wife and children.

"After eleven years, the second came out, also thanks to a reduced sentence. By then, the first had settled down. He very humbly excused himself, and passed the knife to the second. It was no different with the second. Less than two years after his release, he came to visit us and said that he wanted to leave the knife to someone else. Those of us still inside spat on him.

"At last, the third of us was freed. But we had no chance to pass him the knife, because he was sick, so they let him go although his sentence was life, the same as mine. He died almost at once.

"So finally, when my sentence was commuted after nineteen years, the knife passed to me. That was last March. And I was not like the rest. For a forty-year-old ex-politico who gets out after rotting inside for nineteen years, rehabilitation is almost out of the question. I pursued the traitor with more determination than my comrades. This knife-grinding trade didn't just offer the possibility of carrying the knife around legally, it allowed me to earn a living as well. And at last I'm within reach of the bastard."

"You mean, he's in Taejin?"

"That's it. From what I hear, things didn't go too well for him either. At first he got a few favours from the police for having shopped us, but then they dropped him because he was taking bribes. After that he had a hard time of it. It seems that for the last few months he's been working out there on a fishing boat."

He fell silent for a while, then scrutinizing me carefully, he asked, "So don't you want to turn me in?"

His mysterious smile had come back again. Then he fell silent, as if he regretted having spoken so freely, and he didn't say another word until the time came for us to part. The snow had stopped and it was broad daylight when we left the shelter. We walked amost eight miles together in silence, then parted at a fork in the road with the town already in view.

"You come down on your own. It's better they don't see you with me. Just in case there are problems later."

He left me with those words, spoken in the same emotionless voice I had heard when we first met, and went walking firmly ahead. I didn't even say goodbye, and absently watched him go.

Now we have reached the last chapter in my narrative of the events of the winter of that year.

It was about two in the afternoon when I entered Taejin, it was sleeting. I had stopped a couple of hours at a small village to rest and dry my clothes.

I hear that nowadays Taejin has developed into something of a seaside resort, but in those days it was an insignificant little harbour, where nothing ever happened except perhaps in summer. The unfrequented wintry port made me think of a haunted island. The last few miles were anything but smooth, too. This is what I scribbled in my notebook that day, on a page stained by the falling sleet:

Sea! I have come. Why were your calls so insistent?

These last few days, you have summoned me in many forms, called me in a host of different voices. I have seen you in the lowering sky, in the flying snowflakes. I have heard your voice in the howling north wind and in the sad sobbing of the trees along the road. Your call was all round me, in sleep, and dreams, and drunkenness.

Therefore I have come to you like this. Nothing could block my way, not the blizzard, the worst for thirty years, not the lofty mountains without a single proper road. These eighty miles racing through frost and snow have not been too arduous. I did not give up, although my feet are blistered and my face is on fire.

The last few miles before I reached you were the worst. The empty road, exposed on all sides, was whipped by biting sleet-filled winds. The snowflakes falling on my cheeks and neck melted instantly into icy water that ran down over my bare skin. My frozen shoes grew soggy from the slush along the road. My damp hair froze stiff and tugged at my scalp. But I still kept running, like a faithful dog obeying its master's call.

Now tell me. Tell me why you are calling me. I am listening.

For a long while I remained standing silently in front of the sea. Strong winds were pushing endless waves towards the shore, where they slammed against the rocks and clawed at the sandy beach. I was wrapped in a kind of mist, where the drifting milky spray and the snowflakes dropping from the dark sky above mingled.

I still remember it all. The frenzied sea, the dark sky blending with the waves, the solitary seagulls soaring with their dying cries. And the sudden realization of my own miserable insignificance.

I wonder now whether the silence I had fallen into was not another of my vague raptures. And whether in that rapture I was not expecting some kind of communication with the sea. As if I was hoping for the reply to a question I had in fact long since resolved, but which on my own I could not lay to rest, a question that may seem absurd now, but at the time was desperately important to me: should I throw away the cup, or persevere in draining it?

Yet the sea seemed only intent on emitting roars I could not understand. "Answer! Answer!" I went down to the water's edge, as if insisting. The dying waves caressed my frozen feet with a sort of gentle warmth, then, as the warmth reached my knees, stronger waves sent me reeling.

I stood there for a long time, struggling to keep my footing, and gazed at the writhing of the ever darker sky, the ever wilder sea, as I strained my ears. A little way off, a few grey gulls had settled on the back of the tossing waves, and were resting weary wings.

I closed my eyes. It was as if a faint ray of light was slowly rising from the very depths of my consciousness. I had the impression that the sea's mystery was about to reach out and touch me, speak words that would at last bring my wanderings to a happy conclusion.

I waited for it to become clearer and more distinct.

A long moment passed. But finally my eyes were forced open by a violent blow against my thighs and the thunder of an enormous wave striking the nearby rocks. And just at that moment a tiny event occurred on the edge of my still blurred vision. Unless it was an illusion? A tiny grey gull floating not far off was suddenly overwhelmed by the unfurling surf of a mountainous wave.

The bird flapped its wings once, sank, and did not reappear. Even in the state I was in, I prayed and prayed that it would come back up, but there was no sign of it. Then I was sent staggering, as the reflux from the huge wave that had engulfed the bird suddenly crashed twice, thrice, against my back.

From that moment, my body seemed to be entirely dominated by instinct. Despite the seductiveness of the sea's apparent warmth, I strained every muscle to get back onto the shore. That momentary exposure to danger had suddenly set me ablaze with new vitality.

It was an intense, but equally a sad and melancholy flame. For it showed me a true image of myself, as small and weary as that gull the waves had swallowed. There I saw my own wretched existence, buffeted by great waves of absurdity and despair. Then suddenly the roaring of the sea became meaningless, its frenzy nothing more than the empty motion of an inanimate object.

I'm going back home. It's time to finish this too serious game. The sea has turned out to be nothing more than a fraud, like all the other things sent to mislead us. Can anything offer us salvation, when God himself has given up all idea of saving us?

But still the gulls must fly and life must go on. If a gull gives up flying, it is no longer a gull; if a person gives up trying to go on, he is no longer a person. The cup that each receives has to be taken and drained. Despair is not the end but the real beginning of existence . . .

Those are the last lines I noted that day, and they too are marked by stains of sleet. But despite that unexpectedly resolute conclusion, I was unable to overcome an inexplicable feeling of despondency, of grief even, that went with it. No matter how level-headed and rational you are, an experience of despair demands more of you. I know I stayed for a long time leaning against a rock there on the beach, weeping.

Truth to tell, my despair was not yet complete enough to become the starting-point of a new life, but certainly the despair I experienced there at the edge of the sea afforded me an invaluable sense of freedom.

If there are no absolute, objective values that can guide us, our salvation lies in our own hands alone. Our lives are not in the control of any external powers, they necessarily receive their seal of approval and their fullness from what we ourselves decide.

In that sense, my cousin back in Y. had been right. Despair is the purest and most powerful of human passions, and in it lies our salvation. That discovery was determining for my life in the years that followed. For I chose beauty as my absolute value, on account of what I had experienced at Ch'angsu Pass.

Now I am reflecting. A truly artistic temperament builds on an absolute despair concerning beauty. What makes the greatness of the artist is not the creation of beauty, but the fact of taking up the challenge and suffering, while knowing in advance that creation of beauty is impossible. The same is true of this story . . . In the end, if it is found to possess any value, it will not be because of my imperfect portrayal of that winter's beauty and authenticity, but on account of all the nights of weariness and pain I have endured while writing, knowing perfectly well that my task was an impossible one.

* * *

I had more or less regained control of my mysterious grief and despondency when the knife-grinder reappeared. Despite the noise of the waves and the wind, I gradually became aware of someone nearby. I looked around and saw him on the other side of the rock I was leaning against. How long had he been there? I couldn't tell.

I noticed that he looked different, wretched and worn out. The wooden box he had been carrying lay now at his feet, like a defeated warrior's abandoned armour. He seemed deeply absorbed in private thoughts, as he stared blankly towards the sea.

He had not noticed my presence. Seized abruptly with a strange feeling of sorrow, I drew near.

He did not move, though I was only a few steps away. I stood still for a moment, afraid somehow of disturbing him. He was still lost in his thoughts, unaware of my presence, but finally he rummaged for something and drew out the knife I had seen that morning. He stared at it for a few moments, then, as if suddenly making up his mind, he hurled it with all his might towards the sea. The knife curved through a long arc, and disappeared in the waves.

"What are you doing?" I blurted out, feeling strangely shaken and somehow, at the same time, disappointed. He suddenly seemed to acknowledge my presence, and gazed at me sadly for a few seconds, before replying with a sigh:

"Throwing away an illusion I've been carrying around for too long."

His response made me understand why he was looking so crushed and miserable. He had lost the only thing that had mattered to him – his tenacious hatred.

"The bastard was living in a half-ruined hut, with a sick wife and two kids covered in boils. The kids were crying with hunger and the wife was dying. I reckoned it was more of a punishment to let him go on living."

He smiled mournfully. And I knew he was lying, at least the last part. I knew it intuitively, at the sight of that melancholy smile.

"The bastard begged me to kill him, but I refused."

Hearing those words that sounded like another excuse, I suddenly wanted to ask the real reasons for his forgiveness. But another, even stronger impulse, took hold of me. Leaving him where he was, I ran to the bag I had left lying on the other side of the rock. I pulled out the letter written the day before and the bottle of poison I had been carrying around for the last six months, and contemplated them for a few seconds, just as he had stared at his knife.

Slowly he approached me and began to observe my movements.

I wonder if the time had really come or not? Anyway, I wrapped the bottle in the letter and hurled them with all my strength into the sea. They flew in a curve, were swallowed up, and vanished.

"What did you throw away?" he asked in a strange voice.

"Sentimentality. And my knowledge, it was rotten before it was ripe."

A few years later I came across him one day by chance in a small town. He was earning a living drawing pictures with a red-hot iron on wooden boards. It must have been something he'd learned to do in prison. His shop was not very big, but judging by the steady stream of customers, things must have been going well enough for him. I should also mention that he had a pretty young wife with him, and a one-year-old son.

Yet strangely enough I have absolutely no memory of how we parted back there on the beach.

The next day, I was in a train on my way to Seoul. It was a fine bright afternoon in late winter. As the train was passing through a peach orchard, I noticed that the tips of the branches were already touched with red, a sure sign that when spring came the blossom would be more than usually splendid.

From Winter that Year
Translated from the Korean by Brother Anthony of Taizé

MURRAY BAIL

The Seduction of My Sister

My sister and I were often left alone together. She was younger than me, about eighteen months. I hardly had time to know her, although we were alone together for days on end, weekends included.

Our father worked odd hours at an Anglo-American tobacco company. And our mother, she had a job at Myer's. Ladies' shoes, Manchester, toys and whitegoods were some of her departments. She worked Saturday mornings, and there was the stock-taking. She put in a lot of overtime, working herself to the bone. Some nights our mother arrived home after dark, more like a widow in black than a mother, and passed around meat pies from a paper bag, one for each of us, including our father. Otherwise, we were "left to our devices", our mother's term; I heard her explain to a neighbour over the fence.

For a long time I hardly took any notice of her, my sister, always at my elbow, in the corner of my eye. Whatever I was doing she would be there. More than once I actually tripped over my sister. She seemed to have nothing better to do than get in the way. She said very little, hardly a word. She and I had different interests, we were interested in totally different things, yet if I was asked today what her interests were I couldn't say. Tripping over her once too often or else wanting nothing more than to be left alone I would turn and shout at her to go, get lost, even giving her a shove; anything to get rid of her. Half an hour later she would be back, all smiles or at least smiling slightly, as if nothing had happened.

My sister was skinny, not much to look at. She had short hair in a fringe, and a gap between her teeth. If anyone asked what colour her eyes were I could not answer, not exactly. There was a mole above her lip, to the left, almost touching her lip.

Taking an interest in something or standing near a group she had a way of holding her mouth slightly open. I can't remember a single thing she said.

The mole could have by now transformed into a beauty spot, I've seen them on other women. Brothers though are supposed to be blind to the attractions of their sisters.

Our father had a small face, and although he didn't himself smoke the odour of fresh tobacco followed him about like a cloud, filling the passages of the house. I don't know about him and our mother. About their happiness or contentment even it was difficult to say. When our father spoke it was to himself or to his shoes; he hardly looked at our mother. In reply she would say nothing at all. Sometimes she would make a strange humming sound to turn to us and say something unrelated. Arriving home after standing behind a counter all day our mother looked forward to putting her feet up. After the table had been cleared our mother and father often went over the various budgets, income and outgoings, gaining some sort of pleasure or satisfaction from the double-checking. If he saw us watching, our father would give a wink and make a great show of scratching his head and licking the pencil.

It was a short street, the houses dark-brick from the Thirties. Each house had a gravel drive and a garage, although hardly anyone had a car, and a front hedge, every house had its box hedge, except directly opposite us, which was an empty block, the only one left in the street. It was surprising how long it remained empty, swaying with grasses, lantana in the left-hand corner. Who in their right mind would want to live all day looking across at us? Our father winked at us, our mother taking a breath, not saying a word.

It remained then, a hole in the street, a break in the hedges, in the general tidiness, an eyesore to more than one.

Nothing lasts, that is true; it goes without saying. Nevertheless, the morning we woke up and saw pyramids of sand and a cement-mixer on the block it was a shock to the system, the builders more like intruders than new neighbours, trampling over habits and feelings.

Slowly, then rapidly accelerating, a house took shape out of the disorder and commotion; I would have preferred it to last forever, so much there to follow, to take in and assemble in my mind. I can't speak for my sister.

Instead of retreating at right angles to the street like any other house, including ours, it was positioned longways, parallel to the street. It caused our father to give a brief laugh of misunderstanding. He called it "The Barn". Instead of bricks the colour of lamb chops which slowly turn brown, ours, it had cream bricks of a speckled kind, and grey tiles on the roof instead of the painted corrugated iron as ours.

I came home one afternoon late to see my sister standing at our front gate as always, waiting for me; only I could tell by the way she was twisting one leg around the other that she was talking to someone.

The Gills had moved in, their doors and windows wide open. Gordon withdrew a hand and introduced himself. He was their only son; about my age.

The house inside was still smelling of paint. In his bedroom he had a stamp album and cigarette cards scattered on his desk, and merely shrugged at the model aeroplanes suspended from the ceiling, as if he had lost interest in them. We went from room to room, my sister and I. In the lounge Gordon demonstrated the record-player which opened on silver elbows into a cocktail cabinet. Shelves and glass cabinets displayed plates and bowls and porcelain figures. From another room a clock chimed. Now and then Gordon stepped forward to explain something or take it from our hands, then returned to the window, answering a question or my sister's exclamations. Across the street directly opposite stood our house, stubborn, cramped-looking. It was all there was to see.

Mr Gill put down a lawn, bordered by roses, not ordinary roses, but dark roses, and stepping stones of slate to the front door. Mr Gill had a moustache, the only one in the street, and a strong set of teeth. From the moment they met he called my father "Reg", and made a habit of dropping it with informal gravity into every other sentence, sometimes flashing a smile, which pleased my father no end. "Do you think, Reg, this weather's going to hold?" And, if he was in the middle of something, pruning or striding around to open the car door for Mrs Gill, who remained seated looking straight ahead, he'd glance up and with a single nod say "Reg", and return to what he was doing. Even this pleased my father.

It was our mother who suggested doubts. "No one", she was scraping the plates, "is like them, not in this street. They might as well be from another planet."

With his shirt wide open at the neck our father put his finger on it. "They're alright," he smiled, "they're extroverts."

Our mother always looked tired. I wondered why she kept on working, what on earth for, but she went on almost every day of her life, Saturdays included, at Myer's. Through the store she bought a washing machine and a Hoover, demonstration models, otherwise brand-new. In turn the store made a new fridge possible, the varnished icebox ending up in the garage, along with our father's hat-stand, tennis racket in its press, and a God-forsaken electric toaster. Chimes were added to the front door, a new letterbox smartened up the front, father's idea, displaying our number in wrought-iron beneath the silhouette of a Mexican asleep under his hat.

Taking a tour of our house one afternoon Gordon barely said a word. A floorboard kept creaking; I noticed the light was yellowish and the walls, carpets and chairs had a scruffy plainness.

In no time we were outside by the fig tree where I searched around to retrieve something. "That'd be a hundred years old," I pointed with my chin.

To demonstrate, my sister in her cotton dress shinned up into the first fork. Grinning, she looked like a monkey, I could have clocked her one. I glared and hissed at her; but she took no notice, which only gave the impression she was used to such cruel treatment.

I steered Gordon into the garage, my sister scrambling down from the tree, not wanting to be left out. Our mother and father never threw anything away. Poking around I held up things I thought might be of interest, waiting for his reaction. And Gordon too began examining things, the old tools, tin boxes, our mother's dressmaker's dummy before she was married. He squatted down, my sister alongside. It was Gordon who came across the gramophone records, still in their brown-paper sleeves. Reading the labels one by one he carefully put them back.

I thought he was being polite.

"Tell you what," I had an idea. "You go and stand on your front lawn," I glanced up at the sky, "and I'll send a few of these over the roof at you".

"What for?" He remained squatting.

It took a while for the penny to drop.

"See if you can catch them or something, I don't know." I had to push him. "You stay here," I told my sister.

Before Gordon could change his mind I yelled out from the back of our house, "Coming now!" And in a simple quoit-throwing motion sent up in the half-light the great Caruso singing something mournful in Italian. It soared above our iron roof, the disc, and in a moment of dark beauty tilted, almost invisibly, and hovered like the great tenor holding a high note, before returning to earth. My sister and I both had our mouths open. I reached our gate, sister alongside, to see Gordon waiting on their patch of lawn, hands in pockets,

suddenly give a hoarse cry as the black 78 brushed his shoulder and
thudded into the lawn behind him.

Hardly able to run, laughing too much, I crossed the street. "What
d'you reckon?" I gave him a shove. "It almost took your head off."
Picking up the record Gordon wiped it with his sleeve.

Nobody spoke. He could have gone one way or the other, I could
see. I took another look at him, my sister gaping at one of us, then
the other. I ran back to my position, not saying anything.

I sent over *Land of Hope and Glory*, and before he could recover,
The Barber of Seville, followed by the *Nutcracker Suite*. I had others in
a stack at my feet when the street lights came on, and Mrs Gill began
calling in her musical voice, "Gor-don."

Anyone could see he was not suited for sporting activities. The
sloping shoulders, the paleness: even the hang of his arms – uncoordi-
nated. Yet the following night Gordon was in position early, pacing
up and down, looking over to our side.

I waited for it to be almost dark. To my sister I called out, "Look
at me. See how I do it. If you like, you can have a go later."

I began throwing and threw, in quick succession, one musical disc
after the other. They were hard to spot in the night sky, that of course
being the idea, their closeness suddenly revealed by a faint hissing
near the face or back of the head. They were lethal. Quick reflexes were
necessary. And concentrating hard and working on his technique
Gordon took everything I sent at him. He used his feet, swaying from
the hips. With each throw of mine the better he became; and so his
confidence grew. It wasn't long before he began in a lackadaisical
manner grabbing at the black shapes as they came down at him or
past him, managing to pull down in mid-air one in three or four,
without saying a word, even after leaping with an arm outstretched,
thereby putting pressure right back on me on the other side, sister
looking on. Some I tried sending in low or at unexpected angles,
anything to catch him off-balance.

My sister had moved to the front gate where my efforts could not
be seen, where instead she could observe Gordon facing up to the
onrushing discs. For a while the pressure began to get to me; I had
to talk to myself. The heads of a few of Mr Gill's prize-winning
roses were severed; another night, a disc I gave too much wrist kept
on going above Gordon's shout and outstretched arm and smashed
against the mock louvred shutters Mr Gill had bolted to the wall,
showering Gordon with fine-grooved shards. Almost before he could

recover I sent a recital of a legendary pianist, forget his name, Jewish, who died only the other day: wide of the mark, wrong grip, it sailed through the open window of the Gill's lounge room, my sister and I waiting for the crash of all that bone-china, which never came. There were moments or ordinariness, moments of poetry. Simplicity, I realised, produced elegance, not only in the throw, in Gordon's response as well. One night, Melba, collectors' item I'm told, sliced through Mr Limb's new telephone wires next door which fell over Gordon's face and shoulders like string. Gordon froze, my sister too; hand went to her mouth. They didn't have a clue about electricity, Gordon and my sister were not mechanically minded. Realizing he was not about to be electrocuted Gordon kicked the wires and some of his embarrassment aside and went back to his crouch.

Engrossed in our separate tasks we hardly spoke, every throw presenting a different set of problems. It changed Gordon, it opened him up. He'd come around to my side early, rubbing his hands as if it was freezing, my sister looking on.

"One of those records the other night," he followed me into the garage, "boy, was it funny."

I was sorting through the few that were left.

"You ought to hear *Laughing Gas* one day. It had the old man rolling on the floor."

Along with *Little Brown Jug*, the Satchmo selection and *Sing, Sing, Sing* it would have been our father's. Our mother, I was told, had a singing voice. Always with a grin hovering at the ready our father had a taste for imaginary honky-tonk playing; he made the cutlery jump on the table, sister and I watching. I began putting the remaining 78s back in the trunk.

"What are you doing?" Gordon grabbed my shoulder. He began reading the labels. "What about these?"

At that moment I wanted to pause; something felt out of place. Twice he whistled he was ready. I stared at my fingernails, waiting to think clearly. A few houses away a dog barked, and someone was trying to start a motor-bike.

It took less than a week, if that, to go through the remaining 78s, and when they were gone we tried chipped or broken discs, until too difficult to throw or nothing was left of them. Even so, when I realised the entire collection had gone, a feeling spread in my stomach, of corresponding emptiness.

I dismissed Gordon's suggestion we continue, using saucers, his

idea of a joke: saw him nudge-nudging my sister. She was hanging
around us, always there. A glance at her scrawniness could trigger
irritation in me, I don't know why. Anything he said she'd listen,
mouth open in that way. I would have said, look, scram, buzz off;
words to that effect. I was about to, when Gordon reached for
something wrapped in newspaper under the bench, and we squatted,
sister too, I could see her knickers.

Lifting it out I untied the string.

"Eek!" she clutched at him.

I held up a fox with a glass eye.

"O-kay", I swung experimentally. "This'll do. What's the matter?"
I stared at my sister. "I can throw it."

Before she married, our mother dressed up for special occasions,
little hats, veils, dresses consisting of buttons and tiny flowers. One
photo in the album has her on a shopping spree with her mother in
the city, each with a cheesy smile, like sisters. Shortly after, she met
our father, I forget where. Near the back door I was adjusting my
feet, getting the balance right. I swung a few times, began again,
swung once more, again, suddenly letting go with all the smoothness
I could muster, the centrifugal force of the lop-sided fox hop-hopping
me forward like a shot-putter.

Leisurely, the dog-like shape began flying, its tail outstretched. At
the chimney it somersaulted in slow motion against the night sky,
appeared to set course, and with snarling teeth nose-dived straight
for Gordon across the street, chatting to my sister. At her cry he
tried to swerve. The fox followed, sinking its fangs into his throat, as
he rolled on the lawn.

A fox is pleasant to hold, weighted at one end, a living thing. I
never tired of sending it over, enjoying the accelerating moment
of release, then running up our drive to follow its twists and turns,
flash of orange tail, its Stuka-dive forcing Gordon into the acrobatics
of a goalkeeper, exaggerated for my sister, looking on. "Improvisation
is the mother of invention!" I heard him call out. My sister swallowed
anything. At the same time she had a frivolous side; I could imagine
reaching our gate to find her parading in front of him, fox draped
over one shoulder, hand on hip for him.

As mentioned, the houses each had a hedge, except the Gills', which
had the picket fence, leaving the house naked. The Gills didn't
seem to mind, on the contrary. Every other night the lights would be
blazing, more like an ocean-liner than a house, the rest of the street

as dark as the sea. The rectangle of illuminated lawn appeared as a billiard table, the beds of roses, shutters flung open, car in the drive all added up to a welcoming, optimistic air. After the loss of the fox I sent over a rubbish-bin lid, glittering chassis of a crystal-set, tennis-racket in its press, other objects so poor in the aerodynamics department they barely cleared the roof. They were not adding anything; I was beginning to lose interest.

The card table had a way of setting its legs in mid-air, to make a perfect four-point landing on the Gills' lawn; but that only happened, I think, twice.

Our father would begin picking his teeth with a match, and for the umpteenth time tell us what a time he had, the best years, working with cattle in the outback, before he married, only ten months, but enough to deposit a slowness in his speech, a corresponding glaze in our mother's eyes, and a green trunk full of aboriginal weapons in the garage. I had forgotten they were there. Gordon was holding the boomerangs in his hand, authentic tribal weapons, not the tourist kind.

"You might as well put them back," I said. "They're too dangerous." When I turned my sister was already skipping around to the front, Gordon at her heels.

"Listen, will you?" I crossed the street. I grabbed my sister. "You're not going to watch me, right?" I felt her squirming. "Then you'd better keep your eyes open. In case someone's coming, that's why. These things," I sounded prim, "could kill someone."

Gordon was in no doubt as to the serious turn the game had taken. Boomerangs were altogether different to the grimacing masks and decorated shields from New Guinea displayed in the room Mr Gill called his "study". If one caught him in the face it would have been curtains. We knew, Gordon and I, my sister too. Gordon began going through his stretch exercises. Instead of hesitating, let alone calling a halt, I was gripping the boomerang at one end.

I gave plenty of elbow: let go.

By the time I reached the street the boomerang was ahead of me. Gordon on their lawn was shielding his eyes. My sister had moved from the gate to be alongside. The mulga blades came swirling out of the fading light in a fury, seeking him out. Keeping his eyes on it, swerving and ducking at the last moment, he avoided being hit, just. He was impressive, I'd have to say. From then on the vicious insistent things kept coming at him, at the strangest angles, finding him in roundabout ways, where least expected, side-on without

warning or from behind. While I had never underestimated his
confidence, I think I underestimated his abilities in general. He had
a certain course of his life marked out, even then. He would always
succeed where I would not, I could see. In the end my life became
something of a shambles. His would not.

Gordon wore his father's yellow driving gloves and was grabbing
at the boomerangs as they flew past, my sister clapping encouragement whenever he managed to pull one down. Keen eyesight, reflexes
played their part, fair enough, knowing which ones to leave, sure;
but as I watched I began to find his way of crouching and twisting,
particularly in the region of his hips, distasteful. He displayed a
fleshy alertness I found offputting, just as when he received a given
object and turned it over in his hands I saw his arms were precisely
the pale arms with black hairs I found unpleasant, repulsive even. I
have always had trouble with such hairy arms, my sister didn't seem
to mind. Every night her job was to whistle or cough if a motor cyclist
appeared or a pedestrian, such as Mr Limb next door deciding to
stretch his legs, it's all she had to do; otherwise I was throwing blind.
But she was more interested in warning him, Gordon, crouching
there on the slippery lawn; more than once letting out a cry, which
may well have saved his skin. I had to cross the street and tell her
to pipe down, we didn't want the neighbours coming out. If she
didn't we'd have to stop, it would be the end. As I laid down the
law she began to blink, I could see she was about to cry. Gordon
nearby examined his elbow, saying nothing.

Gramophone music came from the Gills' open windows, men and
women moved in the brightly lit rooms, now and then a man leaned
back laughing his head off. This flat boomerang felt longer on one
side, inscribed with dots and whorls. I threw it casually, perhaps
that was it, for as I ran with it up the drive, the thing hovered like a
lost helicopter blade above our chimney, before returning. Slipping
on the gravel I ran back just as our father stepped out the door.

"Bloody crow!" he waved over his head. "Did you see that?"

It clattered into the fig tree, but by then our father had cocked
his ear to the Gills' party noise.

"Benny Goodman", he gave a bit of a jig, "at the Carnegie Hall.
Hello, how's Gordon tonight?"

Gordon pulled up panting, sister alongside. As soon as our father
went back in our mother began getting stuck into him, listing things
missing in him.

"Think," Gordon was shaking me. "Where did you say it landed?"

"I'll find it in the morning. Don't worry about it".

His answer startled me. "Put it off and never find it again. That'd be right."

Already up in the tree my sister dropped it at his feet. Wiping it with his handkerchief Gordon held the flat blade up to the light. Whatever he saw pleased him, for he lunged with both hands at my sister as she passed, ignoring me.

No matter how hard I tried I never managed to make another one return. And when the trunk was empty, even of fighting boomerangs, which Gordon explained were never meant to be thrown, the problem again was finding something to send over. In this and other matters Gordon revealed a single-mindedness I never had. Gordon knew what he wanted, usually had a fair idea. What I thought hardly worth the effort he invariably thought the opposite. Already he had a sureness in summing up the other person, then no longer taking them into account.

Anything I could lay my hands on I was letting go, I found all sorts of things we did not want. Nothing ever meant much to me. Even today I am casual about possessions. With people too I come and go. In this I resemble my casual father, who in the end disappointed people, my mother and others.

In a single night I sent over a pair of suit trousers, striding across the sky, a row of coat-hangers, textbooks I would never open, wooden lavatory seat. I watched as every copy of *Life* presented to me by an amateur photographer uncle changed hands, the history of the post-war world turning over like a newsreel. Patterns form without anyone being fully aware, I see now. Our mother wore the same shoes for a week and a half, our father never changed his hat.

Electric light bulbs lit up the sky, followed by the first fluorescent tube; our pop-up toaster another time trailed its plaited cord. Problems of a technical kind: it took several attempts to hurl the standard-lamp over, a ceremonial spear. The electric radiator made the journey, the single red bar describing quite fantastic arabesques, catching Gordon by surprise, talking in the shadows to my sister. When occasionally she skipped over to my side, expressing interest in what I was doing, I could see she was itching to get back to him and whatever he was saying, on the other side. I set the American alarm clock for seven o'clock in mid-flight, and as it began ringing Gordon reached out and silenced it with one hand. I chucked half a dozen eggs, we kept fowls in the backyard, rotten tomato, a navel

orange, another joke, Gordon collecting it on the neck. He said he
confused it with the moon, but he was talking to my sister, I saw
them. And for the first time my sister turned on me, "That's going
to leave a bruise," as I ran up arranging a country grin, in the manner
of our father.

Eventually we come up against things said by others which cannot
be explained, not at the time. The night our mother talked about
"taking in ironing" it made us laugh our heads off, my father and
I, sister too after a glance, our father laughing the loudest, almost
choking, at the same time placing his weakened hand on my mother's
arm, which she pulled away. "Your mother sometimes comes out
with all kinds of rubbish," wiping the tears from his eyes. At the table
my sister sat demurely. It made me look twice, our mother too. The
few jokes I cracked in her direction, not worth repeating, she ignored.
The usual family racket we made she seemed to find irritating, which
in turn irritated us, at least our mother.

From the beginning, I began to see, I was doing all the work. To
Gordon, I suggested we change positions. Operating in darkness
near our back door I could do my bit with my eyes shut, whereas
on his side light was absolutely essential, he pointed out. "Without
proper light I've no idea what's coming my way." I'm at the receiving
end, let's not forget, he actually said.

Besides, he pointed out, we have each attained a degree of
efficiency in our respective roles. "Isn't that right?" he said to her,
alongside.

The pale ironing board in flight reminded me of the loose skin
above my mother's elbow. Difficult to send up and over it was more
difficult still for Gordon receiving, a matter of manoeuvring desperately to get side-on to the torpedo-shaped thing. At the same time
Mr and Mrs Gill, stepped out for a night at the theatre or somewhere.
By the gate I watched Mrs Gill, fox over one shoulder, although the
night was warm, flash my sister a smile. "So this is Glenys?" I heard
her say. After that she usually stopped to say hello, Gordon looking
casually bored, as Mr Gill strode around to open her car door.

To get my sister's attention Gordon sometimes touched her with
his foot. Other times, talking to me, he'd drape an elbow over her
shoulder. In turn, my sister remained still, no longer jumping about.
He subscribed to American magazines and gave her books to read.

Birdcage, oval mirror reflecting the clouds, a perfectly good floral
armchair.

The smallest things amused my sister. She had what I would say

was a childish delight in small and modest things. It was one of
her attractive sides. And yet when I sent over things carefully chosen
for her she reacted as if they had fallen from the sky into his lap, as
if it had nothing to do with me, on the other side.

I submitted silver coins when I had some to spare. "We're down
to our last shekels," I called, the coins shooting across the sky as
falling stars.

It was she who pointed them out to him, I could hear her cries.
It would have been their appearance among the stars that caught
her eye, not their value; I can't answer for him. As always Gordon
hardly said a word; I mean to me: I could hear him murmuring
to her. Mostly, you never knew what he was thinking; he never
gave much away. Vase of flowers, inner-spring mattress, dustpan
and brush. By the time I'd reach their gate he'd still be talking to
her, my sister taking in whatever rot he came out with. It had been
the same with me. So practised had he become he'd merely extend an
arm and take whatever I'd sent over or simply move back a step,
taking her by the waist, a protective move.

She was out of my hair, I was no longer tripping over her, a good
thing; at the same time, I felt great rushes of irritation at the way
she transferred her attention lock, stock and barrel to him, in that
trusting way of hers, mouth slightly open. If our mother saw two
people with heads together they were "as thick as thieves". And more
than once she said, "No one likes anyone whispering."

A large oil painting from our mother's side used to hang in the
bedroom, a summer landscape, on canvas. It aquaplaned into multi-
ples of parched hills and fat gum trees. Gordon received it with open
arms, my sister helped him lower it to the ground, and listened as
he launched into a lecture, pointing out the strengths and weaknesses
of the composition. After examining it and wiping it with his
handkerchief he pronounced it too fragile to travel, my sister nodding
in agreement.

In the way the boomerang came back over the roof it was only
a matter of waiting before our father's expression returned to one of
smiling slightly. Mr Limb, a bachelor who lived next door, used to
say, "I don't have a hobby or a pastime," and as he reached retirement,
"Most of my life has passed, and now just when I need it I don't
have a hobby or a pastime." The subject of early retirement occupied
his mind so much he suffered excruciating headaches; he took days
off from the work he no longer enjoyed, on medical advice.

Even then I felt sympathy for Mr Limb. I don't know what

eventually happened to him. The umbrella jerked open and parachuted down, ironic cheers from Gordon's side, ashtrays were never used in our house, nest of tables, mother's, and our father's tan suitcase opened its mouth and dropped a sock on the telephone wires.

From my side in darkness I would hear Gordon's voice, followed by her laugh. Rolling pin tumbled over, dusted still with flour. They would have trouble finding the knives and forks. I no longer bothered rushing around to see how the latest thing was received. We were going through the motions, little more. Only later do we realize something of value has slipped away. Whatever had been worth the effort in the beginning was coming to an end; a feeling I would recognize in later years.

I squatted near the garage, my sister, Gordon at her elbow, rummaging through what little was left.

Embroidered tablecloth, their idea, didn't make the distance; I could have told them that. At any given time there is only a limited number of ideas of value, I wanted to say. And before long we exhaust them as well. I remained squatting, watching them. If one of them went somewhere the other one followed. I was left alone, to one side.

That night when my sister came skipping around to my side I thought she was coming around to my way of thinking, whatever that was.

Instead, she had a suggestion, and as I listened I felt my father's grin beginning to run amok; but she was looking away, strangely, and speaking vaguely.

Thinking the thing she suggested was going to be the last I got to my feet, not at all laboriously, and went inside. I came out with it rolled up.

So many things passed through my hands; nevertheless, I found it necessary to use all my skills with this one, and wondering whether it was her idea or his dispatched after some difficulties my sister's favourite party dress. I could follow its progress slowly, walking up our gravel drive. Billowing from the waist it elbowed gently past the chimney. And in its determination, oblivious to me or anybody else, I glimpsed my sister then and in the years to come. She would always be determined, always there, her way, while I felt within a heavy casualness, settled and spreading.

Whatever Gordon was expecting it wasn't this. Directly above him the translucent dress began descending, flapping gently at the edges.

Not sure whether to grab at it with both hands, or perhaps deceived by its slowness, the slow hip and narrow waist movements, he was caught wrong-footed. The white cotton dress smothered him.

I waited for my sister to rush forward and help, as she had all along, but she looked on, not lifting a finger, letting Gordon disentangle himself.

From the gate-post if I glanced across the street I would see Gordon's outline, kicking gravel, my sister discussing something. I had almost forgotten what my sister looked like. The dark bulk of the house now came between her features and me, obscuring aspects of her personality even. Out of habit I hung around near our back door. From inside the kitchen I heard the soft thudding of our mother ironing, occasionally the murmur of our father.

Things at least seemed to be steady there, I remember thinking.

At the sound of her voice, my sister, I stood up. Gordon was one step behind, both hands in his pockets, pursing his lips.

My sister whispered again. Why the whisper? I wanted to ask. Facing her, I noticed a rushed, wide-open expression I hadn't seen before.

Still I didn't say anything. After a while my sister simply went inside, leaving us. He and I stood there. Gordon glanced at his watch. When she came out in her white party dress he stepped forward.

"How am I?" she asked in a small voice. She was speaking to me. The gap opened between her teeth as she smiled.

It allowed me to place my hands under her arms. She was much heavier than I imagined, I could feel the soft swell of her breasts. She allowed my hands to remain there; she was my sister.

I looked at her once more. "Are you alright?" I was on the point of saying. "Is this what you want?" Other questions reached my tongue, but her body had gone completely soft, and by then I had taken an interest in the whole technical question; I began gathering momentum. In an almighty heave-ho, putting my whole body into it, I let go.

Trust and optimism were always her main characteristics. Now she tilted her chin, and dog-paddled among the stars, then clasped her hands more like an angel than my sister. Putting her trust in me she was now putting her trust in him. I concentrated on the mole near her lip, a point of focus, until it too began diminishing, along with the pale hopes of her body, fringe, standing on one foot, listening: all this blotted out by the chimney.

I heard Mr Limb's cough. He was setting out on his evening walk, for health reasons. I felt so much around me slipping, accelerating, beyond my grasp; for I was left with nothing. Running from my side towards the light I began calling my sister's name, to where she had gone.

EXTRACTS FROM NOVELS

LIONEL ABRAHAMS

from *The Celibacy of Felix Greenspan*

Felix's first, short-lived affair had happened when he was twenty-seven and at a breaking-point, and now there had been six more years without a woman. What counted even more than his physical impediments was a personal deficiency: he froze or frightened the women he loved – or merely wanted – at just the moment when he moved to attempt persuasion, because he lacked the male knack of acting calmly while impassioned. As for purchasable women, Johannesburg was gruffly secretive about its accommodations (yet, since this was home, could it ever be secretive enough?) and between his timidity and ignorance he had never found his way to them. Six years had brought him again to a point where the needs of his flesh were terrorizing his thoughts.

All at once the European trip was upon him. Gordon and Katherine Slessor were emigrating and they invited him to accompany them on their preliminary tour. It was the time of the Emergency. They'd had to make their decisions suddenly and his notice was brief, but an unusually profitable business deal by Dad just then made his going possible. This was the sort of miraculous opportunity it would be stupid to turn down. Gordon and Katherine could not be bettered as travel-companions and guides. Besides, there was the hint, in some of the names in their itinerary, that this jaunt could become relevant to his personal emergency. He made the secret acknowledgement that that, in the end, was what he was going for.

They went by sea. The evening before they docked for their half day at Las Palmas, Felix stood with Gordon at the deck-rail listening to his friend's satirical description of what would happen in port: scores of the proper young fellows aboard would stream ashore for their first bit of freedom, and queue up to take their turns with the town's few over-worked tarts. Felix grinned and grimaced at this picture, hiding his dismay.

Next day with Katherine they did the taxi tour of the island and afterwards found they had an hour they could spend in the town. Gordon asked, "What else shall we go and see? The market? Or the cathedral?" He turned to Felix: "Should I get him to take you to a brothel?"

Felix avoided looking at Katherine as he stiffly replied, "Not after what you were telling me last night." He knew an aftermath of faint regret over this rejection of his first opportunity, but that evening in conversation Katherine opened to him a set of ideas which filled his thoughts and coloured his feelings during the last days of the voyage. There was for some people, she said, the privilege of a conscious confrontation with suffering, a high, hard fate to embrace if they dared: it was the way, for them, to an extraordinary fulfil-ment. It could be that for him she was implying. By the means she had revealed, he could – and would, he fancied, after all – rise above the riot of himself and refuse the easy compromise solutions.

On the train from Southampton they bought sandwiches and London newspapers and watched through the windows the unfold-ing of the modest, humane landscape. Katherine and Gordon were palpably filled with satisfaction, with relief almost. Felix could not resist teasing them by pretending that he saw, scrawled on walls in villages, typically South African signs and slogans: "Police State" "Let the people vote" "Slegs blankes" "Gents – Here".

From Waterloo station the taxi route to their hotel took in embank-ments, bridges, palaces and parks, all bland with the sunshine and greenery of a fine summer's noon-day. Where, Felix wondered, was the great black pit of the London the novelists described? But it was not long before something of that other, the darker London of his initial secret anticipation, came mockingly over the scene for him. The Slessors, whose last visit there had been under the shadow of post-war austerity, had a hundred things to remark on, but what fixed his attention in the passing days was their amusement at the prevalence and cunning of prostitutes' advertisements now that street soliciting was suppressed.

He began making explorations on his own, his attention divided between the fable manifest of the city's life and monuments, and the suggestive bits of pasteboard or paper that ought to have been pinned to doorposts and noticeboards. Somehow – had he missed the favoured area? – the invitations he was looking for eluded him. Or he saw things that were too ambiguous to trust. He pored over screen after screen of blatant photographs outside strip clubs, and one day entered one and sat, with a silent audience in a dark shoebox of a place, through a score of would-be febrile turns, with a hot sense of being near his goal and yet cheated and befouled.

At last he found the formula he expected and made his way up three flights of battered stairs, only to be turned away by a suspicious old hanger-on who insisted that "Madam does not work today."

Paris would, must, be different. It was. The Slessors seemed to find its beauty richer and more moving. After their first supper in their hotel on the Ile de la Cité, leaving Felix to settle in his room and explore the immediate vicinity, the pair of them took a long walk to revisit some specially remembered scenes. When they returned Katherine went to bed, but Gordon offered to go out again and show Felix a little of what there was to be enjoyed.

They drank coffee at a sidewalk table in the Place St Michel where they could see the fountain and glimpse, above the roofs, the top of Notre Dame itself. But the setting and the cosmopolitan throng taking the balmy air amid the lights were to Felix a mere papery phantasmagoria obscuring the single elusive reality. As they started back toward the hotel, he said to Gordon, "Please tell me, where are the red lights?"

Gordon looked faintly affronted and embarrassed. "There aren't actually red lights . . ." he said, and a silence fell between them.

The museums and restaurants, the marvels and monuments and shrines he visited during the next few days left Felix chilled, unbelieving, finally hysterical. The more he saw the more he felt the unreality of things and of himself. He moved for hours among silent Rembrandts and Chardins in the Louvre, oppressed by the dull suspicion of some terrific deception somewhere – perhaps in himself, perhaps in the long-awaited masters. But it was the Seine, endlessly varying the reflections of chestnut avenues, palaces, moulded balustrades and bridges, that, because it had the elements of what should be an ultimate loveliness, was the worst, the most desolating of all.

On the fifth evening he took a long ramble with Gordon and Katherine on the Right Bank. Somewhere beyond Les Halles among crooked narrow streets, they saw a woman standing at the kerb, exposed like a statue, her arms folded, a bag dangling from one wrist, her foot beating placid time to the tune she absently hummed. "There's a tart," Gordon remarked. They turned the corner she was standing at, and the next street was revealed as a market place of waiting women and hovering circumspect men.

The scene realised an ancient fantasy of Felix's, long since abandoned as improbable. And yet he walked through the place with a strained aloofness, feeling, despite his friends' amusement at the various miniature comedies of strutting and ogling, chaffing and pricing, a certain shame before them. After a while his awkwardness seemed to be communicated to them and they grew quieter. He wondered uneasily whether Gordon had told Katherine about his mistimed request of the first evening. If so, she would be aware of his hidden excitement over the commerce they were witnessing and of the defection – possibly it was also a kind of betrayal – that it implied. It humiliated him to be exposed – and equally, to have failed.

Nevertheless, two evenings later (it was his earliest opportunity) he set out alone to find that street again. Vague about how they had arrived there, he wandered for nearly an hour without finding the place. He was beginning to feel exasperated when he came not to that street but another, wider, brighter, with hotels sporting illuminated signs, cafés from which music came, and gayer men and prettier, more flamboyant women parading what was less ambiguously a place of pleasure. One girl of a surprisingly proud, fastidious style of good looks – dark and petite and dressed in crisp yellow with a spread skirt that swayed like a bending flower about her slender legs as she paced – drew him. He went happily toward her.

"*S'il vous plaît . . .*" he said, but she passed him without acknowledgement. Either she had not heard him or he had, after all, mistaken her. In fact she was too good to be true in the part. But then he saw her speak to a man and go with him into a hotel. In barely fifteen minutes she was back outside, and almost immediately, before Felix could go up to her, another man approached and she went inside with him.

Felix waited at the hotel door and stepped in her path as she emerged. "*Bonsoir, Mademoiselle,*" he said, and she met him with an immobile look. "*Je voudrais . . .*" he pointed at her, at himself, and turned his lips in a smile. But she shook her head and began to walk away. "*Pourquoi?*" he called. "*Qu'est-ce que? Combien? Oh, God, I've got enough money . . .*"

But she was away, oblivious, the poppy of her skirt swinging with her freedom to take and refuse as she pleased, round a corner out of his view. A minute later he was still dazedly staring for her, anxious to press his right, to argue it out, when she re-appeared at the corner. She halted there when she saw him and gave one more faint shake of her head. Then she crossed the road to where there was a knot of other women. They stared at him and talked among themselves. Then one of them, a tall negress, came over to him. Close before him she stopped and looking in his face nodded gravely like a child.

He felt very weary and remained silent for several seconds, staring bitterly at the girl in yellow. Then half fiercely and half mechanically he said, "*Combien?*"

Quaintly the negress leaned forward and whispered, "*Quatre mille.*" Her price was her secret and their intimacy had begun. Beginning to see her voluptuousness, the piquant ironies of her offer, he nodded and followed where she led. Through a doorway they came to a thickly carpeted staircase with a polished banister. But it was narrow and steep, and half-way up the first flight there was a sharp turn and a tread which afforded only a toehold. He needed a little help and put his hand out toward the woman. "*S'il vous plaît . . . Votre main.*"

She stopped and looked back at him. He stretched toward her the hand he wanted her to seize, but she made no move.

"*Le main,*" he said. Was that the right word? "*Votre main, si'il vous plaît. Assistez moi . . .*"

A small sound came from her as she stared at him, but she remained unmoving.

"*Votre main,*" he groaned, scraping the air with his own hand, and she gave a sort of giggle and muttered, "*J'ai peur,*" the meaning of which he did not remember.

"Just give me your hand," he begged. "*S'il vous plaît, votre main . . .*" And then he understood what it was that she was saying, in a squeaky whisper like an incipient scream, over and over again, "*J'ai peur . . . Ooh, j'ai peur . . .*" Frightened. She was afraid of him.

His air was wild when he got back downstairs to the street, and three women in succession simply turned away as he approached them. After the third bid he walked desperately away out of that street.

In a place that was empty of people he stopped, his face pressed against a darkened shop widow, and stood motiveless for a long time. At last the thought came of returning to the hotel on the Ile and going to sleep. But the thought of that sleep made him more frightened than the negress paralysed on the staircase. If this was how he had to return and go to sleep, with the world all ice and stone and a joke, he would never feel real again. Yet he had done the thing, made the demand, gone all his share of the way, already. What was there left for him to do?

Still, when he at last began again to walk, it was northwards, away from the river. After some blocks he came to another of the prostitutes' beats. It was an ill-lit street with dingy buildings, and the women seemed shadowy and dingy too. Intimidated and drained of lust, he walked slowly along, incapable of action or decision.

None of the figures he saw stirred his desire. Here and there his eye recognized a symbol of invitingness – a swing of hair or skirt, a half-bare breast – but it only sent through him a tremor of hopelessness.

Two blocks down, the street was nearly deserted, but he walked idly on toward the next corner. Rounding it he saw what seemed one last, remote patch of activity. A few girls loitered near a couple of opaque doorways, their flesh and the shadows only different shades of grey. Over the road several more sat at tables by a small drab café. He stopped and leaned against a wall, watching but passive. It was late and growing cold.

At first it seemed that a strange stillness lay upon the street, as though the women and the three or four ruminating men had all strayed here by mistake and were suspended in indifference like himself. One man hung quite immobile save for a hand and a cigarette. Two others exchanged remarks in muttered undertones. One more walked with surreptitious slowness past several of the women and when he paused by one it seemed that a single subdued gurgle of laughter was all that heralded his disappearance with her into the maw of a building.

There was a flicker of movement as one woman ran across the road to the café and spoke to those who were sitting there. They responded with some argument and laughter and after a minute or two she re-crossed and went to stand with a tall, copper-haired girl to whom she made some animated report. Felix began to focus his attention on the full-fleshed looks of the red-head. She gestured at her high-heeled shoes and passed a brisk comment, and the other, with a grin, ran back to the café.

The red-head gave Felix a passing glance, and he prepared to approach her, but at his decision his breath began to race as though he had just made an exertion. While he waited for it to quieten, the messenger returned from the café. She must be some servant or exploiter of the other women, he supposed; she was dressed differently, in denim jeans and a colourless jersey, and since her hair was shingled she seemed to have put aside her woman's guise. He came nearer to the pair, hoping to catch the red-head's eye again.

But his guess was wrong. A man – a middle-aged Oriental in a sports jacket and an open khaki shirt carrying a sandwich-tin – walked without loitering out of the distance straight up to the girl in jeans, and seemingly without a word going between them, she led him through a nearby doorway.

Felix waited a few minutes before gathering himself to move toward the red-head and speak. But abruptly he became aware that someone else was within a yard or two of him and coming nearer. It was the silent smoking man, a big dark-haired young fellow whose blue suit went tight over the muscles of his arms and legs. He seemed to be staring closely at Felix from behind his dark glasses. Felix waited for him to go away. But he stayed, a small muscle working in one of his sallow-skinned cheeks, his fingers trembling as they carried his cigarette from his small bluish mouth. At last he spoke.

"*Je ne parle pas Français,*" Felix answered.

The man repeated his first remark, then made another.

Felix explained again that he did not understand, but the man remained there speaking insistently to him. Yet he did not seem drunk.

A minute later the girl in jeans was outside too. She emerged from the doorway and the Chinese walked away as silently as he had come. She watched the exchange that was taking place for a few moments, then she spoke sharply to the young man. He glared at her, shrugged and walked away.

"Are you English?" she asked Felix.

"Yes."

"Tourist?"

He nodded.

"Where is your hotel?"

"Ile de la Cité."

"So far! This is the quartier Algérien. It is dangerous for you. That man wanted to make trouble." Felix saw, beginning with her face, that after all she was indeed womanly.

He said, "Thank you."

She nodded, then, "What do you want here?" she asked.

"You," Felix said.

She looked at him for a moment in silence, as though not immediately understanding, then solemnly nodded again, and taking his arm led him inside, up a naked old stairway – and into a cell of a room where there was a bed starkly covered with a plastic sheet, a hand-wash basin, and a bidet.

"Please," she said when they arrived, "Five new francs for the room. And twenty francs for me." The price was humble, and the blank way she named it was even more so. It made him momentarily recall the solemn-faced Chinese who had silently come to her and gone again, with the sad quiet sureness of routine. Felix paid her and they undressed only sufficiently and with no kiss or caress came together. It was abrupt and mechanical, yet urgent and reverberating. She let him lie a full minute when the release had come, breathing in grateful stillness. The ablutions afterwards celebrated rather than brought about his cleansing. As they dressed they talked a little, asking for each other's names and origins. When they were ready he thanked her fervently. She, with an unexpected matching fervour, kissed him on the cheek.

Down in the street she urged him to take a taxi for his safety's sake, and he half promised that he would if he should see one. But the midnight streets were empty until he neared Les Halles. There he saw no taxis, but a tide of other life. The area was bustling with the preparations for the morning's trade. Everywhere there were marketeers arguing and hallooing and chalking out the positions of their stalls, like claims on a diamond diggings. Restaurants were open and busy. He entered one where some market women were gossiping at the counter over little glasses of black steaming liquor. He took an onion soup. This, of course, as the Slessors had reminded him, was the famous time and place for it. It was good. While he ate he watched the lively old women at the counter. They were joined by some newcomers whose orders told him that the black drink was mere "café", made festive by the glasses.

When he had finished the vast scalding bowl of soup and left the restaurant, the activity outside was at a pitch, the streets almost blocked by people, barrows, handcarts, piles of gaping crates spilling reds and greens and whites and yellow and purple, and shunting lorries with new freights of dust-breathing dry stuff and juicy perishable produce turning the city's night into the whole cycle of seasons for the burgeoning and reaping of a brief prodigious harvest. Through the maze of it all Felix's path was difficult and even dangerous to follow. But he picked his way, beyond all fear, exulting amid many-scented pyramids of the fruits of the earth.

SLOBADAN SELENIĆ

from *Fathers and Forefathers*

CHAPTER ONE

I am sitting rather than lying, propped up on two plump pillows, in my regally spacious, old–fashioned bed that has been, so far as I'm concerned, the central and safest spot in our safe enclave for two decades now. I hear the ticking of the wall clock. Nine o'clock. I wonder:

Why now, so suddenly? All over again? What is the point of upsetting the bearable stillness of our little enclave? It frightens me. Do I dare proceed any further down this threatening path? Has time made me able to bear a memory that could play havoc with me? How did that thought manage on this particular morning to insinuate its way into our enclave, surrounded by besiegers but safe from the incursion of the outside world which, if the truth must be known, has shown little desire for decades to penetrate the well-buttressed fortress? Elizabeta and I have been living in the fortress for a single day stretched out over twenty years, a day without shape, without name but also without murderous memories to poison it as a maggot would a festering wound. Instead of nightmare-wracked nights in a sweltering bed – emptiness. Painless and sexless. In our little enclave.

Our enclave is perhaps best defined as a one-bedroom apartment, but it eludes all their city planning categories. The apartment is on the second floor of building No. 52 on Milos Veliki Street,* and one reaches it either by going up a broad, white staircase, now cracked and chipped, or with the reliable Schindler elevator that slowly and begrudgingly, like some wheezing old mule, lugs overweight tenants to their destinations. In 1926, when we moved into this build-ing, newly built at the time, the apartment on the third floor made expressly for us was ours alone, but in 1945 they confiscated it and divided it into two unequal parts. The larger part was given to Major Šiljak. The stump was left to us. The only door connecting the parts

* A Street in Belgrade

of the divided apartment has long since been walled up; the main entrance way from the corridor belongs to Šiljak, while the servants' entrance, through the terrace and kitchen, is ours.

That was a long time ago. I've since forgotten. And that partition is on the other side of the hedge that I have raised between myself and life. Whenever I use the word enclave, it always refers only to the present, small size of the apartment, never to the larger, original size. If I want to remember the large one, I have to close my eyes, muster all my strength, and see our former habitat in my mind's eye. Distant, distant.

One enters our current, sole existing habitat from the staircase landing across the kitchen terrace, but that is still not our enclave, it is no man's land, a quarantine zone between the world and the planet of the Medakovics. Our spacious, light kitchen, formerly done in white and black tiles – half of them now gone – is the first room of the enclave. From there two doors, one next to the other, lead to the maid's room (Elizabeta has made it her bedroom) and the pantry (now a bathroom with shower) on the left, while a much wider door to the right leads into the living room, which has a two-fold function at the present stage of its existence. It is my study, but also the living room where we spend our time together. From the dining room, through a large double door with a stained-glass panel – the only bright remnant of former luxury – one goes into a small room (in the original apartment it led to the "small salon" which was connected, by the door now walled in, to the "grand salon"), serving in the enclave as my bedroom. It is rather difficult, therefore, to suggest a pat category for the enclave: it could be treated as a two-bedroom, one-bedroom or studio apartment, if the maid's room and little salon, because of their cramped size, are stripped of the status and dignity of a "room".

But I never think of our apartment as small or large, comfortable or cramped. The enclave is not subject to comparisons of this sort. Its crucial feature is that it is safe, inviolable; that with its terrace, like some medieval drawbridge over a moat two storeys deep, it is sheltered from the world that might want to penetrate our refuge; that it is ours alone, Elizabeta's and mine, from early morning in my regal bed to late at night, which we spend together in the living room, each reading a book by the gentle warmth of the tile stove in which the fire has already died out. The Vatican amid greater Rome. Monaco – an azure dot in endless France.

I know, of course, that the enchanted isolation of our enclave –

from the apartment that it used to belong to, from the building that it fits into, from the streets that surround it, from the city of Belgrade and the land of Serbia – is something we have shaped in our mind's eye, that the hedge around the enclave is spun of the finest silk, still secreted by our lives, submerged under the ashes of past events, but the impression of sovereignty conveyed by this isolation is no less effective and soothing. We are alone. It is bearable. My closer relatives have all died. The distant ones, never fond of us, were easily discouraged; for years they haven't tried to cross our threshold. Elizabeta's are all dead. Far away. In England. So here we are, my wife and I, alone.

Why now, all of a sudden? I've already begun, in this renewed attempt to make my way through the labyrinth of my life, yet I am not able to foresee whither the thread of Ariadne's skein will lead me. Theseus slew the Minotaur and found a way out of his crime. Will I find mine? Will my Ariadne help me at it? Does she have a skein? Should I set out on the journey – I wonder in my spacious and safe bed, though I know that I'm already on my way.

Because, this morning, after such a long time, I awoke with a memory of the young Elizabeta on my mind. I've never been good at blocking out only the murderous memories, while letting the others stack straw by straw of my past life in their sequence. Now I know that the skein of memories leads to a dark knot which I may only be able to untangle at very real danger to my life. But I'm off. Now that I've begun. Cautiously, like someone blind, I grope my way, step by step, approaching the distant abyss, in hopes that the many days and years have bridged it, that under my feet, when I reach it, I'll feel a log that stretches to the other side.

I am able, then, to look at the young Englishwoman whose name, that distant evening in 1924, in the Glengyle Inn pub, I still didn't know.

I am able. Able. That nice, strong, solid word able. Mihajlo used to use it. He learned it from me. He and Elizabeta. He adopted that one and she a few others – almost all the Serbian words she uses.

How stunning my Elizabeta is! Perhaps because I've done so little remembering, I haven't probed the far-off images for such a long time, I haven't spoiled them with too frequent use – now I see the Bristol days with some, earlier unknown, almost tangible vividness. As if they were not mere memories, as if the reality of four decades ago has now come tumbling into my room in all three physical dimensions, unfolding before us, who are numb and shut out from events, sufficient unto itself. Does Elizabeta see what is underway? No, of course not, although it often happens that we think of the same thing at precisely the same moment.

I can see it so clearly. Though she's amid the general fuss, Elizabeta strikes me as lonely among the boisterous company with mugs of dark Guinness in their hands. She is sitting on a stool by the bar, in the middle, between two friends – from this remove they seem like two little girls. She is taller than they are and more mature. A woman. The cloud of her thick, heavy red hair is twisted under the kind of hat they wore then: bell-shaped, tilted forward, like a little haystack perched on the head, it casts a shadow on her face, but not enough to darken the gleaming whiteness of Elizabeta's complexion. Even then I knew that my Englishwoman had the most beautiful colours: skin white as a peeled almond, hair red, but not the pale red that people with freckles have, rather a deeper hue, eyes green as deep ice, "bright as the precious stone on a king's ring", I once wrote. From my place in the inn, I can't see Elizabeta well, or for very long. My colleagues only pretend to pay as much attention to the girls as they do to everyone else having a quick drink after class, but everything they're doing, they do for the girls; they fight to get a word in edgeways and hog attention, they are witty, lively, pushy, too noisy and much less intoxicated than they feign to be.

I was, indeed, a few years older than most of them, but it seemed to me at the time that I'd turned up suddenly, an adult, bitter and experienced, among children. This was certainly far from the case, but at the Glengyle Inn I was seeing my colleagues as boys who had only yesterday worn short pants. Now they had pulled on trousers, donned blazers, ties and kerchiefs, yet all of it fitted them, as Nanka would say, like a tit on a chicken. Contrary to their almost uniform-like clothing, with university badge on their chests, I was dressed after Viennese student fashion, in a manner already outmoded even in Vienna by 1924, with a cane, top hat, the gloved left hand holding the glove of the right hand – and that in itself was enough to set me apart from the casual style, from what I'd call the cultivated air of carelessness that had just begun to creep into student fashion in redbrick, or more recent (as opposed to the older, aristocratic) universities in England.

From this vantage point it is easy to feel superior to my former distress, but attire did cause me grave concern. Was I to adapt to the unusual habits I happened upon on this eccentric island, or should I stay true to myself, though both conspicuous and different? During my first ten days in London, of course, I had already become aware that in my long-tailed topcoat resembling a redingote, with white gloves, with a cane, I looked different from the elegant Englishmen. Since my inborn shyness, inherited from my father, was more pronounced than ever before, I believed that the difference in my dress made me awkwardly, almost painfully conspicuous. This feeling became all the more acute when I arrived among the students in Bristol, and I would certainly have altered my wardrobe if shyness hadn't prevented me once again. One afternoon I went down to T. C. Marsh and Son Limited, a haberdashery some distance from the centre and the university, so that I wouldn't run into anyone I knew, and there I tried on several suits that the congenial salesman recommended to me, as a student. However, when I saw my new appearance in the large mirror – a grey, rather cropped blazer with the garish university badge bearing the inscription VIM PROMOVET INSITAM,* its trousers loose, limp and wrinkled – I was mortified at the very thought of how my fellow students and professors would perceive my haste as a newcomer to conform. At that point I chose the lesser of two evils: be different, a tortuous feat of endurance for my shyness, rather than be the frog that prances after seeing the horse prance.

Indeed, what most overwhelmed me those first days in Bristol was the feeling that I was completely different, and not only in dress; that I'd come from another world to join this carefree and capricious young crowd. Regardless of whether this was, in fact, the case, I felt, though only a few years their senior (there were several, of course, of my age) that I could be their father, with beard and moustache among the clean-shaven; upright, tall and stiff among the boyishly playful. Even had I wanted to, I couldn't have played their monkey-like pranks or laughed at the grimaces that announced their boyish folly, and released their buoyant vitality. Although not yet twenty-two, only just emerged from boyhood myself, I had already tasted tragic experience utterly unknown to these children of peacetime, for two reasons at the very least: first, during the war they were under the age of ten, I was fifteen by the time it ended and second, the English boys fell bravely on land and at sea, in Flanders and on the Somme, but did not endure war on their own soil. The difference vast, the gap irreconcilable. The fact that I felt older and more experienced than most of the students did not, however, impart a sense of security: rather, quite the contrary, a sense of discomfort, because I couldn't

* Power is Enhanced by Knowledge

behave as they did, wayward and frivolous. My rigidity because of unfamiliar customs, and my halting conversation because of meagre vocabulary did not strike me as things reasonable to expect in this novel and unfamiliar world; they seemed shameful. I would usually pretend to understand things that I did not, in fact, follow rather than obstruct the light flow of conversation. This was often without consequence, but I remember the miserable awkwardness when, directly asked how I stood on the topic under discussion, I had to admit that I didn't know what the topic was. Bristol University was, at the time of my arrival, small, so everyone, both undergraduates and postgraduates, in particular those from the same department, would congregate at Victoria Rooms, local tea rooms, inns and playing fields. I was enrolled in the Department of History, taking a course on what we called the History of British Parliamentarianism, but I met many colleagues from other departments as well. All of them, especially during the first few weeks, treated me like a wild animal, with curiosity, at a distance, without understanding. I can hardly blame them. I must have looked strange, always aloof, impeccably turned out, ever serious, melancholic and taciturn. Because I was foreign, a native son of the barefoot people who fought at the battles of Cer and Kolubara, with my bushy, black beard, slightly older, different in every respect, they would have sneered at me sooner or later, with a boyish cruelty, to justify themselves and the social rules of prestige (amusing, wise, proper) that each generation lays down and follows among themselves.

I soon became the butt of jokes, undoubtedly because difference always excites either intolerance or taunts (which I did not, unfortunately, know at the time, so it could be no solace), but also because I was far too serious for my years, and always brooding. I see myself, without a trace of humour, amid that youthful, cynical crowd that considered everything good for a laugh, the best being precisely whatever was the most sacred. Me, with my exaggerated sense of responsibility for every single minute spent at my studies which my fatherland was paying for with sums vast at home, yet such a pittance here, among over-sexed adolescents who proclaimed irresponsible idiosyncrasy to be the fundamental principle of society.

I was literal-minded among the ironic; a newcomer among natives – no wonder I had to undergo several weeks of purgatory, all the more insufferable because I was unable to conceal my sensitivity with ease, calmly ignoring the taunts. They started to ape the way I spoke English, first behind my back, and then to my face, savouring it when they noted that I was unaware of what they were doing. And how could I be, those first few weeks, with an ear unattuned to this foreign tongue? Since idiomatic phrases are the most lively and difficult to grasp in jokes, I often took a simple pun seriously, only realizing my error once the laughter subsided after my untimely rejoinder. It soon became a widespread habit among my young fellow students to pronounce "th" with a Slavic hardness; they would say "It struck my mind" as I had once said, instead of "It struck me"; or Edinburg, instead of Edinbruh, as the name of that city sounds when they say it. Today I know that their behaviour was unruly, improper; the older and more serious of them knew as much from the start, but that didn't help me.

A little Lesley Hayes made my life particularly difficult (he was killed in an automobile accident, most unusual in those days, so whenever I think of him, the feeling of insult mingles with a feeling of some sort of guilt), Lesley with curly blond hair, a face like rubber, in constant motion, restless, childish, with an exaggerated need to be the centre of attention at all times. I must admit that he so caught my turn of speech, the way I twiddled my moustache when I hesitated in mid-sentence seeking an elusive word (I didn't even know I did it until I saw Lesley doing it), the way I adjusted my impeccably creased trousers when taking a seat, how I held my cane, gloves – that it reduced to tears even those who felt that jibes at an odd, standoffish and literal-minded Serb were crude and impolite. No matter how witty and talented an imitator Lesley may have been, success and unrestrained boyish glee went to his head. He couldn't sense the limits dictated by taste, which though somewhat understated in England, are nonetheless righteous as the blade of a sword and deadly for those who blunder. He did himself in through no merit of my own, and soon found that his jibes on my account no longer had a willing audience. The depth of my concern at the time and the importance I placed on improving my status among these new acquaintances is conveyed, however, by the fact that even this morning, here in bed, forty years away from the scene of events, I can still remember with such vividness that sinking feeling of being awkward among others so agile and quick, oafish as if hewn from a single, coarse block, perhaps even – stupid.

The discomfiture of my first days among strangers at the university was aggravated by the unpleasant interruption of a pleasant three-week acquaintance with Robert Rackham who had been residing for several years at Miss Trickey's boarding house where I came upon

arrival in Bristol, in the room next to the one the landlady rented
to me. Miss Trickey was waiting for me at the Temple Meads railway
station, according to our earlier arrangement agreed in writing.
The station seemed gloomy on that bleak September day in the fog
that dampened like a light rain the station platform, the black iron
columns with oval roof, the train, benches, pigeons, people – everything that my curious gaze took in while I went up to two women
and a man who seemed to be waiting for travellers from the London
train. By the time I'd reached them beyond the turnstile, lugging
my cumbersome trunk behind me, worried because of my undignified
twist to the side, the younger woman was already kissing one of
the arriving passengers, so there could be no doubt that my landlady
was the elder of the two. She was in her fifties with a prominent
protruding nose, a huge smile that exposed long and large teeth and
the gums of the upper and lower jaw, which, in spite of the accuracy
of this description, had an air of warmth and innocence about it. On
that grinning head was perched a large and rather striking hat (even
I, uninitiated in nuances of fashion, could tell that it belonged to
some bygone age) that did not fit with the grey double-breasted
overcoat and outsize shoes and almost mannish bearing. All the way
in from Bath on the train, for almost half an hour, I had been composing an English sentence that, as I would later realize, was clumsy,
but fortunately, comprehensible.

"Are you waiting me?" I asked, in response to which large, buxom,
courteously smiling Miss Trickey loudly and cheerily began to bark
out sentences whose meaning I couldn't begin to guess at, but in
one of these I managed to make out the word "Medakovik", and
so established that I had addressed the proper person. I had arrived in
England with a rather high opinion of my knowledge of the language
that I had studied for over a year in Belgrade in private with a
Miss Edith Lamb. I had read a number of English books on my own
and with her guidance and held hundreds of conversations with my
teacher on a wide range of topics. When I bought the *Illustrated
London News* at the port of Calais, I was delighted to confirm on the
Dover boat that I could translate the captions under the photographs
and articles on various subjects without much difficulty. After only
a few days spent in London, however, it became perfectly clear that
I needn't divide the English into the intelligent and the stupid, or the
attractive and the ugly, or the male and the female, but, at least for
the time being, into those I could understand and those whose speech
I was not able to understand at all. I was able to follow educated

people kind enough to make the effort to speak simply with clearly enunciated words. It was harder to understand those who, grown indolent owing to a troublesome spleen, belittled everything with their mumbling, as well as my need to understand what I heard. And I understood absolutely nothing, not a word of what I was told on the streets, in restaurants, in shops, by the conductors, porters, hat-check girls. To make matters worse, for some reason, clearly kindness, these people were the most set on lifting my spirits with an enthusiastic rush of sentences to which I could only respond with a foolish smile and a neutral, utterly unsuitable phrase: "Thank you".

Dragging my cumbersome trunk in my left hand on the short route through the railway waiting room towards the exit where coaches and taxi cars were waiting for passengers, trembling with a presentiment of imminent trouble, I established beyond a shadow of a doubt that Miss Trickey, chatting away at my right, belonged to a group of those English from whose mouths gushed words of a totally unfamiliar form, even when they were ordinary and quite familiar to me in writing. It was only when the large lady, grinning from ear to ear and thrilled about something, took her seat next to me in a coach going up steep Park Road towrds the large university that it suddenly (I cannot explain this belated reaction) flashed through my mind what Miss Trickey meant by the jumbled clutter of sounds she had produced, looking at me in query, at the exit from the railway station.

"Coach or cab, what do you prefer, Mr Medakovik," she had asked, and admitting defeat, without understanding what I would grasp too late, I said: "Yes", which convinced my kind landlady that she would have to decide herself, without any further concern for the personal preference of her new and tongue-tied boarder. I, brimming with gratitude for my landlady's politeness and perception, and buxom Miss Trickey, gazing in delight at the city and citizens moving by us as if we were in a procession, rode ensconced on the back seat of the open coach, oblivious of the fog and damp. Like some great queen mother and the dejected prince, heir apparent, ready to relinquish all worldly honours for the godsend of silence, on we rode, majestic, towards Pembroke Road.

CHAPTER TWO

Dear Stevan,

I am answering your third letter with some delay, after deciding,
this time, to reply to your many questions. As far as I can, of course.
Though you didn't convince me in the first two, you have in the third
that Liza will give you no answers, and I think you should know at
least as much about the woman you want to spend your life with as
I do. I am certain that Liza would not see my well-intended candour
as a betrayal, but I'd rather you didn't show her the letter. At least
not now.

You see, Stevan, although Liza is my closest friend, and I've known
her to apologize – in such a British way! – for burdening me with her
confessions, I'm surprised, as I write to you, to realize that, in fact,
I know very little about her. Or rather – I know only as much as she
permits, and here you are right, this is never a great deal. Do not, my
dear countryman, be so sensitive to Liza's closed nature. As her friend,
and a subject of the English Crown for six years now, I assure you
that Elizabeth's secrecy is not due to feminine coyness, nor is it a
sign of a lack of trust in you. Elizabeth's secrecy is her character, in
part, and also typical of her nation. In an old Anglo-Saxon legend
they tested a hero to see if he was worthy of honour as follows: Is he
virtuous? Is he fearless? *Is he silent?* Do you suppose that I know more
about Archibald, after six weeks of keeping watch at his hospital
bedside and six years of marriage than you do about Elizabeth? But
I have understood something: I know little not because Archibald
has little love for me, but because it is not proper to speak of oneself
to anyone. One of the most English of questions you can hear reveals
the British obsession with propriety: "Do people, generally?" they
ask, when trying to decide upon a course of action.

So, you see, one does not generally confide in others here in
England, which, I'd say, speaks not so much of their coldness and
closed temperament, as you, admittedly with some foundation,
have seen it, but rather of their manners. Confidence here is seen as
indecent exposure, and the capacity of a person to keep his troubles
to himself is proof of resolute character and propriety. I advise you
not to push Elizabeth too hard. Understand that it is difficult for her
to meet your need for closeness, and accept that she can love you
only as she does now.

You see, Stevan, since I am Jewish, I was born with the knowledge that we were one thing, while the Serbs were something else; I found it easy to accept that the English are something else again. You do not have that feeling. You have grown up as a part of the majority, the victors, impassioned, enamoured with yourselves as newcomers on the stage of history always are. When my peers and I, educated in your schools, decided to move from the Sephardic Mahalla into Serbian Belgrade, we did so because we happened upon an open-minded tolerance almost without parallel anywhere in Europe or throughout our Jewish history, a tolerance that had to be tested for centuries before the hermetically sealed ghetto of ours would open, as it did during my Belgrade generation. We have, however, paid the price: we have adopted your language, your customs, we have become – Serbs. My father was a real Jew. Fanatically devoted to Sephardic customs and morals, he lost his life as a Serbian soldier, a volunteer corporal, in a battle against the Turks near the village of Mlado Nagoričane in 1912. I had already finished school, a "Serbian girl of the faith of Moses", with financial support from the Monarchy,* and had gone off, a fiery patriot, to join the Serbian army as a nurse, and yet, here, as you can see for yourself, I still speak of *you* and *us*. *You* are the Serbs or the English; *we* are the Sephardim from the Mahalla, who can quite adeptly become Serbs or English while still remaining Sephardim. I don't doubt that the word mimicry brings associations of negative, unbecoming traits to mind. Not for me. Mimicry is a capacity, I am proud of it, it is proof of my inherited wisdom, perhaps – of my advantage over you. *You.* Unbending and unadaptable. I spent my first year on the Island observing and absorbing. Whenever I caught on to something I would tell myself: "Ah, ha, Rašela, now you know how they do it." Never, Stevan, never once did I ask myself: "Why do it that way?" That's their business. Mine is to watch and to conform. You asked me whether my sons understand any Serbian, and I lied to you. I said they do. They don't. I have never taught them a single Serbian word. Upon occasion I grieve at the fact that my children do not speak the language closest, for me, to what you'd call a mother tongue. They know a handful of words in Ladino. They are fond, though I can't say why, of a verse from an old Moorish ballad:

> Mañanita era mañana,
> al tiempo que albordeaba,
> gran fiesta haciare los moros
> en la bella Granada.

* The Serbian Monarchy

[The next day it was dawn,
The time when they would prepare
A great holiday of the Moors
In lovely Granada.]

– they sing it sweetly together, yet they've never asked me what it means.

Why am I writing all this when you are so eager to find answers to the questions that interest you? Because you must realize that neither you nor Liza have the gift of adaptation, that you are brittle as steel that snaps instead of bending. You told me with a cheery grin about the little war raging between East and West at your dinner table in Belgrade, about your father who takes *milchbrot* with his *café au lait*, and about your nanny who insists stubbornly on *klekovača** and raw onion. She is the Serb, Stevan, not your father. Because she is unable to change. Remember how Njegoš's† Draško saw the Venetians. He was filled with revulsion because instead of the *gusla‡* they played other instruments, they preferred eggs and chicken to mutton; he despised them from the bottom of his soul because they'd "gone mad from their riches, infantile like small children"; their sentiments were "little improvement over the Turk", not to mention that "there could be no talk of heroics here", and that "the world has never seen such disgrace, such creatures". And since they were so different from Montenegrins, Draško came to the proper Serbian conclusion that "they gravely transgressed divine will" because the divine, naturally, is what is Serbian "and that their empire will be struck down" – what else could be expected from something different than what Draško knew?

You and Elizabeth are, at least a little, from time to time, biased the way Draško was, each towards your own world. Difference seems like betrayal and unkindness. You believe that there can be only one truth. If in no other way, Stevan, at least through the difficulty you have had getting used to English customs, do try and see how strange your customs must be to such a stalwart Englishwoman. Why should your nanny be the only one with the right to her *klekovača* and raw onion? During a recent visit, Elizabeth told me that you brought up my adaptability as a model for her. Wrong! I am not a model, not

* A beverage made from distilled juniper berries.

† Great 19th-century Montenegrin poet (1813–51), head of Montenegrin church and state.

‡ An ancient Slavic one-stringed bowed instrument.

for you and not for her. I am Jewish, and that is why I am now English. More so even than Archibald: I exult in the fact that he knows less about me than I do about him. I am Jewish, and that is why I can be Serbian here, with you: to you I disclose realms of my soul that Archibald has never laid eyes upon. And that's it! Let Elizabeth stay English. I recommend the same to her: *pusti Stevana da bude Srbin*.* Do not expect him to become English. Only in that way will you be able to go through life graciously under the same roof, in love and dignity.

If it is any comfort to you I admit that even among the more orthodox of Englishwomen there are few able to refrain from discussing a former marriage. Liza told you: "If you insist, I'll tell you all you want to know, but I'd be very grateful if you could manage to refrain from asking anything." You are not at fault for attributing this to my friend's slyness, assuming that by appealing to your *cŏjstvo*† she had hit the bull's eye on her Serbian target. However I am absolutely certain that Liza is not capable of such slyness. Much too much forethought for Liza. Out of the question! She was not requesting such heroic discretion from you out of cunning, of this I am sure. I will tell you how and why Liza behaved as she did. It was from despair, Stevan. Yes, despair enlightened her because she couldn't imagine telling you about events so painfully bound to her innermost heart of hearts. That is why I will tell you everything that I saw, that I heard from others, and a bit of what I guessed.

Liza did get married a year and a half ago to Richard Harris. She was eighteen, Richard thirty-four, but do not rush to the conclusion that this was a marriage of convenience, even if that might suit your Serbian, or perhaps merely your male, vanity. Richard is a wealthy man, from a family of much better standing than Elizabeth's (his paternal uncle became Sir Robert Harris only a few months prior to the wedding), but at the age of thirty-four he was a handsome, charming man that any eighteen-year-old could fall in love with. Trust my female intuition. Tall, a bit too thin, narrow face, high crown as often seen among Anglo-Saxons, attractive, light brown hair worn somewhat longer than is fashionable these days, elegant in the genuine English way – in other words, showing subtle signs of carelessness in attire manifesting a disregard for elegance (which is only for the parvenus who must prove their social status by what they

* Let Steven stay a Serb.
† The Serbian code of manliness

wear), an Oxford graduate, a civil servant with an almost guaranteed career in the Ministry of Trade (Treasury Department for Colonial Affiliations) – it was as if he were copied out of some guide for the current population of aspiring, young, English brides. I admit that I liked him and I believe I envied his impeccable English tact, an inborn sense for the fine line between the socially decorous and the undesirable. Sarcastic though never caustic, with a mildly suggested disdain for all that was earnest, rather satisfied with himself deep down inside, even when making the harshest jokes on his own account he was slightly but comfortably bored, weary of his success in life, studied in gesture, somewhat affected in speech, the tell-tale signs of a controlled measure of self-complacency. I think that Richard, if I am called upon to judge, was the ultimate Island gentleman. I was still not close to Liza at the time, so it is no wonder that I cannot recall whether she ever spoke of her fiancé. I had a number of occasions, however, to observe them. Richard treated Elizabeth as a child, he took each statement or question she made in earnest with the mild irony of which he was a true master. Liza sometimes pretended not to hear his benevolent sarcasm, but sometimes she showed a little impatience with this treatment. I heard her saying several times: "Come on, Richard, try to be serious, I'm no child." But Richard would still manage to maintain his benevolent, sarcastic tone which he lightened only to make it palatable enough for his annoyed fiancée. He was brilliant in conversation with Liza's and Archie's tiresome aunts, while mocking their behaviour with even greater brilliance as soon as they left the company, yet never awakening the suspicion of those who stayed behind that they might meet a similar fate as soon as they moved on.

I couldn't say whether Liza was, or rather how much she was in love, since she must have been fond of Harris to decide to marry him. Her love, however, no matter how great it may have been, was kept in check. Her feelings for Richard were hardly those of a teenager in love with a fairy-tale prince. Although quite young, Elizabeth had a high opinion of her intelligence and her independence. I think it unjust, Stevan, to attribute too readily all of Elizabeth's apartness to her English origin and her education. Believe me, even the English, the very ones who knew her best, described my cousin as a wilful and intractable young woman. Her rather early decision to go on to higher education upon completion of secondary school, towards starting a professional career at a time when most girls dreamed of the prince who was expected to come out of a fairy tale to gallop off with them into high society was not greeted with particular enthusiasm by her old-fashioned parents. They still believed that marriage was the one and only desirable fate for a girl. And her second, equally important and equally independent decision – to marry at the age of eighteen – not only contradicted her previous professional plans (marriage implicitly meant an end to them) but it confirmed once again that Elizabeth has a mind, not English in its obstinacy and decisiveness, but rather hers alone, and capable of implementing the most unexpected whim by itself, without a second thought. It is not easy, you see, not easy at all to manage Elizabeth, but all her decisions come out of what I would call an honourable character, and though they may occasionally contradict custom, they never contradict the high expectations that my friend and yours has always cherished for herself and those she loves.

However, though Elizabeth didn't lose her head over Richard Harris, rather, I'd say, she entered marriage sober and firm, her father was beside himself with pride and joy. Proprietor of a small real estate agency, the least successful member of a large family (he was youngest of four brothers; my father-in-law was the eldest) he was head over heels in love with his only daughter, and Robert Blake made no effort to conceal his delight at acquiring such an affluent, suave, successful son-in-law from the distinguished Harris family. While Liza's anger at Richard's patronizing manner was controlled, taking the form of slight impatience, her patent annoyance at her father's unconcealed delight, his obsequious bearing towards his future son-in-law was more candid and much more harsh. She'd blush, sometimes she'd even speak sharply with her father, she'd abruptly interrupt the conversation, more humiliated than furious, or even leave the room demonstratively. This, however, did nothing to ruffle Uncle Robert's joy, nor amused and ironic Richard's good mood, for this was merely a ripple in the otherwise smooth, easy, comfortable engagement between Elizabeth Blake and prosperous, charming Richard Harris.

Of course Archibald and I felt the difference between this match, so desirable from every vantage point, and ours, which the family still today regards with undiminished disapproval, not to say rancour. I felt the happy bustle that inundated Liza's home in Reading upon each of several visits, as a reproach, perhaps directed more at me than at Archibald, that I, a foreigner, Jewish no less, had shoved my way into the family. Open reproach, of course, never reached me, but the hints were most frequently, may the Blakes forgive me, clear as a bell. My kind Aunt Penny, or dear Cousin Stella, were obviously aiming at poor Archie when they praised Richard's handsome figure and the good repute of the forthcoming marriage. As we say: *svoga kara, tudem prigovara.** Archie and I, of course, refused to notice the malice and disdain. We've grown accustomed to it, Stevan, and their pointed comments have long since ceased to hurt us. We try to see as little of them as possible and we bear the fate of black sheep in the family without clenched teeth and insult. I am not boasting. It is easy to be superior to Aunt Penny and Cousin Stella.

However, although we may have been able to put up with the nasty allusions of the relatives, Elizabeth, indignant, young – so very young only two years ago! – could not. It may seem a bit odd, perhaps, but I probably never would have become such close friends with Liza if it hadn't been for the family opposition to Archie's marriage that they can't seem to forgive and forget these many years, and their genuine English disdain towards me, a foreigner, which in England, remember this, Stevan, is one of the few unforgivable sins. Liza would always, in every way, show great impatience with the fatuous and unfounded nasty comments of the aunts, old maids who thought of nothing but our life, though it was none of their business. "It's so suffocating in here," she'd rudely interrupt Aunt Penny, who was exclaiming, looking pointedly at me, what an excellent family Richard came from, or Cousin Stella, who spoke of the shower as a foolish European contraption, or Archie's mother, who commented with a sigh how Liza's parents must be so overjoyed about the marriage, or his father, who for no good reason, *s neba pa u rebra*† would suddenly talk about some bloody, stupid foreigner who had bungled everything with his ignorance of customs.

"My, it's stuffy in here," Liza would say, after trying to protect us from the poisonous darts that seemed to hurt her more than they did Archie and myself. "Rachel, let's go for a walk."

Of course as soon as we went out together and were alone, she wouldn't mention the lack of tact of the relatives. Not so. We would dwell on trivia alone, the English way of being noble, perfected for centuries.

Elizabeth is a marvellous person, Stevan. If this letter helps to bring the two of you together, you must know that I do so at great personal sacrifice. Don't be surprised that it took me so long to decide to tell you what I know. When you read everything, you'll see that it hasn't been easy.

---

* Criticize others, castigate kin.
† Out of the blue. Literally: Out of the sky and into the ribs.

Elem* the big day arrived (I mean the precise date – 23 March, year before last, that is 1923). The wedding was held at the local Anglican church and over a hundred people came to the Blakes' house afterwards. I think that Uncle Robert managed to ask every single guest the same question (skipping us, needless to say): "What an impressive crowd, isn't it" – thinking certainly of the numbers, but having the eminence of the invited guests foremost in mind. Liza was quite stunning, quite young and, if I noted well, a little shaken, absent. The newly-weds did not linger with the guests because they had to make the final arrangements before going off on their honeymoon the next morning, off to the other end of Europe, to Dalmatia. Since my part had been considerable in their decision to go to Opatija and Dubrovnik for their honeymoon, Liza caught me, just before they got into the car that was to take them to their new, London apartment and inquired about certain particulars, not because they really interested her, it seemed, but to delay departure a bit longer. I don't know, perhaps I am wrong. I never asked her whether she was, in fact, hesitating.

Everything went off with flying colours which made the subsequent catastrophe all the more staggering. Mr and Mrs Harris did not depart for Dalmatia, and the day after, Elizabeth came back to her parents' home and engaged a lawyer to file for divorce, with "as much discretion as possible". This last part of Liza's request was, of course, logical, but most difficult to guarantee. The scandal was immense; as they say so quaintly in Serbian, *oplahivali su usta*† with Liza and Richard in hundreds of salons at once.

Thus far, Stevan, I have written of what I know. Now I'd have to embark on a bit of guesswork as to what brought on such a sudden and dramatic divorce. I am not, however, prepared to do so. I could relate all sorts of gossip about the motives of one or the other spouse – and we heard versions that would stun you, goodness knows, with their invention – but I am sure that they would be more likely to mislead you than point you in the right direction. I have never asked Liza what led her to such an abrupt decision (I will disclose my conviction that it was Liza who made the decision, for which I find confirmation in the families' attitudes, both Liza's and Richard's), and she has never shown the slightest inclination to inform me of it. The fact that the two of us became fast friends at that very time,

* Well
† They washed their mouths out.

so difficult for Liza, probably lies in Archibald's and my restraint in not mentioning the painful event. I remember quite clearly, that the word divorce was uttered in our household for the first time when it was legally finalized. Archie said, in passing, between two sips of beer:

"I heard the business of the divorce is over."

"Yes, it is," Liza replied.

"Thank God, forget all about it as soon as you can." And that was that.

Translated from the Serbo-Croat by Ellen Elias Bursać

NOTES ON THE AUTHORS

LIONEL ABRAHAMS, novelist, prize-winning poet, teacher, critic, publisher, and editor, was born in Johannesburg in 1928. He encouraged and published young black writers during Apartheid days. Among his publications are several collections of poetry and two novels, including *The Celibacy of Felix Greenspan*, extracted here.

MURRAY BAIL was born in Adelaide in 1941, and now lives in Sydney. His first novel, *Homesickness*, won both the National Book Council Award for Australian Literature and the Melbourne *Age* Book of the Year Award. His subsequent novel, *Holden's Performance*, won the Vance Palmer Prize for Fiction. His most recent novel, *Eucalyptus*, won the Commonwealth Writers Prize and the 1999 Miles Franklin Literary Award.

STEPHEN BECKER is the author of exceptional narrative fiction; his novels include *The Chinese Bandit* and *When the War is Over*, and translations from the French (André Schwarz-Bart's *Les Derniers des justes* and works by André Malraux), history, biography, essays, reviews and screenplays. He died in the spring of 1999.

CAROL BROWN JANEWAY grew up in Edinburgh. After graduating from Cambridge, she worked briefly in London before moving to New York, where she is a Vice President, Senior Editor and Director of International Rights at the publishing house Alfred A. Knopf.

GESUALDO BUFALINO was born in Comiso, Sicily, in 1920. After studying literature he worked as a teacher and turned to writing only after his retirement. He died in 1996. His *Night's Lies* won Italy's most prestigious literary award, the Strega Prize. Patrick Creagh's translation of *The Plague-Spreader's Tale* was published in 1999.

JENEFER COATES edited *Survey*, helped establish *Index on Censorship* and presently co-edits *In Other Words*, the journal of the Translators' Association. She lectures on literature and translation and is completing a study of Vladimir Nabokov.

JULIO CORTÁZAR was born in Brussels in 1914, of Argentinian parents. Before moving to Paris to devote himself to writing and translating in 1951, he worked as a teacher. He is the author of *Hopscotch*, which was lately re-issued by Harvill, along with a new selection of his stories with the title *Bestiary*. He died in 1984.

ADRIAAN VAN DIS was born in the Netherlands in 1946 and, after a career in journalism, made his debut as a writer in 1983. He is the author of three collections of travel writing and several novels, including *My Father's War*.

PAUL DURCAN was born in Dublin in 1944. An acclaimed poet, he has several collections to his name (including *Daddy, Daddy*, winner of the Whitbread Award for Poetry, 1990). His most recent collection, *Greetings to Our Friends in Brazil*, was published in 1999.

JULIEN GRACQ was born in 1910. A schoolteacher for most of his life, he published many novels, including *A Balcony in the Forest*, and *The Opposing Shore* for which he won the Prix Goncourt.

ERNST JANDL was born in Vienna in 1925. After many years as a high-school teacher, he joined a university faculty in 1971. He has received numerous awards and prizes for his poetry both in Austria and abroad and is considered one of the most eminent German-speaking poets and performers.

ISMAIL KADARE, born in Albania in 1936, studied in Tirana and Moscow. Having established an uneasy *modus vivendi* with the communist authorities he eventually found himself compelled to seek political asylum in France. His novels include *The Palace of Dreams*, *The Concert*, *The Pyramid*, *The File on H*, *The Three-arched Bridge*, and *Broken April*. His *Three Elegies for Kosovo* will be published in 2000.

STARLING LAWRENCE was born in 1943. He is the editor-in-chief of the notable American publisher W. W. Norton. He is the author of *Legacies*, a volume of short stories, and a novel, *Montenegro*.

CLAUDIO MAGRIS was born in Trieste in 1939. He is a professor of German Language and Literature. He has translated Henrik Ibsen, Heinrich von Kleist and Arthur Schnitzler, published literary criticism, and attracted international acclaim for his work *Danube*. He was briefly member of the Italian Parliament, the only representative of an independent party. His latest work, *Microcosms*, published by The Harvill Press, won the 1997 Strega Prize.

LUIGI MALERBA, born in 1921, is one of the most widely read and admired Italian writers living. He is the author of more than 20 books, and has been translated into many languages.

JAVIER MARÍAS was born in Madrid in 1951 and published his first novel at the age of 19. He is an accomplished translator of English fiction (including Laurence Sterne and Robert Louis Stevenson) and has reached international recognition with his novels, of which *A Heart so White*, winner of the International IMPAC Dublin Literary Award, is the best known. His short-story collection, *When I Was Mortal*, was published by Harvill in 1999.

JULIAN MAZOR was born in Baltimore in 1929. After studying Law at Yale he joined the Air Force. His first collection of fiction was published to acclaim in 1968. In 1975 he chose to retreat from the literary scene. The story in the present volume is his second published work.

ROBERT MORT was born in Sydney in 1964. After studying psychology, and spending some years in London, he is now a freelance artist and portrait photographer. He has exhibited at the National Portrait Gallery and the Photographers' Gallery and has won the Jane Bown *Observer* Portrait award.

NEVA MULLINS was born in 1953, the daughter of a career soldier. She studied with Peter Taylor as Henry Hoyns Fellow at the University of Virginia. In 1981 she became the first recipient of the Virginia Prize for Literature.

BRUNO K. ÖIJER, born in 1951, made his literary debut in 1973 with a collection of poems, *Song for Anarchism*. He became the leading figure in a group of young Anarchist poets who enlivened Sweden's cultural debate and he is now receiving more general acclaim.

ANNA MARIA ORTESE, the *doyenne* of Italian writers, was born in Rome in 1914 and spent most of her life in Naples and Liguria. Her first work, a volume of short stories, was published in 1937. Her *œuvre* includes *The Lament of the Linnet* and *The Iguana*. She died in 1998.

ALEKSANDR PUSHKIN (1799–1837) is widely regarded as Russia's greatest poet. Apart from lyric poetry and narrative poems like *The Bronze Horseman* (1833), he also wrote prose fiction, dramas, and novels in verse, most notably *Eugene Onegin* (1823–31).

JONATHAN RABAN was born in Norfolk, East Anglia, in 1942. After spending four years as a university lecturer, he became a professional writer in 1969. He is a distinguished critic and the author of, among other works, *Soft City*, *Old Glory*, *Hunting Mister Heartbreak*, and *Badlands*, which won the National Book Critics Circle Award and the PEN Award. He lives in Seattle.

JAMES SALTER was born in New Jersey in 1926. A former fighter pilot, he is the author of a small and very distinct body of work, including *The Hunters*, *A Sport and a Pastime*, *Light Years*, and a recent work of autobiography, *Burning the Days*. He has also worked in Hollywood.

JOSÉ SARAMAGO was born in Portugal in 1922 and has been a full-time writer since 1979. He was awarded the Nobel Prize for Literature in 1998. His distinguished *œuvre* embraces poetry, plays, short stories, works of non-fiction and several novels, including *Baltasar and Blimunda*, *The Year of the Death of Ricardo Reis*, *The Gospel according to Jesus Christ*, *The Stone Raft*, *The History of the Siege of Lisbon* and *Blindness*. His most recent novel, *All the Names*, is published by Harvill in 1999, and his *Journey to Portugal* in 2000. His books have been translated into more than 20 languages, establishing him as Portugal's most popular and influential living writer.

KEN SARO-WIWA was born in Nigeria, where he worked as a university lecturer, writer, and civil servant. Increasingly involved in civil-rights and nature-conservation issues, he became an active campaigner and was executed by the Nigerian government in 1995, despite international protests.

SLOBODAN SELENIĆ was born in Croatia in 1933. A distinguished presence in Belgrade culture, he was Professor at the Conservatory of Dramatic Art, and wrote plays, literary criticism and six novels, including *Premeditated Murder*, published by Harvill. He died in 1995.

LUDMILLA ULITSKAYA was born in Siberia in 1943. She worked as a geneticist before establishing herself in the early eighties as a dramatist and author. Her novella *Sonetshka* was nominated for the Russian Booker Prize in 1992. She lives in Moscow.

YI MUN-YOL was born in South Korea in 1948. Korea's leading novelist, each of his books achieves huge sales in the South, while his entire work is banned in the Communist North. His first novel to appear in English was *The Poet*.

NOTES ON THE TRANSLATORS

PATRICK CREAGH is the prize-winning translator of works by Gesualdo Bufalino, Vitaliano Brancati, Claudio Magris, Anna Maria Ortese, Antonio Tabucchi, Marta Morazzoni and Sebastiano Vassali.

ELLEN ELIAS-BURSAĆ teaches Croatian and Serbian at Harvard University. Her translations include *Words Are Something Else*, a collection of David Albahari's short stories.

TOM GEDDES has regularly translated Torgny Lindgren's novels and stories into English. Other translations include *Long John Silver* by Björn Larsson. His translation of *The Way of the Serpent* was awarded the Bernard Shaw Prize.

IAIN HALLIDAY was born in Scotland in 1960 and grew up in England. Previous translations include work by the verist writer Giovanni Verga (1840–1922). He currently teaches at the University of Catania.

MICHAEL HAMBURGER was born in Berlin in 1924, and came to Britain in 1933. He is an outstanding translator, teacher, and critic of German literature. He has translated works by, among others, Rilke, Hölderlin, Goethe and Celan.

MARGARET JULL COSTA has translated works by Spanish, Latin American and Portuguese writers. She was joint winner of the 1992 Portuguese Translation Prize for her rendering of *The Book of Disquiet* by Fernando Pessoa. Javier María's *A Heart So White*, in her English translation, won the International IMPAC Dublin Literary Award.

CHARLIE MURPHY was born in London in 1948 and now lives in Amsterdam, where he works as a copywriter and translator.

PETER NORMAN is a distinguished translator of Russian poetry including Lydia Chukovskaya's *Going Under*, Anna Akhmatova and Marina Tsvetaeva.

GIOVANNI PONTIERO was Reader in Latin-American Literature at the University of Manchester. Until his death in 1996, he was the principal translator of Clarice Lispector and José Saramago, for the translation of whose *The Gospel according to Jesus Christ* he won the Teixeira Gomes Prize.

SYLVA RUBASHOVA was born in Riga and, after ten years of exile in Siberia, came to the west in 1965. She worked for the BBC's Russian service until 1987 and is the translator of Lydia Chukovskaya's *Akhmatova Journals*.

BROTHER ANTHONY of Taizé has lived for many years in Seoul, where he is Professor of English at Sogang University. He has published translations of three collections of Korean poetry.

GUIDO WALDMAN has translated Italian writers from the thirteenth to the twentieth century (including Italo Calvino and Giuseppe Tomasi di Lampedusa), and also translates from French. His most recent translations include Alessandro Baricco's best-selling *Silk*, which was awarded The Weidenfeld Prize, and La Fontaine's *Contes*.